Edward Everett Hale

Susan's escort

And others

Edward Everett Hale

Susan's escort
And others

ISBN/EAN: 9783743367159

Manufactured in Europe, USA, Canada, Australia, Japa

Cover: Foto ©Andreas Hilbeck / pixelio.de

Manufactured and distributed by brebook publishing software (www.brebook.com)

Edward Everett Hale

Susan's escort

[Page 13

"ONE NIGHT, IN A HIGH GALE, SUSAN WAS DRAGGING HIM BESIDE
HER"

SUSAN'S ESCORT

AND OTHERS

BY

EDWARD EVERETT HALE

AUTHOR OF

"A MAN WITHOUT A COUNTRY" "IN HIS NAME"
"LIFE IN SYBARIS" "TEN TIMES ONE" ETC.

ILLUSTRATED

BY W. T. SMEDLEY

NEW YORK AND LONDON

HARPER & BROTHERS PUBLISHERS

1897

OF the stories in the present volume "Susan's Escort," "Aunt Caroline's Present," "Both Their Houses," "Colonel Ingham's Journey," and "A New Arabian Night" have appeared in HARPER'S MAGAZINE; "One Good Turn," "The Minister's Black Veil," and "Bread on the Waters," in the New York *Independent*; "From Generation to Generation," in the *New England Magazine*; "Only a Fly," in the *Chautauquan*; "Mrs. De Laix's Indecision," in *Once a Week*; "From Making to Baking," "The First Grain Market," and "Pharaoh's Harvest," in the *Northwestern Miller*. "King Charles's Shilling" and "Colonel Clipsham's Calendar" were issued by the McClure syndicate.

A PREFACE

THIS is a volume of what are technically called "short stories." Alas, such stories may seem too long to some readers! And yet the author of such stories always hopes that the reader may wish they were a little longer.

It is difficult to find a fit title for such a collection. It had been determined in council that this book should be called "Short Stories, Old and New." In this title was a subtle reference to the magazine *Old and New*, which is still remembered by its editor. Alas, in the evening paper published the day of this great decision was announced another collection as very meritorious, called, "Short Stories, New and Old."

Those of us who do not dislike the short story, and are willing, in writing, to accept its somewhat stern requisitions, look back, of course, with serious pride, to the methods and the names used by our great American master, Hawthorne. It pleased him to call his first collection "Twice-Told Tales." Would it be possible, with a proper modesty, to name this collection in a like fashion? "Tell it again," the children say, when they are pleased. Such is the highest of compli-

ments, whether to Scheherezade, our great mistress, or
to our dear Stevenson. Might we say, without vani-
ty, "Thrice-Told Tales," or would the transcendental
mathematicians permit us to say "Tales of a Quater-
nion?"

No, you cannot do that. For in this volume are
some tales which have already been printed more than
two million times. The reader will find others which
he has never seen. Some of them are old, as has been
intimated—older than the average reader. Some of
them are fresh, with the vigorous flush of youth, and
stumble as they make their modest bows and courtesies.
So far was that name justified, "Stories, Old and New."
But every person in the Trade sees that you cannot
have a title-page so varied as one which should say,
"Tales, some of which have been told two million
times, while others have not been told at all." The
meanest errand-boy would refuse to carry such a title
from the retail shop to the jobber.

The descriptive title is difficult and dangerous.
When I first submitted a collection like this to the
public, I called it "If, Yes, and Perhaps." "If" was
for the possible stories, "Yes" was for the true stories,
"Perhaps" was for the probable stories. These might
have been, but one did not know; "perhaps" was the
best you could say of them. This volume might claim
a similar character. Some of these stories are true,
some of them are only possible, some of them, let us
hope, are probable. The public, however, could make
nothing of the title, "If, Yes, and Perhaps"; so that,
after struggling through five or six editions, we were
obliged to do what we have done here—to give to the

volume the name of the first story in the collection. And thus we let our dear Susan and her Escort usher in the others.

There are critics, generally of the ecclesiastical type, who disapprove of probable stories. They consider the success of a story-teller to be gained when no one can imagine that his story is true. I had the honor, myself, to be called "a forger and a counterfeiter" by the editor of one of the journals called religious—I do not know why. He had mistaken one of my stories for a narrative of an event in history. He thought, and I suppose still thinks, that a parable should have no resemblance to real life. But the masters in literature are against him. Indeed, we have the highest authority for saying that instruction by parable is that form of instruction which best reaches the masses of mankind, and which is remembered the longest. The critics of a hundred years ago spoke of "Invented Example." No one of them proposed that the example thus invented should appear to the reader incredible. The only value of "invented examples" was that they should, in substance and foundation, conform to life.

For four thousand years, be the same more or less, short stories have been in the world. It may be guessed, then, that they have come to stay. I find none better than those of the Indian sage, Bidpai, and I do not know when he wrote them, nor does any one else. But Mr. Kipling's are as good, when he describes the loves and the hates of the descendants of Bidpai's heroes. If one may judge who has read thousands with delight, and has with equal delight written his share, the days of the short story will not be ended while we have Miss Jewett and Mrs. Slosson and Mr. Wister and Mr. Davis and Mr. Barrie and Mr. Kipling to write them.

EDWARD E. HALE.

ROXBURY, *April* 8, 1897.

CONTENTS

ILLUSTRATIONS

SUSAN'S ESCORT, AND OTHERS

SUSAN'S ESCORT

I

Susan Ellsworth is as nice a girl as I know. I wish that you and I, dear readers, knew more such. She lived just out from Boston; not at Jamaica Plain, but at one of the most convenient stations on that admirable Providence Railroad—my road, so far as a person may be said to own it who by many punch-tickets builds up the fortunes of the stockholders. Susan Ellsworth was and is a school-mistress in one of the public schools of Boston. Like most such ladies, she had a fancy for living at a great distance from her school, and went and came by rapid or slow transit as the gods and Mr. Whitney might provide. This was in the daytime, and was easy.

But Susan had more difficulty in the evenings. Her brothers lived, one in Alaska, one in Yokohama, and a third was studying medicine in Vienna. She was engaged then to a man far away, and is now, if, indeed, she be not married before this story goes to press. Still, she had what I may call a passion for evening concerts and lectures—nay, let me whisper it,

1

for a rollicking, laughing burlesque, if the Vokeses or some other nice people came along, and, most of all, for the opera when it was really good. Now, all these brothers were earning their own board bills, so that Susan Ellsworth was not fleeced by them, as most good school-mistresses known to me are by their brothers. And as her salary was good, she could indulge her passion for these evening entertainments, for she was still young.

She tried at first bold independence. Boston, she said, was a civilized city. The streets were light, and, after electricity came in they were very light even at night. So she pretended to be bold when she was frightened. She went into the station at Park Square by rail. She took street-car or sidewalk to the Institute, the Opera-house, to Mr. Hale's reading, to the Old South lectures, to the Museum, or wherever she went. When the entertainment was over she crowded into a car, or put herself in the wake of some large walking party going her way. And so she pretended to herself and to fellow-graduates from Vassar, to whom she wrote descriptions of her independent Boston life, that she was not afraid.

All the same she was afraid, and knew she was; and she was always well pleased when, just in time for the theatre train out to Readville, she found herself safe in that hospitable station.

And one night her fears were justified. She had gone to a natural-history lecture. It was really the best thing in Boston that winter, the most exciting, the newest, and the most entertaining. So dear Boston had let it wisely alone, and there were not a hundred people in the hall. No one, as fate ordered, went Susan's way, and so it happened that a drunken dog on two legs staggered up to her, and asked if he should not see her home. Susan was horribly frightened. She said nothing, but almost ran. Fortunately that friendly policeman, the old man who patrols that section, came round the corner. She gasped rather than spoke. He saw the trouble, gave the drunken dog a bit of his mind, and walked with Susan to the station. But she had learned her lesson very thoroughly. She dared not try mock courage again, nor purchase her independence so dearly. For a fortnight, almost a month, she was horribly dependent.

"Dear Sarah, if you are going to the opera to-night, may I join your party? I have a ticket, but," etc.

"Dear Mr. Primrose, are you going to hear the bishop? May I," etc., etc.

"Dear Mrs. Armitage, would it trouble you and Mr. Armitage," etc., etc., etc.

And generally it proved that Mr. Primrose was not going, or that Sarah was to stay in town, or that it would trouble Mr. and Mrs. Armitage. Sometimes poor Susan bought two tickets to the opera and treated some cub of a pupil. But this was intolerable in the long-run. She really thought she should have to abjure the world, have her beautiful hair all cut off, give up all the modest amusements and vanities of her life, and enter a convent.

II

But necessity is the mother of invention. One day when Susan was at Hollander's to be measured for a new walking-dress she saw whence her safety might come. For she actually stepped back a moment for a lady to pass her, and then it proved that the lady was no flesh-and-blood lady, but only the frame of a lady, with her frock stretched over her neatly, and a bonnet where the head is usually. Susan recovered herself from her little blunder, passed her hand within the sack, and lifted the pretty creature from the ground. She found that she was by no means heavy.

You see, of course, what she determined on. In two days she had made for herself an Escort. She bought a cheap and light gossamer overcoat, a travelling-cap, a dozen toy masks, and at a second-hand clothing store a pair of badly worn check pantaloons. She also bought rattan enough, and the wire of hoop-skirts, for her purpose. She sewed to the bottom of the pantaloons two right-foot arctics, which Hugh had left when he went to Vienna, because they matched only too well. From the rattan, with an old umbrella slide, she made a backbone and two available legs to support the mackintosh, and on the top of the backbone she could adjust either of the masks which she preferred with the travelling-cap. The whole thing would shut together like a travelling-easel. The mask would go into her leather bag, which, like others of her sex, she carried everywhere. The rest could then be slid into a long umbrella-case, rather large for a patent um-

brella, but not so large as to challenge attention. Susan
finished her little manikin early in the afternoon. The
hours crawled, they stood still, till evening came, when
she was first to put him to his trial. He was to go to
Lohengrin with her, and she had bought only one
ticket for both.

Fortunately it rained like fury. It did not seem
curious that one should carry two umbrellas. She
might be returning one; for virtuous and true people,
like Susan, do return umbrellas sometimes. Arrived
in Boston, Susan went outdoors to that sheltered lee
where you wait for Cambridge street-cars. In an instant she had opened up her new friend to his own
proportions, and in a moment more, by an act not dis-
similar, she opened her own umbrella. A moment
more, and she slid her arm under the cape she had
sewed on his mackintosh, and they crossed Park Square
together.

He was a little man, he stooped in walking, and was
ungraceful in movement. But most men are this and
do thus, as Susan said bravely and truly to herself. He
was not so tall as she; neither were any of the schoolboy cubs on whom she had been depending. He had
nothing to say; neither had they. Better than this,
he said nothing; alas, most of them were not so wise!
He could be squeezed into a very small corner if they
were waiting for a crowd, or at a crossing; but they
stepped out and tried to perform deeds of gallantry.
So that, as she walked with him, delighted to see how
people turned out for them, Susan, as she balanced his
advantages and his disadvantages, said that the good
far surpassed the evil, as Robinson Crusoe did on a

similar emergency, and as the reader will, if he will
fairly compare the plus and the minus of this well-
governed world. Both parties sped down Boylston
Street safely, and arrived without any adventure before the Boston Theatre. There Susan walked into
the alley by the side with him, as if she had been a
carefully attended ballet-girl a little late. In a second
more his face was in her bag and his bones in her light
umbrella-case, and Susan—alone as it seemed, but
really never less alone—was on her way up to the family-circle, where her two umbrellas took place beside
her, in time for her to see daybreak in the opera.

III

Prosperous and happy girl, Susan followed her new
career with success and cheerfulness such as she had
never looked forward to. There was in her life none
of the embarrassment which the other girls felt, who
did not know whether they should or should not insist
on paying their own car fares when their attendants
offered to pay. Her escort never proposed that they
should stop on their way to the train to eat an ice, and
never terrified her by waiting so long in the ice-cream
saloon that she thought they had both missed the train.
Her escort never annoyed her by depreciating Wagner,
or by overpraising that sweet air in *Trovatore*. On
the other hand, she saw in a week that the other girls
regarded her with a certain sort of respect, not to say
admiration and awe, which she had never been conscious of before. To be met in the street, now with a

dark Italian, now with a foolish-looking Irishman, now with a German who scowled and knew everything, now with a light-hearted Yankee who seemed a Harvard Junior or Sophomore—this affected Susan's reputation among her young friends of her own sex. They were not surprised. No; they knew she was well worthy of any amount of admiration. Not surprised—no, only—well—yes, it was different from what it was the year before, when Susan had been poking about as if she were nobody and nobody cared for her.

It would be wrong to say that Susan cared for respect or admiration so cheaply bought. But if you had asked her, she would have owned that she was glad that she was no longer the subject of commiseration among her young friends. In truth, she took a higher grade than a girl engaged to only one person, and hers is a grade much higher than the girl who has six brothers.

Yet I really think it was a mistake that one evening when Susan, having a pocketful of complimentary tickets for the recital, took Mr. Mackintosh into Chickering Hall with her, and let him sit by her side to listen, instead of leaving him with her umbrella in the anteroom. But the recital was really first-rate, so the audience was very small. Susan was very much interested in the success of the young lady who was giving her first concert, and she thought that every seat that was filled was an advantage to her. But you see, of course, that it made other people talk. Here was this handsome young man sitting by Susan, and for a week her fair friends were asking who he was, and how she came to know him. But she did not at first appreciate this, so she made the mistake more than once, and I

think he heard more good music than was good for
him.

But as for her, in "these halcyon days of his first
success," she enjoyed her winter as she had never enjoyed a winter before. If you choose, in Boston, there
is nothing you may not see and hear and know and
understand in the heavens above, or the earth beneath,
or the waters that are supposed to be under the earth.
Susan found her time full, her hands full, her heart
full, and her brain very much more than full. When
she was not in school she was writing up her notes or
reading, that she might be in a measure prepared for
Mr. Barton, or Mr. Goodale, or Mr. Shaler, or Mr.
Wright, or the rest of the *savants*. She knew the difference between a kame and a drumlin; she knew the
difference between a moth and a behemoth, and how
the trunk of one was related to the trunk of the other.
She knew that she was herself an ascidian, and she
was as eager as any one to work out the links which
connected her with her grandfather's great-grandfather.
She dipped into Büchner and Helmholz, and even went
back to Helvetius and D'Holbach that she might get
the doctrine at the fountain. So she understood that
if a giraffe without a long neck only wants one enough,
he will get it by stretching up his neck to the top of
the palm-trees; and that if a seal on the beach wants
a pair of legs, and tries for them hard enough, he will
develop them, and that what there is left of his tail
will dwindle down into insignificance. This is the
doctrine of the *nisus*, or effort. Susan, who was a
good girl, satisfied herself with the effort to be very
wise, and hoped that it would come out all right; but

little did she think all the time how the same doctrine was soaking into Mr. Mackintosh's empty head, and what a nuisance it would be to her.

This is the reason why I feel sure it would have been better to have left him in his case with the umbrellas at the door. But, as you will see, it was an annoyance, if you were walking to a lecture with a party, to have to make some ridiculous excuse for staying outside; and also it seems rather cheap to confess that you always go to the play or lecture with a man who cares nothing about Shakespeare or geology, and prefers to stay elsewhere. It was to the scientific lectures and the really first-class concerts that she took him most, for to those a school-mistress of her grade was almost sure to have free tickets sent her. As to places where she paid for tickets, she never dreamed of taking him into the house there.

But it was really as great a misfortune to him as it was to her. Empty-headed creature as he was, of course he listened to nothing, heard nothing, and understood nothing—at first. And it never occurred to Susan that things would not stay on this easy and cheerful basis. But nothing stays on the thoroughly comfortable basis. People always attempt improvements, which often result in ruin. So it is that Voltaire says that "the better is the enemy of the good."

One night there were some very bright and wonderful stereoscopes. And poor addle-pated Mr. Mackintosh could not help having the rays come through his gray glass eyes into that empty camera-obscura of his head. And of course the picture could not help showing itself all upside-down and hind side before. But it

amused him and pleased him. And that night his
mask had very large ears, so that he could not help
listening a little. And then he listened more. For the
man was gesticulating and quoting and illustrating and
making it very plain, so that if Mr. Mackintosh would
only "make an effort," as Mrs. Chick said, all would be
well. I suppose he did "make an effort," as far as
rattan and whalebone could, and so he formed that
habit, which proved bad for him, of listening to the
man more. As for keeping his eyes and ears open, he
could not help that, for none of the masks were made
with eyes or ears that opened or shut, and he had to
look and listen whether he wanted to or not. The rest
of us are more fortunate.

Susan, quite unconsciously, hurried on the mischief
which had been begun, by talking to him herself as
they walked home from the lectures and concerts. I
do not think she did this for practice in talking. For
she talked a good deal in the school-room, and, though
she is a modest girl, I think she must know that without special practice she is as good a talker as you shall
meet with in a long day. But she was sensitive and
conscious about the deception which she was keeping
up with Mr. Mackintosh—or with the public in the
affair of Mr. Mackintosh. Dr. Primrose preached that
terrible sermon of his about "Truth" just then, and
made it clear that any conscious deception was a lie,
whether you said a word or not. This worried her a
little. For was she not consciously deceiving every
loafer on Washington Street or Boylston Street? Had
she not made Mr. Mackintosh on purpose that she
might deceive them? But a certain under-conscious-

ness that she meant no wrong sustained her against
Dr. Primrose, and at first the stings of conscience only
pricked her so deep as to make her resolve that she
would not be found out—no, not if she met Dr. Primrose and Mrs. Primrose both. So she thought it more
prudent—that was the word she used in discussing it
with herself—to keep up an animated conversation with
Mr. Mackintosh in the street when she observed that
any one was near them. And indeed this proved so
agreeable, as conversation is apt to when you do all the
talking, that she kept it up all the time from the lecture or concert to the station. After they came to the
station she always folded him up in some recess of the
ladies' waiting-room. For Providence Railroad conductors are pitiless, and would have been sure to demand a ticket for him.

"That is a magnificent harmony at the end of the
third act." No audible reply—but one so seldom hears
both sides of a conversation. "I was not sure but
Gloria strained a little in striking the *non;* but it was
all so good that it is absurd to pick out flaws." Again
Mr. Mackintosh's voice is lost as those firemen rush by.
Or, "Could you quite follow him in what he said about
the permanence of type? How can it be, if the type
is permanent, that we should notice the transition, as
Mr. Shaler pointed it out Tuesday? But then, I am
not quite sure if Mr. Shaler and Mr. Barton quite agree
about that. You must remind me to ask him. Or we
might send a note to *Notes and Queries.*" Now, if the
bishop himself had heard that, or Mrs. Bishop, neither
would have minded, or remembered afterwards, that
Mr. Mackintosh said nothing.

IV

But, alas! simple Susan carried on this rattling and interesting conversation quite too far and too long. Mr. Mackintosh had been making all the *nisus*, or effort, he could in listening to the stereoscope man, and he had all the encouragement of the success of the giraffe and the seals. Now, here was this bright, wise, merry Susan Ellsworth, who bore him along, who was the result of just such efforts as he was making. And he found it much more agreeable to listen to her sweet, low-toned voice just in his ear, her breath fragrant as clover, and her hand under his arm beating a pulse in keeping with all she said—he found this much more agreeable than straining his poor little new wits to make out what the man on the platform a hundred feet away was howling about. So he was always distressed when any of her friends joined them to take advantage of his protection, and when Susan turned away from him to speak to Maud or Clara. To say the truth, this did not happen often. For Maud and Clara had the same proper pride about hitching on upon other people's escorts as had governed Susan in her independent days.

While poor Mr. Mackintosh made this *nisus*, or effort, to hear, he was all the time making wild and futile efforts to speak. For these he had wretched organs and more wretched opportunities. For one night in the family-circle, where Susan had unfolded him after they had passed the ticket-gate, he had seen the policeman seize two boys who were catcalling, and hale them off he knew not whither. So poor Mr. Mackintosh was frightened, and did not dare to try experiments indoors. Then, as soon as they came to the railway station, Susan always ruthlessly shut him up, and he had no organization at all. Literally he "went to pieces," and it was not slang to say so. One night, in a high gale, Susan was dragging him beside her—or rather behind her—and he tried to speak, but nothing but a great howl came out, which was half a sneeze. She did not suspect that he had anything to do with it. And the poor creature was dreadfully mortified by his failure.

But another night, very imprudently, she left him sitting in a chair, in the anteroom of the hall of the "Sons of Idleness." The hall had been hired for a "reception" which was given by the graduates of Vassar to one of the professors who was going to Germany on his sabbatical visit. Susan thought she was safe in leaving Mr. Mackintosh in a dark corner without folding him up. And so she was. He sat, with his chin on his hands, as she left him, and thus he had, for once, the chance to try his various gruntings and howlings, and to pass through the experiments of the ascidian to the more articulate language of the man.

Fortunately for him, he had some lessons just when he needed them most and expected them least.

For one of the other escorts, who had been taken into the reception hall, came running out, and helplessly rushed up and down the waiting-room, annoyed that he found no one there. But in his despair he saw Mr. Mackintosh.

"Ugh—ah—glad to see somebody—ugh—could you

—can you—yes—would you tell me, please—ugh, you know—don't you see?—where the water is?—Miss Maelstrom—ugh—is faint—you know!"

Mr. Mackintosh's time had come. Imitation was his cue, clearly, as in Rosenthal and Prendergast. With one sublime effort he echoed the other, wondering, as he did so, whether perhaps he had as much brain.

"Ugh"—tremendously prolonged—"ah"—shorter, but very long—"glad to see somebody"—this hopelessly indistinct from eagerness, like an Edison turned three times too fast; "could you—can you—can you—could you"—this slower—"water—Maelstrom—ugh—ah—yes, you know." But fortunately, in his agony gesticulating like a schoolboy who forgets his piece, he pointed his finger to the looking-glass, where stood pitcher and tumbler in full sight of both of them.

"Ugh — oh — thanks — yes — so much — so much obliged, you know—thanks—ugh, oh, Miss Maelstrom" —and Mr. Knowitz vanished with his tumbler.

Mr. Mackintosh had tried and had succeeded, and on these sounds he practised all the evening.

Would she give him another chance for practice? Alas, no! or it seemed no. That night as they went home there was a great group of Vassarites, all bubbling over with fun—effervescing and spluttering as so many bottles of XX might do which had been warmed at a sociable all the evening. And he thought Susan had never been so remorseless as she was in undoing him that night. The next evening was worse. A gentleman joined her on the other side. And poor Mack-

"HE SAT, WITH HIS CHIN ON HIS HANDS"

intosh was afraid for his very life as they swung along.
It was not till the third night that he had a chance, or
so it seemed to the poor witless creature.

V

But on the third night the chance came. Susan was
in the highest spirits.   The night was clear and cold,
and they devoured the pavement as she rushed him
along. "Well, my dear Mac," said she, mercilessly,
"that was first-rate. I do not wonder women want
to speak, if they could speak like that. Mac, if I
could get Mr. Edison to give me one of his rollers, I
would attach it to you, and you should repeat the end
of Mr. Bryce's lecture."

"Ugh—ah—you know—well—Miss Susan—ugh, ah
—give me a chance—you know—and I will do·'em-all."
The end was badly run together.

"What, you—my dear Mac?"   This was all Susan
said, and she almost dropped him in the gutter in her
surprise, and she lost her own speech for laughing. She
laughed so that she shook him from his cap to his arctics, and all the poor breath he had in his limp ribs was
knocked out of him.   And when she came to herself,
all she could say was, "Poor dear Mac! I beg your
pardon, but"—then she broke down again—"but who·
ever dreamed of your talking?"

But then it was poor Mac's turn. She had to listen,
and he told her, with many unnecessary "ughs" and
"ahs," and "you knows," and "don't you sees," that
he was sure he only needed more practice to speak quite

well.   It was true that he could not manage *r*, and he
always called *th d ;* but so did many gentlemen he met.
He needed extra breath, but "ugh" and "oh" seemed
to help in this.   And when he had not an idea, he
could fill in with "don't you see" and "you know."

"You poor dear thing," said Susan, compassionately,
as she unscrewed his head and put it in her bag, "you
are really eloquent."

VI

But the reader will see that a good girl like Susan
could not shut up the face just now eager in its entreaties, and go to sleep, after she had silenced it, without serious thought.   Here was a matter of conscience
more formidable than that question about veracity
which Dr. Primrose had started.   Was it quite hon-
orable in her, was it fair—nay, was it right—to start
this poor feeble creature in his career, to let him par-
take of a little taste of the wonders of science, of art,
and of music, and then to snuff him out like a candle,
simply because she chose to?   Susan tossed in her bed
a good deal before she went to sleep, with these questions troubling her.   And early in the morning, when
the singing birds first awakened her by their carols to
the rising sun, she rose, screwed Mr. Mackintosh together, tied him to an arm-chair in her entry, and left
him to enjoy the sunrise.   As she went to sleep again
she could hear him practising an imitation of this
morning hymn of the birds, who were Plymouth Rock
cockerels.   The poor brainless creature did not know
any better; he had taken it for granted that these were,

the morning songs of men. Susan was pleased with herself for this act of mercy, and she did not take him to pieces till it was time for her to go to school.

As it happened, he was this time shut up—and, so to speak, ceased to be as an individual—longer than had ever happened to him before. For, to her delight, as the school recess came, Susan received a card, and visit close following, from George Farmer, the fine young engineer officer to whom, as I said, she was engaged. By good luck, and by good strategy of his own, he had got himself ordered to Boston, to make a contract for some ice for the meat-cars of the Cattaraugus and Opelousas Railroad. With good luck, this ice contract and certain subsidiary negotiations were made to last a fortnight, and during that whole time Susan needed no escort other than George, and, in truth, thought very little of any other. But at length the last day of George's visit came, as last days will, and then she began to think how dreadful it would be to have nobody but Mr. Mackintosh to go anywhere with her. Still, she was less disposed than ever to cut off her hair and to retire into a convent.

Wisely, therefore, the girl submitted the question to her lover. But she did it in a guarded way, which I would not recommend to other good girls in a like position; if, indeed, there ever may be such girls. As they came home from the Symphony on that wretched farewell night she said: "George, I want your advice. You are so good, and—and you are never jealous. You see, when you are away, I have no one to go with me to the concerts, you know, and the lectures."

2

"No; you used to boast of your independence when
I first knew you."

"I know—yes, I did.   But I was very foolish."
And then she told him of that horrid fright she had
had.   And he was very angry, and swore—just a little
—and made her promise to run no such risk again.
This made it easier for her to go on.

"No; I knew you would not let me.   That is why I
did not write you about it.   But what I did—you
must not be angry—was to take a poor stick there was,
with nothing to do, to come and go with me.   You do
not mind that, do you?"   And here she looked up at
him with her most roguish and confiding smile.   But
George's face clouded; she could see it did.

"I don't know," said he.   "That would depend.
What sort of a creature is he—an old man?"

"Oh, I do not know.   Don't be jealous, now.   I do not
suppose he is very old; perhaps he is very young.   You
see, he was deaf—and dumb—and blind—and could
hardly walk.   So I did not suppose you would care."

At this George grinned a somewhat ghastly smile,
and said he didn't care quite so much; but asked how,
if the man was deaf, he could enjoy the concerts.

You will observe also that Susan wandered from
Dr. Primrose's instructions.   She said Mr. Mackintosh
"was" deaf and dumb—she hardly dared say "he is"
—and there was conscious deception again.   In answer to her lover she said: "Enjoy the concerts?
Who ever said he enjoyed the concerts?"   She was a
little reassured, as women are, because he had made an
unimportant mistake.   "You do not suppose I ever
bought a concert ticket for him, do you?   No; I take

him as I would a cab after the concert was over.
Dear George, you must not be jealous of him more
than you would be of a cabman."

"You do not take a cabman's arm," said George, a
little irresolutely; and Susan shuddered as she recollected with how firm a grip she had to take all the
arm Mr. Mackintosh had. "What is the wretch's
name?" continued he.

"Name?" said Susan. "Do you ask your cabman's
name? I never asked him. We call him Mr. Mackintosh, from the coat he wears, but I never asked him
his name. I do not believe he has any."

This encouraged George a little; but still he said he
did not think it was nice or wise, and that nobody but
as innocent and sweet a girl as Susy would ever have
fallen into so silly a plan. He even asked if other
girls in Boston had to hire their escorts. At which
Susy said that other girls had escorts who did not live
in the Rocky Mountains, or in Opelousas either; and
at that Mr. George had to come down from his high
horse. It ended by a compromise. She agreed, when
she went anywhere alone, to order a cab regularly at
a stable he named, and he declared that the next time
he came to Boston he should pay the bill. Whether
she would let him or not was left undecided in the
final ceremonies of the farewell. For he left in that
horrible train which goes off at eleven at night, and
there was no question but that he must go.

So all Susan had got by asking advice was that she
was worse off than she was when she asked for it.
This is what is apt to happen, dear Clara, when you
do not tell your whole story to your adviser.

VII

And now she must deal with Mr. Mackintosh alone, by her own unassisted sense, such as it was. Really it was stronger, as the reader has seen, in the inventive and mechanical lines than it was in the philosophical and ethical lines.

Of course she could have left Mr. Mackintosh where he was—his legs and arms in the glazed umbrella-case, his masks in her alligator-skin bag, and his arctics on the floor of her closet. But, as has been said, she did not think this fair. She had thought of burning him up. But she was too strong a Protestant; her reminiscences of Smithfield and John Rogers were too strong, and that she would not do. She had called him into such being as he had, poor creature, and she would not destroy her own work. "That would be simply mean," she said to herself; "that would not be fair."

So she took another morning when the cocks were crowing, and screwed him together, and tied him to a chair as before. Poor Mr. Mackintosh did not know how long he had ceased to exist, any more than Mr. Hyde knew how long Dr. Jekyll had been running the machine. Nor was the poor thing as wretched as the girl chose to fancy him. For, as he had none of that essence which loves and fears, hopes, admires, and worships, he had nothing worth remembering, if he could remember, as he could not; and nothing to look forward to, if he could look forward, as he could not. But this, simple Susan did not consider. She simply screwed him together. He listened to the cock-a-doodles, as he did before; and if he had thought, as he could not and did not, he would have thought that this was thus and then was now.

Then Susan went to bed and slept till the dressing-bell rang. As she dressed, she began a little note to George, for she had promised to write to him twice a day. But after breakfast, before school-time, she came up and brought Mr. Mackintosh into her room and locked the door. He had never been in that room before.

"Mac," said she, "I shall not want you any more. What do you want to do? What do you like to do most?"

"Oh, ugh, ah—you know—don't you see—well, you know—"

And Susan was patient, for she often had such remarks addressed to her by her partners who were not skilful in extempore speech. So she waited. And at last it came, as gas comes after the puff of air in a poor gas-pipe.

"If—you know, Miss Susan—I could go to some of those parties — receptions — like that of the Sons of Idleness. Indeed, Miss Susan, I can talk as well—as the young men I see there."

"I think you can," said Susan. "I should be ashamed of my work if you could not. I had thought of that, Mac. But I cannot do it, for you have no pumps nor patent-leather shoes. And your trousers are not good. I have no money to throw away on parties. Think of something else, Mac."

It is not worth the while to load the page with poor

Mac's "ohs" and "ughs" and other "spaces." In substance he then asked if he might not be a juryman. "I thought I could; you know they do not have to know anything, and, indeed, are better when they do not."

"That is good, Mac. I had not thought of that, but I will," said the girl. And so she took his head off and shut him up, and took this plan into consideration.

But of course she did not assent to it. That same day she read the Court Calendar, and was distressed to think that she had yielded even for an hour. When she went home she put Mac together, and told him that this would not do.

"Then," said he, very piteously, "might I not be an under-editor to an independent journal? You know they do not have any opinions, and are very proud that they do not. I am sure I never had any opinions. I do not know what an opinion is." But this time Susan was not deceived; this was only the jury plan under another form.

Then Mac pleaded, quite eloquently for him, that he might stay just what he was. He had seen the red-capped messenger men at the station. He envied one of them his one arm, because practically poor Mac had no arms at all. "Now I could not go of errands, Miss Susan. But you say yourself I do my work well. You could fasten me at the door, and any one who wanted me would unfasten me."

"My dear Mac, you do not see. The secret would be discovered, and then the roughs would not mind you. Don't you see, Mac, you cannot knock a man down? You might as well be a woman, for all the good you are in your own business, unless people think

"'MAC,' SAID SHE, 'I SHALL NOT WANT YOU ANY MORE'"

you are a man. And if they do think so, it is because I 'consciously deceive' them. Oh dear! Oh dear! I wish you had never been born!" And the poor girl broke out crying. But she did not say, "I wish I had never been born," for the memory of George's last kiss came to her.

"I had thought," said Mac, "of voting. What you say of women reminds me that they cannot vote; but I can."

"No, you can't," said Susan, smartly, for she knew. "You have not registered, and you have not been assessed."

"I could register," said Mac.

"You can't register; it's a very smart person who knows how to register; and, besides, you can't read the Constitution. So it would be of no use if you could register."

"No," said Mac, sadly, "I cannot read the Constitution. You don't think I could be a minister?"

"No, you couldn't. There are some kinds that know very little, but they all have to know something."

"Nor a doctor?"

"N-o, Mac; at least, I believe not. I think they have to know something."

"Nor a lawyer?"

"No, certainly not. You have no eye-teeth. And they have to be cut before you are a lawyer. I heard Judge Jeffries say so."

And then they waited. "I will talk to you again by-and-by," she said. And then she ran down-stairs to meet the postman, and found just a little postal card, on which George had written in French that she was the dearest girl in the world, and that he should always love her. Immediately on this she took Mr. Mackintosh to pieces, dressed herself for the Appalachian Club, went to Boston, and tried her pretty cab for the first time. It was really an elegant little coupé, and the stable-keeper had put the driver in livery. George had written to him from Springfield that the coupé must wait for Miss Ellsworth every evening.

But the next morning Susan brought her little drama to an end.

She screwed Mr. Mac together once more, and said, "Tell me yourself what you want to be."

"Could I not be Vice-President," he said; "till the President died, you know; or Lieutenant-Governor, or something like that?"

"Oh no, Mac; they might not know when to unscrew you."

"Could I not be a trustee? I believe trustees have to be cautious, and not do the rash things other people do."

"I had thought of that, Mac, and I inquired. But you would have to give bonds. Now, no one would give bonds for you. I am sure I would not." This was cruel in Susan; but sometimes she is cruel.

"Then, Miss Susan, why cannot I be what I am?"

"Because I do not want you."

"But somebody else might want me. I could stand in front of tailors' shops with new clothes on. I should like to be that. I see a great many young men who do that and nothing else, and they seem to like it very much."

"You dear old Mac!" cried the girl; "you have

more sense than any of us—at least, more than I have. It is the best sense possible to be what you are, and pretend to nothing more. I knew that, though I have never tried it, for Mr. Emerson says so."

So she went with him to Cutter & Dresser's that very day. They are the great ready-made clothing men. And they took Mac at once off her hands literally. And they put on him that handsome Garrick you saw me wearing yesterday. That was the way I came to know the story.

And—will you believe it?—one day when they had dressed him in a costumer's suit as Dromio of Syracuse, old Mac forgot, and began walking up and down the balcony on which he was standing. The people in the street saw it, and fancied he was a wonderful automaton. They stopped in hundreds to see him, and of the hundreds scores went in to buy.

That was the beginning of the triumphant success of Cutter & Dresser. They owed it all to Susan, and I think they will send her a pair of salt-spoons for her wedding.

ONE GOOD TURN

I

HELEN MELCHER was just going to bed. Twice she looked doubtfully at the old bureau, which had been her mother's; once she half crossed the room towards it. The third time her resolution gave way, and she opened the upper drawer and took out her journal-book. She sat down, opened it, read the last entry, which was, in truth, rather forlorn, paused again, with her pen in her hand; but then, without any further hesitation, wrote quickly and steadily thus:

"*Friday, December 26th.*—Another good-for-nothing day. I have hesitated before I would even waste good ink on telling the story of such wasted hours. I did better in those days of the early journals, which say 'Washed my doll's clothes,' 'Ironed my doll's clothes.' If Clara and John would only let me, now, I would send Bridget off to-morrow, and would wash and iron my own. Why, I should then, at least, be good for something!

"I have no longer even the wretched occupation of going to Dr. Hunter's. He says my wrist is all right, if only I do nothing. And that is just what I am good for. It is lucky for me that he has done with me; for I gave him my last two dollars, and I shall have to go on foot till dividend day if I save this bright quarter for the contribution-box. For that matter, I may just as well stay at home as go out. It is all one with such a do-nothing as I am. I even told John Orcutt, at the doctor's, that his time was more valuable than mine, and I let him take my turn, first among the patients, when he would have been last. Then I sat reading the *American Orthopedist* for the hour, while the others went in. It was just as well. What was I good for? Poor John Orcutt! I wonder if he understood how bitter was my satire!"

And with this exclamation-point Helen Melcher went to bed.

II

The Recording Angel copied Helen's entry into his big book in much fewer words than I have used. They have a shorthand there which we cannot yet imitate.

And the Recording Angel smiled with that grave, queer, sweet smile of his, which no artist as yet has given us on canvas. It had been a busy day with him; for he had had all John Orcutt's entry to make, and all the entries of all the lives in all the places and all the countries which hinged on John Orcutt's. And so the Recording Angel did not think Helen Melcher's day so insignificant as she did.

The truth is that that particular day of hers kept him very busy for a long time, and we shall see. In fact, he had to ask for more assistants, and he had them granted him; for they are very kind there to servants as faithful as he.

III

John Orcutt was not in any sense what you would call an important man. He was an honest, rather slow coach, unimaginative, but perfectly willing to do his duty, if anybody told him just what it was. He was not very bright in finding it out for himself. Indeed, a difference in that very faculty is one of the rather critical distinctions between men. John Orcutt sat in the pew next at the right of Helen's pew. That is the way she came to know his name.

When at Dr. Hunter's that day Helen had bitterly said to him that his time was more precious than hers, and had let him go first into the surgeon's room, he had not enough wit to see that she was bitter or sad. What he knew was that in the printing-office that morning a heavy chase had fallen on his foot. He was lame, and he was afraid that some of the little bones were broken. He had had to take a cab to do the errands which his chief had given him; he had just finished that critical interview with their counsel, Kent & Marshall, about the libel; he was late at Dr. Hunter's, whose office was full when he arrived, and, except for Helen's good-nature, he would have had to sit there an hour.

As it was, it did not take the great surgeon two minutes to tell him that nothing was the matter. In another minute his boot was on, and in another he had called a cab and was driving quickly back to the office.

His chief was delighted to see him.

"I had not looked for you before five," he said, "and you so lame, too! I had just telegraphed Marcy at enormous length; but now you are here, I will leave the office to you and catch the express myself. Personal presence moves the world. I will be back Monday morning. Lead with the judiciary, then take 'Bulgaria' or the 'Fisheries,' then as you choose; only," said the chief, as he pulled on his overcoat and lifted down his travelling-sack, "Claghorn is to say nothing, not if you have to kill him. We say nothing about silver and about Scotland Yard, you know."

And so John Orcutt was left in charge of the journal from five o'clock, Friday, till breakfast-time, Monday, while the great man swung himself to the train and to the capital. And so, also, at the very moment when Helen was making her forlorn entry about John Orcutt in her diary the great chief, thanks to her, was rushing along, asleep, as fast as steam would pull him, two hundred miles from home.

IV

Let us follow his story first, and then we will go back to John Orcutt, in the office. The great editor arrived at the seat of government at last, long after breakfast-time. But he did not stop for breakfast; nay, he scarcely stopped to wash his face and hands. He called a cab, and in ten minutes was at the bureau of his friend, the great officer of state, to whom he had been telegraphing.

"Are you a foreign minister?" said the messenger, who sat at the door, surprised at the unknown visitor.

"I am a domestic minister," said the editor, bluntly, and pushed by the unavailing lackey.

General Marcy, whom he had come so far to see, was at his desk, working as if he were never tired. A young man at another desk looked pale and "dead-beat," and, if he had spoken, would have said that the place of private clerk to a Secretary of State is not the elegant sinecure which men imagine it. A Pueblo blanket lay on a sofa, on one side, rudely tossed, as it had been thrown back after the secretary had caught his hour's nap at three that morning. By each of the gentlemen was a cup of coffee.

The great secretary turned to the editor as he entered, almost as if he had expected him:

"Is it you, my good fellow? It is so like you to come on. But I supposed that was out of the question."

"I thought so myself when I wired you." And then the editor at once observed a certain doubt on his friend's face, and added: "You have my despatch?"

"Despatch. Yes, I think so; of course. When? Gilbert, did we have any despatch from—from Mr.—?"

But he did not add the name. Gilbert had produced the despatch and brought it to his chief. The editor was quite quick enough to see that it had never been read or even opened before.

"You are just in time," said Marcy, not so much as waiting to apologize, "for me to read you the full text of our despatch in its last revision. I had Clinton here, well, till two o'clock last night, and Maxwell and the chief himself sat where you are sitting. These are the rough drafts; most of it, of course, is mine. But the chief himself drew this, and I am bound to say it is in his best style. Mr. Gillott, here, was good enough to make a clean copy while I caught a nap there. I have been sketching the instructions, which will go with it, to Franklin and to Stowell. Mr. Gillott will give us clean drafts of these while I am reading. Put up your feet, and I will read."

So he rang for a cup of coffee and some oysters for his guest, and while Orcutt partook of this scant re-

fection the great secretary read to him that celebrated despatch on the length of the marine league and
the true limits of blockade. Logical and clear, it moved
steadily from point to point, and compelled conviction.
It asserted the rights of mankind in language which was
absolute; it stated the position of the nation in the
maintenance of these rights for the world as for itself.
It ended with ten lines of sharp and indignant comment on the pettiness and duplicity of the despatches,
to which it replied, from two great powers.

The reading occupied the better part of an hour.
When Marcy had finished he and his friend looked
each other steadily in the eye for a minute without
speaking, without winking. But the editor smiled
gravely in approval.

"Will it do?"

"It is simply perfect," said he. "It sends one back
to the Protector and John Milton. While you read I
gradually forgot our modern races, nor remembered
the existence of a leading article. Do? Why, you
redeem diplomacy when you make such a record of
common-sense?"

The secretary was well pleased. He even blushed.
"I am glad you were the first person to hear it after it
was put together."

"So am I," said the other; and again there was a
long pause. The secretary rang for two more cups of
coffee.

"You have something to say," he said, at last.

"Perhaps," said the other. "Yes; I have. Charles
—you men here—you do not know the country as well
as we do."

"You are always saying that," replied the great diplomatist, annoyed.

"Because it is true. You are shut up here in your palaces. You are reading letters from consuls and plenipotentiaries. We are knocking about among men who speak bad English and buy lean cattle to fatten them." And he paused again.

" Yes ?" said the secretary, uneasily.

" And—in a word," said the editor. "Charles—I wish—well—I hate to say it—I wish you would cut off your snapper at the end. It is good as gold. It is better. It is perfect as repartee. It is threat without threatening. But it is threat all the same. Charles, the country will not back you in it."

" Fudge !"

" Charles, I know the country. This country is not prepared for that war. Those ten lines mean war—and will make war. This country will cheer you at the beginning, and abandon you—as sure as you live. Say to your chief that I say so."

" You want me to cut off my perfect conclusion ?"

" Yes. And you had rather cut off your left hand."

" Of course I had," said the secretary. "John, it is the only passage which I care a penny for in the despatch."

" I knew you would say so."

The great man walked up and down his office three times. Mr. Gillott still copied on the instructions. No one said anything.

Then the secretary came to the writing-table, and drew two broad strokes of a pen across the offending passage. He rang and ordered his carriage. " I will take it to the chief. You have conquered, Galilean!"

But neither of them smiled, even. They almost crushed each other's hands as they parted. The editor looked at his watch, and went to his breakfast.

V

Bearers of despatches travel quickly, and in a very few days this critical despatch was read in the chancelleries of both of the sovereigns to whom it was addressed. There was a little sovereign and a great sovereign. The little sovereign would wait to do what the great sovereign bade him; and the great sovereign would do what his great chancellor advised him.

The great chancellor bade his man Friday read the Marcy despatch aloud to him, which he did. The great chancellor then sent the man Friday to bed, and read it again and again himself, before he followed the man Friday's example. The next morning, over his coffee, he read it again. He then summoned the Field-Marshal Julius and the Secretary of the Admiralty, whose name was Nearchus, and he said: "Gentlemen, you may give holidays to your people. This breeze has blown over." And when they both seemed surprised—for their departments had been at work day and night for weeks—the great chancellor said: "Between ourselves, gentlemen, we must not fight till we have a better case. These people yonder put the thing so well that all Europe and all the neutral powers will be with them; and I do not mind saying to you,

3

our friends of the opposition would handle us badly at home. Now, if they had bragged never so little, if I could appeal to wounded pride or national honor, could say they had insulted us, that would be one thing, and we would gladly send you gentlemen to blow them all out of the water or into the land. But as it is—well, I suppose it is as well. The truth is, their paper is better than our paper. Jove! gentlemen, it is as calm as the New Testament." They waited a minute more, and he smiled and nodded : " That is all, gentlemen ; there will be no war."

When the Recording Angel wrote that down in his shorthand he smiled that queer smile again, and he said to himself : " That is pretty well for Helen Melcher's good-natured self-sacrifice."

VI

We must not forget John Orcutt.

John Orcutt was too unimaginative a person to be surprised much at anything. There was nothing in the office of *To-day* which, sooner or later, he had not done. In his time he had swept the floor, he had watered it with a water-pot, he had set type, he had unfolded newspapers from the mail. He had folded other newspapers. He had made out bills and he had collected them. Also he had failed to collect them. He had written book notices and theatre notices, and critiques on Wagner's music. He had reported a baseball match in the afternoon, and with the same pen a discussion on predestination in the evening. He had eaten good dinners with the political clubs, and he had returned from them to write a notice of Browning's last poem. He had been "responsible" before now; and as nothing surprised him, he was not surprised to find himself "responsible" again. While he had been discharging his other offices the chief had been "responsible."

John Orcutt now thought he would take the comfort of being "responsible." The chief's office was much larger than the little cell which he usually occupied. That was one comfort. At his side were the choicest English and French and German papers. While he sat, the grave, pale little boy, who opened the mails and distributed to the different gentlemen their specialties, brought in fresh copies of the *London Spectator*, *Le Nord*, *Le Temps*, the *Revue des Deux Mondes*, and the *Journal Officiel.* For the chief liked to have the first dip into them. And so John Orcutt, having, for a wonder, no inventors to hear with new projects for the enfranchisement of mankind, put a pin into the loose sheets of the *Journal Officiel*, turned to the non-official part of it of course, and began to cut the leaves. He saw in a moment that there was nothing for which his public cared. But there was a curious report on the food of infants, presented to the Académie de Médecine, in Paris, by Léon Broussais. It went deep into detail, and he who did not understand before about goat's milk, ass's milk, cow's milk, and woman's milk did afterwards. John Orcutt looked through the details in the elaborate tables, put the whole in a cover, and sent it to his classmate, Flanders. Thirty-six hours afterwards, on Sunday morning, he found this note on his desk :

"DEAR ORCUTT,—I thank you, or, reverently, I thank the good
God, for your Frenchman and his report.   People will believe a
printed scrap from Europe when they will not listen to an Angel of
Light at home.   Our orphan board met—quarterly meeting—at noon
to-day.   I carried Broussais's paper, and I utterly floored the old
fogies with it.   Dear boy, it means one hundred live babies this summer, cooing and playing in their mothers' arms, instead of one hundred little crosses over mounds in the cemetery.   I cannot thank
you enough.   Shall I send back the paper?
          "Yours always,   W. FLANDERS."

When the Recording Angel entered this business of
the hundred babies on William Flanders's book, he
directed two of his assistants to make cross-references
to that entry in Helen Melcher's book and in John
Orcutt's, and he smiled with that queer smile of his
again.

VII

And, to go back again, John Orcutt still sat, Friday
night, in the "responsible" chair.   To him there came
in the chief of ship-news.

"It is not our affair," said this gentleman.   "But
clearly this complication in the Marquesas Islands is
not understood by the gentlemen in Babylon."

Alas!   John Orcutt felt that he did not understand
it, and could not.   But he did what a responsible editor
should do.

"All right," he said.   "You can leave the papers
with me."

Now there was among the young men who did "general work" — reported baseball matches to-day and
discussions on quaternions to-morrow—one serious fel-

low, named Pringle, whom John Orcutt liked. He
hardly knew why. He had never spoken to the young
fellow, except to nod as they met in the wash-room.
But Pringle was always at his desk five minutes before
he had to be, always was the last man there at night,
even long after the others were gone. In overlooking
proof one week Orcutt had noticed that Pringle's copy
was always clean, and he knew that in eighteen months
he had never been blown up for a lie or an exaggeration. So, as soon as the ship-news chief went out, John
Orcutt struck his bell, and sent for Mr. Pringle.

The young man came, amazed. They were often
sent for in the morning, but never before had he been
in the chief's office at eleven at night.

"What are you doing, Mr. Pringle?" asked John.

"I am making rather a curious tabular statement,
from my own notes, comparing the number of catches
on the fly made in a temperature of 80° against those
made at an average temperature of 60°."

"Would it do as well on Monday, or is any one else
doing the same thing?"

Mr. Pringle was quite sure no one else was doing it.
He had not even suggested it to any of the other men,
so eager was he that *To-day* only should have the glory
of the discovery, if discovery there were. In the slang
of the office he called the glory "Kudos."

"Then I will thank you to take those letters and
papers, which Mr. Atwood has left me, and sift out
this Fiji and Marquesas business. I do not know, but
I suspect that our admiral is wrong. I do not know,
but I think that there is no French admiral there. I
do know that the Babylon papers are wholly wrong.

Have the goodness to look up the international law.
Do not forget the cases of the *Wild-flyer* and of
the *Pilgrim*, which are, I think, the leading cases.
Look at Porter's account of his occupation of Marquesas. Take as much space as you like, but be sure
that we are right and not wrong. I will hold back
the press if you choose. I am sorry to keep you
up."

" That is of no consequence," said the young man,
his face all beaming with delight. " I shall have four
hours clear."

" And I think no one will interrupt you," said John
Orcutt, laughing. " Good-night."

" Good - night, sir." And the happy young fellow
took away the papers.

When the great editor returned on Monday morning he drove directly to John Orcutt's home. It
was in the fifth story of the Wellington Apartment
Hotel.

" Mrs. Orcutt, I am sure you will give me breakfast.
Heaven knows what I might find at my quarters! I
want to talk to your husband." And at this moment
John Orcutt appeared.

" John, I was just in time. They hated me, but they
listened. They had not looked at my telegram, had
not even lighted their pipes with it. John, we saved
them from the greatest blunder they have made yet.
And to say that is to say a great deal, as you know.
But all is well that ends well. They are saved ; the
country is saved ; nay, the world is saved, till somebody somewhere makes another blunder. We will

try to forget this one. Now I want to talk about ourselves. I bought our paper Sunday as I crossed the ferry. Who wrote our leader on this island row?"

The chief's manner was perfectly impassive. He broke his egg without the least feeling. Was the leader all right or all wrong? John Orcutt had not the faintest idea. But the truth must be told.

"Young Mr. Pringle did it," said he. "I told him the truth must be found and stated, and I gave him four hours to do it."

The chief looked gravely at John and nodded. In a minute he said: "I knew you did not write it, nor L'Estrange, nor Walter, nor Webb. Indeed, I did not know we had a man in the office who could write it. No, nor the man in the country. I knew I could not."

John Orcutt was well pleased to find that the article was all right. He had feared, indeed, since Saturday, that it might be all wrong.

"What do you say his name is—Pringle?"

"Yes."

"I guess his father was in the law school in my time. Send him in to me at two o'clock."

At two o'clock Mr. Pringle knocked at the "responsible" door. He knew he was to see the chief. Whether he were to be dismissed from the office or not, he did not know.

But the chief even rose and shook hands. "Mr. Pringle, I am so glad to see you. I ought to be ashamed, but I did not know before yesterday how

we were wasting the force of our office. I think it
may please you to know that when I met Chancellor
Guilford yesterday, as we were coming out of church,
he asked who wrote our articles on international law,
and he said that he should read your paper on the
·Occupation of Rimatàra' to his classes."

Mr. Pringle blushed and stammered out his thanks
and satisfaction.

"Do you read German?" continued the eager chief.

"Of course, sir."

"Good. Please take these Vienna papers, and this
Rundschau—yes—and somewhere here—here they are
—these pamphlets, and look up for us this man Kohlschutter's discussion of Nationality. I thought I
should have to do it myself. I suppose he is a son of
the old Kohlschutter, or maybe grandson. Take all
the time you want. Mr. Orcutt says you only had
four hours Friday night."

"Yes, sir; but I studied that matter in the fore-
castle, when I was before the mast."

"Good!" said the chief again. "Here is a line to
Mr. McElrath. He will fix your salary for the present
at $2000. I will speak to Mr. Orcutt about your work.
Unless you wish, you will do no more baseball at
present. Good-morning. Come round when you can,
and let me introduce you to my wife. You had better move your things into Mr. What's-his-name's
vacant office; next Mr. Orcutt's, you know. Good-
morning."

Before Edward Pringle moved a thing, he went into
the empty office and wrote this despatch to Mary
Underwood:

"DEAR MARY,—My salary is raised to $2000. Say Thursday, or Thursday week.

EDWARD."

And she telegraphed back:

"Thursday week, if you insist upon it. Always yours,

"MARY."

VIII

When the Recording Angel entered this last correspondence he bade his clerks make cross-references to it in the great editor's book and in John Orcutt's book, but he asked to have Helen Melcher's book brought to him, that he might make the entry there with his own hand.

"Somehow," said the Recording Angel, with that grave smile of his, "I am more glad for this one than I am for all the others. Wars and rumors of wars, life and death—yes—yes, they are all very grand and very important; but they are all grand and important only if and as they help to making happy homes.

"And how good it is," he said, as he dipped his pen in his best golden ink, "that when that sad girl did that unselfish thing in that surgeon's anteroom she made this heaven of a happy home for Edward Pringle and Mary Underwood, not for time only, but for all eternity!"

THE MINISTER'S BLACK VEIL

WITH FULL PARTICULARS

[THIS curious and pathetic story has been told by Mr. Hawthorne in his very best style. It is now classical as one of the "Twice-Told Tales." I would not undertake to tell it for the third time but that I do not believe that many readers have seen the original documents. Mr. Hawthorne, indeed, carefully keeps them out of sight, and, with his love of mystery, he leaves the reader to guess what Mr. Hooper's reasons were for wearing the veil, if, indeed, Mr. Hawthorne himself knew. Now the truth is that many a man of to-day, particularly as he steps into a street-car or enters any other public place in what is called our modern civilization, wishes he had a veil on. Women have this resource, and avail themselves of it—how much I do not know ; for, of course, when they are deeply veiled I cannot tell who they are. The only men I ever saw with veils on were some work-men on the Lake Superior Canal. They said they wore the veils to keep off the mosquitoes. But, for aught I know, they may have all been retired clergymen earning their living honestly, and their names may have been "Hooper." But, as I did not ask them their story, we will let them pass, and go back to our own version of the original Parson Hooper and his Black Veil.]

I

Mr. Hooper woke one morning after a broken sleep. He was more silent at breakfast than was his habit. Mrs. Hooper saw this, and she knew the reason. She had seen it while he dressed himself, and she knew the reason then. But all her comment was to hurry into her kitchen a little earlier than usual, and take in her own hand a certain preparation of egg on toast which he was fond of. "If he is worried, he shall have his egg," said the good woman to herself. And Mr. Hooper had it, and ate it all, and thanked her for it. But he talked little at breakfast, and Mrs. Hooper knew why.

A messenger had come from her brother the night before to say that Plinlimmon would sail on Thursday, if the wind served, for England. Now Plinlimmon was to take in his ship the return which Parson Hooper was to make for the last year's purchases in London— for the silk dress, the silk stockings, the muslin neckties, the books, the gamboge and senna and other medicines. Mrs. Hooper's cousin Avery had made and sent out the selection, and had bidden Mr. Hooper send the returns in mink or beaver, clapboards, sassafras, and gold-thread. But, of course, he had left it to Mr. Hooper's judgment how much or how little of each of these various staples should be intrusted Plinlimmon. And here was the great decision to be made to-day. Poor Mr. Hooper must find out how much gold-thread there was on sale, and how much sassafras, and the rest. He must take final advice with her brother and the other merchants, and so do the best possible thing for her cousin Avery. Mrs. Hooper knew too well that she must not oppose him. She had suggested that he should leave the whole affair to her brother, and Mr. Hooper had said "No." She could not understand, he had said, but it was one of those personal things which he must determine.

So he left her, with his brow clouded. He had called her attention to what he supposed to be the rise in the price of gold-thread. He had asked her whether she had heard from "the Indian" anything about the number of minks killed last winter. So far he had confided in her. But only so far. And she knew that he went, in perplexity, to a disagreeable morning.

But if Mr. Hooper was depressed when he left home, he was more depressed when he returned. Yet his brother-in-law had been most kind. He had ready for him, in the little counting-room, notes of the pieces of all the various articles which the Averys had suggested for shipment. He had given his own advice. He had consulted with neighbors; and as Mr. Glover, the brother-in-law, was one of the largest merchants, and as Mr. Hooper's and Avery's little venture was one of the smallest, even Mr. Hooper felt that all possible care had been given as to the grounds for his decision. And he had gone so far as to determine that twelve hundred cedar clapboards, of a fashion that had found favor in London, should be that day packed away in the recesses of the hold of Plinlimmon's vessel. For the rest, he had told Mr. Glover he would decide.

And so he had started to walk home, and to make his decision on the way. Then it was that misfortune began. For, just as he crossed from the counting-room to the more quiet side of the street, that he might meditate undisturbed, excellent Madam Cockrell had seen him, and had borne down on him.

"Dear Mr. Hooper, I am so glad to see you! I am so taken up to-day, and so busy with Ruth and Eunice and all the girls. You do not know, indeed, that Ruth

is to go to Biddeford with Chauncy, and not a thing
ready! I said to my husband that I did not see how I
could go and see your wife, and he did not seem to
think that he could go. But now I have caught you; it
is so lucky, and you will do just as well. Will you tell
Mrs. Hooper that I have seen Dinah, and that Dinah
says that if she will give her up Monday afternoon, so
that she can go up to the Tetlows then and kind of
finish off their washing—she can stop for me half an
hour earlier on Tuesday, and then be at your house by
eleven. Or, if you must have her Monday, and will let
her know by Silas when he passes by, then she will see
Miriam at Judge Lee's," etc., etc., etc., etc. Mr. Hooper could not repeat more of the message, far less Mrs.
Hooper, and least of all this chronicler.

"She said she had caught me," said the poor minister. "How often they say that! As if I were escaping
from my keepers. She 'caught me,' indeed, and after
she had walked half-way home with me without her
hood on, and I tried to think out about the gold-thread
and the sassafras—my dear, I believe I am going crazy.
I was all confused whether your brother said ten or ten
dozen. I do not know, and I know he wants to know
in the morning."

Poor Mrs. Hooper did what she had done hundreds
of times before in similar catastrophes. She sympa-
thized, soothed, and wondered. She led back to the
success about the clapboards. Privately she despatched
Gotham, who was chopping wood, with a note to her
brother. And, before Mr. Hooper had finished the egg
and wine she had hastily beaten up for him, lest he
should be chilled by his walk, a note from the wharf

supplied, in black and white, the necessary information. And, in the secret silence of the study, Parson Hooper recomposed himself as he could to the unusual and disagreeable calculation. What his brother Glover would have done in five minutes this excellent man wasted a day upon, and even then was sure that he did not do it well, because Mrs. Cockrell had "caught him." Not even when Avery's letters arrived, eight months after, and expressed even enthusiasm about the success of the venture, was Parson Hooper wholly soothed.

II

To persons unused to ministerial life in New England at the beginning of the last century, it will seem that no such misfortune could happen again to Parson Hooper within a year. But that is because they are unused to it. His wife could tell them better. The very next day—it was Wednesday—the good man told his wife that he should give the morning to the Goldthwaites at the mills. The troubles of the Goldthwaites were: 1, bodily, in that they were poor; 2, mental, in that they knew not what to do; 3, spiritual, in that each one had quarrelled with each other of the whole clan of Goldthwaites. On Parson Hooper, as the clear-headed, sound adviser and peacemaker of the whole town, devolved the solution of all problems and the reunion of the broken family. And to this work he gave up Wednesday, and went forth as cheerfully as Amadis ever went to battle:

" Lo ! he returned all wounded and forlorn,
His dream of glory lost in shades of night."

To Mrs. Hooper, and to her alone, he told the story
of his discomfiture.

He had seen Seth Goldthwaite alone. That was
necessary. And no one knew he had come in. He
had seen old grandsire Tetlow, who had married the
widow Goldthwaite. This visit also was secret, as if
he had been Nicodemus. He had seen Lucas and Phi-
lemon as they were hewing the timbers for their new
barn. Then he had left them to "cross lots," by par-
donable guile. For both these "contrary" men believed that he was on his way to the school at the
Falls, and he did not undeceive them. His visit to
Fairfax Shipman, who had married Rachel Goldthwaite, must be as secret as the dew from heaven,
and none this side the Recording Angel must know
he took to her ten pieces of eight and a joe from
Mother Tetlow.

"And I went by the quarry, and just as I had to
cross the country road, of all men in the world the
doctor appeared in his gig. Of course he knew me.
Of course he guessed I was going to the school. I
must ride. He would stop and bring me home. My
dear Mary, if I had lisped a word about Rachel Shipman it would have gone over the town. So I had to
go with him. I have been at the Falls since noon.
The doctor has brought me home, and here I am,
with poor Rachel's money in my pocket. My dear
Mary, I wished for the invisible hat of Jack the Giant-
killer !"

And in this grievous wail of the good man the first suggestion of the veil came in.

Before it was light the next morning he had saddled the bay mare. And before the sun rose Rachel Shipman had her money.

III

But the week was not ended. No, indeed. "The end is not yet," as good Parson Hooper would have said. In the long ride to Mr. Shipman's in the gray of the morning he had studied over his sermons as best he might, and in the ride back again he had gone over the order of the argument again. But the whole was hazy, and he knew it was. All intermingled with the logical flow of predestination and free-will, sanctification and duty, came in the refrain of poor Mrs. Shipman's entreating words as she stood on the doorstep and whispered them in his ear. It was a long distance, and of course he was late to his breakfast after he returned. Then he told his wife the whole story. And now he could go into the study and begin his notes for a brief of the sermons. But his mind would not work well. The Goldthwaites and the Shipmans and the Tetlows, and all their gossip, would interfere with the argument. The good man put on his hat and boots, stopped at the dairy door to tell his wife that he was going to walk in the cedar pasture, so as to think out the sermons in the open air, and jumped lightly over the fence into the orchard on his way thither.

Better for him had he taken the longer way; for, as he passed through the orchard, Nick Tainter saw him and joined him instantly.

"So glad to find you, Parson! Didn't dare go in! Miss Hooper said you was busy writin', 'n' I thought I must wait tell ye come out. All night I've been thinkin' about it, 'n' I knew I must come 'n' ask ye. Now, tell me, Parson, ef Solomon's Temple hed a nethermost chamber five cubits high, en the middle chamber was six cubits broad, en the third chamber was seven cubits broad, how would them priests and Levites turn round?" etc., etc., etc., in that strangest and saddest of half coherency and half folly in which the mathematical mind of New England is so apt to give way.

Poor Parson Hooper! he knew the morning was gone for him now. How often the poor man had said that here was the one point where his dear Saviour's example failed him! "He could cure these poor, crazy people," the good parson said, "and I can't." Still he was willing to do his part. He could always soothe, and he would always soothe. How much time or how little he ought to give to them and their vagaries he could never decide. And yet he could never bring himself to accept the more trenchant views of Mrs. Hooper—into which discussion this story need not go. Enough to say that the brief of the sermons was more hazy than ever, and was intermixed now with the dimensions of the nethermost chamber. And to-morrow would be Friday. In a working minister's life, most days are.

When dinner came, Nick Tainter was provided with

a bit of pie and cheese to walk home with, and told to read carefully the books of Chronicles, and good Mr. Hooper, still perplexed, but ready to see the droll side of the adventure, joined the family at their meal. Here was a new element. His wife's pretty sister, Martha Glover, had come down from Boston. She had been expected, but not expected so soon. She was a pet with the parson, as she was, indeed, with all the household. And the blackest clouds of Goldthwaites or of Tainters vanished before her sunshine.

By the time they came to the dumplings, Mr. Hooper was in his best mood, and, with all his latent fun, and with infinite kindness as well, he told the story of poor Nick's troubles about the nethermost chamber, and of his own crafty and ingenious solutions. But then his face clouded a little, and he said, sadly enough : " It is all well enough to laugh at, but what will become of my sermons? I am sure I do not know." And so he told, in a humorous vein, and not as seriously as I have told it, the history of Tuesday and Wednesday and Thursday : how Mrs. Cockrell had "caught him," how the doctor had insisted on his riding, and now how poor Nick had recognized him the moment he leaped the fence. Indeed, if he had not told the story, you would not be reading it now.

"My dear brother Oliver," said the laughing girl, " you must do as I do. You must wear a veil. You are too attractive by half to all these people. Now, what do I do when I want a bit of ribbon, or some buttons, or some muslin, early in the morning before I am dressed in a walking-dress, you know — when I just want to run into Cornhill and out again ? Why, I put on a veil! If I meet anybody, he thinks it is the Governor's cook or one of Judge Sewall's maids. I get my buttons, and nobody is the wiser. I might be a squaw, and nobody would know." And they all laughed at the conceit, which supposed that the light, merry girl should not be recognized anywhere. But she was pleased with her fancy, and she followed it out into its details. And she made the parson and Mrs. Hooper, and even little Deborah Hooper, discuss the color of the veil—whether it should be white, or light blue, or dark blue, or green, or purple. But Parson Hooper said that he wouldn't have it green, because his eyes were strong and good; and as for white, he thought it was unbecoming. "As to that," the merry girl said, "no one could tell until they had tried."

She was sure, she said, that she could find muslin or some sleazy stuff in her sister's boxes or drawers, and that afternoon she should put a veil in every hat in the house. And so she did. While the parson, in the quiet of his own den that afternoon, took a long nap, and then addressed himself to the mysteries of predestination again, Miss Martha captured every hat in the house. In one she sewed a white veil, in one a green, in one a light blue, and in one a very dark blue. She could find no purple muslin, and so had to give up that fancy. But she revenged herself by putting in one a veil of cherry color.

She was wild to try the experiment, and a little before sunset she tapped at his door and said he must come to walk with her. The good man did as he was bid; and, to her infinite joy, as he took the first hat which offered, carrying it absently in his hand till they

had crossed the door-yard, he did not notice the pink
veil till, when the hat was fairly on his head, it fell before his eyes.

The girl screamed with delight at her success. And,
when he fell in with her humor, and walked on with
the veil; when even the two old cows, waiting to be
milked, turned with horror and fled when they saw
him, she clapped her hands with delight and did not pretend to suppress her shouts of laughter. A jolly walk,
indeed, they both had of it, and when they came back
to supper it would be hard to say which of them made
the more absurd and amusing story from the adventure.

"Indeed, my dear sister, you must let him do it! Indeed, my dear Oliver, you must wear one or the other
of them always, whenever you go abroad, if it were
only for the love of me! When Mrs. Cockrell sees you
she will say, 'That man looks just like our dear Mr.
Hooper; but it isn't he, because Mr. Hooper never wears
a veil.' And when the doctor sees you he will say,
'Umph! there's one of Pyecroft's patients; the old fool
has made him wear a veil!' and you, my dear Oliver,
you will be the happiest of men. Your sermons will
be perfectly magnificent, and every day you will bless
your wise little sister Martha."

IV

And so it proved, indeed, that the minister's Saturday
was tranquil and happy. Not that anybody saw him
with a veil on, always excepting Jotham, who saw
everything that went and came. And Jotham asked

no questions. Why should he ask questions? There were many things in that house, from Hebrew down and from Marlborough pies up, which he did not understand. Possibly the presence in the house of a cheery, wide-awake sister Martha, determined to make the best of everything, had its part in the improvement of the minister's spirits. He had his quiet morning in his study. He had his lonely walk in the afternoon among the cedars; and, to amuse Martha, when he went out, he let the rose-colored veil fall over his face. And for half an hour he forgot it, as he wove back and forward that web of foreknowledge into which were wrought the patterns drawn from the Goldthwaites' quarrels. And as he came home in the evening, with the sermon well thought out, he dropped the veil again as he crossed the orchard, so that he might please the laughing girl who awaited his return.

Martha hardly knew one hat from another, certainly did not care, as she stitched the veils into the linings. But Mrs. Hooper knew very well which was the Sunday hat; and when she and Martha started for meeting together in the chaise on the Sabbath morning she left the Sunday hat, carefully brushed, in full sight of her husband, and secreted all the others. Now this hat, as the powers ordered, was the hat with the dark-blue veil. Mr. Hooper always preferred to walk to meeting alone. Indeed, if he could start an hour before the rest, and carry a crumb of comfort to some wretched home, he said that was his best preparation. But this time he followed hard after the party in the chaise. Of course, he had folded the veil back so that it rested above his head, nor did any one suspect that it was

there. But as he walked alone and shook out again
that webwork of foreknowledge on which he was to
preach, again the phantoms of the Goldthwaites' lives
ran across his thought ; and as, in his puzzle, he tried
to wipe the furrows from his forehead, unconsciously
for a moment he lifted the hat from his head. It was
but a moment, and when he put it back the blue veil
fell and floated before his eyes. It did screen out the
sun. It screened off the dust of the road. His puzzled
thoughts did flow more smoothly for the moment. He
would not break that flow for the world, and he let
the veil hang. It was at that moment that Jotham
Lee passed him, as he paced along so slowly and
thoughtfully. It was he who announced, as Mr. Hawthorne has told, to the wondering loafers on the steps
of the meeting-house that "the minister was wearing
a veil."

Meanwhile the bell slowly tolled. It would have
tolled all day if the minister had not come. Mr.
Hooper did walk slowly. The veil soothed him more
than he knew. And even when he approached the
group of those waiting for him he did not know how
late he was. Indeed, he was roused from this thought
only by a coarse oath of that brute, Cephas Goldthwaite, who said, as if half daring the minister to
hear :

"Ef he would wear that rag into meetin', I'd go in
an' hear him, 'n' I have not been into meetin' twelve
months to-day."

Parson Hooper turned on the brute, took off his hat,
and looked at him, with a look of love which might
have softened a stone.

"Go in then, Cephas, with your wife, and I will wear the rag, as you say."

He tore the lining out upon the instant, adjusted the veil over his eyes, and, as the hushed assembly stood on both sides, bowing as he passed, he bowed to the right and left, and, with the mysterious veil upon his face, mounted the pulpit stairs.

Mr. Hawthorne seems to have confounded two traditions of Mr. Hooper's life in the earlier part of his story. But when we come to the scene in church, all the traditions are at one. "That mysterious emblem was never once withdrawn. It shook with his measured breath as he gave out the psalm; it threw its obscurity between him and the holy page as he read the Scriptures; and while he prayed the veil lay heavily upon his uplifted countenance.

"There was something which made the sermon greatly the most powerful effort that they had ever heard from their pastor's lips. The subject had reference to secret sin, and those sad mysteries which we hide from our nearest and dearest and would fain conceal from our own consciousness, even forgetting that the Omniscient can detect them. A subtle power was breathed into his words."

When Mr. Hawthorne goes on to say "that the man of hardened breast" listened now as never before, he recalls the memory of that brutal Cephas Goldthwaite, who had dared the minister to wear the veil. And well may that memory be renewed from that day to this day. It was Cephas Goldthwaite to whom Mr. Hooper was speaking; it was for Cephas Goldthwaite that he prayed with his veiled face turned up to heaven; it

was the certainty of what was hidden in Cephas Goldthwaite's life which gave the dramatic power to the
story of David as he read. And if, after he had begun
the sermon, the puzzle of foreknowledge all drifted
away like a morning cloud, if in place of it the clear
sunlight of the Holy Spirit poured down and lighted
every heart in that amazed multitude, all this was because Parson Hooper had determined that for once
Cephas Goldthwaite should hear the truth of God, if no
word ever spoke to him again. And it was because the
Spirit, thus wooed and thus won, did speak to Cephas
Goldthwaite as he sat there in a maze—because of this
it was that he who came in a brute went out a man.
He pressed his poor wife's hand tenderly before he
left the hard form which was the seat assigned to
them. He shook his brother's hand cordially, as from
different doors they met upon the green—that brother
to whom he had not spoken since his father's funeral.
To grandsire Tetlow as he passed him he said: "Send
round Nathan for a barrel of apples there is waiting";
and as he, of all men, lifted Madam Hooper into her
chaise he said, in a half-whisper: "Mistress Hooper,
do you tell the parson that this day he has saved a
soul from hell!"

Well might the people in that town, and their children to Mr. Hawthorne's day, say that the preacher
"had discovered their hoarded iniquity." They waited,
of course, for a brief interval till he came out, the last
of all. "He paid due reverence to the hoary heads,
saluted the middle-aged with kind dignity as their
friend and spiritual guide, greeted the young with
mingled authority and love, and laid his hands on the

little children's heads to bless them. Such was always
his custom on the Sabbath day. Strange and bewil-
dered looks repaid him for his courtesy."

I do not pretend more than Mr. Hawthorne has
done to give the exact date or place of this strange incident, in which was bound up so much of the future of
that man. As always happens, and as the reader sees,
when tradition once got hold, it had its way. First of
all, the dark-blue veil—torn from one which had once
screened Mrs. Hooper's eyes in snow-storms—became
black as the story passed from generation to generation. As the reader has seen, Mr. Hooper, the happy
husband of a cheerful wife, "became a comely bache-
lor of thirty." He never chose to tell why he wore
the veil at first; nor, indeed, to tell why he wore it
afterwards: and so posterity in its report did as re-
porters will, and made a mystery of shame and peni-
tence, when there was no such mystery in the beginning.
Mr. Hooper found out that his sister Martha was right.
If his veil were down, he could pursue a train of
thought without being asked to remember the appoint-
ments of a washerwoman. He could go on the errands
which he had determined instead of being led to and
fro by the vagaries of wayfarers. He could command
his own time for the service of God and man, instead
of giving it up to chattering with loafers, without apparent rudeness; he could obey that great instruction
of the Master to his disciples, that when they went on
his imperial mission they should not stop on the way
to salute vagrants. "Salute no man by the way," he
would say, seriously, to his wife when she asked him,
cautiously, whether he had better wear his veil on such

or such an errand. If he did wear it, she was sure that
he went on the Master's service.

Little wonder that the good man's life became more
and more serene. Little wonder if his real cheerfulness were more and more tender. Little wonder if
men and women with whom he talked found his words
were more weighty and his counsel more sure. It was
no vain thing for him to take up one of the threads
spun by the Eternal Wheels, as they move in infinite
certainty, and to weave that thread into the pattern of
such a life as a Goldthwaite or a Tetlow was living.
No foolish interruption tangled the thread or broke it.
It came to be an easy thing that the clear mirror
of the good man's thought reflected directly the ray
which fell upon it from the Sun of Righteousness. No
hammer of Thor broke that mirror ruthlessly. It was
left as the God of Heaven made it. Why multiply
words? The good man's eye was single now. And
from this Sunday all that men saw of him was full of
Light.

AUNT CAROLINE'S PRESENT

I.—NOW WE SHALL KNOW

Yes. We were really married.

The minister had said we were one, and he had given us his blessing. He had taken my hand, and the tears were in his eyes as he wished me all happiness. He kissed Eleanor, whom he had christened twenty years before, and he blessed her again. "God bless you, my child!" he said. Then we turned round, so that the other people in the room could see us, and the procession of sympathizing friends came up and wished us well.

The sixth person in the procession was Aunt Caroline. She is Eleanor's aunt, but I like her quite as much as Eleanor does; the kindest, sweetest, most loving aunt that ever came in when she was wanted, and stayed away when she was not wanted; that ever sent ice-cream across to your house on a summer's evening, or called to take your Southern cousins to ride when she knew they bored you to death. Aunt Caroline was sixth in the procession of welcome.

"Dear Felix," she said at once, "dear Eleanor, my present—well, it is too big to be carried about much, and so — well, I have told the man to carry it to your new house, and when you come it will be there before you to welcome you. I do hope you will like it."

" Like it !—of course we shall like it, Aunt Caroline. We should like it if it were only a lump of coal." And in her tenderness Eleanor kissed her aunt again and again.

Fifty times on the wedding journey did we go back to the present, and wonder what it was which was so large. I was sure it was a cast of the Laocoon. Eleanor was quite sure it was a library bookcase. Sometimes I thought it was the *Cyclopædia Britannica* up to Marplot, which was as far as that cyclopædia had then gone. Sometimes I hoped it was Larousse, which would be better still. At last, after such a fortnight of October and red maples, and purple tupelos and glorious sunsets, and cozy reading of Browning by the firesides of comfortable inns — after fourteen days of exquisite life and happy love, we drove up to the pretty little house which was to be our happy home, and I lifted Eleanor from the buggy, and I said, " Welcome home, sweetheart and darling !"

And she kissed me, and she ran before me into the house, and she said, " Now we shall know."

II.—WHAT WE FOUND

Alas! we did know, only too soon.

Bridget had lighted up the new parlor for our reception with the effulgence of her own enthusiasm. There was a large carcel burning on the centre table. This lamp was a present from Uncle Tristram. On the mantel were too bronze branches in which she had placed four red wax-candles, and she had lighted them all. These branches were a present from my cousin Jotham. On the other side of the room, on the piano-forte, were two student-lamps of different patterns. These were presents from Ernest Gabler and Submit Shattuck, and Bridget had lighted both of them.

All this light and sweetness were to do fit honor to Aunt Caroline's present, which was at the other end of the room as we entered, and obtruded itself from the very first instant. Indeed, it was impossible to escape it at any moment while you were in that room. It was a thoroughly horrible picture from the parable of the Prodigal Son. It had escaped by misfortune from some "chamber of horrors." I do not know its real history, though I have, alas! had time enough to study it since those days. But I cannot think calmly on its history; it even makes me sick; and excepting that the name "Melgrum" appears rather prominently un-der the feet of one of the swine, I have no clew to its origin. I can only suppose, as I do, that "Melgrum" was some overgrown oaf in some high-school, who made himself disgusting by caricaturing the boys and the masters. I think the masters, in the hope to be rid of him, reported that he was a genius, and per-suaded some kind brewer to give him money enough to go to Munich to "study art." Arrived there, I think he had just learned what are the crudest, the most fiery and piercing pigments concocted, when he painted this picture, before his studies in anatomy, composition, or perspective had begun. I think the Bavarian government forbade its public exhibition, and that it was then surreptitiously sent to this country for sale. I think dear Aunt Caroline was entrapped or lured into the warehouse where it was exhibited just when the thousand dollars was burning in her pocket-book which she meant to spend for Eleanor's present. I think she told her companion, Mrs. Jabez Flynn, how much she meant to spend, that Mrs. Flynn privately told this to the perjured villain who is the master of the picture-shop, and that he, with an awful audacity, bade the attendant bring this picture forward and place it under the lights for exhibition. I think he mentioned twelve hundred dollars as the price, but consented to be forced down to one thousand. And then and thus I think our fate was sealed.

The size of the picture was eight feet by six. The frame was enormous, and very costly. The conception was absurd. In the middle of the picture you saw a large group intended to represent a company of people feasting, who were the Prodigal Son, his father and mother, and other guests called in on the occasion of his return. A gallery above them in the background was filled with people singing, and under the gallery, but beyond the guests, you could dimly discern other people dancing, with tambourines over their heads. All this transpired under certain columns and arches, but all in the open air. On the right hand, in what would be the distance had "Melgrum" known how to represent distance, stood a man in his shirt-sleeves feeding hogs with Indian-corn. On the other side, of the same size and character, was a butcher cutting the throat of a calf. From something Aunt Caroline

dropped, I believe it was the happy union of three
subjects on one canvas which determined her to buy
the picture. As she said, with real enthusiasm, " It
does not represent a part of the parable; the whole
parable is there."

III.—HOW PEOPLE LIKED IT

Here was the picture, occupying practically the whole
of one wall of our parlor, which was to have been so
pretty—the room in which, as our plans were made,
dear Eleanor was to spend the greater part of her life.
We looked at it a little, we received silently Bridget's
enthusiastic admiration of it, but we passed as quickly as
we could to see how the dining-room was arranged, and
how my workshop looked. And it ended in my putting Eleanor into my own easy-chair there, going back
into her parlor for one of the reading-lamps, and bidding Bridget extinguish the others and the candles.
Eleanor spent the evening with me in my den, and I
read Coventry Patmore's *Betrothal* to her.

But we could not do that all the time. She could
not be in my room when I had men there on business.
She had a feeling of pride, indeed, which for a long
time made her keep up a gallant struggle for the parlor, which was her own room, she said. " Why should
I go up-stairs and sit in a bedchamber, when I have
such a pretty room of my own?" She would say this.
She would say, "I am sure dear Aunt Caroline did not
mean to make me to be a vagrant in my own house."
Queer, now, that sense of pride. I have known men
who had it. I have known men who really thought

that when they had done a gallant eight hours' work down-town they had a right at home to the things home was made for. Philanthropists and politicians and tramps, map-peddlers and others, would follow them to their homes, and yet these men would actually refuse to grind their axes for them there. So poor Eleanor said she would stand for her rights in her pretty parlor. She would not be driven out from it by that hateful butcher; she would not have those dirty pigs trampling over her carpet, she said; she would not hear those tambourine women clinking their old parchment things.

But she overestimated her own abilities. I have noticed that most men do who think they can keep bores out of their houses. I have a large circle of friends in and near Netherstone, and so has Eleanor. They were making their wedding calls, and they always found the Prodigals—as Eleanor called all the people in the picture, quadrupeds and bipeds—had stepped in before them. Eleanor had not simply to keep the odious creatures out of her own mind and heart; she had to keep them out of her visitors'.

"I could bear it," she said, "if I were alone. I can turn my back to it. See, I have my work-table and my things here, and here is my writing-desk I look exactly the other way. But it is the callers. Everybody looks at the Prodigals first and last; and in spite of all my skill it is the central and chief subject of conversation."

In truth, visitors might be divided into three classes as regarded the picture. These were, first, the frank, unpretending people, who did not value their own opinions highly, but still had opinions. These people said —how could they do otherwise?—that they disliked the picture very much. Some of them asked Eleanor how she could have such an absurd thing there. Most of them, it is true, thought this was not kind. But even of this set there were but few who had sense enough and self-control enough to say nothing. Had it been an ugly figure on the paper-hanging, I do not think they would have spoken of it. Had the room been inconveniently low, I do not think many of these people would have said, "How low this ceiling is!" But a mistaken etiquette has come in, and people think they must speak of pictures as you must speak of the weather, of the election, of health, and of the opera. So was it that even judicious people asked if it were painted in Munich, or they were reminded by it of a picture they had seen in Antwerp, or they said the subject had not been often treated, or said it had. The most carefully trained of this class said it was "very instructive." Other some said that it must have taken a great deal of pains and study. And my poor wife— as the various nice people of the town and the neighborhood called upon her—came to know all the possible changes of these judicious remarks, as you know the changes on the nearest chime of bells. She said she could tell what they were going to say before they opened their mouths.

The second class was larger. It was the body of people, quite uninstructed in fine art, who wanted to be instructed, wanted to think right, and wanted to say right, if they could only find out what right was. Well, I have a right to say that there was nobody in

5

Netherstone whose opinion on such matters was regarded more highly than mine. I had shown my photographs at the Lend-a-Hand Club one winter. I was president of the Reading Club, and we had read Mrs. Jameson, and all the people who could had brought pictures. So long as there were art unions, the book-store men always sent the art-union agents first of all to me. Indeed, if anybody in that neighborhood knew what was good in art, I did. Class number two consisted of people who, of themselves, would have detested the picture, but, seeing it in my house, knew they ought to like it. They made horrible attempts to like it. "How very natural that pig's tail is!" "How red the sunset is!" "See how angry his face is!" "It is so interesting to see the costume! I never understood before about the coat of many colors;" and so on. They would keep my poor wife standing before the abomination all through the wedding call. When I came home from the office she would be dead with fatigue, and when I soothed her, and asked the reason, she would sigh out, "Oh, it was the Prodigals again!"

Smallest of all, yet I ought to say most disagreeable of all, the three classes of visitors were those who abused it up and down. Smallest because, as I have hinted, it required courage in my house to say that one of my pictures was hopelessly bad, and had no redeeming point in it. But this the thoroughly disagreeable people of our acquaintance, the people we least liked, sometimes had courage enough to say, or what Mr. Ward calls "cussedness" enough. These people, therefore, were the only people of all who made wedding

calls on us in the month after our return who said
what we ourselves said to each other. Yet such is the
perversity of human nature that we were not pleased
when they did say it; for they seemed to say it because they thought it would displease us. When we
assented moderately, they were not satisfied with such
assent. They required stronger language or none.
But who would, who could, gratify such cynical and
hateful wretches? Were we to give up dear, kind Aunt
Caroline to their gossip and brutal jeers? No, indeed!
The unfriendly criticism was as bad as the friendly.

"It is all horrid, perfectly horrid!" This was my
wife's exclamation to me almost every day.

Yet Aunt Caroline looked in on us herself so often
and so kindly that it was impossible to carry the dreadful thing to the attic, to the cellar, or to the furnace.
And when she came—without saying much about her
own present—she still brooded over it with an eye so
loving and tender, her whole great heart went out to it
with such delight, that for the moment my poor Eleanor
would be rewarded for the struggle she had made.
Now she was glad she had not dashed at that little
pig with her scissors to cut out his "natural tail":
now she was glad she had not brought "Morning Sun
Stove Polish" from the kitchen to rub it over the face
of the butcher who killed the fatted calf. So much
occasional reward had she for a moment as the recom-
pense for days of wretchedness.

After the various wedding calls on us were over, and
after we had returned them, there came a certain lull.
In the midst of it Eleanor made a little visit of forty-
eight hours to Miss Stearns, her dear old schoolmis-

tress. I improved the occasion, and sent for Copperhead, the village upholsterer, and with his aid I moved
the Prodigals into the dining-room. The first time
Aunt Caroline called she looked for it in its usual place,
and her face fell. But I told her boldly that the light
was better in the dining-room, and that I thought the
festivity which was suggested by the picture was ap-
propriate to that altar of the appetites. Dear Aunt
Caroline! she also had perfect confidence in my good
taste in fine art, and she abjectly and modestly assented. So that when my dear wife came home she could
receive a morning visit without terror.

But when one saves at the spigot, one may lose at
the bung. Your skirmishers are successful, but just in
their flush of victory your centre is forced, and the
battle is lost. While we triumphed in the serenity of
morning calls it happened that I had to give a little
dinner-party to Sir William Hartley, the distinguished
botanist, who had brought me letters from Professor
Sabbati. I had sent to Cincinnati for the L'Estranges
to come up and meet him; Armstrong had been very
good and had ridden over from the college; Eleanor's
pretty sister Grace was staying with us; and we had
the two Carter girls, Felix Carter's twin daughters.

I do not say that Eleanor and I had forgotten. That
is impossible. But I always sat with my back to it,
and she with her right side to it, and we had fallen
into the habit of leaving the room without looking at
it. In summer we had a light gauze hung over it, to
keep off the flies.

But it was just before Christmas that Sir William
came with the letter of introduction. No flies then.

The most agreeable of travellers was he. And all the others came, as nice as they could be. He took Eleanor in to dinner, I took in Sarah Carter, and the others were arranged just as they liked. He was telling a very merry story about the Ameer of Cabool as he ate his soup, and he had just come to the point, when Bridget took his plate away, and as he looked up he saw the pigs and the forlorn Prodigal.

Well-bred as he was, he lost command of himself. He faltered, and for a moment said nothing. Then he turned to Eleanor with an agonized smile, and said, "I beg your pardon, I was saying—oh yes, it was the *officinalis*, not the *maritima*, but the two resemble each other closely."

All the other people stared. Of course every one on his side looked up at the wall to see what had dashed him so.

Eleanor declared, as she cried about it afterwards, that from that moment he talked to her as if she were an idiot. And when he went away from Netherstone without so much as calling on her, she said: "I should not think he would. I should not think he would want to see anybody that had such abominations on her walls."

So, when Eleanor went to her mother's at Christmas, I had Copperhead again. This time we moved the hateful thing into my study. I packed up some hundred and fifty books, took down one set of shelves, moved all the encyclopædias into the closet, and old Copperhead and I hung the Prodigals on the vacant wall I thus gained. There was an awful cross light, but this was so much the better. I turned my own desk so that my back should see it as I wrote. As for the visitors, I hoped their good angels would be with them.

Aunt Caroline came in to see Eleanor on her return. It was New Year's Day. She went in to lunch with us. It was so lately that I had told her how good the light was in the dining-room that my heart sank with my mortification when, as she sat at Eleanor's right, just where Sir William Hartley had sat, I saw her look up at the wall, where we had hung Vernet's "Gideon" in place of the Prodigals.

The surprise on her face was very distinct, but the good woman said nothing.

"We have moved the picture—your picture—the 'Prodigal,' into my study," I said. And then, with the audacity of despair, I added, by a sudden impulse, "I am going to have my Bible class there to see it."

Aunt Caroline said nothing, but I hoped she was not displeased.

Before I slept I atoned for that awful lie. I wrote a note to each of the Bible class, and asked them to take tea with us Thursday evening, and they came.

I received them in the parlor. I am always afraid of them on Sunday, when I have prepared the lesson. How much more afraid was I now! But I asked after their fathers and their mothers. Mr. Clarkson, the superintendent, was most cordial and affable. Eleanor, dear soul, showed photographs, and at last the welcome announcement of supper took us all to the table. Meat and drink warm all hearts. I loitered at the meal as long as I dared. But when the last boy had eaten the last bonbon a warning look across the table from my wife compelled me to act.

"Would you not like to come into my work-room, and—and see my great picture of the 'Prodigal Son'?" Thus far I had not lied.

"Oh yes, sir." "Oh yes, sir." "Mrs. Ames told me all about it." "Mrs. Wenceslaus was speaking of it."

I knew that these two people represented two classes of critics. Woe is me!

We filed through the hall into my library. The picture was well lighted. The young people arranged themselves. Mr. Clarkson happened to be at one end of the platoon, and I was at the other. I think two girls giggled, but I shall never know.

I cleared my throat. "The picture is partly what is called realistic and partly allegorical. In the middle you see the great columns divide what may be called the picture of the present from the other pictures, which may be called the pictures of the past. In the right-hand picture of the past you see the poor young Prodigal, pale to show he is hungry, looking eagerly at the husks. You see how the swine are eating them, just as the Bible says. Then in the background, in the picture of the present, you see the dancers; those persons in the gallery are the band of music."

I thought I should die as I went through with this galimatias. Mr. Clarkson with a rod pointed out the different figures as I alluded to them.

No boy spoke, and no girl.

> "There was silence deep as death
> As I drifted on my path,
> And the boldest held his breath
> For a time."

It became oppressive. Even the boys and girls felt
that something must be said, and Jabez Proctor, inva-
riably silent in the Sabbath-school when any subject of
ethics or of faith was discussed, with one great effort
asked: "Be them hogs Berkshires or natives? The
tails is too tight twisted for natives, and the legs is
long for Berkshires."

Mr. Clarkson, with a bold invention, of which I was
not guilty, said, "These are the hogs of the breed of
Edom," but he was hardly heard. A loud guffaw burst
through all the ranks, and but little that was edifying
came from the study of Aunt Caroline's picture that
evening.

The slow world turned still on its axis. At last nine
o'clock came, and the children went away.

IV.—WHAT WE DID THEN

This is only one instance in a hundred of the annoyance given me, and more often given Eleanor, by a
present meant most kindly. It is provoking to have
such a presence in the house asserting itself almost
every hour of every day. You may say one should be
philosophical and forget it. I only wish you would
try. Fortunately for Eleanor and me, March was a
very warm month, and I really saw, on the 10th, two
large flies on my window-pane. Any other year I
should have killed them. But not now. I ran to the
linen closet. With my own hands I brought out the
lace with which we protected the "Prodigal." In a
few minutes it was screened from all danger, and for a

little a weight was lifted from me. Aunt Caroline called the next day, and came into my work-room. I said, with a sense of guilt, "Have you noticed how early the flies come, and how annoying they are?" Aunt Caroline said nothing.

It would be absurd to say we did not enjoy life in that house. We did enjoy it, though not long. At the end of the winter we enjoyed it much more than at the beginning. We understood life more, and of course we enjoyed it more. Eleanor knew me better, I knew her better, and we both knew better what mutual life or double life is—call it what you will, so you know that it is real life. But I do say there was not a fore-noon, nor an afternoon, nor an evening, when the Prodigal Son, or his father, or his elder brother, or the butcher, or some dancer, or perhaps one of the pigs, did not walk out of that horrid picture and interfere with our enjoyment or profit of the day.

I will not say that this was the reason why in the end of the spring we gave up housekeeping for a little. It was my reason, but it may not have been Eleanor's. We dismissed Bridget and Delia. I boxed up a few books, and we took lodgings for the summer on Tower Hill, that most charming and cool of hilltops, which overlooks Narragansett Pier so prettily. Here we spent a pleasant summer. Eleanor sewed and sketched and read to her heart's content. I earned my daily bread with my good-natured old brain and my diligent pen. I took my bath in the surf every morning, and we sat in the shade to see the others bathe. And in the afternoon I read aloud the last Howells of the day. So pleasantly the summer ran by, without husks or swine, without penitent Prodigals or jealous brothers, till September closed in, when one morning I was a little late at breakfast. Eleanor was sitting after breakfast on the hotel piazza with Mrs. Partelow, and I was talking grand politics with Julius Tucker, when Vanderdyke, one of those disagreeable fellows who like to tell bad news, came up to me and said:

" Are not you Mr. Throop?"

I said I was.

" From Netherstone?"

I said yes, I was from Netherstone.

" Then I suppose that means you," he said, and with a certain satisfaction he thrust the morning journal into my hand, pointing out to me a short telegraphic paragraph under the head,

"FIRE IN NETHERSTONE, OHIO.

" A fire in Netherstone, Ohio, yesterday, destroyed the houses of Mr. Felix Throop and Mrs. William Jackson. Loss $15,000."

I called my poor little wife, and told her the disastrous news. We escaped our sympathetic friends at once, and rushed home to the cottage to pack for our return. In less than an hour came a despatch from John Bradford confirming the story. " So late that we saved hardly anything."

Eleanor had borne the news most bravely up till now. But when this despatch came she fairly laughed with joy. She crossed from her trunk and sat on my knee, and said, " I can bear anything, now I know that; I am sure we shall be happy, wherever we begin."

By the afternoon of the next day we were at Netherstone. As we came to the last stop, Eleanor, who had been resting her head on my shoulder, looked up and smiled.

"Felix, there is one comfort," said she.

"Indeed there is," said I.

"We shall never see those horrid pigs again."

"Never," said I. "It's an ill wind that blows nobody any good."

I had telegraphed Bradford to meet us, and he and many of my friends were at the station.

"It was so late," said Bradford, "and so sudden. The wind was hard from the northwest."

"But," said Mr. Clarkson, "there is one thing, Mrs. Throop, which will delight you."

"Yes?" said Eleanor, cheerfully. "What is that?"

"It was the courage and pluck of young Proctor, of the Bible class, you know. When things were at the worst he got three or four of his mates together, they dashed in the blinds and windows of the library, and entered it by ladders. With his own knife he cut the great picture from the frame, and that is saved!"

I

COLONEL CLIPSHAM led a curious life, but, for a man at his age, not an unpleasant one. His professional duties were not oppressive, and he had entered into a career which made it almost sure that they never would be oppressive. He had a very comfortable suite of rooms in his sister's house, and always breakfasted with her family. As will be seen, they did not often expect him at dinner; but nieces and nephews, sister Prue and her husband Wintergreen, were always glad if he did look in at that meal. For the rest, Clipsham was a general favorite in Tamworth, where he lived; and if there were not a german every evening, or a progressive-euchre party on his list, why, there was the Thursday Club, and the Whist Club, and the Chess Club, and the Union, and the Association, and the pretty new room of the Harvard Club. "As to that," said Clipsham, truly, if you had asked him how he spent his evenings, "I am never so happy as I am with a novel or with the newspaper at home." But it was to be observed that he seldom enjoyed this acme of his happiness at the top-notch of his life's tide.

The one thing of which Clipsham's friends were sure was this, that he would never go into public life.

True, he always voted; he even voted for the school committee, which most of the people in Tamworth forgot to do. But it was also true that he did not attend primary meetings. And it was by a series of rather curious circumstances that the public was led to place that confidence in him which has now lifted him so far out of the run of machine-made politics. It is the business of this story to tell, for the first time, so far as I know, the way those circumstances followed each other.

Clipsham was a man of iron memory. And this was not all pig-iron. One might say steel memory, or a memory of watch-springs, if we understood better than we do the action of the mechanism of memory. By this I mean that he recollected what are called little things at the right moment, as well as he remembered the big things all along his life. He remembered that the national debt was $2,198,765,432.10 when it was at that precise amount, but he also remembered that he had told the washerwoman's boy to come round at a quarter past eight Friday evening and he would give him a ticket to the circus. On such a combination, of what I call the pig-iron memory and what I call the watch-spring memory, does much of the good cheer and success of a happy life depend.

But on a fatal day, after Clipsham was thirty-three years old, he thought he forgot something. I do not myself believe he did. If he did, it was before breakfast, when no one ought to be asked to remember anything—not whether Semiramis is the name of an empress or of a toadstool. But he thought he forgot something. And so it was that he went down to Mr.

Backup's shop and bought this calendar, of which I am
going to tell you the story.

There it is.   He gave it to me on the day of his inauguration.   You see it has the days of the week on
one scroll, and the days of the month on another.
Then you turn this cog at the beginning of the month,
and you are ready for thirty-one more days, if there be
so many.   The only defect in the machine is that you
might suppose that there were thirty-one days in February.   But, as Judge Marshall said, "The court is expected to know something."

Now Clipsham is a charming public speaker.   He
tells a story well—in particular, he tells with great
good-humor a story to his own disadvantage.   He remembers well—that has been said.   He passes, by a
sudden change—what do singers call it, modulation?—
from grave to gay, or from gay to grave.   Best of all,
he never says one word about himself.   Then he never
pretends that he does not like to speak.   He does like
to speak.   A man would be an ass who did not like to
speak if he spoke as well as Clipsham does.   He makes
no introductions to his speech.   When he has done he
makes no "conclusion."   Just when you are hoping he
will say more he sits down.   And he never makes a
long speech.   These spring from sterling qualities,
which are not often united in one handsome, graceful,
intelligent young man of thirty-three.

So it is that Clipsham is much invited to public dinners.   As for that, we all are.   But generally the invitation is accompanied with a request that in accept-
ing you will pay for your ticket—a dollar and a half,
or three dollars, or five, or ten—according as the hon-

ored guest of the evening is a college professor, doctor of divinity, an agent from Japan, or a travelling English lecturer. Now, as most of us can bolt our modest dinner of mock-turtle, fried oysters, charlotte-russe, and coffee at any eating-house—even the most fussy, noisy, and showy—for less than the lowest of these prices, our invitations are not so attractive. To Clipsham the invitation always came with a ticket. That is quite a different thing, and Clipsham, who was in a good many college societies, was the great-grandson of a Cincinnatus, and a grandson of a hero of Lundy's Lane, and son of the man who stormed Chapultepec and held the block-house at Gannon's Three Corners—Clipsham, I say, who was a member of the United Guild of Men of Letters, and of the Consolidated Sodality of Lovers of Art—Clipsham, whose good-humor and good-fellowship had related him to pretty much all the associations in Tamworth, and, indeed, in that whole State, found that he was bidden to a public dinner almost every day. Indeed, sometimes the "bids," as his childish nephews called them, overlapped each other.

This was the reason why he dined so seldom with his sister. On the other hand, it was the reason why you met him so seldom at a restaurant or public table.

You would generally find him if you went up-stairs to the great dining-room of whichever Delmonico or Wormley or Parker or Young of Tamworth happened on that day to entertain the "Soul of the Soldiery," or the "Brothers in Adversity," or the "Nu Kappa Omega," or whatever sodality happened to be holding its annual dinner. And if you looked in at the right moment, Clipsham would be making a speech, and a very good speech too.

II

Clipsham's little niece, Gertrude, is the first heroine of this story. And it is on her that the plot turns, more than on Elinor May, who is the other heroine. Gertrude has the run of the house, but never ought to go to her uncle's room unless he asks her. And this Gertrude knows perfectly well.

But on this day of which I speak, some impulse of Satan, as the old indictments would tell you, and Dr. Watts would confirm them, led Gertrude into the "study," as the room was called. The same Manichean divinity whose name begins with S, but shall not be mentioned again, moved her to take down the calendar mentioned before, and to try the screws. She twirled them this way, she twirled them that. Of a sudden she heard Kate Connor, the girl who made the beds.

Gertrude feared detection. She hung up the calendar hastily and fled. But, alas! she left M., which stands for Monday, and 10, which stands for the tenth day of the month, both one notch too high. T., W., Th., F., and the rest all followed M., and the engagements for the month were all set one day wrong.

Kate Connor did not, in fact, enter the room. But guilty Gertrude thought she would, and the result was the same. Gertrude was called by her mother before she had any chance to go back again, and was made ready for a tennis-party at Mrs. Fisher's. And now it is that, strictly speaking, this story begins.

George Clipsham came home to dress for dinner. He stopped a moment, and took down the cyclopædia to look at the account of the battle of Bennington. For he had been turning over a speech which he was to make at a Grand Army gathering, and he remembered that Plunkett's mother was a Stark. He wanted to make a good allusion to Molly Stark and her widowhood. But as he passed his desk he took the fatal calendar, which guilty Gertrude had not had time to hang on its peg. Clipsham hung it up without a thought, but did look to see, to his amazement, that the Grand Army dinner was done and gone yesterday. The calendar said he was to dine with the graduates of the Western Reserve College to-day. "Lucky I did not fire the battle of Bennington at them," said Clipsham to himself; "but what will Plunkett say?"

The truth was that Clipsham had this dreadful cold which you all have had. And just as you and I determined that we would go to Florida another winter if our lives were spared, Clipsham had determined. Handkerchiefs?—he was bankrupt in buying them. Hearing?—he had been stone-deaf all the week. He did not cough very badly, but the cold was just on that juncture of the pharynx with the larynx where it is uncomfortable to have it. He had stayed at home the day before and nursed it—glycerine and whiskey, taken with a very small spoon, was his remedy—and he had persuaded himself that he could go out to-day.

To tell the whole truth, his sister Prue had had pea-soup and salt codfish for dinner the day before, and the children had been very noisy. Clipsham had determined to change the scene. So he had determined to dine with the Grand Army to-day, and now the calendar said the Grand Army dinner was "done and gone." "Well," said Clipsham to himself, "I could not have spoken aloud anyway. And I should not have heard a word they said. Western Reserve it is to-day. Lucky I looked!" And he went on with his dressing, and thought over some old Harvard stories which would do to tell to the Western Reserve graduates.

As he went out, furred, and even veiled, and with those horrid arctics on which made him limp with pain, Prue met him at the door.

"Dear George, you are not going out with that dreadful cough? Why, I was sure of you. I have asked Mrs. Oliphant and the Pryces to meet you, and I have such a lovely pair of canvasbacks."

George intimated that he didn't hear.

Prue shouted her bill of fare, physical and metaphysical, into his ear.

George was sorry. But he was all ready, and to the hotel dinner he went, and left those canvasbacks behind. Prue's would be warm, alas! and at the Hotel Jefferson—that was more doubtful.

iIi

The waiters all know George to a man, and he was shown to the reception parlor instantly. The reader understands what George did not—why a third of the guests were in uniform. Of course they were, for it was the Grand Army of the Republic. But George, who thought it was the Western Reserve dinner, was surprised that the college men wanted to bring out their old blue frocks and bright buttons. "But that was all right," he said, "if they chose to." Oddly enough, his friend Colonel Plunkett was receiving the guests, and Clipsham slipped into his hand the note of apology he had written. Plunkett slipped it into the little pocket of his uniform coat, and found it there two years afterwards, when he dressed for the same anniversary again. Clipsham mumbled an apology to Plunkett, which, quite of course, Plunkett, in shaking hands with half the soldiers in the State, did not hear.

Clipsham is a bright man, and one would have said that he would have caught the thread of the occasion earlier than he did. But he did not hear one word in five that any one said. As for the uniforms, all the world knows that five-sixths of the college men of the West served in the war. Besides, they had introduced Clipsham to Professor Schmidgruber, who had just arrived, as the agent from the government of Hesse-Cassel to study Western education. Clipsham was interested in the savant, and they talked very earnestly, the savant speaking directly into Clipsham's ear.

So it was that when Clipsham got a card at the dinner-table from Plunkett, who was presiding, which said, " You next," he knew that now was his turn to speak, without having known much of what had been said before him.

And a very good speech it was. Not one word about the war, nor the bird of freedom, nor the American soldier, nor Molly Stark, as there would have been had Clipsham understood the truth, that he was speaking to a Grand Army post. Instead of this he spoke, with serious feeling, on the work which educated men can render in any community. What he had been saying to the German he now said aloud. There is the secret of a good speech. He spoke to the men before him as if they were all scholars, all men of conscience, and all leaders in the villages or towns where they lived. He told some good stories, he made some good jokes; but his speech was not in the least commonplace, and it ended with a very serious pledge as to the duty they would all do to their country.

It was received rapturously—yes, wildly. Indeed, as the reader will understand, it was better received than it would have been by the graduates whom Clipsham thought he was addressing. Every one of these good fellows was pleased that one of the most accomplished men of letters in Tamworth spoke to him as an equal with equals. They had only too much of soldier talk, and were glad to hear something sung or said to another tune. Clipsham had gone deeper down than the average and commonplace, as he was apt to do.

Now you would say that, before he left the hotel, he would have found out his mistake, or that, at all events, he would have understood it from the newspapers next

morning. But there you are quite wrong. In the first
place, he only stayed " to listen to two more speeches,"
as he said. For it did not seem courteous to go away
the moment he had himself spoken. In fact, he did
not hear one word of either of them. As for the newspapers, Clipsham generally looked at them, though not
always. He never looked, however, at what the re-
porters called their "sketches" of his speeches. "Why
should I make myself miserable?" said Clipsham.
" Nobody else reads the things, and why should I?"
If he had stayed long at his office next morning, or
looked in at the club, he might have found that his
calendar was all wrong. But instead of this he took
Dr. Schmidgruber to. examine the high - school; so he
remained quite sure that he had spoken to the college
men the night before, and that to-night he was to speak
to the carriage-builders. In fact, as the reader knows,
he would meet the college men, and the carriage-builders' night would not come till to-morrow.

And it all happened just as before, as it says in the
Arabian Nights and in Grimm's fairy tales. Only this
time Clipsham sat at the cross table, because he was to
respond for Harvard, and was among the more distinguished guests. But little did the poor fellow know
what he was to respond for. He did know that the
Carriage - builders' Association of the country brings
together a remarkable body of men. He had dined
with them a year or two before. Their business requires an interest in design, a knowledge of the physical structure of the world, an acquaintance with all
sorts and conditions of men, all combined with remarkable tact and promptness. Observe that carriage-

builders, like railroad men, are always trying to an-
nihilate time, or to give us more of it, which is the
same thing.

"Ye shall become as gods—transcendent fate !"

So Clipsham knew he was to speak to a bright set.
In point of fact, he did speak to the triennial gathering of the graduates of the Western Reserve College,
one of the oldest and largest of the Western universi-
ties. And he told them things which it was very good
for them to hear, but which people did not very often
tell them at these meetings. He told them that man
is man, because he can control matter by spirit; that
this shows that he is a child of God. He told them
that the child of God works with God, and that
here is the difference between work and labor: that
work elevates man, while labor fatigues man. He
charged them to see that the men whom they employed
should not be mere laborers, but should become fellow-
workmen with God. He said they might rest from
their labors, but that their works would always follow
them. And he said, very seriously, that this was no
matter of book-learning; that they would not find it in
Seneca or Aristotle, but that they would find it in pro-
portion as they were men of honor and truth, as they
forgot themselves and consecrated their workshops
into temples.

Then he sat down, and, just as it was the night before, the speech was received with cheers. The truth
is that at any such college gathering in America the
men are only playing at being men of letters. Every
man of us is a workman, or ought to be ashamed if he

is not. As for poor Clipsham, the nervous excitement
of speaking brought on a fit of coughing, and he had
to excuse himself and go home.

He soaked his feet in hot water with mustard, put a
porous plaster on his chest, and went to bed with a
lump of sugar by his side on which he had dropped
Ayer's Cherry Pectoral. But he slept all night, and
did not need the sugar.

Four days went on in this way, with four different dinners. Nobody told Clipsham he was all wrong, because
nobody knew. On the other hand, everybody thought
he was all right, and said he had never made such good
speeches in his life. The next night he really went to
the carriage-builders' dinner. But he thought he was at
the annual meeting of the Chautauquan Literary Circle. That is to say, he thought he was speaking to a
large company of people who, in the midst of every
sort of daily occupation, read regularly in a systematic
course. So in fact he was. And the carriage-builders
liked his speech all the better that he made no pretence,
as they said any other lawyer would have done, to a
knowledge of their business. He said nothing about
varnish, or the strength of ash, of which he knew nothing; and he did not once allude to the hub of the universe, the wheel of time, the chariot of the sun, or Dr.
Holmes's "One-Hoss Shay," which had been worked to
death at their celebrations.

IV

The two other dinners on the calendar that week were at the joint anniversary of the Chautauquan Circle, as has been said, and at the anniversary of the trustees of a fund left for the education of that sub-tribe of Ojibwas whom the first settlers had found fishing on the point which makes Tamworth harbor. These Ojibwas had long since gone where other Ojibwas, I fear, are going. But the fund remained, as funds will, to curse the descendants of the trustees. And the only way which had been devised to use up the annual interest was to have the trustees dine to-gether, with such of their friends as wished to meet them, after they had chosen themselves again into office at their annual meeting. At the Chautauquan dinner, accordingly, Clipsham went rather carefully into a discussion of the movements of American immigration, and the elements which have contributed to the making up of American civilization. This was on Friday, and all through the week Clipsham had never forgotten the day of the week, although that mischievous Gertrude had thrown him out in the use he made of the several days as they came. Meanwhile his cold grew no better. His deafness grew upon him, and he sent for the doctor. The doctor told him he must stay at home. Clipsham said he could well do that, that for once there was no evening engagement; and he looked up the serial called "My Friend the Boss," which he was read-ing, which was full of allusions to his Tamworth friends. Little did he think, as he discussed the side-bone of the nice turkey his sister Prue had provided, that the trustees' dinner was cooling while they awaited his arrival at the Hotel Jefferson. The truth was that they were entitled to that excuse which he wrote at the beginning of the week to Colonel Plunkett, and which Plunkett still had, unread, in the handkerchief pocket of his dress uniform.

But all the staying at home over Sunday, and all the whiskey and glycerine, and all the Cherry Pectoral which could be administered did Clipsham no good, and on Monday morning he asked the doctor if a change of air would not help him. The doctor said of course it would. It was clear it would not harm him, for he was past much harming. He was deaf as a post; his nose and throat and all the passages to them were inflamed, and red with the inflammation; his eyes were drooping with watering, and he said he was as stupid as an owl. The doctor gave his permission for a journey to Colorado. Clipsham looked on his calendar, and with his pencil marked off all the dinner-parties, and wrote letters of excuse for the next three weeks. But there was one engagement he could not manage so easily, for here his conscience pricked him.

It was the city election. Clipsham knew in his heart of hearts that he had not done his duty in this affair. He had not gone to one meeting where his friend Gordon had summoned him, to obtain a competent, nonpartisan school committee. He was afraid there was a "job" at the almshouse, and he had not looked into that. He distrusted the reigning Mayor, yet he had not lifted a finger to dethrone him. Now if he went to Colorado he should be away on election day, and

should not give even one vote against the rascals and
one in favor of honest men.

But Clipsham did so wish to go to Colorado! He
had promised his cousin Lucy that he would visit her
on the way—and she wrote such a pretty letter!

Clipsham compromised with himself. He would go
to Colorado because he wanted to—and his cold was
so bad. But he saw on the calendar that on Monday
night there was a meeting of the Friends of Good
Government at the Mechanics' Hall. He knew who
called this meeting, and that it was in the right interest. John Fisher and all the rest had signed the call.
He would go to that meeting. That would show
which side he was on. He would not go on the noon
train; he would wait until the evening train, which
went at 9.30. And his presence there would, in practice, show his colors as well as if he stayed in Tamworth nine whole days, sneezing and coughing, to vote
at the end of them.

Indeed, he might be in his coffin if he stayed, and a
man cannot vote when he is in his coffin.

So, when Monday came, Clipsham sent his trunk to
the train, ordered a carriage for himself an hour before
the train started, and went down to the hall. The
truth was that the citizens' meeting was not to take
place until the next night. But Gertrude had changed
all that, and Clipsham found, to his surprise, that the
large hall was not lighted. However, the smaller hall
was. An assiduous gentleman whom he did not know,
who had been drinking more than was good for him,
asked him in; and Clipsham, regretting that the friends
of order made so poor a show, went in. As has been

said, he was not used to primary meetings. Once in, it was like all other meetings, though not very large. There were two hundred men there, of whom he did not recognize three. The president was a man who had once tried to sell him a horse. The Mayor was making a speech, and Clipsham supposed from this that that officer had been frightened, and was trying to "get good," as the children say. But whether he knew them or not, they knew him. Three or four showily dressed men met him and led him to a front seat, and expressed their pleasure at his presence. In a moment after, the Mayor's motion was carried, and a committee was sent out—nominated from a list which had been prepared in his office that afternoon—to suggest a ticket for aldermen.

Then it was that another man, who also had been drinking more than was good for him, arose and said that they were honored by the presence of a gentleman whom they had often heard in public, and who was known to be interested in all public affairs, and that he hoped Mr. Clipsham would address them on the great issues before them; and all the people shouted "Clipsham! Clipsham!" Why he was there the leaders wondered, but they supposed, in their low way, that he had quarrelled with John Fisher and his set, and had come over to them to see what they would give him.

The truth was, as the reader sees, that he had come to a meeting which was one day earlier than the meeting which he had meant to come to.

Clipsham himself did not hear the man who spoke, and did not know what they were shouting at. But when another man came to lead him to the platform

he knew what that meant, and he stepped up and sailed
in.   And a capital speech he made.   It was that speech
which put him into what people call public life.   For
my part, I think he had been in very public life before.
He was pleased at being called upon so early; he was
pleased at being recognized as in some sort a leader;
and he said to himself, as he mounted the steps, that
this was what he had come for, and that, if they wanted
him to lead, he had better lead.   He did not quite know
what to do or say about the Mayor.   For here was the
Mayor at his side.   If he had repented of the dirty jobs
he had been in, Clipsham thought, he would let him off;
and he did.   But he did not let off anybody else in that
meeting.   He exposed, from cellar to cupola, the dis-
graceful jobs about building the new school-house opposite Prue Wintergreen's house, and the unkind audience howled with delight as they saw Alderman Bob
Lyon and Councilman Bill Stuggs held up under Clipsham's pitiless ridicule.   One of these gentlemen had
led him to the stand, and the other was secretary of the
meeting; but this Clipsham did not know.   Clipsham
could see that the assembly was a low-lived set, and mad
enough was he with Fisher and the rest who had signed
the call and then stayed comfortably at home.   So,
after dissecting every nasty job which his hearers had
been engaged in for five years, he closed with a really
eloquent denunciation of the indifference of educated
men and holders of property in the management of the
affairs of the city.   His own conscience pricked him,
as has been said, and he spoke all the better for that.
The closing passage, where he describes the rich manu-
facturer, who could not sign his name if the public

schools had not taught him, and could not squeeze on a pay-roll if the public school had not taught him, yet who, when he is rich and prosperous, will not go to a meeting which cares for the schools, and does not know a schoolmaster when he meets him in the streets, has gone into the reading-books; and if you will go to the graduating exercises of the Lavinia Academy you may hear it spoken.

Well, that one fellow held that angry assembly by the mere force of audacity and truth, and they did not even remember that they could pelt him to death with their private gin-bottles and other "pocket pistols." When he had finished his speech he did not wait to hear what followed. He did not care to hear the hisses nor curses. He did see the scowls, but he had not supposed that everybody would like his speech. He bowed himself away from the hall, and in half an hour he was asleep in his berth as his train started for the West.

By great good luck it happened that the chief short-hand man of a newspaper unfriendly to the crew had been sent to "do" the meeting. It was supposed that a square or two of "matter" would be all the result of his probing such an ulcer. But he caught the position in an instant. He wrote down every word of Clipsham's speech, and the next morning Tamworth and the State had it all. Such head-lines!

BILL STUGGS ENLIGHTENED !

A Lively Caucus !

A CITIZEN'S PROTEST !

LIGHT IN DARK PLACES !

And the public soon knew that, for once, the little
coterie which had "run" Tamworth for some years
had been told the truth by one modest, quiet gentleman, who had no axe to grind and no ring behind
him.

That man was Clipsham. While he was doing the
mountains and cañons of Colorado, events were making
him, without the slightest suspicion of it himself, the
most popular man in the State. So soon as there was
a chance, the Friends of Good Government put him
in nomination for Governor — and Governor he was
chosen. He will be Governor till he wishes to go to
the United States Senate.

V

"But who was Elinor May?" asks my kind reader,
Emma, who has followed this little story with the faith-
fulness which has given a charm to other stories, and
who remembers something said in the beginning about
the heroine. My dear Emma, can there be no story
without a wedding at the end? No, there cannot be,
if the story is quite perfect. So you shall hear who
Elinor May was, for it belongs to the calendar also,
and can be told in a few words.

So soon as Clipsham had determined to go to Colorado, the doctor asked him if he should stop in St.
Louis. He said he certainly should. Then the doctor
told him that he must call on some friend of his named
Day, and gave him the address. The doctor took a
card and wrote on it: "Colonel George Clipsham, introduced by Dr. Jones." Clipsham was lying on a long

extension chair, carefully wrapped up in a Zuñi blanket, and he asked the doctor to put down the name and street on this fatal calendar; and there the doctor put it, just as Clipsham bade him. Before Clipsham started upon his journey, he copied all the lines from his calendar into his pocket-book. There was not much, and he did not look at the dates. They came thus:

M. Speak at Caucus.
Tu. Stop over at Aunt Lucy's.
W. Day, 999 Olive Street. (This in the doctor's writing.)

But Clipsham never noticed that the dates were wrong. He copied the entries into his own note-book; and thus it happened, as we say, that many pleasant things followed. Elinor and George do not think anything "happened." They think it was all made in heaven. This I know—that they had that mischievous Gertrude for their only bridesmaid.

For so it was that, on the evening when Clipsham meant to call on Mrs. Day in St. Louis, he was in Chicago. He looked at his diary, and he found this entry. "How queer it is!" said he. "I thought Jones said these people lived in St. Louis"—as indeed Dr. Jones did. But Clipsham had formed the notion that his memory was failing, so he consulted the hotel clerk as to how he should find the street. The clerk never heard of it, but saw in a moment that it should be Ohio Street, and that Clipsham had copied it wrong. Clipsham went to No. 999, as he thought he had been bidden. Here he sent in the card: "Colonel George Clipsham, introduced by Dr. Jones." After a moment's delay he was admitted, and a very charming lady came forward to meet him. Clipsham bowed, and said she was very kind to be so informal, and to permit him to be, but he was a traveller, and had but one night in Chicago; and then he was presented to Elinor, and I think the whole thing was pretty much finished then, as far as he was concerned—and so would you, if you knew Elinor Clipsham as well as I do. Then there was a little inquiry about Dr. Jones. But that did not come out very well. In the first place, Clipsham did not hear very well. In the second place, he was a good deal preoccupied with Elinor. In the third place, the Dr. Jones he was talking about was the leading physician of Tamworth, and the Dr. Jones they were asking about was the Rev. Dr. Jones, president of the theological seminary at New Berea. But she was well-bred; she saw there was some mistake, and she let it pass.

A very pleasant evening Clipsham had. It proved that he heard Miss Elinor much better than he had heard anybody for a fortnight. The journey had been of use already. Then they fell to singing duets, even on this slight acquaintance. She plays a charming accompaniment, and he sings admirably when he has no cold. She was tolerant that evening, though his voice was all wrong. Then, when her father came in, it proved that they were all going to Colorado Springs on the next day but one; and so it was very easy for Clipsham to make up his mind that he had business which would keep him over a day in Chicago. Although he did not tell them so, he made his resolution to stay before he left the house.

When he had gone away, Elinor's mother said she

pitied him because he had such a horrid cold. "But, mamma," said Elinor, "did you ever know a cold make a man say 'Day' instead of 'May'? He kept calling you 'Mrs. Day.'"

Mrs. May had not observed this; but it was even so. As for Clipsham, when he met them at the train, and took his seat with them in the same Pullman, he was no such fool but that he could see that their seats were taken for Mrs. May, Mr. May, and Miss May. But then he supposed the P. P. C. man had written this wrong. When, however, the names which they had themselves put on the books with which they travelled proved to be May, Clipsham gave up his conviction that he knew their names better than they did. As he went on, indeed, he began to be wondering whether he could not persuade Miss Elinor to change hers. He was very soon on that plane of conversation where he called her "Miss Elinor."

Yes, a Pullman is a very nice place when the company is good. They sang in the twilight, for Clipsham's voice improved very fast, and his hearing gained so that he could hear Miss Elinor, even when she spoke in very low tones of experiences of hers which she would not care to have that Russian merchant hear who was on his way to Alaska. The Pullman people had not then advanced so far as to have a piano in the car between the saloon and the smoking-room. But these two people found that they could sing without any accompaniment. At the stations Clipsham always managed to bring in something: if there were no flowers there were queer crullers, or if there were no crullers there were fossils. Sometimes there was half an hour's detention, and then he and Miss May would have a good, brisk, constitutional walk together.

Now, Clipsham had mining interests in Colorado, and Mr. May had smelting interests; and while Mr. May attended to the smelting, Colonel Clipsham would wait with them. And while Clipsham inquired about the mining, the Mays were not far away. And the "Garden of the Gods" was more divine than ever, when they dismissed the carriage one evening, and under the moonlight walked home together, while those old divinities looked down, in still approval of what these younger people said and did. Altogether, the journey out, and the journey there, and the journey home, were charming. Clipsham never received one newspaper all the time, and he did not dream that he was growing famous. As for the Mays, they never asked nor cared whether he was a public man or a private man. It was enough for them that Rev. Dr. Jones had recommended him. Nay, they did not long think of that. For, give him a chance, George Clipsham is anywhere his best recommendation. He is a modest man, but you cannot be with him a day without seeing that he is a brave, quiet, true, Christian gentleman. He thinks very little of himself, but is glad—nay, eager—if he can, to make other people happy and good, and to serve the world where he has a chance to serve it.

Nothing, indeed, could have been better or brighter or more happy in its results than this Colorado journey. Clipsham threw off his cold entirely, and before the journey was over he had undertaken to take care of Elinor to the end of her days, if she would let him. She, on her part, has taken such good care of him from that day to this that he has never made the wrong speech in the wrong place, and he has never had that "horrid influenza" again.

When he came back to Tamworth, in all the exuberance of his new life, he did manage to ask Dr. Jones how he had contrived to write "Day" instead of "May." For the calendar still hung there, and there was the "D," perfectly plain, in the doctor's handwriting.

Then it was that a thorough examination and explanation ensued, and then Gertrude, in tears, confessed to her mother, for she, poor child, had never forgotten her sin. But she had perfect absolution. A beautiful doll, open-eyes-shut-eyes, was given her, and she has never been scolded from that day to this.

You would say that Clipsham would have called on Mrs. Day in St. Louis on his first visit there. But he has never done so. His wife says she is afraid to have him. He says he has found out that there are no nice daughters there.

Both he and Elinor bless Gertrude every day of their lives for her little experiment on his calendar.

I

"Only think, Matty, papa passed right by me—when I was sitting with my back to the fire and stitching away on his book-mark, without my once seeing him! But he was so busy talking to mamma that he never saw what I was doing, and I huddled it under a newspaper before he came back again. Well, I have got papa's present done, but I cannot keep out of mamma's way. Matty dear, if I will sit in the sun, and keep a shawl on, may I not sit in your room and work? It is not one bit cold there. Really, Matty, it is a great deal warmer than it was yesterday."

"Dear child," said Matty, to whom everybody came so readily for advice and help, "I can do better for you than that. You shall come into the study; papa will be away all the morning, and I will have the fire kept up there, and mamma shall never come near you."

All this, and a thousand times more, of plotting and counterplotting was going on among four children and their elders in a comfortable, free-and-easy-seeming household in Washington, as the boys and girls, young men and young women, were in the last agonies of making ready for Christmas. Matty is fully entitled

to be called a young woman when we see her. She
has just passed her twenty-first birthday. But she
looks as fresh and pretty as when she was seventeen,
and certainly she is a great deal pleasanter, though she
be wiser. She is the oldest of the troop. Tom, the
next, is expected from Annapolis this afternoon, and
Beverly from Charlotte. Then come four boys and
girls whose ages and places the reader must guess at
as we go on.

The youngest of the family were still young enough
to write the names of the presents which they would
be glad to receive, or to denote them by rude hiero-
glyphs, on large sheets of paper. They were used to
pin up these sheets on certain doors, which, by long
usage in this free-and-easy family, had come to be regarded as the bulletin-boards of the establishment.
Wellnigh every range of created things had some rep-
resentation on these bulletins—from an ambling pony
round to a "boot-buttener," thus spelled out by poor
Laura, who was constantly in disgrace, because she always appeared latest at the door when the children
started for church, to ride, or for school. The youngsters still held to the theory of announcing thus their
wants in advance. Horace doubted whether he were
not too old. But there was so much danger that nobody would know how much he needed a jig-saw that
he finally compromised with his dignity, wrote on a
virgin sheet of paper "jig-saw," signed his name, "Horace Molineux, December 21," and left his other presents to conjecture.

And of course at the very end, as Santa Claus and
his revels were close upon them, while the work done

had been wonderful, that which we ought to have done, but which we had left undone, was simply terrible. Here were pictures that must be brought home from the frame-man, who had never pretended he would send them; there were ferns and lycopodiums in pots which must be brought home from the greenhouse; here were presents for other homes, which must not only be finished, but must be put up in paper and sent before night, so as to appear on other trees. Every one of these must be shown to mamma, and approved by her, and praised; and every one must be shown to dear Matty, and praised and approved by her. And yet by no accident must Matty see her own presents or dream that any child has remembered her, or mamma see *hers* or think herself remembered.

And Matty has all her own little list to see to, while she keeps a heart at leisure from itself to soothe and sympathize. She had to correct the mistakes, to repair the failures, to respect the wonder, to refresh the discouragement of each and all the youngsters. Her own Sunday scholars are to be provided with their presents. The last orders are to be given for the Christmas dinners of half a dozen families of vassals, mostly black, or of some shade of black, who never forgot their vassalage as Christmas came round. Turkey, cranberry, apples, tea, cheese, and butter must be sent to each household of these vassals, as if every member were paralyzed except in the muscles of the jaw. But, all the same, Matty or her mother must be in readiness all the morning and afternoon to receive the visits of all the vassals—who, so far as this form of homage went, did not seem to be paralyzed at all.

For herself, Matty took possession of the dining-room as soon as she could clear it of the breakfast equipage, of the children, and of the servants; and here, with pen and ink, with wrapping-paper and twine, with telegraph blanks and with the directory, and with Venty as her Ariel messenger—not so airy and quick as Ariel, but quite as willing—Matty worked her wonders, and gave her audiences, whether to vassals from without or puzzled children from within.

Venty was short for Ventidius. But this name, given in baptism, was one which Venty seldom heard.

Matty corded up this parcel, and made Venty cord up that; wrote this note of compliment, that of inquiry, that of congratulation, and sent Venty on this, that, and another errand with them; relieved Flossy's anxieties, and poor Laura's, in ways which have been described; made sure that the wagon should be at the station in ample time for Beverly; and at last, at nearly one o'clock, called Aunty Chloe (who was in waiting on everybody as a superserviceable person on the pretence that she was needed), bade Aunty pick up the scraps, sweep the floor, and bring the room to rights. And so, having attended to everybody beside herself, to all their wishes and hopes and fears, poor Matty—or shall I not say dear Matty?—ran off to her own room to finish her own presents and make her own last preparations.

She had kept up her spirits as best she could all the morning, but at any moment when she was alone her spirits had fallen again. She knew it, and she knew why. And now she could not hold out any longer.

She and her mother, thank God, never had any secrets.
And as she ran by her mother's door she could not
help tapping, to be sure if she had come home.

Yes, she had come home. "Come in!" and Matty
ran in.

Her mother had not even taken off her hat or her
gloves. She had flung herself on the sofa, as if her
walk had been quite too much for her; her salts and
her handkerchief were in her hands, and when she saw
it was Matty, as she had hoped when she spoke, she
would not even pretend she had not been in tears.

In a moment Matty was on her knees on the floor
by the sofa, and somehow had her left arm round about
her mother's neck.

"Dear, dear mamma! What is it? What is the
matter?"

"My dear, dear Matty," replied her mother, just
succeeding in speaking without sobs, and speaking the
more easily because she stroked the girl's hair and
caressed her as she spoke, "do not ask, do not try to
know. You will know, if you do not guess, only too
soon. And now the children will be better, and papa
will get through Christmas better, if you do not know,
my darling."

"No, dear mamma," said Matty, crossing her mother's purpose almost for the first time that she remembered, but wholly sure that she was right in doing so—
"no, dear mamma, it is not best so. Indeed, it is not,
mamma! I feel in my bones that it is not!" This she
said with a wretched attempt to smile, which was the
more ghastly because the tears were running down
from both their faces.

"You see, I have tried, mamma. I knew all day
yesterday that something was wrong, and at breakfast
this morning I knew it. And I have had to hold up—
with the children and all these people—with the feeling that any minute the hair might break and the
sword fall. And I know I shall do better if you tell
me. You see, the boys will be here before dark, and
of course they will see; and what in the world shall I
say to them?"

"What, indeed!" said her poor mother. "Terrible
it is, dear child, because your father is so wretched. I
have just come from him. He would not let me stay,
and yet for the minute I was there I saw that no
one else could come in to goad him. Dear, dear papa,
he is so resolute and brave, and yet any minute I was
afraid that he would break a blood-vessel and fall dead
before me. Oh, Matty, Matty, my darling, it is terrible!"

And this time the poor woman could not control
herself longer, but gave way to her sobs, and her voice
fairly broke, so that she was inarticulate as she lay
her cheek against her daughter's on the sofa.

"What is terrible? Dear mamma, you must tell
me!"

"I think I must tell you, Matty, my darling. I believe if I cannot tell some one I shall die."

Then Mrs. Molineux told the whole horror to Matty.
Here was her husband charged with the grossest plun-
der of the Treasury, and charged even in the House of
Representatives now. It had been whispered about
before, and had been hinted at in some of the lower
newspapers, but now even a committee of investiga-

tion of Congress had noticed it, and had "given him
an opportunity to clear himself." There was no less a
sum than forty-seven thousand dollars, in three separate payments, charged to him at the Navy Department as long ago as the second and third years of the
war. At the Navy they had his receipt for it. Not
that he had been in that department then any more
than he was now. He was then chief clerk in the
Bureau of Internal Improvement, as he was now com-
missioner there. But this was when the second Rio
Grande expedition was fitted out; and from Mr. Molineux's knowledge of Spanish, and his old connection
with the Santa Fé trade, this particular matter had
been intrusted to him.

"Yes, dear mamma!"

"Well, papa has it all down in his own cash-book;
that book he carries in his breast-pocket. There are
the three payments, and then all the transfers he made
to the different people. One was that old white-haired
Spaniard with the hair-lip, who used to come here at
the back door, so that he should not be seen at the
department. But it was before you remember. The
others were in smaller sums. But the whole thing was
done in three weeks, and then the expedition sailed,
and papa had enough else to think of, and has never
thought of it since, till ten or fifteen days ago, when
somebody in the Eleventh Auditor's office discovered
this charge, and his receipt for this money."

"Well, dear mamma?"

"Well, dear child, that is all, but that now the newspapers have got hold of it; and the Committee on Re-
trenchment, who are all new men, with their reputa-

tions to make, have got hold of it, and some of them really think, you know, that papa has stolen the money!" And she broke down, crying again.

" But he can show his accounts, mamma !"

" What are his accounts worth ? He must show the vouchers, as they are called. He must show these people's receipts, and what has become of these people; what they did with the money. He must show everything. Well, when the *Copperhead* first spoke of it— that was a fortnight ago—papa was really pleased. For he said it would be a good chance to bring out a piece of war history. He said that in our bureau we had never had any credit for the Rio Grande successes; that they were all our thunder; because *then* he could laugh about this horrid thing. He said the Navy had taken all the honors, while we deserved them all. And he said if these horrid *Copperhead* and *Argus* and *Scorpion* people would only publish the vouchers half as freely as they published the charges, we should get a little of the credit that was our due."

" Well, mamma, and what is the trouble now ?"

" Why, papa was so sure, that he would do nothing until an official call came. But on Monday it got into Congress. That hairy man from the Yellowstone brought in a resolution or something, and the committee was ordered to inquire. And when the order came down, papa told Mr. Waltsingham to bring him the papers, and, Matty, the papers were not there!"

" Stolen !" cried Matty, understanding the crisis for the first time.

" Yes—perhaps—or lost—hidden somewhere. You have no idea of the work of those days—night work

and all that.   Many a time your father did not undress
for a week."

"And now he must remember where he put a horrid
file of paper eleven, twelve years ago.   Mamma, that
file is stolen.   That odious Greenhithe stole it.   He
lives in Philadelphia now, and he has put up these
newspapers to this lie."

Mr. Greenhithe was an under clerk in the Internal
Improvement Bureau, who had shown an amount of
attention to Miss Matty which she had disliked and
had refused to receive.   She had always said he was
bad, and would come to a bad end; and when he was
detected in a low trick, selling stationery which he
had stolen from the supply-room, and was discharged
in disgrace, Matty had said it was good enough for
him.

These were her reasons for pronouncing at once that
he had stolen the vouchers and had started the rumors.

"I do not know.   Papa does not know.   He hardly
tries to guess.   He says either way it is bad.   If the
vouchers are stolen, he is in fault, for he is responsible
for the archives; if he cannot produce the vouchers,
then all the country is down on him for stealing.   I
only hope," said poor Mrs. Molineux, "that they won't
say our poor old wagon is a coach and six," and this
time she tried to smile.

And now she had told her story.   All last night,
while the children were asleep, Mr. Molineux had been
at the office, even till four o'clock in the morning. taking
old dusty piles from their lairs and searching for those
wretched vouchers.   And mamma had been waiting—
shall one not say, had been weeping?—here at home.

That was the reason poor papa had looked so haggard at breakfast this morning.

This was all mamma had to tell. She had been to the office this morning, but papa would not let her stay. He must see all comers, just as if nothing had happened, was happening, or was going to happen.

Well! Matty did make her mother take off her sacque and her hat and her gloves. She even made her drink a glass of wine and lie down. And then the poor girl retired to her own room, with such appetite as she might for taking the last stitches in worsted-work; for stippling in the light into drawings; for writing the presentation lines in books; and for doing the thousand little niceties in the way of finishing touches which she had promised the children to do.

Her dominant feeling—yes, it was a dominant passion, as she knew—was simply rage against this miserable Greenhithe, this cowardly sneak who was thus taking his revenge upon her because she had been so cold to him. Or was it that he made up to her because he was already in trouble at the office and hoped she would clear him with her father? Either way, he was a snake and a scorpion, but he had worked out for himself a terrible revenge. Poor Matty! she tried to think what she could do, how she could help, for this was the habit of her life. But this was hard indeed. Her mind would not take that turn. All that it would turn to was to the wretched and worse than worthless question, what punishment might fall on him for such utter baseness and wickedness?

All the same, the children must have their lunch, and

they must not know that anything was the matter.
Oh dear! this concealment was the worst of all!

So they had their lunch; and poor Matty counselled
again, and helped again, and took the last stitches and
mended the last breaks, and waited and wondered,
and tried to hope, till at five o'clock an office messenger
came up with this note:

"4.45 P.M.

"DEAR MATTY,—I shall not come up to dinner. There is pressing
work here. Tell mamma not to sit up for me. I have my key.

"I have had no chance to get my things for the children. Will
you see to it? Here is twenty dollars, and if you need more let them
send in the bill. I had only thought of that jig-saw—was it?—that
Horace wants. See that the dear fellow has a good one.

"Love to Tom and Bev. Ever your   PAPA."

"Poor, dear papa!" said Matty, aloud, shedding tears
in spite of herself. To be thinking of jig-saws and of
the children in all this horrid hunt! as if hunting for
anything was not the worst trial of all, always; and at
once the brave girl took down her wraps and put on
her walking-shoes, that her father's commissions might
be met before their six-o'clock dinner, and she determined that, first of all, she would meet Tom at the
station.

At the station she met Tom. That was well. Matty
had not been charged to secrecy. That was well. She
bade Tom send up his valise and walk up the avenue
with her, and he did. She told him all the story, not
without adding her suspicions and giving him some
notion of her rage.

And Tom was angry enough; there was a crumb of
comfort there. But Tom went off on another track.

Tom disbelieved the Navy Department; he had been long enough at Annapolis to doubt the red-tape of the bureau with which his chiefs had to do. "If the Navy paid the money, the Navy had the vouchers." That was Tom's theory. He knew a chief clerk in the Navy, and Tom was for going at once round there.

But Matty held him in check, at least for the moment. Whatever else he did, he must come home first. He must see mamma, and he must see the children, and he must have dinner. She had not told him yet how well he looked and how handsome he was. And there were a few minutes as they walked homeward, and he must help her about the jig-saw and some other things for the children. Ah! happy she would have been last Monday had anybody given her twenty dollars, with *carte-blanche* for spending it; and now, how wretched it all was! But, all the same, the jig-saw was bought, and mamma and Beverly and Laura and Florence—indeed, everybody but Tom and Matty herself—were cared for out of this hateful twenty-spot—hateful, though it were so kind.

And they came home to dinner. And as dinner closed, Beverly came in, noisy and cheery, from the Southern train, and he found *his* dinner ready. And after Tom had seen him, Tom slipped off—pretended he had unfinished preparations to make. Tom went right to the department, forced his way in. because he was Mr. Molineux's son, and found his poor father with Ziegler, the chief clerk, still on this wretched and fruitless overhauling of the old files. Tom stated frankly, in his offhand and businesslike way, what his theory was. Neither Ziegler nor Tom's father believed in it in the least. Tom knew nothing, they said. The Navy paid the money, but the Navy was satisfied with our receipt, and should be. Tom continued to say, " If the Navy paid the money, the Navy must have the vouchers," and at last, more to be rid of him than with any hope of the result, Mr. Molineux let the eager fellow go round to his friend Eben Ricketts and see if Eben would not give an hour or two of his Christmas-eve to looking up the things. Mr. Molineux even went so far as to write a frank line to Mr. Ricketts, and enclosed a letter which he had had that day from the chairman of the House committee—a letter which was smooth enough in the language, but horribly rough in the thing.

Ah me! Had not Ricketts read already in the *Evening Lantern* a terrible attack on Molineux, stating that he had not appeared before the committee at noon, because he had not dared ; and that the committee itself deserved to be impeached because Mr. Molineux was not already under arrest. " But if a purblind committee thus sleeps at the post of duty, an Argus-eyed press and an awakened country," etc., etc., to the end of that chapter. Eben Ricketts had read, and was willing, if he could, to serve.

So he, with Tom, went round and found a Navy Department messenger, and opened and lighted up the necessary rooms, and there they spent six hours of their night before Christmas.

Meanwhile Beverly finished his fruit, had a frolic with the children, and then called his mother and Matty away from them.

"What in thunder is the matter?" asked the poor boy.

And they told him. How could they help telling him? And so soon as the story was finished the boy had his coat on, and was pulling on his boots. He went right down to his father's office; he made old Stratton admit him, and told his father he had reported for duty.

Neither of them had come home at four o'clock in the morning. Mrs. Molineux and Matty got such sleep as may be imagined. The children were only crazy to know what Santa Claus would put in their stockings.

And so went by the eve of Christmas for that family.

II.—CHRISTMAS MORNING

And at last Christmas morning dawned, gray enough and grim enough.

In that house the general presenting was reserved for evening, after dinner, when in olden days there had always been a large Christmas-tree lighted and dressed for the children and their little friends. As the children had grown older and the trees at the Sunday-school and elsewhere had grown larger, the family tree had grown smaller; and on this day was to be simply a typical tree, a little suggestion of a tree, between the front windows, while most of the presents of every sort and kind were to be dispersed—where room could be made for them—in any part of the front parlors. All the grand ceremonial of present-giving was thus reserved to the afternoon of Christmas, because then it was certain papa would be at home, Tom and Beverly would both be ready, and, indeed, as the little people

8

confessed, they themselves would have more chance to be quite ready.

But none the less was the myth of Santa Claus and the stockings kept up, although that was a business of less account, and one in which the children themselves had no share, except to wonder, to enjoy, and to receive. You will observe that there is a duality in most of the enjoyments of life; that if you have a long-expected letter from your brother who is in Yokohama, by the same mail or the next mail there comes a letter from your sister who is in Cawnpore. And so it was of Christmas at this Molineux house. Besides the great wonders, like those wrought out by Aladdin's slave of the lamp, there were the wonders, less gigantic but not less exquisite, of the morning hours, wrought out by the slave of the ring. How this series of wonders came about the youngest of the children did not know, but were still imaginative enough, and truly wise enough, not to inquire.

While, then, the two young men and their father were at one or the other department, now on step-ladders handing down dusty old pasteboard boxes, now under gaslights running down long indexes with inquiring fingers and unwinking eyes, Matty and her mother watched and waited, till eleven o'clock came, not saying much of what was in the hearts of both, but sometimes just recurring to it, as by some invisible influence—an influence which would overcome both of them at the same moment. For the mother and daughter were as two sisters, not parted far, even in age, and not parted at all in sympathy. For occupation they were wrapping up in thin paper a hundred barley dogs, cats, eagles, locomotives, suns, moons, and stars, with little parcels of nuts, raisins and figs, large red apples, and bright Florida oranges—all of which were destined to be dragged out of different stockings at daybreak.

"And now, dear, dear mamma," said Matty, "you will go to bed—please do, dear mamma!" This was said as she compelled the last obstinate eagle to accept his fate and stay in his wrapping-paper, from which he had more than once struggled out, with the instincts of freedom. "Please do, dear mamma; I will sort these all out, and will be quite sure that each has his own. At least, let us come up-stairs together. I will comb your hair for you—that is one of the little comforts. And you shall get into bed, and see me arrange them, and if I do wrong you can tell me."

Poor mamma, she yielded to her, as who does not yield, and because it was easier to go up-stairs than to stay. And the girl led her up and made herself a toilet-woman indeed, and did put her worn-out mamma into bed, and then hurried to the laundry, where she was sure she could find—what Diana had been bidden to reserve there—a pair of clean stockings belonging to each member of the family. The youngest children, alas! who would need the most room for their spread eagles and sugar locomotives, had the smallest feet and legs. But nature compensates for all things, and Matty did not fail to provide an extra pair of her mother's longest stockings for each of "the three," as the youngest were called in the councils of their elders. So a name was printed by Santa Claus on a large red card and pinned upon each receptacle, FLOSSY or LAURA, while all were willing to accept of his bounties contained within, even if they did not recognize yarn or knitting as familiar. Matty hurried back with their treasures. She brought from her own room the large red tickets, already prepared, and then, on the floor by her mother's side, assorted the innumerable parcels, and filled each stocking full.

Dear girl! she had not wrongly guessed. There was just occupation enough, and just little enough, for the poor mother's anxious tired thought. Matty was wise. She asked fewer and fewer questions; fewer and fewer she made her journeys to the great high fender, where she pinned all these stiff models of gouty legs. And when the last hung there quietly, the girl had the exquisite satisfaction of seeing that her mother was fast asleep. She would not leave the room. She turned the gaslight down to a tiny bead. She slipped off her own frock, put on her mother's heavy dressing-gown, lay down quietly by her side without rousing her, and in a little while—for with those so young this resource is wellnigh sure—she slept too.

It was five o'clock when she was wakened by her father's hand. He led her out into his own dressing-room, and before she spoke she kissed him!

She knew what his answer would be. She knew that from his heavy face. But, all the same, she tried to smile, and she said:

"Found?"

"Found? No, no, dear child, nor ever will be. How is mamma?"

And Matty told him, and begged him to come and sleep in her own little room, because the children would come in in a rout at daybreak. But no, he would not hear to that. "Whatever else is left, dear Matty, we have each other. And we will not begin—on what will be a new life to all of us—we will not begin by 'bating a jot of the dear children's joys. Matty, that is what I have been thinking of all the way as I walked home. But maybe I should not have said it but that Beverly said it just now to me. Dear fellow, I cannot tell you the comfort it was to me to see him come in! I told him he should not have come, but he knew that he made me almost happy. He is a fine fellow, Matty, and all night long he has shown the temper and the sense of a man."

For a moment Matty could not say a word. Her eyes were all running over with tears. She kissed her father again, and then found out how to say, "I shall tell him what you say, papa, and there will be two happy children in this house, after all."

So she ran to Beverly's room, found him before he was undressed, and told him. And the boy who was just becoming a man, and the girl who, without knowing it, had become a woman, kissed each other; held each other for a minute, each by both hands; looked each other so lovingly in the eyes, comforted each other by the infinite comfort of love, and then said goodnight, and were asleep. Tom had stolen to bed, without waking his mother or his sister, some hours before.

Yes, they all slept. The little ones slept, after all their being so certain that they should not sleep one wink from anxiety. This poor jaded man slept because he must sleep. His poor wife slept because she had not slept now for two nights before. And Matty, and Tom, and Beverly slept because they were young, and brave, and certain, and pure, and because they were between seventeen and twenty-two years of age. This is all to say that they could seek God's help and find it. This is to say that they were wellnigh omnipotent over earthly ills—so far, at the least, that sleep came when sleep was needed.

But not after seven o'clock. Venty and Diana had been retained by Flossy and Laura to call them at five minutes of seven, and Laura and Flossy had called the others. And at seven o'clock, precisely, a bugle-horn sounded in the children's quarters, and then four grotesque riders, each with a soldier-cap made of newspaper, each with a bright sash girt round a dressing-gown, each with bare feet stuck into stout shoes, came storming down the stairs, and, as soon as the lower floor was reached, each mounted on a hobby-horse or stick, and, with riot not to be told, came knocking at Matty's door, at Beverly's, and at Tom's. And these all appeared, also with paper soldier-hats upon their heads and girt in some very spontaneous costume, and so the whole troupe proceeded with loud fanfaron and drum-beat to mamma's door, and knocked for admission, and heard her cheery "Come in." And papa and mamma had heard the bugle-calls, and had wrapped some sort of shawls around their shoulders, and were sitting up in bed, they also with paper soldier-hats upon them; and one scream of "Merry Christmas!" resounded as the doors flew open; and then a wild ravage of kissing and hugging as the little ones rushed for the best places they could find on the bed, not to say in it. This was the Christmas custom.

And Tom rolled up a lounge on one side of the bed,

which, after a fashion, widened it; and Beverly brought
up his mother's easy-chair, which had earned the name
of "Moses' seat," on the other side; and thus in a minute the great broad bed was peopled with the whole
family—as jolly, if as absurd, a sight as the rising sun
looked upon. And then Flossy and Beverly were de-
puted to go to the fender and to bring the crowded,
stiff stockings, whose crackle was so delicate and exquisite. And so, youngest by youngest, they brought
forth their treasures — not indeed gold, frankincense,
and myrrh, but what answered the immediate purposes
better: barley cats, dogs, elephants, and locomotives;
figs, raisins, walnuts, and pecans.

Yes, and for one noisy half-hour not one person
thought of the cloud which hung over the house only
the night before!

But such happy forgetfulness cannot last forever.
There was the Christmas breakfast. And Tom tried
to tell of Academy times, and Beverly tried to tell
stories of the University. But it was a hard pull.
The lines under papa's eyes were only too dark. And
all of a sudden he would start, and ask just the wrong
question. Matty had put the newspapers out of the
way. Not that she had looked at them, but the
chances were too bad but that there would be something cruel about the investigation. And nobody
asked for the papers! That was perhaps the strangest
thing of all. And poor blundering Laura must needs
say "That is the good of Christmas, that there are no
horrid newspapers for people to bother with," when
everybody above Horace's age knew that there *were*

papers somewhere; and soon Horace was big enough to see—what he had not been told in words—that something was going wrong.

And as soon as breakfast was done Flossy cried out, "And now papa will tell us the story of the bear! Papa always tells us that on Christmas morning. Laura, you shall come; and, Horace, you shall sit there." And then her poor papa had to take her up and kiss her and say that this morning he could not stop to tell stories, that he had to go to the department. And then Flossy and Laura fairly cried. It was too bad. They hated the department. There never could be any fun but what that horrid old department came in. And when Horace found that Tom was going to the department too, and that Bev meant to go with him, he was mad, and said he did not see what was the use of having Christmas. Here he had tin-foil and plaster up-stairs, and little Watrous had lent him a set of Government medals, and they should have such a real good time if Bev would only stay. He wished the department was at the bottom of the Potomac. Matty fairly had to take the scolding boy out of the room.

Mr. Molineux, poor fellow, undertook the soothing of Flossy. "Anyway, old girl, you shall meet me as you go to church, and we will go through the avenue together, and I will show you the new Topsy girl selling cigars at Pierre's tobacco-shop. She is as big as Flossy. She has not got quite such golden hair, but she never says one word to her papa, because she is never cross to him."

"That's because he is never kind to her," said the quick child, speaking wiser than she knew.

For Matty, she got a word with Tom, and he too promised that they would be away from the department in time to meet the home party, and that all of them should go to church together.

And, accordingly, as Mrs. Molineux with her little troop crossed F Street they met the gentlemen all coming towards them. They broke up into groups, and Tom and Matty got their first real chance for talk since they had parted the night before. No! Tom had found no clew at the Navy Department. And although Eben Ricketts had been good as gold, and had stayed and worked with Tom till long after midnight, Eben had only worked to show good-will, for Eben had not the least faith that there was any clew there. Eben had said that if old Mr. Whilthaugh, who knew the archive rooms through and through, had not been turned out, they could do in fifteen minutes what had cost them six hours, and that old Mr. Whilthaugh, without looking, could tell whether it was worth while to look. But old Mr. Whilthaugh had been turned out, and Eben even did not know precisely what had become of him. He thought he had gone back into Pennsylvania, where his wife came from, but he did not know.

"But, Matty, if nothing turns up to-day I go to Pennsylvania to-morrow to find this old Mr. Whilthaugh. For I shall die if I stay here; and all the Eben Rickettses in the world will never persuade me that the vouchers are not in that archive room. If the Navy did the work, the Navy must have the vouchers."

Then Matty ventured to ask, what she and her mother had wondered about once and again, why these par-

ticular bits of paper were so necessary. Surely other
vouchers, or certified copies, or books of account could
be found somewhere !

"Yes; I knew you would say so. And if it were
all yesterday, and were all in these lazy times of peace,
you would say true. But, you see, in the first place,
this is ever so long ago. Then, in the second place, it
was in the heat of war, when everything was on a gigantic scale, and things had to be done in unheard-of
ways. Then, chiefly, this particular business involved
the buying up of I do not know who among the rebels
in Texas, and among their allies on the other side the
Rio Grande. This old Spaniard, whom mamma remembers, and whom I just remember, he was the chief
captain among the turncoats, and there were two or
three others, F. F. men, in their places—'First Family
men,' that means, you know—but after they did this
work they did not stay in their places long. No, papa
says he was mighty careful; that he had three of the
scoundrels sworn before notaries, or rather before one
notary, and had their receipts and acknowledgments
stamped with his notary's seal. Still, it did not do to
have a word said in public then. And after everything
succeeded so perfectly, after the troops landed without a shot, and found all the base ready for them—corn
and pork, and just where they wanted it—why, then
everybody was too gratified to think of imagining that
papa had stolen the money that bought the pork and
the corn."

"I wish they were only half as grateful now," he
said, after a pause.

"Tom," said Matty, eagerly, "who was that notary?"

"I thought of that too," said Tom. "There is no doubt who it was; it was old Gilbert. You must remember his sign, just below Faulkner's, on the avenue. But, in the first place, Gilbert died just after our reaching Richmond. In the second place, he never knew what the papers were; and he executed twenty such sets of papers every day, very likely. All he could say, at the very best, would be that at such a time father brought in an old Spaniard and two or three other Greasers, and that he took their acknowledgments of something."

"I do not know that, Tom," said the girl, without flinching at his mannish information. "If notaries in Washington are anything like notaries in novels, that man kept a record or register of his work. If he was not very unlike everybody else who lives and works here, he left a very destitute widow when he died. Tom, I shall go after church and hunt up the widow Gilbert. I shall ask her for her husband's books, and shall tell her why I want them."

The girl dropped her voice and said: "Tom, I shall ask her IN HIS NAME."

"God grant it does any good, dear girl," said he. "Far be it from me to say that you shall not try—"

But here he stopped speaking, for he felt Matty's arm shake in his, and her whole frame trembled. Tom had only to keep his eyes before him to see why.

Mr. Greenhithe, Matty's old admirer, the clerk who had been dismissed for stealing, was standing, impudent, on the steps of the church, and even touched his hat to her as she went by.

Tom resisted his temptation to thrash him then and

there. He led his sister within the door of the church, but did not go in with the others. He took her on one side, under the gallery stairs.

"Matty, I believe I will tackle that man!"

"Oh, Tom!"

"Yes, Matty, I can keep my temper, and he cannot keep his. He has one advantage over most knaves, that he is not only a knave of the first water, but he is sometimes a fool, too. If it were only decent and right to take him into Downing's saloon and give him just one more glass of whiskey than the blackguard would care to pay for, I could get at his whole story."

"But, Tom, I thought you were so sure the Navy had the papers!"

"Well, well!" said Tom, a little annoyed, as eager people are when other eager people remember their words against them, "I was sure—I was wholly sure—till I left Eben Ricketts last night. But after that—well, of course we ought to pull every string."

"Tom!" (this with a terrible gulp)—"Tom, you don't think I ought to speak with him?"

"Matty!"

"Why, Tom, yes; if he does know—if he is holding this up in terror, Tom, I could make him do what I chose once, Tom. You don't think I ought to try?"

"Matty, if you ever speak to that snake again I will thrash him within an inch of his life, and I will never say a word to you as long as you live!"

"That's my dear Tom!" And, hidden as they were under the stairs, and crying as she was under her veil, she flung her arms around him and kissed him.

"All the same," said Tom, after he had kissed her

again and again—"all the same, I shall find out, after
church, where the snake is staying. I shall go to the
hotel and take a cigar. I shall offer him one, and he
is so mean and stingy that he will take it. Perhaps
this may be one of his fool-days. Perhaps somebody
else will treat him to the whiskey. No, Matty, honor
bright! *I* will not, though that ten cents might give us
all a merry Christmas. Honor bright, I will not treat!
But I am not a saint, Matty! If anybody else treats,
I must not be expected to be far away."

Then he wiped her eyes with his own handkerchief
and led her into church. Their own pew was already
full. He had to take her back into Dr. Metcalf's pew.
So Matty was spared one annoyance which was prepared for her.

Directly in front of her father's pew, sitting in the
most conspicuous seat on the other side of the aisle,
was the hateful Mr. Greenhithe. Had he put himself there to watch Matty's face? If he did, he
was disappointed. If he had persuaded himself he
was to see a pale cheek or tearful eyes, or that he
was going to compel her to drop her veil, he had
reckoned quite without his host. Whenever he did
look that way all he saw was the face of Horace.
Horace was engaged in counting the large tassels on
his side of the pulpit curtains; in counting, also, the
number of small tassels between them, and, from the
data thus obtained, in calculating how many tassels
there must be on all the curtains to the pulpit, and how
many on the curtains behind the rail to the chancel.

Mr. Greenhithe, therefore, had but little comfort in
studying Horace's face.

Just as the Creed was finished, when the rest of the
church was still, the sexton led up the aisle a grim-look-
ing man with a shaggy coat and a very dirty face, and
brought him close to the door of Mr. Molineux's pew,
as if he would fain bring him in.   Mr. Molineux was
at the end of the pew, but happened to be turning away
from the aisle, and the sexton actually touched him.
He turned round and looked at the stranger, evidently
did not know him, but, with the instinct of hospitality,
stepped into the aisle and offered him his seat.   The
stranger was embarrassed, hesitated as if he would
speak, then shook his head in refusal of the attention,
and, crossing the aisle, took a seat offered him there, in
full sight of Mr. Molineux, and, indeed, of Matty.

Poor girl! The trifle—of course it was a trifle—
upset her sadly.

Was the man a marshal or a sheriff? Would they
really arrest her father on Christmas-day, in church?

III

Yes, it was, as you have said, a very curious Christmas service for all those people.

What Horace turned his mind to, at intervals, has
been told.

Of the older members of our little company who sat
there near the head of the side aisle, it may be said, in
general, that they did their best to keep their hearts
and minds engaged in the service, and that sometimes
they succeeded. They succeeded better while they
could really join in the hymns and the prayers than

they did when it came to the sermon. Good Dr. Gill, overruled by one of those lesser demons whose work is so apparent though so inexplicable in this finite world, had selected for the text of his sermon of gladness the words "Search and look." And so it happened—it was what did not often happen with him—he must needs repeat those words often—at the beginning and end, indeed, of every leading paragraph of the sermon. Now this duty of searching and looking had been just what all the five elder members of the Molineux family had been solidly doing—each in his way or hers, directly or by sympathy—in the last forty-eight hours. To get such relief as they might from it they had come to church, to look rather higher if they could. So that it was to them more a misfortune than a matter of immediate spiritual relief that their dear old friend, who loved each one of them with an intimate and peculiar love, happened to enlarge on his text just as he did.

If poor Mr. Molineux, by dint of severe self-command, had succeeded in abstracting his thoughts from disgrace almost certain—from thinking over, in horrible variety, the several threads of inquiry and answer by which that disgrace was to be avoided or precipitated—how was it possible to maintain such abstraction while the worthy preacher, wholly unconscious of the blood he drew with every word, ground out his sentences in such words as these:

. "Search and look, my brethren. Time passes faster than we think. Our gray hairs gather apace above our foreheads. And the treasure which we prized beyond price in years bygone has, perhaps, amid the cares of

this world, or in the deceitfulness of riches, been thrust
on one side, neglected, and at last forgotten.   How is
it with you, dear friends?   Are you the man?   Are
you the woman?   Have you put on one side the very
treasure of your life—as some careless housewife might
lay aside on a forgotten shelf this parcel or that, once
so precious to her?   Dear friends, as the year draws to
a close, awaken from such neglect.   Brush away the
dust from these forgotten caskets.   Lift them from
their hiding-places and set them forth, even in your
Christmas festivities.   Search and look!"

Poor Mrs. Molineux had never wished before so
earnestly that a sermon might be done.   She dared not
look round to see her husband for a while, but after one
of these invocations—not quite so terrible as the rest,
perhaps—she stole a glance that way, to find that she
might have spared her anxiety.   Two nights of "searching and looking" had done their duty by the poor
man, and, though his head was firmly braced against
the column which rose from the side of their pew, his
eyes were closed, and his wife was relieved by the certainty that he was listening, as those happy members
of the human family listen who hear best when their
lids are tight pressed over their eyeballs.   As for Beverly, he was assuming the resolute aspect of a sailor
under fire, and was imagining himself taking the whole
storm of Fort Constantine as he led an American
squadron into the bay of Sevastopol.   Tom did not
know what the preacher said, but was devising the
method of his interview with Greenhithe.   Matty did
know.   Dear girl!   She knew very well!   And with
every well-rounded sentence of the sermon she was

more determined as to the method of her appeal to Mrs. Gilbert, the widow of the notary. She would search and look there.

Yes; and it was well for every one of them that they went to that service! The sermon at the worst was but twenty minutes. "Twenty minutes in length," said Beverly, wickedly, "and no depth at all." But that was not true nor fair. Nor was that, either way, the thing that was essential. By the time they had all sung

"Praise God, from whom all blessings flow,"

even before the good old doctor had asked for Heaven's blessing upon them, it had come. To Mr. Molineux it had come in an hour's rest of mind, body, and soul. To Matty it had come in an hour's calm determination. To Mrs. Molineux it had come in the certainty that there was One Eye which sees through all hiding-places and behind all disguises. To the children it had come, because the hour had called up to them a hundred memories of Galilee and Nazareth, of Mary Mother, and of children made happy, to supplement and help out their legends of Santa Claus. Yes, and even Beverly the brave and Tom the outraged, as they stood to receive the benediction of the preacher, were more of men and less of firebrands than they had been. They all stood with reverence; they paused a moment, and then slowly walked down the aisle.

"Where is your father, Horace?" said Mrs. Molineux, a little anxiously, as she came where she could speak aloud. Horace was waiting for her.

"Papa? He went away with the gentleman who

9

came in after service began. They crossed the street, and took a carriage together."

"And did papa leave no message?"

"Why, no! He did not turn round! The strange man—the man in the rough coat—just touched him and spoke to him half-way down the aisle. Then papa whispered to him, and he whispered back. Then, as soon as they came into the vestibule here, papa led him out at that side door, and did not seem to remember me. They almost ran across the street, and took George Gibbs's hack. I knew the horses."

"That's too bad," said Laura; "I thought papa would walk home with us and tell us the story of the bears."

Poor Mrs. Molineux thought it was too bad too, but she said nothing.

And Matty, when she joined her mother, said, "I shall feel a thousand times happier, mamma, if I go and see Mrs. Gilbert now." And she explained who Mrs. Gilbert was. "Perhaps it may do some good. Anyway, I shall feel as if I were doing something. I will be home in time to finish the tree and things, for Horace will like to help me."

And the poor girl looked her entreaties so eagerly that her mother could not but assent to her plan. So she made Beverly go up the avenue with her — Beverly, who would have swum the Potomac and back for her, had she asked him—as he was on his way to join his father at the bureau.

As they came out upon the broad sidewalk, that odious Greenhithe, with some one whom Beverly called

a blackguard of his crew, pushed by them, and he had
the impudence to turn and touch his hat to Matty
again.

Matty's hand trembled on Beverly's arm, but she
would not speak for a minute, only she walked slower
and slower. Then she said, "I am so afraid, Bev, that
Tom and he will get into a quarrel. Tom declares he
will go into Willard's and find out whether he does
know anything."

But Beverly, very mannish, tried to reassure her
and make her believe that Tom would be very self-
restrained and perfectly careful.

On Christmas-day the Jew's dry-goods store which
had taken the place of old Mr. Gilbert's notary's
office was closed—not perhaps so much from the Is-
raelite's enthusiasm about Christmas as in deference
to what in New England is called "the sense of the
street." Matty, however, acting from a precise knowledge of Washington life, rang boldly at the green door
adjacent, Beverly still waiting to see what might turn
up, and when a brisk "colored girl" appeared Matty
inquired if Mrs. Munroe was at home.

Now all that Matty knew of Mrs. Munroe was that
her name was on a well-scoured brass plate on the
door.

Mrs. Munroe was in. Beverly said he would wait in
the passage. Mrs. Munroe proved to be a nice mother-
ly sort of person, who, as it need hardly be said, was
stone-deaf. It required some time for Matty to adjust
her speaking apparatus to the exigency, but when this
was done Mrs. Munroe explained that Mr. Gilbert
was dead; that an effort had been made to continue

the business with the old sign and the old good-will,
under the direction of a certain Mr. Bundy, who had
sometimes been called in as an assistant. But Mr.
Bundy, after some years, paid more attention to whiskey than he did to notarying, and the law business
had suffered. Finally Mr. Bundy was brought home
by the police one night with a broken head, and then
Mrs. Gilbert had withdrawn the signs, cancelled the
lease, turned Mr. Bundy out-of-doors, and retired to
live with a stepsister of her brother's wife's father
near the Arsenal—good Mrs. Munroe was not certain
whether on Delaware Avenue, or whether on T Street,
U Street, or V Street. And, indeed, whether the lady's
name were Butman, before she married her second
husband, and Lichtenfels afterwards, or whether his
name were Butman and hers Lichtenfels, Mrs. Munroe was not quite sure. Nor could she say whether
Mrs. Gilbert took the account-books and registers—
there were heaps on heaps of them, for Mr. Gilbert
had been a notary ever since General Jackson's day—
or whether Bundy did not take them, or whether they
were not sold for old paper, Mrs. Munroe was not
sure. For all this happened—all the break-up and
removal—while Mrs. Munroe was on a visit to her
sister not far from Brick Church, above Little Falls,
on your way to Frederick. And Mrs. Munroe offered
this visit as a constant apology for her not knowing
more precisely every detail of her old friend's business.

This explanation took a good deal of time, through
all of which poor Beverly was fretting and fuming and
stamping his cold feet in the passage, hearing the occasional questions of his sister, uttered with thunder

tone in the "sitting-room" above, but hearing no word of the placid widow's replies.

When Matty returned and held a consultation with him, the question was, whether to follow the books of account to Georgetown, where Mr. Bundy was understood to be still residing, or to the neighborhood of the Arsenal, in the hope of finding Mrs. Gilbert, Mrs. Lichtenfels, or Mrs. Butman, as the case might be. Readers should understand that these two points, both unknown to the young people, are some six miles asunder, the original notary's office being about half-way between them. Beverly was more disposed to advise following the man. He was of a mind to attack some one of his own sex. But the enterprise was, in truth, Matty's enterprise. Beverly had but little faith in it from the beginning, and Matty was minded to follow such clew as they had to Mrs. Gilbert, quite sure that, woman with woman, she should succeed better with her than man with man, Beverly with Bundy. Beverly assented to this view the more readily because Matty was quite willing to undertake the quest alone. She was very brave about it indeed. "Plenty of nice people at the Arsenal," or near it, whom she could fall back upon for counsel or information. So they parted. Matty took a street-car for the east and south, and Beverly went his ways to the Bureau of Internal Improvement to report for duty to his father.

This story must not follow the details of Matty's quest for the firm of "Gilbert, Lichtenfels, or Butman." Certain it is that she would never have succeeded had she rested simply on the directory or on such crude information as Mrs. Munroe had so freely given. But

Matty had an English tongue in her head, a courteous,
which is to say a confiding, address with strangers; she
seemed almost to be conferring a favor at the moment
when she asked one; and she knew, in this business,
that there was no such word as fail. After one or
two false starts—some very stupid answers, and some
very blunt refusals—she found her quarry at last, by
as simple a process as walking into a Sunday-school of
colored children, where she heard singing in the basement of a little chapel.

In a few words Matty explained her errand to the
superintendent, and that it was necessary that she
should find Mrs. Gilbert before dark.

"Ting!" One stroke of the bell called hundreds of
eager voices to silence.

"Who knows where Mrs. Gilbert lives? It is at Mrs.
Butman's house or Mrs. Lichtenfels's."

Twenty eager hands contended with each other for
the honor of giving the information, and in three minutes more Matty, all encouraged by her success, was on
her way.

And Mrs. Gilbert was at home. Good fortune number two! Matty's star was certainly in the ascendant!
Matty sent in her card, and the nice old lady presented
herself at once—remembered who Matty was, remembered how much business Mr. Molineux used to bring
to the office, and how grateful Mr. Gilbert always was.
She was so glad to see Matty. And she hoped Mr.
Molineux was well, and Mrs. Molineux and all those
little ones! She used to see them every Sunday as they
went to church, if they went on the avenue.

Thus encouraged, Matty opened on her sad story,

and was fairly helped from stage to stage by the
wonder, indignation, and exclamations of the kind old
lady. When Matty came to the end, and made her understand how much depended on the day-book, register,
and ledger of her husband, it was a fair minute before
she spoke.

"We will see, my dear; we will see. I wish it may
be so, but I'm all afeard. It would not be like him, my
dear. It would not be like any of them. But come
with me, my dear, we will see—we will see."

Then as Matty followed her through devious ways,
out through the kitchen, across a queer bricked yard,
into a half-stable, half-woodshed, which the good woman unlocked, she went on talking:

"You see, my dear child, that though notaries are
called notaries—as if it were their business to give notice
—the most important part of their business is keeping
secrets. Now when a man's note goes to protest, the
notary tells him what has happened—which he knew
very well before; and then he comes to the notary and
begs him not to tell anybody else, and of course he
does not. And the business of a notary's account-books,
as my husband used to say, is to tell just enough and
not to tell any more."

"Why, my dear child, he would not use blotting-
paper in the office! He would always use sand. 'Blotting-paper? Never!' he would say. 'Blotting-paper
tells secrets!'"

With such chatter they came to the little chilly
room, which was shelved all around, and to Matty's
glad eyes presented rows of green and blue and red
boxes, and folio and quarto books of every date from

1829 to 1869—forty years, in which the late Mr. Gilbert, and Mrs. Gilbert after him, had been confirming
history, keeping secret what he knew, but making sure
what, but for him, might have been doubted by a scep-
tic world.

Things were in good order. Mrs. Gilbert was proud
to show that they were in good order. The day-book
for 1863 was at hand. Matty knew the fatal dates
only too well. And the fatal entries were here.

How her heart beat as she began to read :

Cr.	To Thomas Molineux, Esq. (B. I. I.)	
Official authentication of signature of Felipe Garza	$1 25	
Same—Authentication of sig. of José B. Du Camara	1 25	
Same—Authentication of sig. of Jacob H. Cole.	1 25	

And this was all! Poor Matty copied it all; but all
the time she begged Mrs. Gilbert to tell her if there
were not some note-book or journal that would tell
more. And kind Mrs. Gilbert looked eagerly for what
she called the "diry." At the proper dates, at intervals
of a week or two, Matty found similar entries, the
names of the two Spaniards appearing in all three, but
other names in place of Cole's, just as Tom had told
her already. By the time she had copied all of these
Mrs. Gilbert had found the *diry*. Eager, and yet heart-
sick, Matty turned it over with her old friend.

This was all :

"Mr. Molineux here. Very private. Papers in R. G. E."

And then followed a little burst of unintelligible
shorthand.

Poor Matty! She could not but feel that here would

not be evidence good for anything, even in a novel.
But she copied every word carefully, as a chief clerk's
daughter should do. She thanked the kind old lady,
and even kissed her. She looked at her watch. Heavens! how fast time had gone! And the afternoons
were so short!

"Yes, my dear Miss Molineux, but they have turned, my dear; the day is a little longer and a little
lighter."

Did the old lady mean it for an omen, or was it only
one of those chattering remarks on meteors and weather-
change of which old-age is so fond? Matty wondered,
but did not know. Fast as she could she tripped bravely
on to the avenue for her street-car.

"The day is longer and lighter."

Meanwhile Tom was following his clew in the public
rooms at Willard's, to which, as he had prophesied, Mr.
Greenhithe had returned, after the unusual variation
in his line of a morning spent in the sanctuary. Tom
bought a copy of the Baltimore *Sun* and went into one
of the larger rooms resorted to by travellers and loafers, and sat down. But Mr. Greenhithe did not appear
there. Tom walked up and down through the passages a little uneasily, for he was sure the ex-clerk had
come into the hotel. He even went up and looked
in at the ladies' sitting-rooms to see if perhaps some
Duchess of Devonshire of high political circles had
found it worth while to drag Mr. Greenhithe up there
by a single hair. No Mr. Greenhithe! Tom was forced
to go and drink a glass of beer to see if Mr. Greenhithe was not thirsty. But at that moment, though

Mr. Greenhithe was generally thirsty in the middle of the day, and although many men were thirsty at the time Tom hung over his glass of lager, Mr. Greenhithe was not thirsty. It was only as Tom passed the billiard-room that he saw Mr. Greenhithe playing a game of billiards by way of celebrating the new birth of a regenerated world.

What to do now! Tom could not, in common decency, go in to look on at the game of a man he wanted to choke. Yet Tom would have given all his chances for rank in the Academy to know what Greenhithe was talking about. Tom slowly withdrew.

As he withdrew, whom should he meet but one of his kindest friends, Commodore Benbow! When the boys made their "experimental cruise" the year before, they had found Commodore Benbow's ship at Lisbon. The commodore had taken a particular fancy to Tom, because he had known his mother when they were boy and girl. Tom had even been invited personally to the flag-ship, and was to have been presented at court but that they had sailed too soon.

To tell the whole truth, the commodore was not overpleased to see his protégé hanging about the bar and billiard-room on Christmas-day. For himself, his whole family were living at Willard's, but he knew Tom's father was not living there, and he thought Tom might be better employed.

Perhaps Tom guessed this. Perhaps he was in despair. Anyway, he knew "Old Benbow," as the boys called him, would be a good counsellor. In point of statistics, "Old Benbow" had just turned forty, had not a gray hair in his head, could have beaten any one in

Tom's class, whether in gunnery or at billiards; could
have demonstrated every problem in Euclid while they
were fiddling over the forty-seventh proposition.   He
was at the very prime of well-preserved power, but
young nineteen called him "Old Benbow," as young
nineteen will, in such cases.

Bold with despair or with love for his father, Tom
stopped "Old Benbow," and asked him if he would
come into one of the sitting-rooms with him.   Then he
made this venerable old man his confidant.   The commodore had seen the slurs in the *Scorpion*, and the
Argus, and the *Evening Lantern*.   "A pity," said he,
"that Newspaper Row, which can do so much good,
should do so much harm.   What is Newspaper Row?
Three or four men of honor, three or four dreamers,
three or four schoolboys, three or four fools, and three
or four scamps.   And the public, Molineux—which is
to say, you and I—accept the trumpet-blast of one of
these heralds precisely as we do that of another.   Practically," said he, pensively, "when we were detached to
serve with the Thirteenth Corps in Mobile Bay, I found
I liked the talk of those light-infantry men—who had
been in every scrimmage in the war—quite as much as
I did that of the band-men who played the trumpets
on parade.   But this is neither here nor there.   I had
read this rigmarole.   I thought of coming round to see
your father, but I knew I should bother him.   What
can I do, my boy?"

Then Tom told him, rather doubtfully, that he had
reason to fear that Mr. Greenhithe was at the bottom
of the whole scandal.   He said he wished he did not
think that Mr. Greenhithe had himself stolen the papers.

" If I am wrong, I want to know it," said he. " If I am right, I want to know it. I do not want to be doing any man injustice. But I do not want to keep old Eben Ricketts over at the department hunting for a file of papers which Greenhithe has hidden in his trunk or has put into the fire."

" No, no, no, indeed!" said " Old Benbow," musing. " No, no, no!"

Then, after a pause—" Tom," said he, " come round here in an hour. I know that young fellow your friend is playing with—and I wish he were in better company than he is. I think I know enough of the usages of modern society to 'interview' him and his companion —though in that regard times have changed since I was of your age. Come here in an hour—or give me rather more, come here at half-past two—and we will see what we will see."

So Tom went round to the Navy Department. And here he found the faithful Eben—faithful to him, though utterly faithless as to any success in the special quest which was making the entertainment of his Christmas holiday. Vainly did Tom repeat to him his own formula:

" If the Navy did the work, the Navy has the vouchers."

" My dear boy," Eben Ricketts repeated a hundred times, " though the Navy did the work, the Navy did not provide the pork and beans; it did not arrange in advance for the landing; least of all did it buy the Greasers. I will look where you like, for love of your father and you, but that file of vouchers is not here, never was here, and never will be found here."

An assistant like this is not an encouraging adviser. And, in short, the vouchers were not found in the Navy Department in that particular midday search. At twenty minutes past two Tom gave it up unwillingly, bade Eben Ricketts good-bye, washed his hands from the accretions of coal-dust, which will gather even on letter-boxes in Navy Departments, and ran across in front of the President's House to Willard's. He looked up at the White House, and wondered how the people there were spending their Christmas-day.

Commodore Benbow was waiting for him. He took him up into his own parlors.

"Molineux, your Mr. Greenhithe is either the most ingenious liar and the best actor on God's earth, or he knows no more of your lost papers than a child in heaven. I went back to the billiard-room after you left me. I walked up to Millet—that was Lieutenant Millet playing with Greenhithe—and shook hands. He had to introduce me to your friend. Then I asked them both to come here; told Millet I had some papers from Montevideo that he would be glad to see, and that I should be glad of a call when they had done their game. Well, they came. I am sorry to say your friend—"

"Oh, don't, my dear Commodore Benbow, don't call him my friend, even in joke; it makes me feel awfully."

"I am glad it does," said the commodore, laughing. "Well, I am sorry to say that the black sheep had been drinking more of the whiskey down-stairs than was good for him, and, no fault of mine, he drank more of my Madeira here than he should have done;

and, Tom, I do not believe he was in any condition to keep secrets. Well, first of all, it appears that he has been in Bremen and Vienna for six months—he only arrived in New York yesterday morning."

Tom's face fell.

"And next—you may take this for what it is worth, but I believe he spoke the truth for once—he certainly did if there is any truth in liquor or in swearing. For when I asked Millet what all this stuff about your father meant, Greenhithe interrupted, very unnecessarily and very rudely, and said, with more oaths than I will trouble you with, that the whole was a damned lie of the newspaper-men; that they had lied about him (Greenhithe) and now were lying about old Molineux. That Molineux had been very hard on him, and very unjust to him, but he would say that he was honest as the clock—honest enough to be mean—and that he would say that to the committee if they would call on him—and so on, and so on."

"Much good would he do before the committee," said poor Tom. And thus ended Tom's investigation.

"Come to me if I can help you, my boy," said "Old Benbow." "It is always the darkest, old fellow, the hour before day."

Tom was astronomer enough to know that this old saw was as false as most old saws. But with this for his only comfort he returned to the bureau to seek Beverly and his father.

Neither Beverly nor his father was there. Tom went directly home. His mother was eager to see him. She had come home alone, and, save Horace and

Laura and Flossy and the Brick, she had seen nobody but a messenger from the bureau.

The Brick was the family name for Robert, one of the youngest of this household.

Of Beverly's movements this day the story must be more briefly told. They took more time than Tom's; as much, indeed, as his sister's after they parted. But they were conducted by means of that marvel of marvels, the telegraph, the chief of whose marvels is that it compels even a long-winded generation like ours to speak in very short metre.

Beverly began with Mr. Bundy at Georgetown. Georgetown is but a quiet place on the most active of days. On Christmas-day Beverly found but little stirring out of doors. Still, with the directory, with the advice of a saloon-keeper, and the information of a police-officer, Beverly tracked Mr. Bundy to his lair.

It was not a notary's office; it was a liquor-shop of the lowest grade, with many badly painted signs, which explained that this was "Our House," and that here Mr. Bundy made and sold — with proper license, let us be grateful — Tom-and-Jerry, smashes, cocktails, and did other deeds "without a name." On this occasion, however, even the door of "Our House" was closed. Mr. Bundy had gone to a turkey-shooting match at Fairfax Court-house. The period of his return was very doubtful. He had never done anything but keep this drinking-room since old Mrs. Gilbert turned him out-of-doors.

With this information master Beverly returned to town. He then began on his own line of search.

Relying on Tom's news, he went to the office of the Western Union Telegraph and concocted this despatch, which he thought a masterpiece:

> "GREENSBURG, Westmoreland Co., Pa.
> "*To Robert John Whilthaugh:*
> "When and where can I see you on important business?   Answer.
>   "BEVERLY MOLINEUX, for THOMAS MOLINEUX."

Then he took a walk, and after half an hour called at the office again. The office was still engaged in calling Greensburg. Greensburg was eating its Christmas dinner. But at last Greensburg was called. Then Beverly received this answer:

> "Whilthaugh has been dead more than a year.
>   "GREENSBURG."

To which Beverly replied:

> "Where does his wife live, or his administrator ?"

To which Greensburg, having been called a second time with difficulty, replied:

> "His wife is crazy, and we never heard of any property.
>   "GREENSBURG."

With this result of his investment as a non-dividend member of the great Western Union Mutual Information Club, Beverly returned home, chewing the cud of sweet and bitter fancies.

"There is no speech nor language," sang the choir in St. Matthew's as he passed, "and their voice is not heard. But their line has gone out through all the earth," and Tom heard no more, as he passed on. As he walked, almost unwillingly, up the street to the high steps of his father's house, Matty, out of breath, overtook him.

"What have you found, Bev?"

"Nothing," said the boy, moodily. And poor Matty had to confess that she had hardly more to tell.

They came into the house by the lower entrance, that they need not attract their mother's attention. But she was on the alert. Even Horace and the younger children knew by this time that something was wrong.

Horace's story about the strange man and papa was the last news of papa. Papa had not been at the bureau. The bureau people waited for him till two, and he did not come. Then Stratton had come round to see if he was to keep open any longer. Stratton had told Mrs. Molineux that her husband had not been there since church.

Where in the world was he? Poor Mrs. Molineux had not known where to send or to go. She had just looked in at the doctor's, but he was not there.

Tom had appeared first to her tedious waiting. Tom would not tell her, but he even went and looked in on Newspaper Row, which he had been abusing so. For Tom's first thought was that a formal information had been lodged somewhere, and that his father was arrested. But Newspaper Row evidently was unsuspicious of any arrest. Tom even walked down to the old jail, and made an absurd errand to see the deputy-marshal. But the deputy-marshal was at his Christmas dinner.

10

Tom told all this, in the hall, to Beverly and to Matty. Everything had failed, and papa was gone. Who could the man in the shag coat be? The three went together into the parlor.

For a little, Matty and Horace and Tom and Beverly then made a pretence of arranging the tree. But, in truth, Mrs. Molineux, in the midst of all her care, had done that while they were all away.

Dinner was postponed half an hour, and they gathered all in the darkness, looking at the sickliest blaze that ever rambled over half-burned Cumberland coal.

The Brick came climbing up on Tom's knees and bade him tell a story; but even Laura saw that something was wrong, and hushed the child, and said she and Flossy would sing one of their carols. And they sang it, and were praised; and they sang another, and were praised. But then it was quite dark. And nobody had any heart to say one word more.

"Where is papa?" said the Brick.

"Where indeed!" everybody wanted to say, and no one did.

But then the door-bell rang, and Chloe brought in a note.

"He's waiting for an answer, mum."

And Tom lighted the gas. It popped up so bright that little Flossy said:

"The people that sat in darkness saw a great light."

This was just as Mrs. Molineux tore open the note. For the instant she could not speak. She handed it to the three:

"FOUND! Home in half an hour. All right. Thank God!
"T. M."

"Saw a great light indeed," said Horace, who for once felt awed.

IV

For half a minute, as it seemed afterwards, no one spoke. Then Matty flew to her mother and flung her arms around her neck, and kissed her again and again.

Tom hardly knew what he was doing, but he recovered self-command enough to know that he must try to be manly and businesslike, and so he rushed downstairs to find the man who brought the note. It proved to be a man he did not know. Not a messenger from the bureau, nor one from the Navy Department—least of all an aid of the assistant marshal's. He was an innocent waiter from the Seaton House, who said a gentleman called him and gave him the note, told him to lose no time, and gave him half a dollar for coming. He had asked for an answer, though the gentleman had not told him to.

Tom wrote:

"Hurrah! All's well. All at home.—T."

and gave this note to the man.

They all talked at once, and they all sat still without talking. The children—must it be confessed?—asked all sorts of inopportune questions. At last Tom was even fain to tell the story of the bear himself, by way of silencing the Brick and Laura; and, with much cor-

rection from Horace, had got the bear well advanced in
smelling at the almond candy and the figs, when a carriage was heard on the street, evidently coming rapidly
towards them. It stopped at the door. The bear was
forgotten as all the elders in this free-and-easy family
rushed out of the parlor into the hall.

Papa was there, and was as happy as they. With
papa, or just behind him, came in the man with the
rough coat, whose face at church had been so dirty,
whose face now was clean. To think that papa should
have brought the deputy-marshal with him!

For by the name of the deputy-marshal had this
mysterious stranger been spoken of in private by the
two young men since the fatal theory had once been
advanced that he had come into the church to arrest
Mr. Molineux.

The unknown, with great tact, managed to keep in
the background, while Mrs. Molineux kissed her husband, and while Matty kissed him, and while among
them they pulled off his coat. But Mr. Molineux did
not forget. He made a chance in a moment to say:
" You must speak to our friend who has brought me
here. No one was ever so welcome at a Christmas dinner. Mr. Kuypers, my dear; Mr. Kuypers, Matty, dear.
These are my boys, Mr. Kuypers."

Then, as the ladies welcomed the stranger and the
boys shook hands with him, Mr. Molineux added—
what hardly any one understood — " It is not every
friend who travels fifteen hundred miles to jog a
friend's memory."

And they all huddled into the parlor. But in a moment more Mrs. Molineux had invited Mr. Kuypers if,

after his journey, he would not like to go to his room. And he, with good feeling, which he showed all the evening, gladly took himself out of the way. And so, as Tom returned from showing him up-stairs, the parlor was filled with those "God made there," as the little boy used to say, and with none besides.

"Now tell us all about it, dear papa," cried Tom.

"I was trying to tell your mother. But there is not much to tell. Poor Mr. Kuypers had travelled all the way from Colorado the moment he heard I was in trouble. Yesterday he bought the *Scorpion* in the train and found the committee was down on us. He drove here from the station as soon as the train came in. He missed you here, and drove by mistake to Trinity. That made him late with us. And so, as the service had begun, he waited till it was done."

"Well!" said Bev, perhaps a little impatiently.

"But as soon as we were going out he touched me, and said he had come to find me in the matter of the Rio Grande vouchers. Do you know, Eliza, I can afford to laugh at it now, but at the moment I thought he was a deputy of the Sergeant-at-arms?"

"There!" screamed Tom. "I said he was a deputy-marshal!"

"I said, 'Certainly,' and I laughed, and said they seemed to interest all my friends. Then he said, 'Then you have them? If I had known that I would have spared my journey.' This threw me off guard, and I said I supposed I had them, but I could not find them. And he said, eagerly—this was just on the church-steps—'But I can.'

" Then he said he had a carriage waiting, and he bade me jump in.

" So soon as we were in the carriage he explained— what I ought to have remembered, but cannot now recollect for the life of me—that after General Trebou returned from Texas there was a court of inquiry ; that there was some question about these very supplies— the beans and the coffee particularly. They had nothing to do with the landing nor with the Mexicans. And the court of inquiry sent one day from the War Department, where they were sitting, to our office for an account, because we were said to have it. Mr. Kuypers was their messenger to us, and, because we had bound them all together, the whole file was sent as it was. He took them, and, as it happened, he looked them over, and, what was better, he remembered them.

" Well, that court of inquiry was endless, as those army inquiries always are. Mr. Kuypers was in attendance all the time. He says he never shall forget it, if other people do.

" So as soon as he saw that we were in trouble at the bureau—that *I* was in trouble, I mean," said Mr. Molineux, stoutly—" he knew that he knew what nobody else knew—that the vouchers were in the papers of that court of inquiry."

" And he came all the way to tell ? What a good fellow !"

" Yes, he came on purpose. He says he could not help coming. He says he made two or three telegrams, but every time he tried to telegraph he felt as if he were shirking. And I believe he was right. I believe we should never have pulled through without him. 'Personal presence moves the world,' as Eli Thayer used to say."

"And you found them?" asked Mrs. Molineux, faintly essaying to get back to the story.

"Oh yes, we found them; but not in one minute. You see, first of all, I had to go to the chief clerk at the War Department and get the department opened on a holiday. Then we had no end of clerks to disturb at their Christmas dinners, and at last we found a good fellow named Breen who was willing to take hold with Mr. Kuypers. And Mr. Kuypers himself"—here he dropped his voice—"why, we have not three men in all the departments who know the history of this government, or the system of its records, as he does!

"Once in the office, he went to work like a master. Breen was amazed. Why, we found those documents in less than half an hour!

"Then I sent Breen with a note to the Secretary. He was good as gold; came down in his own carriage, congratulated me as heartily—well, almost as heartily —as you do, Tom; and took us both round, with the files, to Mr. McDermot, the chairman of the House committee. He was dining with his mess at the Seaton House; but we called him out, and, I declare, I believe he was as much pleased as we were.

"I only stopped to make him give me receipts for the papers, because they all said it was idle to take copies, and here we are!"

In the hush that followed, the Brick made his way up on his father's knee, and said:

"And now, papa, will you tell us the story of the bear? Tom does not tell it very well."

They all laughed—they could well afford to laugh now—and Mr. Molineux was just beginning upon the story of the bear when Mr. Kuypers reappeared. He had in this short time revised his toilet, and looked, Mrs. Molineux said, in an aside, like the angel of light that he was. "Bears!" said he. "Are there any bears in Washington? Why, it was only last Monday that I killed a bear, and I ate him on Tuesday."

"Did you eat him all?" said the Brick, whose reverence for Mr. Kuypers was much more increased by this story than by any of the unintelligible conversation which had gone before. But just as Mr. Kuypers began on the story of the bear, Chloe appeared with beaming face and announced that dinner was ready.

That dinner which this morning every one who had any sense had so dreaded, and which now seemed a festival indeed!

Well! there was great pretence in fun at form in marshalling. And Mr. Kuypers gave his arm to Matty, and Horace his to Laura, and Beverly his to Flossy, and Tom brought up the rear with the Brick on his shoulders. And Mr. Molineux returned thanks and asked a blessing all together. And they fell to on the turkey and on the chicken-pie. And they tried to talk about Colorado and mining; about Gold Hill, and Hale and Norcross, and Uncle Sam and Overman and Yellow Jacket. But, in spite of them all, the talk would drift back to Bundy and his various signs, "Our House" and "Tom-and-Jerry," to the wife of Mr. Whilthaugh, to Commodore Benbow, to old Mrs. Gilbert and Delaware Avenue. And this was really quite as much the fault of Mr. Kuypers as it was of any of the

Molineux family. He seemed as much one of them as Tom himself did. This anecdote of failure and that of success kept cropping out; Waltsingham's high-bred and disguised enthusiasm for the triumph of the office, and the satisfaction Eben Ricketts would feel when he was told the Navy never had the vouchers—all were commented on. Then Mrs. Molineux would start and say, "We are talking shop again. You say the autumn has been mild in the mountains?" and yet in two minutes they would be on the trail of "Search and Look" again.

It was in one of these false starts that Mr. Kuypers explained why he had come, which, in Horace's mind, and perhaps in the minds of the others, had been the question most puzzling of all.

"Why!" said Horace, bluntly—"had you ever heard of papa before?"

"Had I heard of him?" said Mr. Kuypers. "I think so. Why, my dear boy, your father is my oldest and kindest friend!"

At this exclamation, even Mrs. Molineux looked amazed, Tom laid down his fork and looked to see if the man were crazy, and Mr. Molineux himself was thrown off his balance.

Mr. Kuypers was a well-bred man, but this time he could not conceal his amazement. He laid down knife and fork both, looked up, and almost laughed as he said, with wonder:

"Don't you know who I am?"

"We know you are our good angel to-day," said Mrs. Molineux, bravely, "and that is enough to know."

"But don't you know why I am here, or what sent me?"

Mr. Molineux said that he understood very well that his friend had wanted to see justice done, and that he had preferred to see to this in person.

"I thought you looked queer," said Mr. Kuypers, frankly; "but still I did not know I was so changed. Why, don't you remember Bruce? You remember Mrs. Chappell, surely?"

"Are you Bruce?" cried Mr. Molineux—and he fairly left his chair and went round the table to the young man. "Why, I can see it now. But then— why, you were a boy, you know — and this black beard—"

"But pray explain—pray explain," cried Tom. "The mysteries increase on us. Who is Mrs. Chappell, and, for that matter, who is Bruce, if his real name be not Kuypers?"

And they all laughed heartily. People got back their self-possession a little, and Mr. Kuypers explained.

"I am Bruce Kuypers," said he, "though your father does not seem to remember the Kuypers part."

"No," said Mr. Molineux, "I cannot remember the Kuypers part, but the Bruce part I remember very well."

"My mother was Mrs. Kuypers before she married Mr. Chappell, and Mr. Chappell died when my brother Ben was six years old and little Lizzy was a baby."

"Lizzy was my godchild," said Mrs. Molineux, who now remembered everything.

"Certainly she was, Mrs. Molineux; and last month

Lizzy was married to as good a fellow as ever presided over the melting of ingots. We marry them earlier at the West than you do here.

"Where Lizzy would have been," he said, more gravely, addressing Tom again, "where my mother would have been, or where I should have been but for your father and mother here it would be hard to tell. And all to-day I have taken it for granted that to him, as to me, this has been one part of that old Christmas! Surely you remember?" He turned to Mrs. Molineux.

Yes. Mrs. Molineux did remember, but her eyes were all running over with tears, and she did not say so.

"Mr. Molineux," said Bruce Kuypers, again addressing Tom, "seventeen years ago this blessed day there was a Christmas morning over beyond Massachusetts Avenue such as you never saw, and such as I hope you may never see.

"There was fire in the stove because your father had sent the coal. There was oatmeal mush on the table because your father had paid my mother's scot at your father's grocer's. But there was not much jollity in that house, and there were no Christmas presents but what your mother had sent to Bruce and Ben and Flora, and even to the baby. Still, we kept up such courage as we could. It was a terribly cold day, and there was a wet storm.

"All of a sudden a carriage stopped at the door and in came your father here.

"He came to say that that day's mail had brought a letter from Dr. Wilder, of the Navy, covering the full certificate that William Chappell's death was caused by exposure in the service. That certificate was what my mother needed for her pension. She never could get it, but your father here had sifted and worried and worked. The *Macedonian* arrived Thursday at New York, and had Dr. Wilder on board; and Friday afternoon your father had Wilder's letter, and he left his own Christmas dinner to make light my mother's and mine.

"That was not all. Your father, as he came, had stopped to see Mr. Birdsall, who was then Speaker of the House. He had seen the Speaker before, and had said kind things about me. And that day the Speaker told him to tell me to come and see him at his room at the Capitol next day. Oh, how my mother dressed me up! Was there ever such a page seen before? What with your father's kind words and my dear mother's extra buttons, the Speaker made me his own page the next day, and there I served four years. It was then that I was big enough to go into the War Department, and Mr. Goodsell—he was the next Speaker, if you remember—recommended me there.

" After that," said Bruce Kuypers, modestly, " I did not see you so often, but I did use to see you sometimes, and I did not think"—this with a roguish twinkling of the eye—"that you forgot your young friends so soon."

" I remember you," said Tom. " I used to think you were the grandest man in Washington. You gave me the first ride on a sled I ever had—when there was some exceptional fall of snow."

" I think we all remember Mr. Kuypers now," said Matty, and she laughed while she blushed. " He al-

ways brought things for our stockings. I have a
Noah's ark up-stairs now that he gave me. In my
youngest days I had a queer mixture of the name Bruce
and the name Santa Claus. I believe I thought Santa
Claus's name was Nicholas Bruce. I am sure I did
not know that Mr. Bruce had any other name."

"If you had said you were Mr. Chappell," said Mr.
Molineux, "I should have known you in a minute."

"But I was not," said the young man, laughing.

"Well, if you had said you were Bruce, I should have
known."

"Dear me, yes. But I have been a man so long—
and at Gem City nobody calls me Bruce but my mother
and Lizzy. So I said I was Mr. Kuypers, forgetting
that I had ever been a boy. But now I am in Washington again, and I shall remember that. Things
change here very fast in ten years. But not so fast as
they change at the mines."

And now everybody was at ease. How well Mrs.
Molineux recalled to herself—what she would not speak
of—that Christmas-day which Mr. Kuypers told his
story of! It was in her young married life. She had
her father and mother to dine with her, and the event
was really a trial in her young experience. And then,
just as the old folks were expected, her husband had
come dashing in, and had asked her to put dinner a
little later because he had this good news for the poor
widow Chappell. And she had to tell her father and
her mother when they came that they must all wait
for his return.

The widow Chappell was one of those waifs who
seem attracted to Washington by some fatal law. It

had been two or three months before that Mr. Molineux had been asked to hunt her up and see for her.
A letter had come asking him to do this from Mrs.
Fales in Roxbury, and Mrs. Fales had sent money for
the Chappells. But the money had gone on back rent
and shoes and the rest, and the wolf was very near
the Chappells' door when the telegraph announced the
Macedonian. Mr. Molineux had telegraphed instanter
to this Dr. Wilder. Dr. Wilder had had some sense
of Christmas promptness. He remembered poor Chappell perfectly, and mailed that night a thorough certificate. This certificate it was which Mr. Molineux
had carried to the poor old tenement above Massachusetts Avenue, and this had made happy that Christmas-
day—and this.

" Why," said Mr. Bruce Kuypers, almost as if he
were thinking aloud, "it seems so queer that Christmas comes and goes with you and you have forgotten
all about that stormy day and your ride to Mrs. Chappell's. Why, at our place we drink Mr. Molineux's
health every Christmas-day, and I am afraid the little
ones used to think you had a red nose, a gray beard,
and came down chimneys!"

"As at another house," said Matty, "they thought
of Mr. Bruce—of Noah's-ark memory."

"Anyway," said Mr. Molineux, "any crumbs of
comfort we scattered that day were *bread on the
waters!*"

_____

Of Mr. Kuypers's quick journey the main points
had been told. Six days before, by some good luck,
which could hardly have been expected, the Gem City

Medium's despatch from Washington was full enough to be intelligible. It was headed " Another Swindler Nailed." It said that Mr. Mallinox, of the Internal Improvement Office, had feathered his nest with $500,-000 in the war, in a pretended expedition to the Rio Grande. It had now been discovered that there never was any such expedition, and the correspondent of the Associated Press hoped that justice would be done.

The moment Bruce Kuypers read this he was anxious. Before an hour passed he had determined to cross to the Pacific train eastward. Before night he was in a sleeping-car.

Day by day, as he met Eastern papers, he searched for news of the investigation. Day by day he met it. But, thanks to his promptness, he had arrived in time. They were all hushed to silence when he told his growing anxiety from day to day; and when he told how much he was moved at finding that he should arrive on Christmas-day they were certainly as much moved as he.

And after the dinner another procession, not wholly unlike the rabble rout of the morning, moved from the dining-room to the great front parlor, where the tree was lighted, and parcels of gray and white and brown and yellow lay around on mantel, on piano, on chairs, on tables, and on the floor.

No! this tale, too long already, will not tell what the presents were to all the ten—to Venty, Chloe, Diana, and all of their color. Only let it tell that all the ten had presents. To Mr. Kuypers's surprise—and to every one's surprise indeed—there were careful parcels for him, as for the rest; but it must be confessed that

Horace and Laura had spelled *Chipah* a little wildly. The truth was that each separate person had feared that he would feel a little left one side, he to whom so much was due that day; and each person severally, down to Brick himself, had gone secretly to select from his own possessions something very dear, and had wrapped it up and marked it for the stranger. When Mr. Kuypers opened a pretty parcel, to find Matty's own illustrated Browning, he was touched indeed. When in a rough brown paper he found the Brick's jack-knife, labelled *"For the Man,"* the tears stood in his eyes.

The next day the *Evening Lantern* contained this editorial article:

"The absurd fiasco regarding the accounts of Mr. Molineux, which has occupied the correspondents of the provincial press for some days, and has even been adverted to in New York journals claiming the title of 'metropolitan,' came to a fit end at the Capitol yesterday. The wiseacre owls who started it did not see fit to put in an appearance before the committee. Mr. Molineux himself sent to the chairman a most interesting manuscript volume, which is indeed a valuable historical memorial of times that tried men's souls. The committee, and other gentlemen present, examined this curious record with great interest. Not to speak of the minor details, an autograph letter from the late lamented General Trebou gives full credit to the Bureau of Internal Improvement for the skill with which they executed the commission given them in a department quite out of their line. Our brethren of the *Argus* will be pleased to know that every grain of oats and every spire of straw paid for by the now famous $47,000 is accounted for in detail. The authenticated signatures of the somewhat celebrated Camara and Garza and the mythical Captain Cole appear. Very valuable letters, throwing interesting light on our relations with the government of Mexico, from the pens of the lamented Adams and Prigg, show what were the services of those two Spanish turncoats and their allies.

"We cannot say that we regret the attention which has thus been given to a very important piece of history, too long neglected in the rush of more petty affairs. We take the occasion, however, to enter our protest once more against this preposterous system of 'Resolution,' in which, as it were, in echo to every *niaiserie* of every hired pen in the country, the House degrades itself to the work of the common scavenger; orders at immense expense an investigation into some subject where all well-informed men are fully advised—and at a cost of the national treasure."

Etc., etc., etc., to the end of that chapter.

But I fear no one at the Molineux mansion read the *Lantern*. They had "found a man" and did not need a lantern to look farther. It was as Mr. Molineux had said: "He had cast his bread upon the waters, and had found it after many days."

GENERAL GLOVER'S TRUE STORY

[THE following story is better than most stories are, because it is exactly true, excepting the names given to the parties and places. The gentleman whom I have called "General Glover" has permitted me to put it in writing, that it may give the same courage to other persons which it has given to him and to me. But, at his request, I have changed every name in the story from those which he gave me; and I assure the most curious reader or critic that he will find it impossible to ascertain by any conjecture who are the parties described. No incident, however, in the story, is drawn in the slightest degree from imagination. I tell the tale as it was told to me, and print it after it has had the revision of "General Glover."—E. E. HALE, writing in 1888.]

———

I was riding across country to Duluth when my old friend General Glover came into the palace-car. We two were born at very nearly the same time; we like each other and respect each other. We have knocked about the world a good deal, and do not meet each other as often as we wish we did; but when we meet we begin where we left off, and enjoy the meeting. At least, I am sure I do, and I think he does.

As soon as the first inquiries were passed I said to him: "I want you to tell me again your story of the letter you wrote to a stranger. At the time you told me I repeated it to my wife, and afterwards to one or two other persons; but now I am afraid to tell it, it is so strange, and I am always thinking that my imagination has added something to it."

General Glover looked at me with a surprise not wholly of amusement. It was quite clear to me that the story was a serious matter to him, as it was to me; and he told it to me for the second time. I think it was four years ago since I heard it first, and it speaks as well for my memory as for his that I should recognize each slightest detail as a thing which had impressed itself upon his careful mind, so that this narrative was identically the same as the first was. It was as if you had struck a second impression from a stereotype plate which you had not used for four years.

" I was sitting at my desk at Xeres," he said, "and working through my daily mail. My custom was to attend to the business of the firm first, and to leave the personal letters to be answered in the afternoon. It was now afternoon, and I turned to the six or eight letters which I had for answer.

" Among these was one from a man for whom I had secured a place in the Navy in the outset of the Civil War. If you remember, I was then at the head of the Bunting Board, and had a great deal to do with the enlargement of the Navy. Also, I was myself connected with the service. I had been in service on the seaboard all my life, and knew, naturally enough, a great many sailors in the merchant marine. Hundreds of such men came to me, and it was with my recommendation of them that they received their places in that volunteer service which was of such infinite advantage to the country in the war. Among these hundreds was a good fellow who had been, I should say, in the coasting trade; but I do not remember what he had been. He wanted to serve the country, and, at my recommendation, he was appointed, as other men were appointed, a master's mate. As a master's mate he did his duty, rose to be a master, afterwards obtained a lieutenant's commission, and so went wellnigh through the war, until, by an accident—not, I think, a wound— he was so far disabled that he could no longer go to sea. I did not know this at the time; there was no reason why I should know it; I had nothing to do with him, and he had nothing to do with me. He was to me no more than one post in this rail-fence which we are passing now is, as distinct from another. I had signed the papers, I suppose, during the war, of thousands of men who had more or less to do with our Bunting Board, and this man, his name or his affairs, made no more impression upon me than the rest of them did.

"But among the letters of this particular afternoon, as I said, was a letter from this man. It was a gentlemanly letter, short and to the point, in which he told me that he received his appointment on my recommendation; that, after some years of service he had been obliged to cease going to sea, on account of the accident of which I speak. He now asked me if I were willing to write to the head of the Pension Bureau to ask that his claim might be examined and acted upon immediately. He said that neither he nor his counsel had succeeded in obtaining any letters from the Pension Office telling them when action would be taken on his claim. He remembered that I was the person who originally introduced him into the Navy, and he thought a letter from me might obtain an answer where he had failed.

"I recalled, as well as I could, the circumstances in which he first came to me, and I said, in a short letter, what I could do to his advantage, in order that he might use my recommendation, so far as it went, in his application, and then I went on with my other letters.

"I had finished the whole correspondence when something, which I do not understand and you do not understand, made me take this letter to him out from the pile. I opened it, looked at his letter again, and looked at the letter which I had written to the Pension Bureau. Clearly, I had done all he asked me for, and I folded both envelopes again and sealed them. I went on with my other work. Still, I was haunted with the feeling that this thing was left unfinished, and I opened both the letters once more. I read his letter again, I read my letter to the Pension Bureau, and I read the note which I had written to him. This time, after reading his letter to me and mine to him once and again, I enclosed in my envelope to him some money, without saying why, for indeed I did not know. This 'finally finished' my correspondence, as I supposed; I sealed the letter again, and, finding that I could do nothing in my office, put on my coat, took all the letters I had been writing, passed from my private room through the counting-room, and left the letters for the mail.

"But I was not permitted to leave the door of the office. In obedience to the impulse which I had now obeyed twice, I went back to the mailing-box, took out my letter to him again, went back to my private office,

and read it once more; read his letter now for the third
or fourth time, and this time wrote a new letter to my
old friend Colonel Sharp, who lived in the town from
which the officer had written to me. I asked Sharp to
be good enough to find him, to find what his condition
was, and that of his family, and if he found that they
needed any help, to render it to them at my expense,
if it should be necessary. I sealed and stamped this
letter, added it to my mail, and this time I was permitted to leave my office and to go to my home.

"We had a nightly mail at that time from Xeres to
Abydos, which was the city in which he was living,
and, as I learned afterwards, my letter to him arrived
the next morning. It will save trouble if I give you a
name for him. We will call him Needles, though that
is not his name.

"Thirty-six hours after I had written I received his
reply. I have it now, and I will show it to you at
some time. It was a most modest and simple narrative
of the steady decline of his fortunes since the accident
which I have described. It seemed he had a wife and
four or five children, of whom he spoke with pride and
confidence. But he had been educated as a sailor, and
knew no arts but those of a sailor; he had no way of
earning a living, now that he could not go to sea; and
he had gone through all the misery of sickness, en-
forced idleness, of his income becoming less and less,
until it was nothing.

"He and his wife had sold every article of property
and dress which they could sell for the food and
clothing of their children. They had been obliged to
withdraw their children from school, because they

could not present a proper appearance there. It was under such circumstances that, needing his pension, of course, he had written to me the modest letter which I had received, asking for my assistance in hastening the decision on it.

"On the night before his present writing—that is, on the evening which immediately followed the after-noon of my writing to him—he and his wife and children were cowering around the little stove which warmed their lodging. The fire in it was maintained by coals and cinders which the children had picked up in the street. He had not a cent to pay for any article of food, and he and the children were all hungry. They reviewed the position as well as they could, and it was then that his wife said that she was sure that brighter times must be before them. For she still believed that God did not mean that people should perish who had not intentionally offended Him or fought against His law. She knew that they had done their duty as well as they knew how, and she believed that God would carry them through. She had no ground for this belief excepting her certainty that neither she nor her husband nor her children had intentionally done what was wrong. With such comfort as they could get from such expressions as hers they all went to bed, the earlier because they had nothing to eat, and perhaps because the fire was not very satisfactory.

"For the same reason they slept, or stayed in bed, late in the morning. One is not tempted to rise early when he has nothing to do and nothing to eat. But they did rise, though late, and were rekindling the fire, I think, when the postman stopped at the door, and brought in the letter which I had three times opened, and in which I had, as I say, enclosed the money.

"Needles wrote to me that when the bill fell to the ground from the letter, as it did, he felt as he should have felt if it had dropped from the hand of an angel. He had not asked me for money; he had not asked anybody for money. He asked me for my influence in the Pension Bureau. Without asking, the money had come. He felt, and his wife felt, as if it had come in answer to their prayer."

As General Glover told me this story I was reminded of a phrase of my friend Mr. Naylor, who used to say that there was no condition in human life in which a check on New York would not answer most purposes. It was clear enough that the crisp greenback which had been enclosed in General Glover's letter had been quite as valuable a workman in that starving family as Aladdin's slave of the ring would have been.

A skilful child was at once despatched to buy the materials for breakfast, and they were well engaged in the first meal which they had eaten for several days when another party appeared upon the stage. This time it was not the postman; it was Colonel Sharp, to whom General Glover's fourth letter had been written. I wish I could give the reader an idea of General Glover's description of Colonel Sharp's methods. He sat, cheering all parties by his lively talk—I wish I were talking with him now—and when he saw that the breakfast was well finished he took Needles with him to the great post-office at Abydos. Colonel Sharp was a pretty important person in that city, and, breaking all lines of defence, he soon found himself with Mr. Needles in the private room of the postmaster, whom, for the purpose of this story, we will call Mr. Rowland Hill. General Glover went on to describe the interview.

"Sharp told Mr. Hill that there was a deserving man who had served the country, and that I was interested in him, and Hill shook hands with official cordiality, and said he should be interested in any friend of mine and his.

"Colonel Sharp said that he wanted Hill to appoint Mr. Needles to a good place in that post-office. Mr. Hill at once assumed the official air of distress, and explained how many hundreds of applications he received every day from very deserving people; but he would put Mr. Needles's name on the list, and would send for him the first time he had an opportunity.

"Colonel Sharp said, at this, that he was very glad Mr. Needles interested Mr. Hill, that neither of them was much occupied, and that they would stay in the private office until the opportunity should occur. At this announcement that the office would need three permanent chairs for some time, Mr. Rowland Hill was more startled. 'In short,' said Colonel Sharp to him good-naturedly, 'the official methods will not answer in this case. Mr. Needles deserves the place; he must have the place; General Glover and I both mean that he shall have the place; and you may as well give it to him now as to give it to him next week.' There are men who can say such things, who have earned the right to say them by long and distinguished service to the country. Mr. Hill knew perfectly well that this was one of those cases, and when, therefore, Mr. Needles walked home that morning to his wife it was to explain to her that he was to go on duty in the post-office of Abydos, with a proper salary, that afternoon.

" All this he explained," said General Glover, " in the letter of which I told you, which I received thirty-six hours after I enclosed the bill to him."

Here ends the first half of General Glover's story to me as he told it on the train. I wish the reader to observe, however, that this first half is accompanied by a second half, which transpired several years after.

Mr. Needles did his work so well in the new office that every one liked him. Had it not been indoor work, and he a sailor, needing outdoor life, this story would end here. But the close confinement of the office was bad for him, and the doctor told him that he could not stand it. He did not write this to General Glover till he had found where he must go. Then it proved that in a bureau which is under the Treasury, which I will call the Bureau of Red Tape, they needed an outdoor invoice man. It was work that he could do, and he applied to be transferred there. He wrote to General Glover, to tell him why he wanted to remove, and asked for his help at Washington.

Help at Washington, indeed! The head of the Treasury had been at the general's side in those old days of '61 and '62, and, as soon as the mail could send it, the new appointment was made secure.

And from that time, for many years, there was no correspondence between General Glover and these friends.

Yes! years passed away; I do not know how many. General Glover, who is a man of a thousand duties, all of which he does well, went hither, went thither, and may not have thought of the letter or the answer once in a month. Needles never wrote to him. He never wrote to Needles. As I said, borrowing his phrase as we flew along in the express train, one such man, till the letter came, did not differ from another more than one post in a rail-fence from that which is next to it.

But the letter, and what came from it, made a difference. Yes, and the memory of that letter, and the picture of the stove, and the children and their mother sleeping late, and all the rest which I have told you, did sometimes come back to General Glover.

And so when, as I say, years had gone by, as he was one day making a visit in the great roaring city which I have called Abydos, he told the story, as he told it to me and as I have told it to you. He was making a call at the Hotel Esterhazy on Mrs. Fonblanque, whom perhaps you know, and he told this story.

"You say he lives in this city?" said she, very much interested in the story. "Do you never go to see them?"

"No," he said; "I have never been to see them."

"Might I see them? Where do they live? What is his name?" she asked, somewhat eagerly.

And the general confessed that since he began to tell the story he had been feeling for the name, but it had escaped him.

"If you had not asked me, however, I think I should have caught it. Queer that I cannot recall it."

"And you have not seen him?" said she.

"No. I should not know the man from Adam if he came in at that door." And at that instant, as if the man were coming, a knock was heard at the door. A servant entered with a card "For General Glover."

The general read it, and bade the man say he would see the gentleman in the reading-room. He turned to Mrs. Fonblanque: "What were you asking me?"

"I was asking the name of the man whose story you told me."

"Yes—you were. And I did not know it."

"You said," continued she, "that you should not know him if he came in at that door."

"I did so. And here is his name."

"Do not tell me that this is that man's card."

"It is his card, and I am going down to see him." So he left Mrs. Fonblanque to her reflections.

Sure enough, there was his friend. He was twenty years older than when, as a young man, he flung himself into his country's cause. There were the marks of his accident, and there were the marks of his twenty years' work. And both these men went back, in memory, to those eager days when the war began. But it was not of them that the younger had come to talk. He was in trouble again. "You will think I am always in trouble, and you will think I always fall back on you."

General Glover is not one of those people who turn over their own benefactions like savory bonbons; he does not often think of them indeed. He said, cheerily, that, quite on the other hand, it was long since he had heard from his friend.

"Nor would you hear from me now," said the other, "if I could help it. But I cannot help it. I come to you, of course. My life is all to change, and I do not know how. I come to you to ask. I should do wrong," he said, very seriously, "connected as you and I have been, if I did anything without your advice—nay, without your permission."

The general looked at him with surprise. But the man was not weak—he was not chattering compliment. He was speaking with the deepest seriousness. "My life, since I entered the Navy, has been all wrought in with your instructions. I should be wrong if I did not come for them now."

Then he unfolded his budget of miseries, and explained that he was worse off than he had been that day of the postman and the letter. Worse off, because a second fall is worse than the first.

This was the story:

At the time when he was transferred from the post-office to the Bureau of Red Tape, at the general's intercession, it had been necessary, under such civil-service rules as then existed, that he should file a proper certificate of character, and he had done so.

Now this certificate, alas! was headed by the most distinguished of General Glover's friends in that city, Governor Oglethorpe!

But in the course of five or six years there had grown up a great feud in the party, and Governor Oglethorpe headed one side and Mr. Clodius headed the other.

And a week before the time we have come to, Mr. Clodius had been appointed from Washington to be the head of our Bureau of Red Tape.

And every man in the office knew that all their certificates had been examined on Wednesday, and that all Governor Oglethorpe's men would be dismissed on Friday.

It was now Thursday evening.

"I only heard of this to-day," said the officer we are interested in. "I would not tell my wife. But she knew something was the matter. But when the evening paper came, I saw you were here at the Esterhazy; and then I knew it was all right."

"All right, dear friend!" said the general, in real distress. "It is all wrong. I do not know this Clodius —have hardly heard of him. I am out of politics these five years. None of them know me or care for me. I cannot help you."

"Oh yes, you can help me," said the man, simply and confidently. "And you will. That is why I came. I told my wife it was all right—and it is."

"My dear fellow, you understand nothing about it. Even the people at Washington do not care for me now. They have forgotten me. I would gladly help you; but I am as powerless as a child."

Still he was touched—how could he help being touched?—by the man's simple faith.

"Of course, I will write a letter for you. But it will do no good. Your Mr. Clodius cares nothing for me or mine. Stay here, however, and I will go and write it."

So he crossed the hotel floor to the private office, where, not the "gentlemanly clerk," but Mr. Mann, the wise director of the whole, was sitting.

"Mann," said the general, "do you know this Clodius?"

"I should think I did," said he. "He sat in that chair half an hour ago. William!" and he struck his bell. "See if Mr. Clodius is in 75."

"No, no; I do not want to see him. But who knows him well enough—well, to tell him a story?"

"I should think I did. I have got him this office in the Red Tape Bureau. He would not be there but for me."

"Is that possible?" said the general, a little awe-struck. "I want to tell him about one of the people in it."

"There are paper and ink. Write a note to me, and it shall go to him. Man to be kept in? He shall stay in. If there is anything Clodius wants, it is to oblige me. At least, those were the last words he said to me when he left this room."

The general wrote his note, in a few lines, as such men can. Mr. Mann endorsed it, "Please see to this." The waiter took it to 75.

There came back a card, with "All right—Mr. Clodius." And fifteen minutes after General Glover had left the reading-room he returned with this card to his friend.

"I told you so," said the man, eager, modest, and simple in his gratitude. "I told you that it would be wrong for me to do anything without consulting you."

And General Glover went back to Mrs. Fonblanque, and told her the end of the story.

I told a story somewhat like this to a very wise man last week, and he forced himself to say: "Yes, it shows how closely we are all jumbled together in this little

world." But he forced himself to say this, and at the
bottom of his heart he was wondering if it did not show
a great deal more. And General Glover thinks, and
Mrs. Fonblanque thinks, and Needles thinks, and his
wife thinks, and I think, that it shows a great deal
more.

We think that outside the people that write letters
and put them in the post-office there are unseen people
who tell them what to say. We think that behind you
and me, who come and go, there are sometimes unseen
hands which show us where to go and where to come.

And those of us who write stories sometimes put into
them such tales of crisis as that in which Jane Eyre
hears the cry of her lover, though he is two hundred
miles away. But we do not put in such things merely
to serve the purpose of the story. We put them in because, if we did not put them in, the story would not
be true to life.

A STORY OF TRUE LOVE

I

"I SHALL not go, old fellow ; that is the whole of it!"

"I shall be awfully lonely," said Fritz, in reply.

"Of course you will, and of course I shall. But some time or other we must be lonely. Each of us has been lonely before."

"But what will mother say?"

"That I have to find out this morning," said Romayne. "And I will put it through before I am an hour older. I tell you, old fellow, the way is to make up your mind, and then hold on. Wax in your ears, like that old fellow we had to do in the Greek; 'no such word as fail,' and all that. I thought this all out at church, when he was talking about something else. The minute I heard Lucia say that mother was going to turn that black gown again, I said, 'Why should she turn it?' I have seen it turned four times already. And then, of course, it came over me that the gown was to be turned so that she need not buy a new gown. And she did not want to buy a new gown because she wanted me to go to Princeton. Then I said: 'Princeton be hanged! I will go into business.'"

"And you never thought of me, Ro," said Fritz, a little sadly.

"Dear old fellow, yes, I thought of you. But the difference is, you like it and I hate it. You know the difference between an abscissa and a horseshoe when you see them; I have to look in a book to see which is which. You will have your part, which is harder than mine. You will have to live alone in those college barracks, and we shall only have good times together in vacation. I shall stay, and do something I like every blessed day of my life. Do not make it any harder for me. I am going to see mother now."

"In short, my dear mother, for this once I must have my way." And he kissed her tenderly, and stroked her smooth cheek with his hand.

His mother was crying; but when she paused before answering those words, he felt that she yielded the point. He knew how she hated to give it up; he hated to pain her; but he had determined the night before. He had gone on his knees in prayer that he might carry through his wish; and though he had often prayed before, he had never knelt to pray. The boy determined; he meant to succeed; and he succeeded.

Their father had died so long ago that there was little left to either boy of his presence but the memory of his form. Three little girls and two boys had cowered around Mrs. Montague on the day of the funeral. Of these, the younger did not remember their father at all, and Romayne and Fritz only remembered that he kissed them when they went to bed, and told them how he used to ride to mill with a bag of corn. Then had come happy years to them, and even to their mother—not so desolate and black as she had imagined they would be, in foresight. The girls grew up cheerful and light-hearted. The boys were ready, obedient, well-meaning, unselfish, and brave. They breakfasted on milk and oatmeal, where, had their father lived, they would have breakfasted on beefsteak with an omelet. But they were as sturdy and strong on the one diet as on the other. They enjoyed life; they made life cheerful in the household; and, had Mrs. Montague known it, the mere necessity that they should go on all her errands, should split the wood for the fires and kindle them in the morning, should black their own boots, and in general be their own servants, was giving them an education which they would certainly have lost, had not Mr. Montague been thrown from his horse, and had not the handsome salary stopped which he had received as treasurer of the Kosciusko Rolling-mill.

"Fritz shall study enough for him and me, dear mother; and I will work enough for me and him, and for you and Effie and Lucia and Poll."

"I do not know what you will do," said she, and she kissed him heartily. "But I do know you are a good boy, and for just this once, I suppose, you must have your way."

But she had a good crying fit after she left him. She did come down to tea, but she said little. She left them all at their evening occupations very early, and said she had something to do up-stairs. This was a thing which had never happened before; nor did it ever happen again. For years, with bated breath, it was spoken of as "the night mamma went up-stairs."

But indeed it marked an epoch. The next morning, when they met for breakfast, Romayne had gone down town. He had "gone into business," whatever that meant. He had made the fire; the teakettle boiled— if the proofreader will let us say so—but he was not there. They breakfasted without Romayne.

II

For after the boy had milked the cow himself, as he always did, and had made his breakfast of a quart, more or less, of milk and a dozen biscuit, more or less, he had left a line with his mother, to say that she might not see him till evening. Nor did she. Every evening, at a late supper, he turned up, always with some amusing tales of the day's experience in this difficult matter of "finding a place." His sisters and Fritz observed, among themselves, that these stories were rather vague, and did not hang very closely together. But Mrs. Montague was somewhat preoccupied. So, if the boy must "go into business," he must; what "business" was, she scarcely knew; but she did know that he might be trusted to do nothing dishonorable, and that when anything permanent came to his hand she would know as soon as any one. If he were not to answer the wish and prayer of her heart by going to college, it was of little account to her whether he went to work with Mr. Black or Mr. White, Mr. Green or Mr. Brown, or whether he sold stocks or sugar, coffee or coal. She knew that some of her nicest friends were "in business," and that some of the nicest of them had a good deal of money. If this should happen to Romayne, why, there would be some compensation for her distress that he would not go to the university.

Accordingly her distress was all the more agonizing, and the first blow the boy had given her was repeated in one twice as hard, when, at the end of the month, he told her that for all those thirty-one days, Sundays excepted, he had been at work with Mr. Galen, the plumber.

That his father's son should be a plumber! She thought her heart would break; she was sure it would.

But when people think their hearts will break they do not. The very fact that they can stop to think about it shows that the shock is not fatal. And Mrs. Montague did survive this disgrace, as she called it, to her family for many years. Oddly enough, as will happen to people of her build, she came to persuade herself that she had seen the advantages of the plumber's business, and had been the person to suggest it to Romayne. She sometimes even wondered if it would not have been better if Fritz had gone to the Galens' with his brother —Fritz, who, after some years, was a leading professor in the University of New Padua. The introductory section of this story was needed only that the reader might understand better the relations in which Romayne lived with the people of the little city which was their home, and so might follow intelligently the details of this little story.

The boy had that heavenly gift with tools with which some people are born, and some, alas! are not—like this author, and possibly this reader. It is a gift as distinct as that for music or for painting. From the first moment when he offered himself on trial to old Galen, old

Galen loved him, he held the pipe in such a loving way, and used the solder so that hardly a drop fell upon the tiles. Both the younger Galens took to him also. He was not afraid of work; he was not in the least above his business. If the work were dirty, why, it was dirty, that was all; there was water enough and soap enough when he chose to be clean. So was it that when he had passed that first month of experiment which old Galen had insisted on, he knew more of the business than nine boys out of ten would have known in three months, and old Galen then gladly made with him the permanent agreement the announcement of which had so distressed his mother.

Then in the evening he was forever reading—hydraulics, hydrostatics, any book on physics in the public library, he devoured them all. If he understood them, well. If he did not understand them, he knew that he did not, and highly resolved that some day he should. By the time his two years with the Galens were up he knew as much of their business as they did, and of its principles and theory he knew a great deal more; and he had money enough of his own in the savings-bank to be able to go to New Haven, and for six months to take such a course as he had blocked out for himself in the Sheffield School.

Meanwhile, every housekeeper understands how it was that Mrs. Montague became reconciled to his career. Actually in the house with her was some one who understood the unintelligible—nay, who could do the impossible. This mysterious cobweb of pipes beneath her feet, which modern civilization hides so carefully, because it is all-important that it should be visible—her own son knew about it all. As some sainted "beloved hearer," sitting Sunday after Sunday in her pew, admires the esoteric wisdom of the dear "rector," who understands all about foreknowledge, and evolution, and Gnosticism, and sanctification, and Tract No. 90, and the fall of man, and the Isidorian Decretals, of which she knows nothing — nay, is in that second or third power of ignorance that she knows that she knows nothing — so Mrs. Montague admired as she loved this more than prophet, who knew where the traps were, and why they were there; who never mistook an outlet pipe for an inlet pipe, and to whom a self-acting valve was as little mysterious as a waffle-iron was to her. More than this, the prophet could do the thing he said should be done. More than this, he was her own dear, handsome boy, who was so sweet and cunning when he was a baby. Most of all — for there was a climax—he sent in no bill at the end of the quarter. All housekeepers will now understand why Fritz's college charges were paid so easily; all sanitarians will understand why the doctor's visits became so few. And when Romayne returned from New Haven, when he went into partnership with young Mol. Galen, and they took the old stand, with the new title of "Sanitary Engineer," one understood how Mrs. Montague delighted in the new rugs Romayne gave her for a birthday present, and how she enjoyed the bays and the landau in which he insisted she should ride on Saturday and go to church on Sunday.

Romayne had been a favorite in the town since those days when he was such a cunning baby. As why should

he not be, indeed? People do not give their plumbing
orders to a young man because he was a pretty baby;
but when they have always known him and always
liked him, and now he understands his business, they
are glad they can give him their plumbing orders. The
town was growing like fury in wealth and population
—growing faster than any town in the State—as every
American town always is that one ever hears of. Business came to the sanitary engineers on the right hand
and on the left. The State insane asylum was established in Verona, and Montague & Galen's bid was a
mile below anybody else's bid. And when the work
was done, Dr. Berzelius spoke of it in the Convention
of Alienists at Saratoga as a miracle of intelligent engineering. Simplicity and strength are as possible in
plumbing as in a pyramid; and Romayne said in all
quarters that they proposed to finish every job so that
they might never see it again. He had an excellent
staff under him. His own success attracted young fellows like him from the high-school, who saw now that
the profession on which depends the purity of every cup
of cold water which one Christian gives another is a profession quite as well worth following as any. So the
firm of Montague & Galen was a prosperous firm, extend-
ing its business not only over all that State, but over all
the region around it.

III

And while every one with whom we have to do
was virtuous, they still had cakes, and what they liked
better than ale; that is to say, the plumbers and the

plumbers' boys did their work well for eight hours a day; they slept nine hours every night, and this left seven hours to each for his meals, for his dressing and undressing, and for any avocations which he might pursue outside his vocation. Saturday afternoon nobody plumbed at all—no, nor soldered. So there was plenty of opportunity for " a little conversation." " What is it all for," says Mr. Emerson, "but a little conversation?" And on very much the same lines of time, Romayne's sisters studied their French verbs, practised their music, kneaded the bread on Wednesday, and attended to their other duties, while they also found several hours a day for " a little conversation." And the young people of New Padua also had discovered many agreeable methods for using the conversation hours. Indeed, it was as pleasant a place as I have ever known. There were horseback parties and picnic parties, pondlily parties and bathing parties; there was a Chautauqua Circle and an Exclamation Society and a Frank Stockton Club. They had everything except hornets' nests to make them comfortable, and they enjoyed life, or, as the vernacular says, they " had a good time," as young people know how. Years went on, and the business of the firm extended with every year — you might almost say that it extended itself. That early phrase of Romayne's, " We never want to see a job a second time," went far and wide, and eventually the firm took it as a sort of trade-mark. It made the heading of their note-paper, so that they had not to seek for business in general. It was only on a great occasion, like that of the completion of the hospital, that they appeared as competitors for a contract. Indeed, after their reputation was established, builders and contractors came to seek them.

Nobody enjoyed this popularity more than Mrs. Montague. Indeed, as has been said, she came to think that it was largely of her own making. She early persuaded herself that it was she who had sent Romayne to Mr. Galen, and had conceived the idea of training him as a sanitary engineer. And now, as her household cares diminished under Romayne's almost lavish provision for her comfort, she felt it her duty to give her leisure time to enlarging the business of the firm. Romayne would have gone wild had he known that such touting and solicitation were going on in his interest as his mother carried forward all the time. But, in truth, it came to be considered a sort of joke among the people of the county. Mr. Whitbread could not stake out the corners of a new wing to the bakery but Mrs. Montague's bays would be seen at Mrs. Whitbread's door. Mrs. Montague would make a state call on that lady, and before she had gone would say she hoped Mr. Whitbread would not forget old friends in contracting for the water-works. All this eagerness of hers was bred by a passionate love of Romayne; from her conscientious determination, formed on that first night when he " went into business" and she went up-stairs, that, in every way in which a mother could, she would go into business too, and would loyally support him.

To her point of view all public institutions were accounted as the best conceivable, or of the lowest degradation, according as they did or did not use the traps and faucets in which our firm was interested. She made herself a life member of the Indian Association because when she called at the office in Philadelphia she saw that Mr. Welsh had the right faucets and water bowls; and she threw her whole influence against the State administration because in the Capitol at Harrisburg she saw that theirs were all wrong.

Romayne had to caution her once and again, as far as a son can caution a mother whom he loves. For the rest, when some ill-natured person brought him a bit of gossip about one or another success of hers as a drummer, he had to make as light of it as he could, to persuade himself that the story was an exaggeration, and to trust that such things did not happen often.

IV

It was necessary to explain Mrs. Montague's methods and her enthusiasm in the cause of sanitary reform, that the reader may understand a breach which she brought about, wholly unintentionally, in the social life of our little community. We have always been on good terms with the people in what we call the other village, although, in a way, we pity them. Their population is not so large as ours by five or six hundred; indeed, had our census been as well taken as theirs there would have been more difference. But they are always fussy about such things, and took more pains with theirs than we did with ours. They have their own post-office, which is foolish in them, and they are apt to drive to the O. and C. depot instead of coming over to our station, which is all a piece of their independent

nonsense. for which we do not care a straw.   But they
are good people all the same, though none of them
come to our churches; and when they have to come to
our stores, as they do, we are always glad to see them.
Some of our ladies exchange calls with some of their
ladies.   Well, there was a Mrs. Hood over there, a lady
indeed, and she had established a seminary for girls.
It was a good plan, we all thought, for she had been
left at her husband's death with several young daughters of her own, and we thought they could help in
the school, and would count more in the catalogue.
Mrs. Hood made a very good school of it; she advertised it in our county paper, which was a good move
of hers, and it became very popular.   The other village
—they call it New Padua, though it should really be
only another ward of our city—is but a mile and a half
from us.   So that from the Montague house, which
stands quite high, you could see perfectly easily when
Mrs. Hood built a brick L to her husband's old house,
and, indeed, the *Argus* announced that this new building was necessary as a dormitory for the seminary.
Then was it that Mrs. Montague reflected, for the first
time, that Mrs. Hood was a stranger in the neighborhood, that she was a Presbyterian like herself, and that
everything made it proper that she should go and call
on her, and pay her the civilities which one of the old
families ought to be ready to offer.   Mrs. Hood's children, it is true, had all been born in New Padua, and
it had never occurred to Mrs. Montague before that
she owed these courtesies.   But she had not had this
carriage long, and she had more time now than she
once had.

So she made her visit, and was very pleasantly received. Mrs. Hood is a charming person, and she sent for that pretty girl Rosaline French, one of the scholars, when she proved to be a second-cousin of the Montagues. There was some sponge-cake, and some phosa, which was then a new brew, to which Mrs. Montague was not accustomed. So the visit went off very nicely, and Mrs. Hood had said she should be glad to be the collecting agent for the Indian Association in New Padua, and Mrs. Montague rose to go. It was then that Mrs. Hood said that Michael had better drive out by the back way, because the front avenue was so lumbered up with timber for the new wing; and then that Mrs. Montague, availing herself of the chance, said, so graciously:

"When you come to the finishing, and put in your bath-tubs and your pipes, you must come and make my boy a visit. Here is his card. Perhaps you do not know that Montague & Galen are all my boys. I call the Galens so, for they are very nice fellows. And really, Mrs. Hood, when health is at stake one cannot be too careful."

To which last remark Mrs. Hood assented very cordially, and indeed a little at length, as a school-mistress should.

"And then," said Mrs. Montague, when she described the interview to Fritz, "she had the impudence to say that she should take great care of the plumbing; that she had consulted Professor Thingamy about it, and had made her contract already. Impudent minx! I could have struck her."

It was this interview, more important in village pol-

itics than can be imagined, which made a certain divi-
sion in the social relations which I have described as
so harmonious before. Fritz thought best not to tell
his brother of it at the time, but Romayne found it
out soon enough, for all that. As it happened, indeed, I think Romayne knew quite as much about
the Hood affair as Mrs. Montague did. For though
he had never seen Mrs. Hood, he had seen her oldest
daughter, and had liked her very much. There was
a party at the Hoods', and in a frolic somebody had
proposed blindman's - buff, and Romayne had been
blinded and had caught Miss Hood. For him that
was the beginning. He guessed her—well, I do not
know how, for he had really never seen her to know
her before. Afterwards there happened one of those
queer accidents which bring people together. He
bought the resin for the firm, and such paints and
whiting and chemicals as they used a good deal of, at
an old-established drug-store. It had grown up to be
a large wholesale business from being the little variety
store of the village. A queer place it was. It had the
little six-by-eight panes to the windows which it had in
Mad Anthony's time, when Utrecht was laid out—long
before the name was changed. When you went in, it
was a perfect curiosity shop. There was a tortoise-
shell which Hugh had brought up from the pond when
he was a boy ; there was an alligator which he had shot
in the St. John's River years afterwards ; and scattered
along on the shelves the dusty relics of two generations
of village shopkeeping—boxes, flower-pots, jugs—all
without a label or a mark, but remembered, I suppose,
somewhere in old Roger's brain. A shop without a

sign, which never advertised, and yet which did half
the business of the manufacturers of the county in
chemicals and other drugs.

At the door of this museum Romayne drew up one
day, held the reins in his hand as he pushed the door
open, and cried, "Mr. Roger, you may as well wire for
half a ton of copperas; we haven't as much as I thought."
And he had just taken his seat again in his wagon,
when a lady called to him from the steps, and to his
surprise he saw his pretty friend Miss Hood.

"I beg your pardon," said she, "but Mr. Roger isn't
in. I was waiting for him. But I will leave your
order with him if you like. He cannot be gone far,
for I found the door unlocked, as you did."

No, Romayne would not think of troubling her with
the order. Indeed, he remembered that he must see Mr.
Roger about some resin. He left the horses, and for
twenty minutes had a nice talk with her in the snuffy
old shop. It was astonishing how well they knew
each other when Roger came in from the post-office,
where fortunately the mail had been late. And this
was only their second time of meeting!

The second time, but not the last. Fortune favors
the brave and the young. Romayne was hand in glove
with our new Presbyterian minister. He was a very
good fellow, who had come to us about the time when
the new firm was established. He liked Romayne, and
Romayne had frozen to him at once. He was in and
out at Lawrence's every other day, to talk about the
Christian Endeavor Society and the Sunday-school and
the Board of Charities, and he was very fond of Mrs.
Lawrence, who often made him stay to lunch. At

lunch one day whom should he meet but Miss Hood.
It proved that Mrs. Lawrence had been a scholar at the
seminary, and knew her. Afterwards he met her there
again, and one day he walked home with her. I do
not say that Lawrence tried to make a match between
them, or that his wife did. Let us hope they had other
business in hand, and left such matters to take care
of themselves, which is generally safe. But I do
know that, without any arrangement on anybody's
part, Romayne was a little apt to find out the days
when Miss Hood made Mrs. Lawrence a visit. And if
he had then known that his mother had been over to
see her mother, and to ask for a job for him, his wrath
would have been awful.

He was destined to find it out, however, by slow degrees. When his mother gave a great party to the Sul-
lys, who came up to Verona when their son was married,
she invited half the county and nine-tenths of the New
Padua people, but sent no cards to the Hoods. It was a
regular out-of-door fête, where there was, as Red Jacket
would say, all the room there was; and really, to ask
the Higginses and not ask the Hoods was a very marked
thing. But Mrs. Hood was even with her, and when,
in June, Dr. Witherspoon came to make the annual address at the exhibition, and the seminary sent out an
elegant invitation card engraved in Philadelphia, there
was one of these cards exhibited in every parlor in
Verona except at Mrs. Montague's. And yet, I suppose that there was not a man in the place who
wanted so much to be invited in a regular way to the
exhibition as poor Romayne Montague. But young
people cannot always have what they want, and so he

had to sit in the gallery as the exhibition went on, just
as all the uninvited towns-people did. And he could
not show his face at the reception, as every other young
man did, whether he hailed from Verona or New
Padua.

V

But Romayne was not the man to be turned from a
plan by one bit of pasteboard more or less—no, not
though the pasteboard bore upon it an engraving from
Philadelphia. He had found out that he liked Miss
Hood better than he liked any other girl that he ever
saw; and he did not care if her mother was such a
fool as to leave plumbers out from her parties. As to
his mother, he had asked no questions when she had
omitted the Hoods and the seminary girls from her
list. He had thought it a pity that twenty or more
of the young people whom every fellow wanted to see
should not be at his mother's party. But he had long
since learned that her ways were past his finding out.
He would have been glad if he could have had a card
to Mrs. Hood's. But if he could not—why, he could
not. And he would find out whether her daughter had
any objection. He followed up such chances as Mrs.
Lawrence's cordiality gave him. He knew he could
make other chances. And it was not long, indeed, before he had an opportunity.

Oddly enough, it was all about copperas again. The
half-ton had all gone in some purification that was
needed at the town-house, and, with a pleasant memory of the day he ordered it, Romayne drove round

13

again to Roger's. The old fellow came out on the
steps as the bays stopped in their quick career. He
was still holding in his hand a great bunch of lavender
he had brought in from the garden. Under his heavy,
beetling brow there was a good-natured smile, for
Romayne was one of his favorites; and would have
been one had he not been so good a customer. He
told him to come in, that he had a new line of goods to
show him, and Romayne readily assented. To his surprise, he found Miss Hood there again, and, for the first
time, he united her and Roger in his thought, supposing
now that there was some relationship of which he had
never heard. The old fellow must be her granduncle.

What was the new "line of goods" I never heard.
I know that Romayne never knew. What with the
lavender, and some thyme and sweet-marjoram which
old Roger went and brought, and a botanical discussion
about the *Didynamia* and *Labiatæ*, and the microscope
which was produced, and the length of some doubtful
stamens, half an hour went by, and the new line of
goods was never produced. Then Miss Hood rose and
said she must go. To Roger she said, "To-morrow
morning, if you please, Mr. Roger." And Montague
was watchful enough to observe that she did not say
"Uncle George" or "Cousin George." Then, as she
went to the door, and he with her, it was impossible
that they should not see the high black cloud in the
west. It was impossible that he should not protest
against her walking home. He did protest; he begged
her to let him take her home under the protection of
his buggy, and she very prettily and very pleasantly
acceded.

I do not know whether she had any idea of what was going to happen. I do know he did. He did not care a cent for the shower after she was fairly in the carriage with a rug and the boot over her knees. And he drove very slowly.

Then he said, squarely: "I was mortified and sorry that my mother and I were not asked to your mother's party, Miss Hood. Plumbers have dirty hands while they are at work, but they are very necessary people in modern civilization."

The girl was astonished, as well she might be; but she was quick and well-bred, and she rallied in time to say that he must not hold her responsible for her mother's visiting-list. He observed with interest and with a certain pleasure that she made no pretence of mistake or omission.

"I do not care much for your mother's visiting-list," said he, in reply. And then he added: "I leave my mother's severely alone. But I care a great deal about yours, Miss Hood. You are good enough to let me take you home now. I wish I might have the honor and pleasure of calling to-morrow, as the old-fashioned people did, to be sure that you have taken no cold."

She was again surprised. But, as before, she was self-possessed when she answered, and her answer was a difficult one. For she knew that, after what had passed between their mothers, Mrs. Hood would not let him come into the house. She did what was wise, therefore. She answered one part of the question, and let the other go.

"Indeed, Mr. Montague, I rate your profession very highly. I have cause to—have I not?—from the mo-

ment I take my bath in the morning till I turn off the
cold water when the girls go to bed. You do not know
that I have the gymnastics in charge. And with sixty
girls there is a deal of hot and cold water. It was
Eve's cosmetic, you know."

But he would not laugh; he would have an answer
to his question, and he said so. And she, poor child,
had to face the music, as our national proverb says.

"Mr. Montague, my mother and your mother do not
understand each other, so that I cannot ask you to the
house. It is not my house. But—" And she paused,
for she ought not to have said "but."

He waited thirty seconds, and the bays walked slowly.

"But?" said he then, with a tone of inquiry.

And now there was a pause of a minute.

"But?" he said again, as before.

"You ought not to make me say, Mr. Montague,"
said she. "But we are not fools, either of us. I have
a great respect for plumbers; I have said that. I will
add that I am always glad to see the head of the profession in this county, though I must not invite him to
my mother's house. I am glad to see him at the Chautauqua, at Mr. Roger's, at Mrs. Lawrence's. I am glad
to accept his invitation to ride in his buggy when it
rains, although I observe that he does not ask me to
his mother's house."

This was bravely said and well said. And from that
moment all things went well with Romayne and Miss
Hood. She had not permitted any nonsense of the
novels to stand between her and one of the most intelligent young men of the region. She had not been un-

womanly; she had not made any advances. But, as
she said herself when the conversation began, she had
not acted like a fool, or as the average novel of the
first half of the century would have required her to
act.

It may be observed here that one difficulty which the
American novelist has in creating a plot for his country
which would pass muster in Europe is, that the greater
part of his country men and women do not act like
sheer fools in delicate or difficult circumstances. Now
half the received plots require action of this sort, or
there is no story. This observation, thrown out by a
friend of the court, is commended to the critics.

So, as I said, the affairs of these two people sped well,
notwithstanding the objections of the two mothers. If
they did not meet at his home or at hers, there were a
plenty of places where they did meet. They met at the
Chautauqua Circle and at the Exclamation Club. When
the young people made a horseback party, and the
Hood girls joined, it seemed natural that Romayne, on
the Iowa gray, should take care of Miss Hood on that
pretty pacer she had bought from Miss Vernon. When
Romayne spoke at the town meeting which Mr. Garfield had set agoing, the Hood girls were there; and
when Mol. Galen walked home with Bianca and Tom
with Portia, who were both grown-up young ladies now,
it was quite of course that Romayne should walk home
with their sister. In such rides and walks and talks
they found out everything about each other. She
found that he was generous, impetuous, and true. He
found that she was true, impetuous, and generous.
They had common tastes, which came out in their bot-

anizing, in her water-colors and his scientific draughts-
manship, in his study of physics and hers of the higher
mathematics, where she had the school professors to
help her.   They read the same books; she knew the last
half of stanzas of which he could quote only the first.
They had the same memories of Rollo, and had wondered together about the lady and the tiger.   Severest
test of all, and most charming, she was perfect in her
Miss Austen, and in any competitive examination would
have done as well as Romayne if questioned about Mr.
Knightley, John Knightley, Isabella, and Mr. Elton.
With these like regards for little things, who shall wonder if they agreed on the greatest thing of all?   One
happy day, as they returned together from an excur-
sion of the Mountain Club, in which, indeed, they had
early been lost, so that they heard little of the stratifi-
cation, and nothing of the erosion—when, as they returned, he asked her the central question, whether she
would receive him in her house if she had one, or would
come and live in his if he had one, then, without a
" but," she said she would, as frankly as he had asked
her.   And it was not long before she said to him that
from that first day at Roger's she had seen how different he was from other men.   "From the blindfold
day?   Did it begin with the blindfold day?"   It did
with him; he was sure of that.   She would not say it
did with her, but there was a charming blush when
she said nothing.   And what "it" was was clear to
both of them.

VI

If Romayne had a hard task when, at sixteen, he told his mother that for one month her son had been a plumber, he had a harder task when, as a young man of position in the town and respected of all men, he had to tell her that he was engaged to be married to the daughter of Mrs. Hood, of the " Female Seminary." She did not stop to ask whether a seminary could be male, or how it could be female; she did not devote herself to any such side issue. She cried, with scorn, " One of those Hood girls!" and then declared that she would hear no explanation. There was no excuse and could be none. For her, she should leave the county, or would do so if she could sell the house. No, she did not know the girls apart; she did not know how many of them there were; and none of them should come into her house. If, on these terms, Romayne chose to marry her, he might marry, that was all.

Whether Mrs. Hood expressed herself with a like severity did not appear. So far as the social politics or interests of our village went, it was of the less importance. We had a strong party, led by the Lawrences and by old Mr. Roger, who thought well of the Hoods, and who repeated Mrs. Montague's ejaculations only with amusement, not to say ridicule. For Romayne himself, he did not seem to suffer so much under his mother's displeasure as she might have wished. Perhaps he remembered that other outburst of displeasure, when he had taken Saturn for the star of his fortune, and had gone into the mysteries of lead and solder.

He told his lady-love of his mother's wrath, in terms
as much modified as the truth would permit, as they
took a charming drive one day up that pretty pass of
Winnococksen River, where he knew they would meet
nobody.   She was tender and sympathetic and wise.
So sympathetic was she, and so sorry that she should
come in between him and his mother, that he pressed
her a little to know precisely what did pass on that
fatal first interview, when the peace of two houses was
interrupted and the course of true love ruffled.   He
had never heard the story from his mother—indeed,
he had never heard it at all, though he had often
heard of it.   To his surprise the dear girl seemed confused by his request, and answered it but lamely.
Why, indeed, should they not have had their plumbing
done by our home talent?   Why should they send to
Philadelphia, or Lancaster, or wherever they did send
to?   He did not know who his rival was, and he did
not care—or he said to himself that he did not care.
All the same, he was surprised, not to say annoyed,
that Juliet, who was so frank about everything else,
should not answer a plain question.   And he said so
to her, bluntly.

Juliet was more confused than before.   For a minute
she said nothing.   But after a minute she rallied.   She
turned in the carriage, so that she could look him in
the face, and said: "Romayne, you do not want me
to give my mother away, as you boys say in your
horrid slang.   Really, I do not know just what either
of our mothers said to the other.   It is better that I
should not know, and I think better that you should
not know.   And I am sure you and I have much more

important things to talk of." And she looked so pretty that he could not help kissing her. How could he be expected to? And why should the bays be in such a hurry? They would not often be in a shady pass as lovely as this. The bays were made to walk more demurely; Juliet and Romayne made their peace under the shade of the maples and in the echoing of the babble of the brook.

But when Romayne gathered up the reins again, and let the eager bays resume their trot, he said, with a good-natured laugh, "All the same, there is a mystery, I see, and I suppose I shall never know what it is."

"Mystery there is," said Juliet, "if you choose to call it so. But if you command it, rash boy—as the people in the *Arabian Nights* do always, though for their own ruin—if you demand it, I will reveal it to you that night when your dear Father Lawrence makes us one."

"If that night ever comes," said Romayne, impatiently. "I never knew days pass by so slowly."

"Do not say that of to-day, dear boy. I am sure the sun is setting only too soon."

VII

Of course Mrs. Hood had to let Romayne come into her house now. There was a certain stiffness about her welcome at first, but Bianca and Portia and the other sisters were always cordial, and Romayne would not be made a stranger. The whole establishment

might be called well-nigh perfect of its kind. Romayne
did not wonder, after he had seen the arrangements,
that the school was so popular. The school-girls
seemed to come and go as if they were at home, and
surely no one of them could ever have had a home
more comfortable, not to say more luxurious. Everything was on that scale of generous living which the
true American likes, not to say is used to; and everything had a certain elegance which the true American
does not always know how to maintain. It was not
that the things were expensive, though some of them
were. It was not that they were pretty, though most
of them were. The charm of the place was that who-
ever was the lady director—and director it was clear
there was—had put in just what she chose, just what
she liked. She had not thought of money one way or
the other.

"Wealth, as mere wealth, is of course simply vulgar,"
said Mrs. Hood one day, putting in eight words what
Romayne felt was the spirit or essence of her vigorous
use of money. But, all the same, it was clear that
there was in this establishment money enough to use,
and this was another mystery to him. People who
had a million in the new four-per-cents were not apt
to keep boarding-schools. And people who lived by
keeping boarding-schools were not apt, so far as he
knew, to have a dozen good horses in the stables, to
have Corots and D'Aubignés on the walls, to have
orchids and allemandias from their own greenhouses
and early strawberries from their own hot-beds. But
as to the origin of all these things, Romayne asked
no questions, not even of Juliet. He was going to

take her, priceless as she was, for her own dear sake. He asked no questions about dowries or settlements, and nobody asked him any. He gave little thought to these mysteries. His only eagerness was to have a day appointed for the wedding, and then to drag along the hours by what strength he could till that day should come. He had bought his own house on the Willow Road, just as you drive out from the town to the Bromwich turnpike. Mrs. Hood and Juliet were making visits to Philadelphia to select the furniture. When he could go with them, all went well. When they would not let him go, or when he had to go off to see the work at McGraw College or at Titusville, all was horribly gray and cold. Still the world turned on its axis and revolved around the sun at the rate, for the first movement, of about fourteen miles a minute in that latitude, and for the other movement at the rate of more than a thousand standard miles a minute. So that Master Romayne was scarcely within the truth when he said that time went slowly. It did not go as fast as he wished. But it did move with the same rapidity which is observed by mercantile men when they have large notes falling due.

Meanwhile he was attentive to all the ladies at the seminary. He made friends with Mrs. Hood and all Juliet's nice sisters. He tried to devise little attentions which he could pay to each of them. In a hundred ways he made the sisters understand that it is a good thing to have a new brother. It is said that women despise the girl whom their brother marries, because they never wanted to marry him themselves. This is not always true. And far less is it true, as

Miss Brooks could tell us, that sisters despise the man who is going to marry their sister.

"What is that everlasting book?" said Portia one day to Bianca.

"The book, fortunately, is not everlasting; it is *Geology in Thirteen Lessons*. My class is at the seventh, and I am at the tenth. I have to be well up, for that Beryl Hitchcock is as quick as a flash, and knows much more than the book does."

"It is just so with Rose and Lily in the botany," said poor Portia. "But I switch them off on analyzing, and they go to work on that, and forget that I have not asked any questions. Now, when you study mineralogy and geology and such you cannot switch them off on analyzing. It would not do to put a pound of dynamite under the school-house to see if the foundations are on a rock. Poor, dear Juliet, who will do the hydrostatics when she is away? She is in the experiment-room now."

"Portia, you do not want to talk about experiments," said Bianca, resolutely, for she knew very well that Portia had something on her mind. For herself, therefore, she must postpone the study of the ice sheet till she was alone. "Do you remember what the child said in *Venetia:* 'I do not want to talk of butterflies, nurse. I want to talk of widows.'

"But, Portia," continued Bianca, knowing her sister was the least bit slow, "I am sure you do not want to talk about widows. You want to talk about brides or bridegrooms, or one bride or one bridegroom."

"I don't," said Portia. "I want to talk about wedding presents. It is so hard to get anything for a man.

You know I had made up my mind—" And then followed all the pros and cons about a landscape by Richards, which she had seen; about a complete outfit for a travelling artist, all because poor Romayne had brought to Portia a little water-color sketch of his own; and then about a fac-simile of the folio Shakespeare. As Bianca knew, Portia had fully resolved, as much as four times, to buy each of these, for this part of this discussion was not new.

Bianca gently intimated that the things cost no more and no less than they did when Portia made her last decision, and that probably Romayne's tastes and wishes had not changed.

"He has not changed, but I have changed." Bianca looked up, amazed at Portia's tragic air. "You know, mamma said we must economize. Mamma said I could not take Juliet's place, and you could not. She did not know who could. And she said something about reefing sails which I did not understand. Only this I do understand, and that made me wonder why you bought the caramels yesterday—that we may be poor, very, very poor. Mamma said this about the sails Sunday, and I have walked to the village every day since, to train myself to do so when we give up the coupé."

Bianca tried to be sympathetic, but she could only scream. "You poor, darling, good girl!" said she; "is this your mystery? Dear mamma must be more careful in her oracles. Why, my child, the school will be fifty times as prosperous when we have a man on the home staff. I should not wonder if it ceased to be a seminary and became an institute."

VIII

Terror in Portia's heart, rage in Mrs. Montague's heart, in Romayne's heart wonder whether the week would never end—these are the emotions to be depicted by those who act in our little tragedy. For Bianca's heart, I think a willingness to let things take their course; and for Juliet's, who shall tell "a maiden's meditations, fancy bound"? And the world spun round, though Romayne thought it did not; the moon rushed round a quarter of her revolution; the week came to an end; even the day came to an end.

They had no minister at New Padua, or rather he had a sore throat, and was studying evolution at Halle. So our Father Lawrence went over there to marry them. All the people went over. Strangest of all, Mrs. Montague went over.

"Not that I go willingly," she said to Effie at the last moment, as the girl arranged some magnificent diamonds which Romayne had given his mother; "I do not go willingly, and no one thinks I go willingly. But who knows? They may be married by the bishop. They were never very sound. Then there must be some one to give my son away."

For Mrs. Montague leans to the third primitive secession, and is doubtful about other rituals than her own. So she went to her martyrdom. She herself saw to the toilets of her daughters, in a fashion, so that those wretched girls at the Hoods' should not in any sort eclipse them. How many there were she did not know, she said; she believed they made up most of the scholars. Her own "exhibit," as the managers of fairs say, was perfect. Her coachman Michael was in a new livery with an immense favor. Otto was on the box with Michael, with a bigger favor. Only Fritz was in Mrs. Montague's carriage; and the girls, with Romayne, were in their own carriage behind, with Anders as grand as Michael, and François with him on the box, each with gorgeous favors. Even the horses had favors covering the blinders, which the grooms had compelled the chambermaids to make for them. Then, in that great drag which the Montagues send to the station for their guests, followed every man and woman of the staff of the house. Actually old Katy, the housekeeper, who had carried Romayne to the font when he was baptized, locked the side door and put the key in her pocket. For there was not one person in that house who would stay away from Romayne's wedding. Had Mrs. Montague stayed, I do not know who would have got her supper.

"I should have been frightened out of my skin," said she.

And at the seminary everything was elegant and just right. It was "ever so pretty." Since Mrs. Hood bought the Flinders lot, and made her own avenue through the maples, the approach to the house has been "about as fine as they make." To-night this was blazing with electric light, and the designs for the illumination, without being showy, were all convenient, pretty, and, to us country people, wholly new. The greenhouse must have been emptied, I should have said, such was the show of plants at the entrance. But afterwards, when I took Bianca in there to get a part

of this story from her and to have "a little conversation," I did not see but it was as brilliant as ever.
Anyway, we entered through a tropical garden. I saw
that dried-up Mr. Roger from the apothecary store,
and Hugh Roger by him. Juliet had not forgotten
her old friends.

We were shown to various disrobing-rooms by pretty maids, who had little favors of orange blossoms.
Strauss's orchestra from New York was playing music
so ravishing that I would have pardoned Father Lawrence if the service all went out of his head as he
listened. Romayne came up with me and some of the
other fellows. He made his sister carry in for Juliet
the great blue box which held her bouquet.

A minute more and Effie came out again, blushing
her prettiest, and said, "Juliet wants to see you, Ro."

And Ro went into that mysterious bride-chamber,
which he had never seen before. And there stood his
own dear girl, wonderful and gracious. Her veil lay
across a great table waiting for the bridemaid to put
it on her at the last moment. The damask in which
Madam Mifflin, her great-grandmother, had been married had been dug out of a Ginevra chest. Madam
Mifflin's skeleton was not found with it, for she lived
to dance at Madison's second inauguration. This bro-
cade was to be worn to-night. And Romayne said,
" Oh, my darling, I am afraid to kiss you. "

"Never fear that," said she. "We will do it again
when I am ninety to remember to-night by."

"It seemed to me," said he, "that the day would
never be done."

"But it is, you see. When will you learn to be reasonable? Romayne, when you say such things I am afraid for you."

"Afraid for me, Juliet?"

"I am afraid that you will forget that the pressure increases with the squares, and even with the cubes, and if your lower ranges are to stand it long, you must put in heavier tubing."

"Oh, now you can laugh; you may say anything," said the happy fellow, only wondering that she chose to chaff him just now.

"You goose!" said she; "do you not know why I have called you?"

"I hoped you called me to marry me," said he, ruefully.

"I called you to explain to you the mystery."

"My darling, you are so beautiful, I forgot there was a mystery."

"That is enough," said Juliet. "I thought you were perfect; now I know you are. All the more shall you know." Then, with a tragic pause: "Do you see this key? Do you see yon door? Open it." And she stood silent, not quite daring to look up.

Romayne opened the door. Within was a perfect plumber's equipment—pincers, clippers, big solderers, little solderers, bismuth strip, super-strip, sub-strip, saws, augers, test bottles, cinnamon and rose-water, piping of every size—all were there.

"Romayne, your own Juliet does the plumbing for the seminary. This is my mystery—and my mother's."

[THE artist Turner is said to have slipped away from London once in the month of May, to have gone down to Hull in a pea-jacket, and persuaded a whaler to take him as a passenger. So he had a chance to study arctic fogs and icebergs, and the various forms of tempest, to his heart's content. And there are critics who think they can trace in his work afterwards the result of this weird experience.

We were talking of this vacation of Turner's one Christmas evening, which we spent together—the Inghams, the Carters, and the Hackmatacks—at Haliburton's house. A funny smile came over Ingham's face, which George Hackmatack understood, and he said at once, "What do you know of Baffin's Bay, Ingham?" for George knew that Ingham's smile meant that he had gone beyond Turner.

Now Ingham is a silent man, especially in the matter of his own achievements. He is much more apt to squeeze the sponges of the people around him, and to make out their biographies, than to give anybody much hint of his own. But the children began an attack when they found there was a chance of a story, and we gave him no mercy till he began.

When he had finished, I did not wonder that he had never told it before.]

I

COLONEL INGHAM'S NARRATIVE

It was all a philosophical experiment. I had given a great deal of thought and study to the problems of Sleep. I once lectured on Sleep all through the Western cities, with illustrations by the audience. That was,

however, my last winter on the "Lyceum Platform."
The committees thought I ought to furnish my own
illustrations. Since then I have only been asked to
lecture in the charitable courses, where they do not pay.

It is queer, when you think of it, that the problem
has not been worked out before. Here is this untiring
soul, clothed upon with a body which grows tired. The
body needs rest, and finds it in sleep. Where is the
man meanwhile? This infinite soul, who half an hour
ago was listening to Isaiah, or walking with Orion across
the heavens, where has he gone while the body is covered up in bedclothes? You do not think the soul has
pulled the blanket round his neck, do you?

I had brooded over this a good deal, when one night,
as my terrestrial globe stood in a strong light from a
kerosene lamp, which made a very decent sun for it, I
was showing Blanche Stockhardt, who is one of my
pets, how nearly opposite to Jerusalem is Pitcairn's
Island, the modern paradise, and then I turned it to
make noon over this Boston of ours, and to show the
child how it was midnight in China.

Of course at that moment the mystery of Sleep was
explained to me, and it has been no mystery since.

You see, do you not? The soul has no care about
distance. Of course the moment when this body does
not need him, though for only an hour of night, the
soul has only to pass across there where it is day, and
start up another machine, which is just ready to be
awakened.

In that moment I saw that there are two of me—one
here in Boston, and the other there in the Chinese
Empire. I did not then know the name of the place,

but as soon as I got Franquelin & Huc's map I found it. Here it is (said Ingham, crossing the room): it is in this little oasis in the great desert of Cobi. It is a place called Pe-ling, but it is not to be confounded with the Pe-ling Mountains. They are quite different, as the Chinese post-office once explained to me. This Pe-ling is a little leather town, where they have a one-horse sort of a tannery. The other, as I call him, wakes when I sleep. His name out there is Kan-schau. He is a man who keeps account of skins as the people bring them in. He is a sort of civil-service man, who gets his income once a month from the government.

[I need hardly say that we were aghast when Ingham went into this detail on subjects of which we thought he could not possibly know anything. But we knew him quite too well to interrupt. When his engine is thrown off the track it breaks all travel on all lines for that day, and numberless jack-screws are needed before any traffic can be renewed. So we let him go on.]

II

You know I had had to do with that region, only it was farther north. I spent the better part of a summer once working with the telegraph at Nofpo Ston, a pretty place on Lake Baikal, on the Russian side of the line. There we had more or less to do with Chinese traders, and I made one of them teach me a little colloquial Chinese by the Mastery method of Prendergast. It only requires you to commit one hundred and seventeen words to memory in sixteen different phrases. So soon as Blanche Stockhardt had gone I found my

Chinese lexicon, and wrote the other body a note, asking about his health and his habits. The next day, as I tell you, I hunted up the Franquelin atlas, and found the place. I did not know his name—I mean, of course, my name—out there. But I directed the note, which was written in the first-chop, gold-button, highest Mandarin language of all, to "The Most Sensible Man in Pe-ling."

But this was the letter which, as I said, was returned to me by the Chinese post-office, with the statement that they had searched all through the Pe-ling Mountains, and there was no such person there as the one mentioned on the letter. The truth is that our Pe-ling—our antipodes on the parallel of latitude—latitude 42° 23′ north, longitude 110° east, has, as I said, nothing to do with the Pe-ling Mountains. It was, on the whole, much better that that letter did not hit him; for, when I got no answer, I hit on a much better plan. And so it was that I saw Turner, as I tell you.

[He had not told us any such thing. But this is Ingham's way. And, as I say, it is so risky to interrupt him that we always let him go on.]

It occurred to me one day that—if the Chinese body kept at the accurate distance of longitude, as, in theory, it certainly would—when I, Fred Ingham, walked north on the 70th meridian, Kaolin, as I then called my other machine, would walk north on the 110th. If I walked or rode west to Albany—four or five degrees of longitude—Kaolin would, of course, go west on his parallel—say to Ling-shaw. Clearly enough, then, if I wanted to talk matters over with him, he and I had

only to go to the north pole—I on the meridian of 70°,
and he on that of 110°. And on this simple plan I
went to work. It is a much easier business than you
think it, when you begin to think, as everybody does,
by supposing an expedition there to be a government
affair, with measurements of magnetic force, and declination, and dip, and all that.

I cared nothing for the dip—what I wanted was to
see my other self, Kaolin.

[" I should think he was beside himself when he started," said
George, in a whisper. But, for reasons stated, no one dared speak
aloud. Little Annie pulled at George eagerly to keep him quiet.]

Of course (continued Ingham), if a man cares about
the difference between *Tetrapus arcticus* and *Tetrapus
borealis*, he must carry a lot of books with him and a
man of science. If he carries a man of science, he must
carry the man's rations and his cook, and a man to drag
his sled, and so on. Hence what are called "expedi-
tions." But if a man is only going to see a friend, or
to see himself, as I was " *veluti in speculo* "—as the Vul-
gate hath it—and if he only cares for *Tetrapus arcticus* as so much good carbon and nitrogen, to be torn in
pieces and devoured for the body's fuel, why, he goes
as I might go to Young's or to Parker's for my lunch,
without an " expedition " to carry me.

I began by running down to New London. All this
was long ago, and they still carried on the whale-fishery
there. Yes, Ned, I went to your cousins, or your wife's
cousins, those princes, the Perkinses: they were in that
business then.

Then and there I learned, what I fancy most of you

do not know, that there is such a charm about that
arctic life that the whalemen always want to be left for
the winter when the ship comes home with oil. This
is the way that the trade has been carried on of late
years. You send up a ship, as soon as the ice is open,
with a full crew. You join the men you left the last
autumn. They have been fishing from the shore all
the time except in the very dead of winter, and trying
out their oil. You take on board the oil they have
made, and spend the summer making more. Then you
bring back all your oil. But the point is, as Mr. Per-
kins told me, that all the men are eager to stay. It is
a reward to stay. You leave those who have behaved
well, and the half which comes home is sour and disappointed.

Well, I did not tell my whole plan to the Perkinses.
They agreed to send me as far north as they could.
They agreed to take aboard an extra boat for my purposes. As it proved, their captain — no, it was not
Budington, it was another man—advanced my plans in
every way, though he did not quite know what they
were.

[No one had said it was Budington. But the reader must understand, once for all, that this ejaculatory or parenthetical manner is in
Ingham's way, and must be taken for granted.]

So I got my traps together and started. We were
to put in at Upernavik, as they all do. Yes, there is a
Lowernavik, or was, but that has nothing to do with it.
The Governor was very civil—only too civil. His
daughter was pretty. You remember her picture. No,
not in Hayes's book: before that. No, not in Parry's:

she was a baby then. I have her picture somewhere.
And it was at a party he gave us and some English-
men from Hull that I met Turner.

Had you rather I should tell you about Turner, or
about Kaolin or Kan-schau? For really I am talking
too much. I am doing all the talking.

[And Ingham looked at his watch. The children cared nothing
for Turner: they hardly knew who he was. They clamored for the
north pole and Kau-schau; and Ingham, well pleased, went on.]

III

As I said, I had no scientific purposes. I was not to
write a book, or to present a report. I was not even
going into society, as men call society. I was only
going to meet my other self—not my better half, whom
I already knew I had left at home. (And here Ingham
looked affectionately at Polly, who was knitting by the
fire.) I wanted to see myself just as others see me. So
I meant to rely, as at bottom all the grandest expedi-
tions rely, on the native Greenlanders. I found plenty
of them ready to be hired. I had not to tell them
whether we were going north, south, east, or west.
Enough for them that they had good guns given them,
such a harpoon and such shark hooks and cod hooks
as they never saw before, promise of good wages, and
instructions to report on board the *Sarah*, with eight
dogs, on the morning she sailed.

Then came a great piece of luck. Baffin's Bay in winter is much like this water-bottle when it left the ice

machine, and had a solid block of ice frozen in it close to each side. Baffin's Bay, on the 20th of June, is much like this same bottle now, where the ice block floats as it chooses in melted water. It is as the turn of a straw, it is the chance of the wind, whether the "pack" of ice hugs the east coast or the west. By good luck that spring it held close in to the west coast; by good luck the winds were northeasterly, and the "pack" all drifted west. We cracked north in the *Sarah*, in no time. The captain meant to leave me at the beginning of Smith Sound, but he found that open, and he said he could not resist the temptation of sailing up. It was early July. The days were all one; the sun was "ever so high" at midnight. The sky—oh, it was so clear!—as if we had been in Spain. In one day —we hardly tacked twice—we ran all through that rather critical channel, which took its discoverers all summer, and my good captain said he was fairly tempted to run to the north pole.

But of course he was for whales, and must not go exploring. He landed me and my traps, and my two men, and my eight dogs, and my whale-boat, under the lee of a bold cliff that runs out—say here, if you will look at my map, Clara. Here is Baffin's Bay, this will do for Kennedy Land, and here we are at Cape Douglas-Digges. They gave us three cheers. I gave them three, and the Greenlanders howled something; the dogs howled more. They filled away for the south, and we sent our blessing with them. No, I did not feel lonely. A man carries the middle of the world with him. The world is just as level, as hilly, as large, as small, there as it is anywhere. The sea was all open at the north, only the wind hauled a little more into the north. I did not like that then, but it proved an advantage, as you will see.

A good whale-boat like that will carry, with crowding, eighteen men. We were but three, with eight dogs and with Jan's sled, which I laid bottom up over the bow, and the dogs rather liked to crawl in underneath to sleep. I liked to have them, for they are not very sociable brutes, and they have few entertaining tricks. I had no reason for staying a moment at Douglas-Digges. Jan and Hans were the most good-natured men-Fridays who ever walked in salt-water to pack stores away. We hauled and lifted, and got the bags and the little barrel and the two boxes fitted to my mind, after some trial. Then I stepped my little mast, Jan called in his dogs, whipped the sulky ones, and I cast off; she had been fastened to a bowlder of basalt which had rolled down from the cliff, and the tide was on the flow.

I had rigged her with a leg-of-mutton sail—just as we saw those boats at Huelva, George. Jan generally sat forward on his sled. But I could tend the sail as I sat in the stern. You know you steer a whale-boat with an oar.

Well, you do not care anything about our log. But the truth is that that day's success and the next told the whole story. Days we call them. But really when at midnight you have the sun nearly as high as our noon sun is at Christmas, you do not say much about this day or that day. Briefly, I cracked on, sometimes eight knots an hour, as I sailed for forty-one hours. I could not go quite to the north. But my

boat sailed very well into the wind. I soon got tired
of holding an oar for a rudder, and so did Hans, and
we lashed our steering oar to a davit and a cleat. I
made very long tacks, running once twenty-nine knots
on the same course to the east of north, and once fifteen
knots and more to the west of north. The wind came
round to the west and southwest. I thought then, and
afterwards I was sure, that in those forty-one hours of
that steady pull I made near two hundred miles north-
ing; that is, you see, nearly three degrees. And, as I
say, with that one long bit, in less than two days from
the *Sarah*, it proved that my success was won—if it
were success, after all.

Forty-one hours, on the whole, towards the pole,
brought me, alas! to land again. I was afraid it was
land first when I was taking the sun's declination,
which I did every hour. I had, indeed, nothing else to
do. The sea was as dull there as it always is. I
thought my horizon was bad, and then with my binoc-
ular I became sure it was not the sea. Sure enough,
"low land, and all was well"—no longer. For when
we came to that beach our hard work began. I had
brought rollers from Upernavik, and when we beached
her, heavy as she was, we harnessed the dogs, and with
their help we dragged her high and dry, above any
tide, upon a sort of dry lichen there was, where we
could see that deer had been. To my horror, however,
there was neither ice nor snow. There was a low hill,
but I got little comfort from the prospect at the top.

Here, you see, I was about five degrees, say three
hundred and fifty miles, from the pole, and I and two
men and eight dogs were to travel there and back in,

say, twenty-five days. It was as if you had to go to
Syracuse and back, from Boston, with no road. The
vehicle was a large two-handed boy's sled—not what
you call a double-runner, Dick, but twice as wide and
twice as long as your clipper-sled—rigged with a pole
for two men to haul at. But the land coast ran sheer
east and west, and I would not lose even a day by
cruising along either way. Right over the lichen I
started due north, harnessing the dogs to drag, and
taking enough canned food for ten days for me and
Jan and Hans. If the guns would not do the rest,
why, we must come back.

Awful work that first day, and the second! We
made only twenty-three miles north in both. Then we
came to the strangest flat steppe there is this side of
Siberia, ankle-deep in lichen, what people call reindeer-
moss, I suppose. The sled flew over it as it would over
rough snow. If we had not watched those brutes they
would have dragged it away from us and mankind.
At last we took turns in riding, merely to keep them
back after they fed. Fed? Yes. They had blood and
fat and all things they liked, more than was good for
them, for the deer would stand to be shot. They were
no more afraid of us than the paroquets were of poor
Cowper. Their tameness was shocking to me. As for
fire, the only trouble was to keep from setting fire to
too much of this lichen, and so setting the north half of
the world in a blaze. This lucky hit lasted us three
full days more. We could not keep at our work more
than eleven hours a day; but in those eighty hours,
more or less, we did make nearly a degree and a half
of latitude. When we came to the sea again we were

two hundred and fifty miles farther north than man
had ever been known to be.

But we did come to the sea. And now we had no
boat, and it was quite too cold to swim far; that is, the
water was. I had no quarrel with the air. Happily the
tide was out, the beach was wide, and the coast trended
north-northwest, a point west. How well I remember!
Over the beach sand, though we were dead tired. I
forged on, fairly running the dogs, for I knew this sand
gave easy dragging compared with what the upland was
beginning to be. The lichen had given out, or was
giving out, and there were loose stones, as there had
not been before. That was Tuesday, as I well remember. Till Friday night, I know, we ran the dogs, or
made them work all through the hours of low tide, six,
and sometimes seven. Five or six hours at high tide
we all slept—and I tell you the dogs slept sound—on
the upland. No trouble about their eating or ours;
only a monotonous bill of fare. Seals galore! a stupid
seal at every headland, and lying on the shore in herds
or flocks sometimes, so that they were fairly in the
way. You do not like train-oil, Clara, because you
always see it rancid; but in the open air, warm from
the blubber, if you had been walking and running a
week, you might fancy it.

That coast is just like the Jersey shore. It is flat as
your hand, as we say. There is one stretch where we
ran almost due north thirty-six miles, if the sextant
did not lie. In those days between Tuesday and Friday I made more than two degrees. Still open sea
on the west of me. If I had only had my whale-
boat! But I did have the dogs, and they were as

well as horses—are said to be. My horse is always sick.

It was that lucky bit of beach—beach hardly broken by a crack of inlet—which gave us our last success. Sometimes we had to go into the water knee-deep at some inlet, and once I went in as high as my armpits. That time it was a carry—when we floated the sled, and swam the dogs, and took the bags and boxes and the barrel in our arms. But the hard run afterwards warmed us very soon, I can tell you, and dried us.

And now, if you have counted, you can see we were near half-way. I mean we were near the pole—and the pole was, of course, half-way back to Douglas-Digges. By my last three declinations, when I came into camp that Friday night—night we called it—in broad sunshine, I was only twenty-four miles and a little more from the pole—twenty-one minutes of latitude, Dick, if you are particular: quite as close, that, as the vernier of my sextant would read for me.

But here the shore began to trend west, and even south of west. I had been conscious for some time that I was running up a bay like Chesapeake Bay, and I was now near the head of it. I fed the dogs on the last seal we had killed—you knock them on the head with an axe, Harry—and we all got into our bags for sleep, I a good deal excited now as to the issue. Before supper was done it had clouded over. I was glad I had made my observations. When I took the sun at noon—which was after we camped—I had staked out a north and south line. By this I tested my compass, which pointed about south-southwest. The variation was 152° south. So untrue is it that the constant needle points to any pole—but its own.

When I waked in the morning it was snowing, and my bag had six inches of snow on it. Yes, Clara, you sleep in a bag of felt, inside a bag of canvas, inside a bag of India-rubber cloth. After you are in the bag you button it up over your head, with only a little nose-hole for air. So it does not much matter whether it snows or not. I rolled Hans over Jan and waked them, and explained that we were to leave their dear sea and cross the land again. Hans said we should find deer, but I doubted. I only told them both that we had not far to go. Nor had we. Rough it was, very hard it was, while the snow lasted. But by noon this cleared away, and at six I let them camp. There was old snow, and in an hour they had built a snow hut under the lee of a hill. We slept like bears, and the next day—Sunday—there were but eleven miles, as I counted, between me and the pole.

IV

I let Hans, who had hurt his foot, stay in the hut with the dogs.

The sun had come out again. The world was white with new snow.

I was almost provoked that the country was so uninteresting.

It was not flat.

It was not mountainous.

There was no great cup in the midst of which a pole rose high to the sky.

There was no sugar-loaf, like the Peak of Teneriffe, rising in my horizon northward.

There was only a vulgar rolling country, beautiful as new snow is always beautiful, but as little varied— well, as that stretch is between Tobolsk and Smilkelsk, if you take the lower road.

I bade Jan take his gun, and put in his pouch a can of beef. For me, I carried nothing but hardtack and cartridges.

It was Sunday morning.

Up and down. Not a tree, not a bush, not a rock, not a sound, not a beast, not a bird. I was sorry we had not worn our snow-shoes. But Jan drew the empty sled: he was sure we should strike a deer.

Up and down. North, still north. One hour, two hours, three. About eleven I called a halt. I ate two or three biscuits, and gave Jan as many.

Why was I so hopelessly sleepy?

Half an hour's rest; and as I was rousing myself I saw poor Jan, without an apology, drop bodily on the ground and go to sleep.

It was not cold enough for him to be stupefied. Why were we so sleepy?

On the whole, I thought I would leave Jan. He had cleared the snow to the ground. And I covered him with a heavy bearskin he had upon the sled. My march was now less than an hour. I would take his beef for a lunch. I knew he would sleep till I came back again.

North for the last tramp of all!
I took the sled with me.

As I pulled up a long slope there is, just before
you come to the pole itself, it seemed to me that I
should die with sleep. Still, of mere will power, I
pressed on until I turned the summit, and looked still
north.

A wide, flat plain a hundred feet below me stretched
I cannot tell how far away. Perhaps a mile and a
half from me a black spot. Was it a man? The bi-
nocular settled that. It was a man, and he was lying
on a sled, asleep.

But for me, had it been the angel Uriel, I could not
have gone to him. I was dead with sleep. I just remember having sense to unroll my bag, which I carried
as a knapsack, and crawling into it, and then I was at
once unconscious.

How long I slept I do not know, but it must have
been hours: that I knew afterwards.

When I awoke I did not know where I was. But I
heard snoring. The bag was not buttoned. I had
been too sleepy.

I pushed my head out, and at that moment a man
fell heavily to the ground at my side. He had fallen
asleep as he sat watching me.

He was in the winter costume of Northern China—
a fur cap, a fur pea-jacket, trousers of deerskin. I had
seen hundreds of such traders on the Baikal.

It was Myself — my Other Self! He had come to
meet me! I was wholly prepared to speak to him. I
cried to him in these words:

15

But he heard nothing; he lay like a log.

I shook him. I rolled him over. He only groaned in his sleep. But it was as if he were dead—only he breathed. Then I remembered how I had been sleeping! I remembered how stupidly Jan was sleeping!

Could it be?—it was—that Jan's other self was three miles south of us, on the opposite meridian!

And I? and Kaolin? Of course he must sleep while I waked; I must sleep while he waked. This was the basis of the whole journey.

No one had ever thought that one soul could carry on two bodies at the same time. Of course, then, we could not talk to each other.

All we could do was to write, and await an answer.

I wrote in my best handwriting, in Chinese, this note:

"My brother—nay, myself; I see you are well. My name is Frederic Ingham. What is yours? What grief that we cannot hear each other's voices, or see each other's eyes?"

Then I crept into my bag, and forced myself to go to sleep. I did not sleep long. When I woke there was a note in my hand, which said:

"I am called Kan-schau. My rank is of the blue button of the province of Fi. I am the government inspector of furs. May your waking be joyful!"

I think he saw the situation, and poked me hard as his last conscious act. But this made no difference. I should have waked, of course, as soon as he slept. I had with me Wells's Smaller Dictionary, and I made out most of what he wrote. Then I bethought me what I should say. What did I want to say? What do you ever want to say in a letter? Of course he knew what I was, and I knew what he was, for I was he, and he was I. So far there was no need to write.

As for the inspection of furs, I cared nothing for that. Nor did he care, I think, much about my home-mission work in District K.

It seemed a pity to talk politics. As to fine art, I did not know the Chinese words for "realistic," or "Pre-Raphaelite."

It is not the first time that, having an opportunity to address a friend, I found that I had very little to say to him.

What I did was this—always a good thing to do: I opened my can of beef, which I had taken from Jan, and placed under it a bit of hardtack. I wrote:

"Feed yourself from my stores. Eat of my bread and meat. If only you might sit with my family at my table! But, alas! our destiny forbids."

Then I crept back into my bag, counted ten thousand, and imagined a flock of sheep jumping over a wall, until I lost myself in slumber.

I awoke to find this note:

"I am made new by your bounty. Eat of my last bird's-nest. It is indeed life to death, and strength to faintness. We must now turn our backs on each other. But I leave a guide for your instruction."

Dead asleep I found him, but this message, and a Chinese envelope with his Chinese address, were in his hand.

I fastened in a parcel a volume of my essays, a small flask of cordial, and a picture alphabet for his children. I wrote my address on an envelope, and on the parcel I placed a card with this:

"FAREWELL.

"We shall not soon meet again. I shall rejoice in your joy, I shall sorrow in your sorrow. Polly, my wife, will gladly hear of the welfare of yours. Farewell."

I left it in his hands, but as I did so that horrid drowsiness came over me. I fell; but waked to find, in a sort of Pidgin-English, this billet by my side. I was alone.

"By-by. Top-notch muchee good for him all the ways. By-by. Two Lapland men behind this Kan-schau. Muchee-muchee, him go and help them. By-by."

Could my gold-chop Chinese be as bad as his English? The prints of his feet in the snow were clear enough. But he had gone. I looked at the sun, which was near noon when I left Jan, and it was now quite on the other side of the sky. I looked at my watch, which Bond had made for me, for safety's sake at this point, and had arranged for it a dial of twenty-four hours. It was half-past twenty-three o'clock. Poor

Jan had been asleep twelve hours, or had waked to find me gone.

I retraced my own steps, and found him just rousing. I knew one of Kan-schau's Laplanders was going to sleep at the same moment.

Jan never knew how long he slept. In three hours more we had joined Hans, and with two snow-rabbits which he had knocked over, and a few specimens of *Grassus inequalis* which he had killed for the dogs, we all feasted. We all slept twelve hours. I suppose Kan-schau was making a long pull home.

I have never seen him again.

THE President of the United States could not sleep.

He had been in bed an hour. He had calculated the interest on the national debt at three per cent., at three and a half, and at four per cent., and still he could not sleep. He had estimated a payment of $9,000,000 a month for one year, $10,000,000 a month the next year, and so on, and when it would all be paid.

And still he could not sleep. The truth was that the President had spent the afternoon at the reception of Mr. Jaffrey, who was then the Secretary of State. Mr. Jaffrey had four handsome daughters, to be remembered among the finest women in the world. The President and Miss Gertrude were on the pleasantest terms. He sat by her an hour as she presided at the coffee-urn, and without so much as thinking of it he drank a great deal more coffee than was good for him, or, at the least, for his sleeping faculty.

So it was that he lay awake. He thought it was his anxiety about the interoceanic canal. It was not. It was Miss Gertrude's coffee.

The President pulled out his repeater and struck it.

One and two quarters.

He lay calculating the national debt, as he thought, for about ten hours. Then he struck the repeater again.

One and three quarters.

He calculated more. He calculated, at compound interest, four and a quarter a year, how large a sinking-fund would pay it if Thus and So.

He struck his repeater again, after what he thought eleven hours.

Two o'clock.

"This will never do," said the President. "I will do as Aaron the Wise would have done." He tumbled out of bed, he lighted the gas, he began to dress, and rang for his valet, who was a black man from a Carolina plantation, named Mesrour.

"Mesrour, go across the square to Mr. Jaffrey's, and say I want to see him."

"Yes, sare," said Mesrour, who was surprised, but pretended to be surprised at nothing.

Mr. Jaffrey also was surprised. But he also, like a loyal and well-bred diplomatist, pretended to be surprised at nothing.

"Jaffrey," said the President, as he met him under the great porch of the White House, "it is pleasanter out-doors than in. I cannot sleep, and I have called you that we may go to walk together, and see how my people live."

"I hear and I obey," said Jaffrey, pretending to laugh, but thinking in the bottom of his heart that there were disadvantages in being the recipient of Executive favors.

"You see, Jaffrey, I have not many subjects. In Virginia yonder they are the Governor's subjects, and in Baltimore yonder it is the same, with another Governor. Only the people of this city, and the red-skins and those who skin them in the Territories, who are my real subjects. And of these here I do not know how they live. Let us go and see. Will not that be a good thing to do? Perhaps there are reforms needed. Perhaps I may send a special message to the House. Or the Commissioners of the District would take a hint from me—eh, Jaffrey?"

Jaffrey tried to rise to the occasion. He saw that the President was in earnest, and really wanted to do the right thing. For him, he had been happily in bed, and he wished he were there still. But he and the President had gone through too many campaigns together in the field and in the caucus for him to flinch now. He knew and he respected this tender spot in the President's heart, and if an hour's tramping up and down the Avenue would help him, why, Jaffrey was not the man to say no.

"No, Mesrour, you need not go," said the President to the faithful negro, who followed them out into the night, as he would have followed his master under a shower of fire, unless he had been sent back.

So the two walked down the Avenue towards the Capitol.

And the poor President was disappointed. There was a moon. The shadows were picturesque. But it was all commonplace, Western, and dull. He had hoped—well, after midnight, you know, alone and on foot, you know— But things would not look strange.

The grog-shops were all shut. Even at Willard's there was hardly a light. Hardly a hell in the second story had a light in the windows.

"Jaffrey," he said, rather sadly, for he was disappointed, "were you ever in Bagdad?"

"Oh yes, when I was minister to Persia, you know. The Secretary sent me word about some excavations—Mosul, Nineveh, or somewhere—and I went down to Bagdad."

"And is Bagdad like Washington, Jaffrey? Is the street—the main street, you know—quite as well lighted and quite as dead after midnight, or are there—well, are there dervishes and nautch-girls and calenders?"

"What is a calender?" said Jaffrey. "There was a calender in 'John Gilpin,' but I never knew what he was or did."

"Nor I," said the President, "no more nor the dead, as my excellent Mesrour would say. But, Jaffrey, look yonder. What is that? That is not commonplace."

And he pointed down one of those dirty streets to the south of the Avenue, which no one by any accident goes into if he can help himself, where was a tall column of yellow fire. "There is an adventure," said the bebored and *ennuyé* President. "Let us go and see."

Mr. Jaffrey also was curious. He thought he knew Washington, and he knew that there was no foundery in those regions. When they came near the spot it seemed more mysterious than ever. The flames rose behind a high brick wall. In front of this a modest brick house, of the kind which ambitious speculators built seventy years ago, before men knew which was to be the court end of Washington, was brilliantly lighted. A duet of a piano and violin was heard from within.

The President bade Jaffrey ring, and he did so.

"I have a desire to enter this house," said the President, "and to see who is giving this concert."

"They are a party who have become intoxicated," replied Jaffrey, "and I fear that we may experience ill usage."

"I must enter," said the President, "and you must devise some stratagem by which we can obtain admission."

"I hear and I obey," said Jaffrey, laughing as before; and at that moment a neatly dressed negro girl opened the door.

"Madam," said the courtly Jaffrey, "we are two merchants from St. Louis, who have been in Washington some days. A merchant here invited us to an entertainment to-night, and we went to his house. We ate and drank with him till it was time to depart, and going out into the night we have missed our way to the hotel, and we do not know its name. We trust, therefore, in your generosity that you will admit us to pass the rest of the night in your house. By doing this you will obtain a reward in heaven."

The girl ran back, evidently consulted with her mistress, and then opened the inner door, and said, "Come in." The President entered, therefore, with Jaffrey. They left their hats where they were bidden, and passed into the concert-room. The performance went on as if they had not been seen. But as soon as the sonata ended, the party present arose, and a lady said:

"Welcome are our guests; but we have a condition to impose upon you, that ye speak not of that which doth not concern you, lest ye hear that which will not please you."

They answered, " Good," and from that moment they were treated as if they had always been companions of their hosts.

In the next moment a black butler threw open the large door which parted them from a dining-room, and said, " Supper is served, madam."

The company went in in form, the President and Jaffrey making the last two of the long procession.

The President took his seat rather timidly, the more so that Mr. Jaffrey was taken quite to the other end of the other side of the table. There were flowers arranged in high vases, so that he could not so much as see his faithful companion. He was received with more display of courtesy than would have been shown were this an ordinary boarding-house, but certainly with less interest in his personality than if, when he was Secretary of State, he had presented himself as a guest at the English minister's. On one side a lady sat, on the other a large man—" gentleman," the President would have said, had he met him in a legislative assembly. The gentleman seemed to present the President to the lady as he sat down. But if he did, the President was none the wiser.

The table was elegantly furnished and decorated. The President fell into talk with the gentleman by him. In a little the lady opposite spoke to that gentleman. The talk was on some matter of detail as to what would turn up the next day in the Senate, whether it were best that the ladies should take some friends to the gallery. It happened that the President knew the order of business, and he gave the information needed, and so, without formality, he soon found himself in conversation with the others, and recognized as if he were a familiar member of their company.

One seat was still vacant at the end of the table, and one nearly opposite the President. But this was not for many minutes. Before the next remove two young men came in, looking a little flushed in the face, but perhaps even more carefully dressed than any one else; although, as the President had observed, with some little annoyance, every one, excepting himself and Mr. Jaffrey, was in full evening dress. When these two young men came in they were greeted by a cordial hand-clapping, which ran all around the board. They smiled and bowed, but said nothing, and applied themselves one to his fillet of beef and one to his roast capon.

So soon, however, as this course was removed, in the little lull while the servants were changing the plates and rearranging the table, the lady who sat at the head, far away from the President, struck her glass with her knife, and thus secured absolute silence. "We will hear the report," she said. And all cried, "Hear! hear!"

The young man with light hair rose to his feet, seemed embarrassed, but read from a slip of paper, "Nine ounces silver, four ounces nickel, two pounds seven ounces and a half copper."

The announcement was received with new hand-clapping. Then the other, who had black hair, rose and said, "One ounce seven pennyweights gold," and the applause was renewed. But nothing more was said. The servants brought round the next course, and the dozen streams of broken conversation began to flow again. As for the President, he was a good deal troubled. Where was he, and what was this report? Were these people debasers of the currency? Was he sharing the food of a lot of people virtually counterfeiters? He shuddered as he remembered the denunciations in the last report of the Mint Master, who had been bitter in his protests as to the quantity of degraded money which came in to him.

But the President was wary. He showed no fear. He did let his fork fall upon the table, so as to judge for himself by the ring whether it were silver or albata. Silver unmistakably! With the indifferent tone of an old diplomat, he said to the lady by him:

"I am very stupid. Am I growing deaf? I did not understand where all this bullion came from."

"Not understand? Why, it came from the straw, of course."

"Straw?" said the President—"what straw?"

"Why, where do you suppose you are?" said she, amazed in her turn.

"I suppose I am at an elegant dinner-party, by the side of a very charming lady."

"As you will," said she; "certainly she is by the side of a very flattering gentleman. But, pardon me, I do not know what countryman you are. I do not recognize your *patois*. Still, it is not in many countries that a table like this—what shall I say?—grows on every tree. That is a bad metaphor." And she laughed very prettily.

"Certainly not in any country I have visited," said the President.

" And certainly the club here, the ladies and gentlemen around us, would not expect the lady president
yonder to furnish it for them every night."

The President started when he heard the lady president spoken of. But he saw in a moment that he need
not be afraid.

" Of course, then," she continued, " it would not be a
club. It is a club—well, because the suppers come
from the straw."

" What straw?" said the President again, somewhat
stupidly.

" Why, what straw is full of gold and silver and
nickel and copper? Do you not know? Why, indeed,
did you come? The only straw which yields such
returns as they have reported is the straw from the
street-cars. Our friend here contracts to furnish clean
straw every morning, and her people clean out the cars
at midnight. Valentine and Asa yonder are the smelt-
ers. They graduated at the Argo Works in Colorado.
The club lives on the products. Why, if they had
reported only two ounces copper, seven ounces nickel—
voilà tout!—we should have had short commons to-
morrow night—a fish-ball and a cracker and a glass
of water each. But if a traveller like you knows what
gold is worth, you see we shall not starve—at least, for
twenty-four hours."

The President felt as if he had already been repaid
for his adventure, and understood better than before
what became of the national currency.

But he tried to conceal any annoyance, and indeed
he unbent to the Bohemian carelessness of the occasion more than he had done, poor man, since he was

at an Alpha Delta supper in New Padua. Once and
again he led up to talk which he thought would show
who his neighbors were. But, ah me! though he was
an old diplomat, these people were too much for him.
He had wormed secrets out of Bismarck in Berlin; he
had been more than a match, in his Western frankness,
for Clémenceau; and Sagasta had told him secrets
which he never told to any other man. But the woman
at his right and the man at his left told him no secrets,
and at the end of two hours the President did not
know whether they knew who he was, and he did
know very well that he did not know who they were.
It was more than two hours, it was nearly three, when
the Queen of the Feast clapped her hands and pointed
to a gentleman who had sung one or two merry songs
before. At the signal he began to sing "We won't
go home till morning," and the whole company joined
in the chorus. With the last words, the stately butler
flung up the heavy curtains of the one window, and lo!
in the east the first streak of dawn. In less than two
minutes the President and Jaffrey found themselves on
the sidewalk walking up the Avenue.

As they walked home the President was silent till
they came to Fourteenth Street, and Mr. Jaffrey, if
possible, was more silent. But as they turned in at
that side-gate by which you go up to the White House,
the President said to the Secretary:

"Jaffrey, this is very mysterious."

"Yes, it is very mysterious," said the other.

"We cannot have such things right under the shadow
of the Capitol without inquiry." And the President

spoke with a certain firmness of tone which terrified
his Secretary. For Mr. Jaffrey knew very well that
when he spoke in that tone he was immovable. In
truth, it was the power to speak in that tone which
had made him President.

Mr. Jaffrey thought, indeed, that any inquiry into
the proceedings of a horde of Bohemians would be
absurd. It would be sure to get into the papers, and
there was no saying where it might end. But he knew
the President's tone, so he made no opposition. But
he said: " Yes, indeed, there must be an inquiry. I
will send a note to the Commissioners of the District."

" Fiddle-stick!" said the President. "Commissioners
of the Town Pump! I shall make the inquiry myself."

"Make it yourself!" said Mr. Jaffrey, startled out of
his usual tact. "But you have no authority in this
District. You are not even a Justice of the Quorum."

"Quorum be hanged!" said the President. " I shall
make the inquiry." And Mr. Jaffrey knew he had lost
the point by the suddenness of his ejaculation. The
President at once thanked him for his good company,
and said, " I think I shall sleep now."

Poor Mr. Jaffrey went home quite sure that he
should sleep now.

The next morning the President sent over to the
library of the Department of State, and bade them send
him the *Arabian Nights*. Then, while the office-seekers
were kept at bay by his private secretaries, the President lighted a cigar, and found what the Caliph Haroun-
al-Raschid would have done in the same circumstances.
He varied the detail so as to fit the civilization of the
nineteenth century and the longitude of Washington.

He struck the bell, saw the steward, and ordered a specially nice lunch at two o'clock for about four-and-twenty people. Then with his own hand, on gilt-edged note-paper, he wrote an invitation which said that the President of the United States invited to lunch that day the lady of the house where he had supped last night, and all her guests.

"There," said he to himself, as he sent off the note by his private messenger; "let us see how much power that has, though I am not a Justice of the Quorum." Then he sent a message to Mr. Jaffrey that he must come to lunch, and gave the next three hours to the office-seekers.

But at two o'clock the office-seekers had all gone, and the President was in that pretty oval room which so often changes its name and its furniture at the White House, waiting for his guests. Nor did he have to wait long. A series of coupés and other carriages drove up under the *porte-cochère*, and twenty-four ladies and gentlemen were shown in by the ceremonious butler. The President recognized at once his courteous hostess of last night. She made her apologies very simply for those of the company who had been called out of town. In a moment more, lunch was announced. She took the President's arm; Mr. Jaffrey gave his to another lady who had come in the same carriage with her, and the rest followed, much at their own sweet will. The talk at table was quite as gay as it had been the night before. But the President had a better chance than the night before to talk with his very agreeable companion.

When at last they were playing with their iced fruits,

the President spoke a little louder than he had done, so that all other conversation was hushed. He said : "Ladies and gentlemen, I was very much interested in your club last night, and greatly enjoyed your hospitality. My curiosity was excited, but I was not so rude as to ask questions of my hosts. My morning sleep has not allayed it, and, as you see, I am now fortunate enough to reverse our positions. A host may ask questions where a guest must be silent." Then he laughed. "I shall question you now."

" As you please," said the lady; and, as it happened, all the others said, " As you please."

Then Mr. Jaffrey remembered how he had told the President that he could not make any inquiry, and here was the inquiry half over.

" All my life long," said the President, "since I read the *Arabian Nights* and 'John Gilpin,' I have wanted to know what a calender was. Am I right in thinking that some of you are calenders ?"

With one voice, even to Mr. Jaffrey's surprise, all the twenty-four answered, " We are all calenders."

" The wish of my heart is answered," said the President.

" Easily gratified, Mr. President," said the first of his guests.

"I will gladly tell you what are my functions as a calender," said a gentleman near him.

THE STORY OF THE FIRST CALENDER

" A calender is defined by Mr. Lane as ' a royal mendicant.' We are all royal, because we are born from the sovereign people. We are all mendicants, because we live by our wits on the work of the industrious. My business and that of my wife is to stretch new boots for millionaires. They send to us their boots as they come from the makers. We walk in them a few days, till that horrid new look is gone, and then we send them to our patrons. It is not the easiest way to earn one's living, but it does not involve the hardest toil. The business grows upon our hands, or, I should say, on our feet, and we are bringing up to it our sons and daughters."

Then the Bohemian opposite told his story.

THE STORY OF THE THIRD[*] CALENDER

" My business is to write autographs for collectors. My sons are both dressed neatly in the uniform of pages at the Capitol. Every one in the House end of the building thinks Gustavus is a Senate page; every one at the Senate end thinks Horace is a House page. They are pretty boys, and, for a dollar, either will take the autograph-book of any travelling fanatic and have it filled the same day with distinguished names. If you have little poems written you must pay two dollars. I sit down-stairs in the committee-room of the 'Committee on Cross-purposes.' It is very seldom that any one comes in. If he does, he thinks I am private secretary to somebody else. My boys' books are filled much faster than any of the other pages', so that we are very popular. Frankly," he said, laughing, " I cannot often attend a party like this, for these are our best hours, and each hour of them is worth ten dollars."

---

[*] For reasons only known to the elect, the story of the Second Calender is untold in correct editions of the *Arabian Nights*.

THE FOURTH CALENDER'S STORY

"This is an off week with me. There are six of us in all; three work one week, and three another. I and my two friends"—and two stout gentlemen bowed as he waved his hand—"run an elevator on the Sixth Avenue in New York. It takes belated travellers up to the Diedrich Street station of the elevated road. The contrivance is simple—two scales, one at the top, one at the bottom, connected by ropes which pass over pulleys. I and my friends weigh more than six hundred: the average passenger weighs only a hundred and fifty. When from above we see three people on the lower scale, we leap upon the upper, and it goes down at once. Then we run up-stairs as quickly as we can, leaving, however, number three to take the money, while he who did take it becomes number one, and goes up with us. As you see, Mr. President, we have to run up-stairs all the time for a week, always going down on the elevator. It is a very fatiguing occupation, but it is very lucrative, and so we are able to lie off half the time."

All this time Mr. Jaffrey was looking straight at the lady opposite him, and pretending not to know her. But now it was her turn, and she said:

STORY OF ANOTHER CALENDER

"My business is to return calls for the wives of Senators and Secretaries. I make Mrs. Jaffrey's calls every Thursday. I do not know what she does that morning after ten o'clock. I go to her house then with a visible pair of curling-irons. But when I go down-stairs I hide them in a muff, and have her card-case and her list. Then the coachman drives me up and down the different streets, and I leave her cards for her. I can do it quite as accurately as she does, and sometimes I think I do it better. As for my husband here—"

"Stop! stop!" cried Mr. Jaffrey; for he was afraid she was going to say that the husband made his calls for him.

Then, amid general laughter, they heard

THE STORY OF THE LAST CALENDER

"My business," he said, in rather a foreign accent, "is to provide what we call Dromios; you say substitutes. On the regulation list of Adams, Allison, Amos, Anderson, Andrews, as you hear it called in the House, when the yeas and nays are ordered, there are many gentlemen who would like to do something else, if only the press were not after them in their absences. For two dollars a day we provide substitutes for them, well got up. For three dollars we give a man who will frank the documents."

"How much a day if he draws the checks?" said Mr. Jaffrey, laughing. But the President hushed him down. He was now intensely interested. He heard this calender's story to the end. When Mesrour came in the moment after with a message, the President pretended there was an important despatch. Of course the party melted away. Only the President kept Mr. Jaffrey and this last calender.

When they were quite alone, he said to the calender, "Have you — have you — could you find a man who would—who would personate me?"

"Of course, Eccellenza," said the Italian. "Our Mr. Jones did you last night at some private theatricals in Baltimore. He is as like as the figure yonder." And he pointed to the mirror.

"Jaffrey," said the President, "you know I am dead sick of all this. If I could have a change! The thing will kill me if I cannot run away before the session ends."

Jaffrey was beside himself with alarm. But it was just like last night. The President had the bit in his teeth again.

"Six long weeks before the adjournment. I might have a month shooting buffaloes in Manitoba, and leave this man here. Jaffrey, dear fellow, let me go!"

Jaffrey remonstrated. He took the President into a corner, and pleaded with him. But you might as well plead with a northeast wind.

"Jaffrey, I will go. That is all." Then turning to the Italian, and speaking in his choicest Tuscan, he said: "Domani, sarò eternamente obbligato," and the man withdrew. Again Mr. Jaffrey begged and begged. But the President was like iron.

And the next day the man came with the simulated President. The real President was startled himself— Jaffrey was more startled—when the creature threw off the mackintosh which disguised him. Once and again he and the President even deceived the wary Secretary, alert though he was, by changing places when he was talking to the Italian. The President's madness was complete. This man should not leave the private office. He would leave it himself. He called

Mesrour. It proved that his carpet-bag was ready packed. He covered himself with the stranger's water-proof, and he and Mesrour went to the B. and O. station, leaving poor Jaffrey in agony with the other.

But things did not work so badly, after all. The new incumbent was very teachable. Fortunately a great general died, and all public receptions were given up. Then it was said that the President had a cold, and could not be abroad. Then he did go abroad, and to every one's amazement developed a very marked passion for driving four-in-hand. At last, on the Fourth of July, there had to be a levee. The President said one or two queer things, but the court journals said the reports of them were all lies. On the whole, Mr. Jaffrey's times were not so hard as he feared—by no means so hard as when his chief was at home. For many days he had a despatch from a Mr. Thompson at the Northwest: " All well." " O. K." " Quite right." At last these stopped; and then Jaffrey knew that his friend was in Manitoba slaughtering the few remaining buffaloes. But the lull in despatches was longer than he liked. Mr. Jaffrey began to be uneasy, when, late one night, the door-bell rang, and Mesrour appeared! His story, alas! even with all his reiterations, was a very short one.

All had gone well as far as the Butte à Carcajou. Then they crossed to the Dog Knoll. Jaffrey verified these names afterwards. They forded the White Sand River in a torrent of rain. Then Mesrour's story was unintelligible, until, after they had crossed Bar River three times on one accursed morning, they came too suddenly on a herd of buffalo. The beasts did not flee, as they were meant to do; they turned and charged the little hunting-party. The President was the last to turn his horse; the poor creature stumbled, fell upon his master—and, on the instant, five hundred buffaloes passed over them!

A wretched rag from his coat and a few fragments of letters, with what was left of a gold repeater, were all which Mesrour could bring to verify his tale.

The body had been buried where it fell.

Mr. Jaffrey retired for an hour, leaving poor Mesrour asleep on a lounge in the reception-room. Then he came and waked the faithful negro.

"Not one word of this to any man."

"Nevare, massa!"

"Nor woman!"

"No! nor woman, massa."

"Go back to your duty at the White House to-night. Say you have been west on a private message."

That is what Mesrour did. No public announcement of the President's death was thought necessary by the Secretary of State. Times were prosperous. As always, the country governed itself without much regard to Washington. The incumbent of the White House confided in the Secretary, and the Secretary confided in the incumbent of the White House.

"And so," said Scheherezade, as she finished her story—"so ended the tales of the calenders. But this is nothing to the story of 'Newspaper Row,' if it please your Highness graciously to lengthen our lives, and to hear it to-morrow morning."

But this was the end of the Arabian Nights' Entertainments in Washington.

I.—THE FLY

Mrs. Mitchell was a good housekeeper, and hospitable. She was so good a housekeeper that, in that business, she had risen to the highest rank. That is to say, she was not hospitable to flies. Housekeepers of the second rank are so governed by a chance remark of Uncle Toby's as to think there is room enough in their houses, at least in winter, for the flies and for all other guests also. So they let the flies go into one cell and another, and lay the eggs which will make the next August miserable to all. Mrs. Mitchell had risen above this form of hospitality, and her house had no room for flies.

So after she had bidden Lawrence good-bye, instead of returning to her knitting she went to the window to catch and kill a large fly that was trying to pass through it. Lawrence was on his way to New York. With his overcoat on one arm, and his umbrella in one hand, with a rather large valise in the other hand, he had come in to take leave of his grandmother. He had put down the valise that he might kiss her better. She had risen from her deep, easy-chair to kiss him. She had said:

" Do not work too hard, dear boy, and I pray God every night to bless you."

"Good-bye, grandmamma."

"Good-bye!"

And they both thought it was all over.

But it was not all over; in fact, as it proved, this was the beginning, or the prologue before the play. For when Mrs. Mitchell went to the window, and struck it rather hard in her pursuit of the fly—struck, indeed, two or three times—Lawrence, who was rapidly passing in the shrubbery below, thought she had remembered some forgotten commission, and was tapping on the window for him to return. So he set down the heavy valise on the ground, ran back to the side steps, ran up them two at a time, ran into her room, and said:

"Yes! What is it, grandmamma?"

"My dear boy, there is nothing. Oh, you thought I called you? Oh no, I am sorry you came back. I was only catching this fly!" And she showed what was left of it on a napkin.

Lawrence laughed, really good-naturedly. Of course he was tempted to do something else. But he only laughed, said "Good-bye" again, and ran down the steps. He rescued the valise from the care of an old statue of the god Terminus, who was watching it, and ran, a little faster than before, through Billy Kelley's alley. Billy Kelley's alley was a short cut by which he came to Vinton Street, which took him to the electric car. He had not been late for this car, but he was not early for it. It was the car which would take him to the northern stations, where was the train which connected with the Cattaraugus and Opelousas, which, at Trefethen, connected with the Midlands, which would take him to the Hudson River at Albany, and so on to New York, where he was going. So he ran through Billy Kelley's alley. The weight of the valise helped him in running down Vinton Street. But it did not help him quite enough, for he was a hundred paces short of the electric track when the "Limits" car passed, the through car which he needed for the northern stations. He waved his umbrella. But the conductor was looking the other way, and the motor-man did not look at all. If they had seen him they would both have laughed and gone faster. So Lawrence had to wait for the Bradstreet Avenue car, and to take his chances of a connection at Cheever Square.

He looked at his watch rather uneasily, but said, aloud, cheerfully in tone, "Ça ira. We will put it through." Nor did he once say to himself, what is the first thing which occurs to me and my intelligent readers, "If it had not been for grandmamma's ridiculous fly, I should have hit the Limits car." But if he had said this, it would have been true.

II.—BRADSTREET AVENUE

The Bradstreet Avenue car was an open car, with the seats running across. If it had not been a car of that build, this story would never have been written, far less printed; for then all would have been changed.

Lawrence's seat was the last of those in front of the smoking people. He lifted in his valise and followed it. The two women who sat next the street preferred to have him pass them, treading upon their twenty

toes, and, of necessity, wiping the mud from his boots
upon their dresses.   For reasons known to themselves
and to no others, they refused to move in so that he
might take the outer seat.   So he was the better
placed in the little incident which followed.

This was the little incident : As the car ran happily
along James Street, which runs along the edge of the
water at the foot of the hill, Lawrence, who was reading a newspaper, felt a jar, heard a crash, looked up
and saw a large horse in front of him in the car, in
place of the people who had been on the seat.   In an
instant more his own car rose from the right-hand
track, rolled over, and while Lawrence guarded his
head with his arm he rolled over with it.   Something
struck him on the head, and for the next nine hours he
knew nothing.

But I know all, and the reader of these lines shall
know all.   What Lawrence could not have told, I tell.

Pinckney Street, Myrtle Street, and Chestnut Street
descend at right angles to James Street, and cross it.
The hill by which they descend is as steep a hill as will
tolerate the ascent or descent of horses.   Indeed, no
one who could help it would drive up or down Pinckney Street.

But there is one set of men who cannot help it.
They are the men who drive the city's ash-carts.   For
every one has coal fires on Pinckney Street, and there
are many ashes left—nay, some cinders—which must
be carried away.   And on this particular day when
Lawrence was in the Bradstreet Avenue car, on his
way to the northern stations, that he might go to New
York and make his fortune, ash-cart No. 47 was stand-

ing at the door of Mrs. Cowan's house, No. 89, with a very heavy load, the horse facing downhill. The wheels were very carefully blocked, and the stout stick made for the purpose held up the thills. At that moment little Jonas Cowan, with a yellow paper kite, rushed out from the back passage of his mother's house, into which the ash-man had just plunged. Jonas Cowan trailed behind him his yellow paper kite, that it might have the better chance in the street. Jonas was still in petticoats, and knew as little about kites as the reader knows about quaternions.

The kite passed within three feet of the nose of the horse of the ash-cart. The horse started. Pegasus would have started. A saw-horse would have started if it could. The horse started. The guardian stick flew up. The wheels cleared the stones which blocked them. The whole ton of ashes pressed heavily down on the poor horse. He could not help himself—he trotted. He then broke into a run. He rushed down Pinckney Street just as the Bradstreet Avenue car passed it. And he did the only thing a horse with an ash-cart behind him could do—he leaped into the open car.

It was this horse whom Lawrence saw—almost with his last intelligent sight of anything—before the policeman in attendance picked him up and carried him to the hospital.

III.—THE HOSPITAL

The humorous disposition of motor-men and conductors, which makes them look cheerfully on the misfortunes or failures of passengers, has been referred to.

But this disposition did not prevent the officers in charge of the Bradstreet Avenue car from feeling the seriousness of the position when it was overturned.

They rang in the police and emergency corps. Two or three ambulances were in attendance before the wreck was wholly cleared away, so that the bed of an ambulance was ready for Lawrence before the stanchion of the car was lifted off his thighs, binding him to the broken floor. Fortunately for him, perhaps, he was insensible, and knew nothing of the handling, rough of necessity, by which he was lifted to this bed.

It was in the middle of the night, in the faintest twilight given by a screened lamp, that he looked around him first, in the white bed in which they placed him in the hospital. The first thing he really learned was that his arm was tied so that he could not move it. The next was that when he tried to move his legs the effort cost him great pain. This accounted for certain very absurd dreams which he now vainly tried to recall, which had been haunting him just before. His effort was enough to make his attendant lean over the bed and speak to him.

In a whisper this man said, kindly, "How do you feel now?"

"Feel?" said Lawrence, "I feel as if I were tied into a bed and could not get out of it. How in thunder did I get here?"

"You must not speak aloud. You will wake the others. You are all right. Only there was an accident, and you were knocked in the head." And then for the first time Lawrence made out that he had a cloth round his head. That is to say, this was the first time that he knew when the good-natured attendant removed the compress and replaced it by another newly wet with iced water. He was not much disposed to talk. He asked some questions about the horse, the sudden apparition of which he remembered, and then obeyed the nurse's requisition, put gently in manner but firmly in substance, that he should hold his tongue if he could, and that he had better go to sleep. With some little help he found an easier attitude for himself, and then, sooner than he expected, he obeyed both injunctions.

And this was the beginning of weeks on weeks of hospital life. His right arm had been broken in two places, above the elbow and below. Both fractures were simple, there was no difficulty about placing the bones, and the surgeons were encouraging about them. For the rest, one thigh was terribly scraped and scratched and torn in its fleshy integuments, and groups of doctors came and felt and poked and punched, to determine what were certain internal injuries, real or suspected, probable or doubtful. At first they affected to withdraw from the bedside before they talked of these. But after a few days, when Lawrence had approved himself a person of nerve and sense, such affectation came to an end, and they discussed his make-up in his own hearing, much as if he were the stenographer taking notes of their conversation. All this added one entertainment, and that one of the most important, to Lawrence's monotonous day. They told him squarely, very soon after he had won their confidence, that it would be some weeks before they should let him go.

The hospital people had not found who he was till late in the evening. But then the contents of his valise had revealed his name, and his aunt's address had been found. In the morning she appeared, and his cousin Frank, a bright boy, who from that time was his best medium in communicating with the outward world. After a day, the authorities permitted Lawrence to dictate a letter. At his bidding Frank wrote the president of the International Lubricant Company, Limited, to explain what was the accident which had happened to Mr. Lawrence Mitchell. The letter said, in a somewhat bold, copy-book hand, that it would be six weeks probably before he would be able to report at the Lubricant office. He explained also that, so soon as his trunks arrived in New York, whither they had been sent, there would be found in the tray of No. 2 the memoranda on the destructive distillation of colza, petroleum, lard, and sperm oil, with Mr. L. M.'s notes on the same. For the use of these reports and notes, Mr. L. M. enclosed his key.

At the end of ten days a note, which Lawrence thought rather stiff, was received in reply from the president. In a way it expressed a certain regret for the accident. It said that the tables and notes had been found, and were in the hands of Mr. Vance, who would address Mr. Mitchell a separate note regarding them. The key was enclosed, carefully done up in a small envelope. The trunks were awaiting Mr. Mitchell's order. It would be impossible for the International Lubricant to wait six weeks for the opportunity to retain his services. And accordingly the president hoped that Mr. Mitchell would consider their contract at an end. He hoped also that Mr. Mitchell would soon be restored to health. And he had the honor to be the most humble and obedient of Mr. Mitchell's servants. And this was all.

After Lawrence had read the letter, it happened that Frank came in, and brought his grandmother for her first visit to the hospital. Dear old lady, she was most kind and sympathetic. She was most eager to have him well enough to come to the house again. She had brought the *Chautauquan* and a couple of other magazines to cheer him. He kissed her affectionately as she went away. But as she and Frank left the ward, he wrote with his left hand in his note-book:

"How little dear grandmamma thinks that I am laid up here, and have lost my salary, and a position for life, because she killed that old fly. *Ça ira!* We must put this through."

IV.—THE TERRACE

We measure life now by inches and now by miles, now by hours and now by years. To Lawrence, when he saw the horse in front of him, the next second seemed of paramount importance; its weight and worth were more than all other seconds together. But, only half an hour before, he had been looking forward for five years at once, thinking of the time when Mr. Olive, the treasurer and selling agent of the International Lubricant, would probably withdraw from active duty, and when there would be a promotion, all along the line, among the subordinates in that concern.

And now that Lawrence was in bed, the important

17

part of life, far the most important part, seemed the
period before the doctors let him get out. He could
not compare against this the period before he should
be at the World's Fair, or at his next Commencement,
or before the end of the century.

Even before he was to get out of bed there was
another period which had a special interest. If all
went well, and there was no risk of bad weather, or of
taking cold, his bed could be put on the rails and run
out upon the Terrace.

The Terrace was on the same floor. At ten every
morning, if the sun shone bright, the fortunate beds on
his right hand and on his left were pushed out upon
the Terrace. What was much more important, the
people in the beds went also. Neither bed nor inmate
returned till nearly four, if the weather were bright.
And in dear, glowing, golden October the weather,
thank God, almost always was bright. A young doctor with the least possible German lisp, a man with
curly golden hair, who always seemed to Lawrence
like Apollo when he came into Vulcan's smithy, told
Lawrence that before many days, if all went well, he
should go upon the Terrace. So was it that he counted hours and days between the now and the Terrace,
ten times as closely as he counted them between now
and New-year, or between now and his birthday.

At last the happy day came. The modest elms in
the hospital garden showed their best golden leaves
against the dark blue of heaven. A maple, which good
old Dr. Chittenden had sent from Vermont thirty years
before, blazed its most brilliant scarlet. A gingko-tree,
which was the gift to the garden of young Dr. Isukara

from Nagasaki, was contributing the orange. And the
day was simply heaven to Lawrence, as in triumph the
casters of his bed ran down the slope of his threshold
and he was under the open sky of God. Not Baron
Trenck, when he emerged from the water-passage on
the north side of the glacis at Magdeburg, was happier. And I do not think that Baron Trenck was half
so grateful.

And it lasted. When Frank's school was out, he
hurried to the scene. For all worthy men and boys,
and all good angels, had known that on this day, the
11th of October, as if to celebrate the greatest event in
modern history, Lawrence was to be moved to the Terrace. He had wanted nothing till now but to look on
the gingko and the sassafras and the maple and the
elms and the green grass and the blue sky, and on the
white beds and blue parasols of the others. And now
he was not tired of their endless variety. But now he
let Frank bring him a light table, with the last two
numbers of the *Chautauquan*, and *The Making of Modern Europe*, and Prof. McClintock's *Mediæval Poetry*.
Not that he wanted to read himself, but the others
might. And it looked social to have a book or two.

And Frank showed him a spring butterfly he had
been making from a long Waterbury watch-spring and
four bits of binders' board. And they entertained
each other, and, as it proved, all their neighbors on
the Terrace, as they made him flap his ungainly wings,
now slow, now fast; fast when he struck down, slow as
he caught the upward slope and made time to strike
fast again. The butterfly would fall now on No. 37,
now on No. 11, and Frank would run and bring him

back. And all the Terrace, or their end of the Terrace, watched for these uncertain visits. Frank had brought his lunch, but at ten minutes of two he had to go away to school.

Then the pretty girl who was reading to No. 29 went away. And the sun went round towards the west, as the sun will, so that No. 29 had to move her parasol to the other side of her bed. No. 29 was next Lawrence, but through the morning the pretty girl had sat between him and No. 29, and the parasol had cut off even his sight of the pretty girl. Now he could see that No. 29 was a pretty girl also—perhaps the sister or the cousin of the reader.

Now Lawrence told his attendant that he might put up his pillow two or three holes higher, and that he would try to read. They let him read now as much as he wanted to, because he did not read with his hips or right hand.

So he could see that No. 29 was peeping in between two uncut pages of a magazine. She had tried to cut them with a spoon, but it had no edge; and then with a hairpin, but the paper was too strong, and the hairpin only bent in her hand. So it was that Lawrence carefully threw his tortoise-shell knife, with its ivory paper-cutter open, across to No. 29, and said, pleasantly, "Try this cutter." And those were the first words he ever spoke to Clara Fitch.

Now she started, for she was really surprised, and thanked him very prettily. And when she had cut her magazine, and read it all, she asked him if he would not like to see it. And he stretched his left arm as far as he could to take it, and then offered her his *Song and*

Legend of the Middle Ages. And it proved that she had had to give up her Chautauqua reading in the spring, and she did not know what the new year's course was. And he asked her to look at the Romance ballads, and he said he remembered a better translation of Aucassin than Bourdillon's, and repeated some of it. And she asked him to read an amusing story in her magazine about the last scholar in an old school. And the time seemed very short before the attendants came and trundled them all off again, like so many people in Noah's Ark, to the compartments where they belonged.

V.—THE INTERNATIONAL LUBRICANT

Meanwhile the affairs of the International Lubricant dragged and halted wretchedly. This Mr. Vance who was to write to Lawrence personally about the destructive distillation of oils, did write to him personally. And Lawrence, though he thought he had been badly treated, wrote him in Frank's best handwriting a careful and exhaustive letter on the subject, telling him some things he did not know, and making some suggestions as to business which he had not the courage to take.

The truth was that Mr. Vance looked on the whole work of the International Lubricant as a contrivance for putting in his pocket three thousand dollars every year. Whether their oils made things go easier he did not care, he hardly knew. Now Lawrence was glad enough to have his salary once a month—he would not have objected if it had been called his wages, for then he would have had them every week. But as he read, and tried experiments, and destroyed oil by distillation in them, he was always hoping and fancying, and praying indeed, that some wheel somewhere would run easier because he worked. There was a little poem he was forever humming, about a railroad fireman who was hurrying to his sweetheart on a train; and Lawrence, as he hummed, was always thinking that some of his oil was on the slide of the piston of that man's engine. When a formula came out, in his planning, rather better than the one he had tried before, he made some little side figures on the back of an envelope, to see how far it might abridge the passage of a steamer across the Atlantic. He did not dirty his fingers with this colza because he was A by himself A, or Lawrence by himself Lawrence, but because he was partaker in a great firm called "The Universe."

But Mr. Vance did his work as Vance by himself Vance.

The same difference was once observed between two women who were grinding in the same mill. One of them was taken and the other was left.

Mr. Vance had no tears when he was told that this wide-awake, inventive, destructive, and constructive young man of science was not, after all, to be taken into the works. He had not opposed the appointment. But certainly he had not suggested it. When, therefore, the president had told him that Mr. Mitchell could not come for some weeks, that there had been a bad accident, Mr. Vance said he was very sorry. This was not true. Then he had taken the occasion to say that his office was very much pressed—that he had

hoped Mr. Mitchell would relieve him. Then he had
waited a moment for the president, and the president
had said nothing. Then Mr. Vance had said that perhaps they might make some temporary arrangement.
And still the president said nothing. Then after half
a minute more Mr. Vance said that there was an intelligent young man who had been doing some calculating and copying for him at home, who understood
the detail already, and that perhaps he might take him
into the office as an assistant till some better arrangement could be made.

This is the sort of half-plan which hard-pressed presi-
dents are apt to be pleased with. And the president
of the I. L. said that if the young man had some
experience Mr. Vance might engage him, and Mr.
Vance suggested a low salary for the young man. So
that was settled.

Now the young man of experience was in fact a
brother of Mrs. Vance, who had been dismissed from
his last employment because his cash would never
balance at night. By employing him in Lawrence's
place the I. L. saved, or thought it saved, eighteen
hundred dollars a year.

Had Mr. Vance ever heard of Lawrence's grandmother, or had Eugene, who was the brother of Mrs.
Vance, they would have said, "We owe this good fortune to the old lady's wish to kill that fly." In a way
they did, but not wholly. If Mr. Vance had not been
what he was, and the president what he was, things
would not have fallen out that way.

VI.—THE TERRACE AGAIN

Meanwhile Lawrence, who had no longer to look forward to his first day on the Terrace, looked forward for his second and third and fourth. And there is no harm in saying that he looked forward with hope that the good angels might appoint his place next to the place of No. 29, whom he soon came to know as Miss Clara Fitch. On the second day he had no such luck; and it was impossible to ask her to ask her push-people to put her next to him. Lawrence did not know whether he wanted to be out early, so that no other bed might be thrust before his, or late, so as to urge his pusher to put him next her. He did what was wise—that is, he took his pushers into full confidence. If he had not, they would have known what he wanted. And it was just as well that they should know. He had already made himself a favorite with everybody, and the pushers were as eager as he was to secure his object.

Whether they told the pushers of the women's ward what they wanted I do not know, nor will this reader ever know. Only this I know—that the chances, by the law of chances, were 476 to 1 that these two patients would not come together on any special day on the Terrace; and that, as things went, ordered or not I do not say, it "happened," as we are fond of saying, that, four days out of five of that autumn, Lawrence was rolled to the berth on the right or left of Miss Fitch, or Miss Fitch rolled to the place on the left or right of Mr. Mitchell. For this the reader may account as he pleases. Besides this I only know that of the arrangements necessary for this purpose Miss Clara Fitch knew nothing. Nor can I tell what she wanted. What Lawrence Mitchell wanted I have told already.

So it was not on one day only that these young people were able to exchange their magazines, their paper-knives, or their fans. And Lawrence began to give Frank more specific orders as to what he was to bring from his grandmother's house, or from the libraries, or from the book-stores.

Miss Fitch's cousins came with a certain regularity to read to her, between eleven and two. These hours Lawrence and Frank had to themselves, either for studies of lubricants, or for discussions about the model of the *Vigilant* and *Valkyrie*, or for experiments on the butterfly. But about a quarter before two the visitors went away, and the patients were screwed up in their beds to have their mid-day meals. These did not last long, and then there were nearly two hours when Lawrence could direct his attention and attentions to his pretty neighbor, and gratify, so far as he and Frank and the telegraph and the mail and the special-delivery stamps could, any wishes she had expressed the day before. Frank brought him, very early in the affair, a lovely long beefsteak-and-chop-turner, far more available for passing things from bed to bed than any other kind of tongs.

For instance, one happy Tuesday, when the raw-boned and skinny cousin left, with ill-disguised satisfaction, as the dinner-trays came, Lawrence began at once with Miss Clara.

" Your cousin is reading you 'The Ring and the Book.' "

" Yes," said she, good-naturedly, but pretending to yawn, "and I am dreadfully tired. We are working at the third explanation of the mystery. It is very subtle, but it is very long."

" If I had to initiate anybody into the great company of Browningites, I should not begin at that end," said Lawrence, boldly.

" Is not one end as good as another ? They used to tell me to begin with the inner end of my embroidery silks, but I did not know that you handled poets in that way."

" They say," said he, " that you can read Emerson up the page as well as down. But, with Browning, you have to begin with the beginning, and go step by step to the end."

"Do you ever get there ?" said she, laughing.

"Indeed you do, indeed you do, if you do not break your neck in a hurry at the first. But how is it, Miss Fitch, that you did not begin in our dear Chautauqua ? That was what started me."

" Chautauqua ?"

" Yes, but long before you began. I have their volume here. Let me read you some of my favorites."

How fortunate that Lawrence should have had the volume! Fortunate, but that he had foreknown, foreseen, and prepared for the whole conversation! When Skin-and-Bones finished her screed of the " Ring and the Book " on Monday, Lawrence had telegraphed to Frank to bring him his nice volume of the Chautauqua selections from Browning. Thus it was that he " hap-

pened to have" that little volume lying at his side.
And so it was that they had that pleasant afternoon as
he read her his favorites. And so he ventured to say
when they parted, " I hope we may be near each other
again."

And near each other again they were, as has been
said. Four pleasant days out of five they were near
each other. And if it rained, and Lawrence had to
stay in the ward, the imprisonment seemed to give him
only new opportunity to show Miss Fitch how long his
arms were.

Lawrence did not dare send a regular order for
flowers to Galvin to be delivered every day to Miss
Fitch in Ward C. C. But he did make Frank bring
him cut flowers every day, and with the beefsteak-
tongs it was easy to pass a carnation or a maurandia
across to her.

Of course there would come botches. That odious
fifth day would come, when the men's ward was too
late, or Ward C. C. was too late, so that Lawrence had
to get along as he might with a deaf Swede on one side
of him and a cross Russian on the other. But when
this happened he called it "the fortune of war," and
made plans more extravagant than ever for the next
day. The pushers and nurses never saw his temper
ruffled.

VII.—FOLGER FITCH

Sometimes there was an embarrassment of riches on
the Terrace. People knew at what hour they might
come, and they did not always come at the hour when

there was most room for them. Frank was furious
one day when he had brought a long new Waterbury
watch-spring, and some butterfly wings twice as large
as they had ever tried, and all was ready for an experiment on a magnificent scale—he was furious because an old gray-haired college professor came in just
as his cousin Lawrence got to work. The tools and
the tray had to be pushed aside, while the two men
talked about the correlation of forces, and poor Frank
was left to walk up and down the garden and blow
thistledown.

Miss Fitch had three regular visitors, who came in
turn. Lawrence did not know their names, but practically he and Frank had christened them Nasturtium,
Clover Blossom, and Skinflint. I do not say that
Lawrence ever used these names, but he understood
them when Frank used them. To the great surprise,
not to say anger, of Skinflint, when she arrived on
time one day, with her "Ring and Book," she found a
good-natured looking gentleman sitting on the camp-
stool which she generally filled. And while she would
gladly have stunned him to earth with one of her chill-
ing Medea glances, it was hardly reasonable for her to
do so, because, as she saw, he was poor dear Clara's
father.

For Mr. Folger Fitch had given up a day from the
works that he might come down to the hospital himself and see how his darling Clara was coming on.

Now, whatever were the senior cousin's duties or
rights in the business, it was clear that Clara's father
had as good rights, or better. Clara herself was very
quick and very good-natured. She was really greatly

obliged to her three cousins for the promptness with which they had rallied to care for her as soon as they heard of her accident. And she did not choose that Miss Astræa should be hurt, even if she were unreasonable. So she told her that she must not go away; she made her father understand that now was a good minute for him to see the superintendent, and as he turned to go to the office she introduced him to Lawrence.

"Father, this is Mr. Mitchell. He was hurt when I was, and he is very careful for all of us."

So Folger Fitch and Lawrence Mitchell began talking together. Mr. Fitch bowed courteously, gave his hand to Lawrence, and hardly let him speak before he thanked him, he really knew not why. Lawrence, who was waiting for Frank's arrival, showed him where Frank's seat was, and begged him to sit down. As he did so, Lawrence laid down his paper. He knew Mr. Fitch at once as one of the largest manufacturers of light wagons in the country. And he said, "What I am reading will interest you. It is Sir Charles Trefethen's paper on the effect produced by high rates of speed on the lubricants employed."

At once he dashed into conversation. There followed what is one of the happiest bits of talk always, when an accomplished man of science, who has touched a subject from the theoretic end, meets an accomplished man of affairs, who has begun at the end of practical experience.

Clara had to call, laughing, to her father once, to tell him he must really go and thank the superintendent and the doctor, and that then he might come back and talk as much as he would. He laughed and said to Lawrence that he always obeyed her. But he was soon back again, and the two plunged into questions about patent axles, and metal on metal, what friction was and what it was not.

Lawrence delighted him by showing him a computation he had made in his absence, on a bit of blotting-paper, as to the number of years of efficient life added to the people of the United States if only some invention made the light carriages of the United States do their average work of a day in five minutes less time than was needed the year before. He laughed, and said:

"When they broke me to pieces the other day, because my car, for want of proper oil, perhaps, was not fifteen feet farther forward, I was on my way to the International Lubricant Company, where I was to be a superintendent."

Folger Fitch's face clouded as he said, "I know them."

Lawrence wondered on what unfortunate subject he had spoken then. In an instant he changed it.

"I wonder you gentlemen leave your carriages to the chances of wayside blacksmiths and hostlers. Why not oil a carriage as carefully as a sewing-machine? I should like to show you my drawings for a self-oiler, which I would fill at New-year's Day, and which would need no other oiling for a year."

"Have you thought of that?" said Folger Fitch. "I have, too."

And at that moment Miss Astræa abandoned her book at last and gave him a chance to speak to his daughter.

VIII.—FREEDOM

And at last it proved that there were no internal injuries in Lawrence's make-up, and, perhaps, never had been any. Auscultating and thumping and rubbing and rolling him over and back revealed nothing amiss. The two breaks in the arm had knit firmly. The wounds in the leg had healed, as a healthy youngster's will. And the doctor and the surgeon and all said that the rapid recovery was due mostly to his patience, that he had never complained, and had shown no desire to go away. He might go now, as soon as he chose, if only he would report once a week at the hospital, for them to make wholly sure of the "internal injuries." So his grandmother's carriage came, and Frank, in great state, to take him away.

Lawrence sent his card round to Ward C. C., where was Miss Clara, not so fortunate. But she was much better, and very pretty she looked, as he came to say good-bye. And Lawrence made the nurse say that Dr. Lavender had said that the next week Miss Fitch might drive out for an hour. And Lawrence made her promise that he might bring his grandmother's carriage to take her. And so it was.

Miss Astræa had to go, too, and Lawrence could say nothing, as he turned from his seat to speak to them, but that black was black and white white, and matters of equal import. Still, he was driving the horses that were dragging her carriage, and he had so far a sort of charge of her. That was as it should be, and sometime he would say something more to her.

And the day came when he did. With an occasional
ride, with a bunch of flowers to-day or a new book to-
morrow, or a call on the Terrace, he managed to keep
up a flitting and occasional intercourse with Miss Clara
until the happy day when she also was told that her
cure could be perfected outside the hospital doors.

It was determined that before she took the long
journey to Phaetonville, where the works were, she
should spend a week at the Trefoils' house. For Clara
had been on her way to the Trefoils' on that fatal
morning when the little boy's kite frightened the horse
that ran away with the cart which smashed the car in
which Lawrence and Clara, all unconscious of each
other's existence, were sitting.

And before Clara could go about freely, there were
long mornings when she could sit in Mrs. Trefoil's
back parlor, and Lawrence would make long morning
visits there. Florence Trefoil was the cousin whom
he and Frank liked best of the three hospital visitors.
She was the one whom they had nicknamed Clover
Blossom, because one morning she had a clover blossom in her button-hole. And it almost always happened that when Lawrence called on Clara, Florence
would be summoned from the room just for a minute,
and often these minutes extended to hours. Or sometimes Florence had to go to the weekly meeting of the
Society for the Employment of the Upper Classes.
And in these long visits of Lawrence's to Clara, after
he was quite sure that he did not tire her, he read
Browning to her, or Austin Dobson. Or sometimes
he did not.

But it was not long—it was before the visit was

over—that he had persuaded her that that fortunate and happy ride in the James Street car, which was the first ride they ever took together, was not to be the last—not by any means.

> "Why not forever ride, we two,
> With life forever old, yet new?"

He was sure he did not know. And Clara, dear child, she did not know either. And she was very sweet and pretty when she told him so.

So it was that the very next day he made his grandmother order out the carriage—which was a property quite distinct from the victoria or the carry-all or the village-cart, and seldom appeared—and old George the coachman got himself up in special magnificence, and took the state whip and held it more vertically than ever. Lawrence helped his grandmother up-stairs, and she made the state call on Mrs. Trefoil and Angela Trefoil and Florence, and on our pretty Clara, in the most cordial and tender way. And Miss Astræa, the other cousin, happened in to make an incidental inquiry about the choice of a treasurer for the Occupation Society, and she joined in the congratulations and general overflow of enthusiasm, with just acridity enough to remind them all that they were human. It was well that they should remember that life is not made up of such fortunate events as accidents to street railways.

Just as Lawrence's grandmother had finished her visit—as they came to that sacred period in such occasions when everybody stands up for a quarter of an hour and is particularly cordial because they are all saying good-bye—the dear old lady turned to Lawrence and said:

"My dear boy, as I have sat at home, and sent to inquire after you, I have thought so often that if you had not come back to speak to your old grandmother again, you would have taken another car, and all this would not have happened."

"My dear grandmother," said Lawrence, "IF is a very wicked word. But on this occasion, if I had not seen you that last time—why, the world would have come to an end."

IX.—LUBRICANTS

In New York things did not move so smoothly. In the office of the International Lubricant there seemed to be more grit and drag, and consequent friction, than anywhere else.

Six months before, the half-yearly accounts had shown some bad falling off in sales, a heavy accumulation of manufactured goods, and the loss of some old customers. The president tried to persuade himself and the few stockholders who came to the annual meeting that this was only a temporary check. It was true that they passed a dividend, he had said; but that would not happen again. The absence of their largest orders, those from Hubbs & Tyre, was due only to the death of old Mr. Hubbs. The president had written to Mr. Tyre, and he was sure that matter would be made all right and any difficulty smoothed over. Every one knew that the great depression of business had checked travel, the president said. If people did not travel they did not oil the wheels, he said. And so the lubricants were stored up in the warehouses, instead of being used up on the axles. But this was, of course, but temporary, he said, and the lubricants existed all the same. They would be sold, sooner or later, and then the company would have their dividends again.

This seemed to him very satisfactory. But the younger stockholders grumbled. And it was after a motion from Mr. Hustler, an attorney who always made a fuss at corporation meetings, that the directors who were re-elected had promised to take some new steps to keep the old corporation even with the time.

It was in taking these new steps that they had hunted up a young scientific expert named Lawrence Mitchell, with whom the reader is acquainted. When people talked of putting new life into the company, he was the new life. Unfortunately, grandmamma's fly and the means taken for its destruction had interfered with Mr. Mitchell's duties in lubricating the machinery of the I. L. corporation. And, in fact, as all hot wheels will do when they are hard driven, its working wheels grew hotter and needed more attention.

Neither Mr. Vance nor the president was the person to give them that attention. Far less was Mr. Eugene Ripka, who had been called in to assist Mr. Vance. Mr. Vance had long since passed that dangerous line in business which marks the point when a man is glad because the mail is small and the morning visits few. Mr. Vance was glad when he could shut his desk at half-past three and take it for granted that nobody would come in before the office closed at four. He had come to that very dangerous point when an official says, "I do not see that we can do anything about it," and when he is very glad to say so. And his new clerk, Eugene Ripka, was only too willing to indulge him in these early departures. " I shall not go till five, sir, if you care to leave the office to me." Mr. Ripka came early, and opened the letters. He stayed late, sent off the mail and filed the copies. There never was a summer when Mr. Vance was able so often to take the early afternoon train to his suburban home.

This was very pleasant for Mrs. Vance and her boys and girls. But, in spite of such prosperity, the sales of lubricants did not seem to advance. Mr. Vance and the president had one or more conversations in which Mr. Vance recommended the renting of the upper story of the larger factory to some enterprising young electric - light men. But this annoyed the president, who was trying at the same moment to find store-room for the oils which no one had ordered. When the principal of an establishment wants to enlarge its work, and the chief agent wants to let its vacant rooms, you may be quite sure that its affairs need more than mechanical oiling.

So sure is this sign that the story need not stop to describe Mr. Hustler's unfriendly visit to the office, nor how he insisted on examining the books. Nor need we tell in detail how he insisted that the president should call a special stock-meeting, and, when the president refused, how he obtained the necessary signatures and called it over the president's head. When the meeting was held, at half-past ten one morning in the office, poor Mr. Vance was beside himself because he could not get the safe open. He had two or three locksmiths to help him. For Mr. Eugene Ripka had not come in, and only he knew the combination. When the safe was opened, in personal presence of the stockholders, the books were there. And Mr. Vance showed, with some pride, quite a large cash balance which he had been hoarding with a view to a dividend. But, alas! inquiry at the banks where this balance was kept proved that Mr. Eugene Ripka had drawn it all, at several distinct periods of the day before; and inquiry at his rooms showed that he had not been seen since six in the evening.

He has never been seen by Mr. Vance or the president since, and the International Lubricant is in the hands of a receiver.

X.—THE MORAL

A brief statement of this appeared in the *Argus* the day after Lawrence and Clara were married. He showed it to her in the palace-car as they started on their wedding journey. He told her the story, as from time to time he had heard it from his uncle Mr. Smiley, who was one of the smaller stockholders.

"They would say," said he, "that all this happened because my grandmother killed a fly. But it did happen, if anything happens, because Mr. Vance is lazy, the president is obstinate, and this Mr. Ripka is a rascal."

Then, after a pause, he said:

"Some would say that you and I are in this car because my grandmother killed a fly."

And Clara said, "But it does happen because you are brave and kind and loving and true—" And he interrupted her to say, "And because you are the dearest girl who lives."

But Clara checked him and said:

"Because we are all under guidance, and God is on the side of people who try to do their duty."

And he said, "And also, because some things are written in heaven."

When they came to New York they went to Tiffany's and picked out a curious pin, made to represent a large fly in enamel. It had two eyes made from small diamonds.

They sent it as their wedding present to grandmamma.

JOHN RICH AND LUCY POOR

I

I LIKE John Rich. I always liked him. We went
to school together, and he "prompted" me one day
when the master asked me what was the southern cape
of Greenland. I thought it was Cape Good-bye, but
John Rich told me it was Cape Farewell. So I got an
"approbation card," and John Rich got a bad mark
for "communicating."

People say John Rich is lazy. I do not think so;
and after I have told this story I want some intelligent
reader to tell me if he thinks so. The fact is that
some people always think "them littery fellows" are
lazy. Because we do not always work with our coats
off, and because our hands are not blistered, people
think we are lazy. Just read this story, and then write
and tell me if you think so.

John Rich was in love with Lucy Poor, and she with
him. But her father disliked their marriage, because,
he said, John was only one of those literary fellows,
and that he had no regular income. He said if John
would go into a bank, or apply himself to business,
that would be one thing. But he said that to have
nothing but writing for a business, that was another.

John was what is called a hack-writer. Macaulay

says the race of Grub Street hacks is extinct. I do not know where the Grub Street hacks have gone; John Rich is not at all extinct. Dr. Johnson, who was a hack himself, and a very good one, too, does not use the word at all, as I found when I wrote my excellent story of the journey Joshua Cradock took in a hack. He went half round the world in one, and his wife went round the other half in another, and they met at Lake Baikal. But the modern dictionaries will tell you that in literature a man is a hack who writes what other people want him to write. Some of them add that he is underpaid.

Now I have a certain respect for people who do what they are wanted to do. There are people who will only do what they themselves want to do. And I observe that they are rather proud of this. But I was brought up in the Christian religion, in which people are taught to work for others, if it is honest work. So I have a certain affection for hacks. Whether John Rich is lazy, because he is a hack, you shall see.

II

It is true that John Rich never works in the half-hour after breakfast. Not if he can help it. But on this day I am telling you about he lay on the sofa, which is a good long sofa and wide, and read *To-day*. Now *To-day* happened to say that Mr. Gansevoort's income had been "sworn," whatever that is, at three hundred and fifty thousand dollars for the last year. For this was all in the antediluvian days of the income-tax.

John Rich said to Miss Clara, his secretary:

"Miss Clara, they talk of this three hundred and fifty thousand dollars as if it were a large income. Will you tell me what Monte Cristo's income was?"

Miss Clara said that she believed Monte Cristo's fortune was seven million dollars, and that his income was, if estimated at five per cent.—and here John Rich interrupted her, and said:

"Yes, I thought so. Five times seven is thirty-five. That is only three hundred and fifty thousand dollars a year. And Gansevoort has the same income as Monte Cristo. Would you mind telling me how much that is in a day—I mean, how much it makes if there are three hundred and thirteen days in a year? Leap-year does not come often."

Miss Clara did her little sum promptly, and said that Monte Cristo's and Mr. Gansevoort's income was eleven hundred and eighteen dollars a day. Did he mind the cents?

No, John Rich said he did not mind the cents.

"I was thinking," he said, "that when you and I do four thousand words in an hour, at three cents a word, that is one hundred and twenty dollars an hour. Nine hours would be one thousand and eighty dollars. There will be thirty-eight dollars more needed, and we should do thirty-eight dollars in nineteen minutes more."

Miss Clara said yes. But she said that really there were more than thirty-eight dollars to care for; there were thirty-eight dollars and twenty-one cents.

"Could you get Miss Annie and Louise and Hattie and that little black-eyed girl to help us? Perhaps Ysabel would come, and Helen and Mabel."

Miss Clara said she would see. If not, there was the German lady, who would like to come, and Mrs. William Penn, who was on the staff before she was married, was now on a visit in town. She would like to come.

So John Rich asked her to telegraph to these ladies, and if they could not come to make up the full staff of ten. And he never said another word about it. Miss Clara did the whole. How well she did it you shall see.

III

John Rich, you must know, is a favorite with editors. I will tell you why. First, as has been intimated, he is not above his business. He is a hack, and he knows it. This means that he is willing to do what other people want, as well as he can. He has no nonsense about its being another man's place to do it, or that this or that should not be expected of him. Then he has no nonsense about waiting for an inspiration, if the work has to be done to-day. His work is ready, I mean, when he says it shall be. If you write to him for an article on Baffin's Bay, and he says you shall have it February 31st, you will have it on the 31st of February, whenever that day comes round, as well done as he can write it. Maybe Admiral Belcher would make a better article, but this is John Rich's best, and you know it is. There it is, absolutely ready for the press. Not a comma wanting — not a gaiter button, as Napoleon the Little said. And it is just as long as he promised, and as short. Did his first note say four hundred and twelve words? The second note, which goes with the article, will not say, "I have overrun your limit, but you can cut it down."

More than this, he never rolled up any copy in his life. He would die first.

Now from all this it happens that his copy is ready for press the moment it enters the editor's office. Suppose that editor wants to go to the farewell dinner to Sir Walter Besant, and suppose he has two forms of the magazine to make up. Here comes in John Rich's article at the moment when the editor's cab-horse is pawing impatiently at the door, as John Rich would not say. The editor is perfectly sure that he has what he asked for. He sends the article up to the printing-office, knowing that it will be all right. It will not say that William III. was the uncle of John Lackland. Far better than this, it will not overrun the space given to it. Its proof has been read in the typewriter copy before it came to the editor. So the editor gives it out at once, goes to the dinner-party, and the next time he meets John Rich asks him for six more articles.

All which it might be wished that young writers would remember.

In the case of our story, John Rich told Miss Clara that she might write to Mr. McClure this note:

"DEAR MR. McCLURE,—I will send on Mondays for your syndicate a leader for weeklies of eight hundred words. The old terms. Let me know if you wish them longer or shorter.
                    "Always yours,   JOHN RICH."

And he said to Miss Clara:

"Same to Irving Syndicate, New Syndicate, American Syndicate, Bacheller Syndicate, and Live Question

Bureau, only changing Monday, of course, to Tuesday, Wednesday, etc. One a day here." And Miss Clara wrote the six notes that morning, and he signed them. Then he dictated these notes:

"DEAR ALLEN,—I will begin 'The Memoir of the Century' at once. You suggested eight thousand two hundred words a number. Let it be so. The book is mine after twelve months. The old rate.

"Always yours,   JOHN RICH."

And he said to Miss Clara:

"Same to L'Estrange for the serial novel. Say we will send the title when he wants it. They like it to run ten numbers.

"Same, changing what is necessary, to Harry. He wants short love stories, alternating with adventure. Look at his note. I think they are seven thousand four hundred words—something to fit their pages. Of course, we do what they wish."

Then John Rich made some notes on his blotting-paper, and asked Miss Clara to look up the advertisement of the *Chicago Herald's* prize competition. "I do not mean to try for their stories. We have too many now to write. But what they call an Epic pleased me. I will try that on alternate days for ten days. That will give you young ladies an hour off on those days. You can arrange about the hours with the other ladies. I like to have you first after breakfast, and first after lunch. And, Miss Clara, please have a riding-skirt here, or wear up something in the morning with which you can mount a horse. Pleasant days we shall want to get some air. And, if you can help it, do not engage any one who is afraid of a boat, or who

does not row well. We shall want to be on the river
or the harbor afternoons. Before breakfast I like to
be alone."

"I could come round then just as well," said Miss
Clara, inquiringly.

"Oh no," said John, "we will take it easily. I
should be sorry to forget how to make p and q. As
things stand, there are eleven letters of the alphabet
which I write in exactly the same way.

"Now we will clear off the mail, and then we can
go to work to-morrow morning."

IV

And so they did, if you call this work. Lucy Poor's
father does not, as I told you. Tuesday morning John
Rich got out of bed at twenty-three minutes before
seven, as he always does. He dressed, and in his room,
by his desk, found a nice cup of coffee ready for him.
He wrote that leader, which I think you may remember, called "Forests and Sinking Funds." The New
Syndicate placed it in twenty-three Sunday papers on
the twelfth day after. Then John Rich took *To-day*
and lay on the sofa till his breakfast-bell rang. He
was ready for his breakfast, and his breakfast was
ready for him. Then he walked round the garden, he
wrote Lucy Poor a little note, he ordered Doogue to
send her a box of flowers. She lived, alas! eight miles
away, at Waban. At half-past eight Miss Clara came
in. She was quite ready for the ride. But they had
their stent of four thousand words to do first. John

lay on the sofa, she sat at her desk, and he dictated.
It was that story of "The Pine-tree and the Palm."
You read it that day you went up the North River,
when you forgot to look at the scenery. John had it
all in mind—had had it in mind since he thought of it
at the Alpha Delta dinner. Both he and Miss Clara
were in good condition for writing, and in thirty-two
minutes and fourteen seconds the work was done in
her pretty short-hand.

John had been putting on his shoes and gaiters ever
since the fence broke down—in the story, you remember—while the blind boy ran for the doctor, and missed
the way.

"Boot and saddle!" he cried, when he saw that Miss
Clara's pencil had reached the bottom of page twenty.
"Boot and saddle!" and they both mounted. He lives
just out of town. Miss Clara rides well, and they go
so often that the horses, though they are hired, know
their riders. They both knew, Miss Clara and John
Rich, that they had saved the time for the ride by
writing fast, and that Madame Gutenschrift would be
at her desk in sixty minutes from the time they started.
But, with the Park and the Arboretum and the Brook-
way and the Fen-way, you can have a good scamper
in eighty minutes, and so at one minute past ten John
was at the work-room again, and Miss Clara hanging
up her hat before she sat down in the Round-room at
her pet typewriter.

Typewriters are quite human, and they know their
mistresses and are known of them.

V

As for John Rich, he went into his own room and shook hands with Madame Gutenschrift, who was an old friend. I do not myself think that madame writes nearly as fast as Miss Clara does. But she thinks she does. And it made no difference; for in the *Memoirs* you have to look up the authorities, and there is more or less walking around and marking passages for copying.

"Good-morning, madame. You look as if you were glad to be at honest work again." Madame laughed, and said that everything seemed natural. And John began, even as he unbuttoned his gaiters:

"On the 1st of January, 1801, men thought that," etc., etc. Is it not written, or printed, in the first volume of the *Memoirs of the Nineteenth Century?* He walked up and down for a little while. He then lay on the sofa with a rug drawn over his feet. Sharp at eleven Nora came in with two cups of coffee, that kind which is the color of the cheek of a brunette in Seville, and with a little plate of those nice stamped biscuits, like miniature waffles, which come in tin boxes from Peek & Frean. John stopped long enough to thank Nora, and he sipped his coffee as he walked up and down. As for madame, she had to take her chances for hers when he paused in dictation to take down a volume of the *Annual Register*. So they forged on, she, brave little woman, never flinching. Her book was paged, as all the books were, and ruled for two-hundred words a page, so that he need only

look over her shoulder to see where they were. But
he knew the rate so well that he did not even look
over her shoulder. The stream flowed on placidly and
surely till quarter of twelve, and then he said :

" Where are we, madame ?"

" We have just turned thirty-nine."

" Good," said John. " I guessed as much. I hope
you are not too tired. We are nearly through."

This meant that the little woman, with all his stops
and waits, had written her seven thousand eight hundred words in an hour and three-quarters. Two hundred words more filled the morning's stent, and in less
than a hundred seconds John dictated them, coming
out at " may be surprised to hear that at such an era—"

"That will do for to-day, madame. There will be
lunch in the Round-room, and some of the other ladies
are there. I shall walk in the garden."

VI

John Rich had, and still has, what the makers ad-
vertise as a "gentle lure to exercise." It is a very
small sickle on the end of a hoe-handle. It is a tool
with which you can stir up the hard ground or cut
out pigweed or "pussly" without stooping. As John
walked round with his gentle lure you might mistake
him for a shepherd with his crook if the costume had
fitted. So John walked up and down in his garden for
the hour from twelve to one, most of the time in the
hemlock avenue. But when he came to a bed of
shortia or of pansies he would tickle the ground with

the gentle lure.   He was turning over the lines of the
prologue of the prize poem.   This is a good place to
say that it took the prize four months after.

He had just finished, to his mind, that fine verse
which you will remember, which ends with the line,

> "Where should the soldier rest but where he fell?"

when the rattle of a carriage drew him to the garden
gate that he might be hospitable.

The carriage was the Poors' carry-all.   But, alas!
Lucy was not in it.   Mr. Poor and the two smallest
children and Mrs. Poor made the party, with Asaph,
who drove.

"No, we cannot stop a minute.   We are late now.
Only Lucy sent round these lilies-of-the-valley to Miss
Clara, and I believe there is a note for you."

And so the carry-all drove away.   And as it went
Mr. Poor said, in a half-whisper, which even Asaph over-
heard, and in a grumbling tone:

"Think of a young fellow like that, who might be
at honest work, fooling round in the garden at one
o'clock in the day!"

Mr. Poor did not refer to what he was himself doing.

VII

John went in, called Miss Clara from the Round-
room, and gave her Lucy's flowers.   This was after
he had read Lucy's note.   Then he dictated to Miss
Clara the verses he had been hammering on while he
used the "gentle lure."   It took literally but two min-

19

utes—" it is so hard to make them in poetry." Then he
called Miss Clara back with him to the Round-room,
where all the staff were, coming or going. Madame
Gutenschrift even had her "things" on, for some afternoon shopping, before she began to put her eight
thousand words through the typewriter.

The buzz of talk ceased, a little slowly, as they saw
that the chief had something to say.

"Ladies, all," he said, "here is a note from Mr. and
Mrs. Viking, who will like to take us all, or as many
as will go, off in the *Undine*. There is just a good
sailing wind, and she will be at the Point at sharp
2.40. We shall go from here in the electric, and those
of you who want to get your best bonnets must turn
up as you can. We may not be back till eight. But
there will be some sort of shebang to bring us
home."

At this announcement there was general glee, for the
girls had all rather be on the sea, in decent weather,
than in the work-room. Then John Rich took his
own lunch—clam chowder *ad lib.*, and coffee likewise.
Then he lay down and slept an hour. This gave him
and Miss Clara just ten minutes to go to the Point, and
at sharp 2.40 they, with all the young ladies, were
on the *Undine*. Old Captain Carver, the skipper,
nodded with an approving smile, hauled in the gangway plank with his own hand, and cast off.

The *Undine* swept out gracefully, and all was well.
The girls all adjusted themselves to their favorite seats,
lounging-places, and partners, as if Mrs. Viking's hospitality were not a novelty to them.

As for John Rich, he called Miss Ysabel; they found

a cool place in the shade of the forward water-tank, and he began on the serial novel.

"I do not know that you will agree with me," he had said to Miss Clara. "You and I take the short story first, because we have to be fresh then. I have put the serial novel after lunch—well, you see, don't you? Then the 'Reminiscences,' and the 'Calendar,' and the 'Personals'—any fool could do them, even if he were sitting on a jury."

So he gave Miss Ysabel four thousand words of the serial. It was written on the Trollope plan, which is a very good one. You take a skeleton story down from your closet, and hang upon it the talk and the incident of the last twenty-four hours. Miss Ysabel writes fast; she did the four thousand by quarter-past four. Then John had a frolic with Oscar Viking, chasing him from one end of the boat to the other, and hiding from him in the launch. But by half-past four Oscar was tired. John beckoned Miss Louise, and they finished the first part of the serial. It was going to the *Century*, and they like eight thousand two hundred words there.

Mrs. Viking liked to put the children to bed early, and so the yacht rounded to at the Point just at seven o'clock. John and Miss Clara went up in the street-car together, on the back seat.

"We have had a good time," he said, "and now there is nothing to do which will keep anybody awake. A fly could do the 'Personals' and the 'Calendar' and not know he had touched them."

"That indeed," said Miss Clara; and she bade him good-bye. Then the car stopped and she went home, sure she should find a nice letter from Will Watrous. And she did. Good girl. She went to bed early, and she slept as good angels sleep, and was up at five in the morning, so that all her day's work was on typewriter before eight the next day.

As for John, he went into the house with Miss Louise and Miss Mabel. As he said, they had nothing but the "Personals" and the "Calendar," the least possible work, though the best paid, as a reckless world orders. Every girl had brought in her contribution in writing that morning. Miss Clara had told them that they had to furnish ten each. John had marked with red pencil all there was in his mails, and these Miss Lilian had copied. After afternoon tea on the deck he had dictated every word of gossip which Mrs. Viking had told him, or of such as her husband had brought from the club. So now, as he took scrap by scrap from the trayful of this stuff which lay beside him, he had only to read, hardly to change the language of the words before him, as he dictated :

"Miss Alice Black has accepted the position of governess in the family of Rev. Dean Golightly in Copake."

"Mr. Frank Jones has joined the party to go to Baffin's Bay in search for Mr. Peary."

"Mrs. Cleveland has changed her nurse, and Miss Bridget Sullivan takes the place of Miss Nora Shay," and so on, and so on.

"The only thing you have to be careful about," said John to Miss Louise, who was new at all this, "is that by no accident shall one word of the least possible interest, value, or use to anybody creep in. That belongs in the news columns, but not in 'Personals.'"

And so Louise went off to copy her four thousand words, and by 9.30 Miss Mabel had taken hers. Those were the scraps of history of what has happened on the 21st of July, since on that particular day of the month Adam asked Eve to give him an old-fashioned white rose. Of course John had made ready for this all through the last year. All is, as you read, when there is a date in history, you mark that passage for copying. taking care only to mark about four thousand words a day. These index themselves as soon as they are copied, and when you get round to that day in your work, why, there you are. It is the only work, except "Personals" and "Pleasantries," which does itself and requires no thought. So it is best to leave it to the end of the day.

Then John took his hat and went down to the Castle Theatre, where they were doing *A Fool and His Money,* and they did it very well. John had a good laugh with the Trenholms for an hour, and came home and went to bed.

Lucy Poor's father was also at the Castle Theatre. He did not like to talk to Lucy about her lover, for he was fond of her, as every one is. But as he undressed that night he said to her mother:

"That lazy dog, John Rich, was lounging at the theatre to-night; and this afternoon as we came up the harbor I saw him fooling with some boys on Viking's boat. You know what he was doing at his own house when we called there. He certainly knows how to waste time better than any one I ever saw."

Mrs. Poor did have the spirit to say, "My dear Le-

onidas, if you had not been in those three places you
would not have seen him."

Then Leonidas changed the subject, and they went to
bed.

And so on, and so on, and so on.   As the reader has
noticed in reading biography, the life of "these littery
fellars" furnishes little incident.   John rose the next
day at twenty-three minutes before seven, and the next,
and the next, and always.   On the particular Wednesday which is the second day of this story, he wrote his
"Syndicate Leader" for the Irving Syndicate instead
of McClure's Syndicate, but that change is not much of
an "incident," even in a short story.   At eight Miss
Clara came in as fresh as a rose.   She did not say so,
but she had just had another charming letter from Will
Watrous.   It came in her morning delivery.

"Were the girls tired last night?" said John Rich, a
little anxiously.

"Tired?   Not a bit!   It was a nice lark."

Did Miss Clara think they could stand the pace?
Why, of course she did.   Of course they could.   Really
there was more force than was needed.   There was
always one understudy to fill any gaps.

"That's the use of the Champollion finger-board,
and having you all write alike.   When we go into
politics we will make everybody do that.   Let it be
our 'Leader' for the American Syndicate."   And Miss
Clara made a minute on Thursday's tickler.

"Are you ready?"

"Quite so."

And so they finished "The Pine-tree and the Palm"

—two thousand words more—and began "The Pink Pond-lily" for *Scribner's*.

After lunch Miss Clara was able to bring John the day-book of the day before, with the total.

" We overran a little," she said. " Without counting the Epic, we made forty-one thousand words."

They never counted, nor pretended to count, the tens and units. Hundreds were all they cared for.

" Without the Epic," said he. " That is, after all, the fun of the competitions. They introduce the element of uncertainty. If not, I would have written to Aldrich and Stedman and Miss Thomas and Miss Munro and asked them squarely if they were going into this one. But one always enjoys a lottery."

And so they went on. The only really uniform thing was John's walk with his "gentle lure" every second day as he worked out the Epic. For the rest, madame did not always have the "Memoirs," nor Ysabel the serial, nor any one person what John called the "idiot's work," of evenings.

" It is but fair to change hands," he said. " No one can stand the same thing forever. I should die if it were not for the variety."

At the end of the month Miss Clara showed to John Rich the ledger account made up to the thirty - first day :

Twenty-six days, as per footing, page 111. . 1,108,600 words
An Epic, " The Sword and Plough "...... 1,300 "
  (Epic uncertain until October 15th, when prizes will be awarded.)
1,108,600 words, at 3 cents a word, is........... $33,258.00
  Of this, $11,120.00 has been paid on the delivery of manuscript and deposited.

The inexperienced reader should understand that there are three classes of publishers:

1st. Those who pay on the delivery of goods. Such are *Harper's*, *McClure's*, the *Century*, and the *Outlook*.

2d. Those who pay on the printing of the articles. Such are the *Thunderer*, the *Unfortunates'*, and the *Firefly*.

3d. Those who say they will pay on delivery, and do not pay at all. Such are the *Penny Trumpet* and the *Catch-me-not*.

So that afternoon John Rich wrote a note to Philetus Baring, who was his classmate, and asked him to buy as many Refined Sugar bonds, which guarantee seven per cent. interest, as $11,120 would pay for.

The President of the hour had proposed two or three wars the week before, so the market was deranged, and John got his seven-per-cents. at ninety-five and a quarter.

The next morning he excused Madame Gutenschrift, ordered a cab, and went down-town to the Threadneedle Street of the town. Philetus gave him the bonds, and told him the market had already rallied.

John took his bonds to the Second National and deposited them as collateral. The well-pleased cashier was glad to lend him $10,000 at four-and-a-half per cent. on such excellent gilt-edged security.

John went back to Philetus's office and bought $10,000 more of bonds. He carried these to the bank and deposited them, and the cashier lent him $9000 more on that security.

John went back to Philetus and bought $8400 more of bonds. And so on for an hour he went backward and forward. At the end of that time, by the prudent use of his $11,000, he had bought some $50,000 face value of seven-per-cent. bonds. He would receive on them $3500 a year. On $40,000 of the money he would pay $1800 interest. That is to say, he would receive $1700 to pay him for his two hours' work in going backward and forward from the bank to the broker. But he took all the risk of the Sugar Company's going to the dogs.

"For my part," said John to Miss Clara, when she entered the transaction on the books, "I had rather have written a short story. But this is what men call 'doing business.' You do not add a barleycorn to the wealth of the world, but somebody pays you a thousand or two dollars for doing it."

Mr. Poor was the brother-in-law of an under-teller in the Second National. So he heard of this transaction, which should have been confidential; and he began to wonder if John Rich had in him, after all, the making of a man of business.

Things would not always run so smoothly. For, alas, this is a finite world! One Friday afternoon, for instance, John had gone out to meet an engagement. He had pressed every one in the morning, and so had gained an hour, and he had told Miss Louise that he must keep her half an hour late and she must stay to dine. All this that he might preside at the annual meeting of the Society for Providing Occupation for Badly Educated Ladies, of which he was vice-president. Mrs. Randolph, the president, had "had a stroke."

He gave his hour and a half to counting in a quorum,

laying on the table, and ruling on points of order—all of it good honest time, worth five cents for every second—and he came home. On his desk was a pencil note from Lucy:

"I came round hoping you could join me. So sorry you are out! Here are some pansies for your button-hole."

So much for public spirit and saving the world!

But John Rich fined himself for this. The next morning, before Miss Clara began on the short story for the day, he said:

"We have had forty-five days of this, Miss Clara. How do the girls stand it?"

"Oh, Mr. Rich, you know they enjoy it! You know how fond they are of each other! They count it all a lark — it is so much better than office-work, you know."

"And you," he said, almost paternally, "how do you stand it?"

"Do I look ill?" said she, turning round with her pretty blush. "Miss Lucy said I was the picture of health."

"Then you would try three months of it?"

"Three months? Three years!" said the brave girl.

"Three months let it be," said John. "And write for Miss Annie. I see that old Mr. Lancelot is dead, and she will be free again."

"I hope she takes no one's place?" asked Miss Clara, anxiously.

"Oh no! We cannot spare one of them. We may need one or two more."

So the stent was increased some days from nine hours to ten. And they contracted for twelve chapters of " Reminiscences."

The next month followed much as by pattern. You see that this " litrary fooling "—as Leonidas Poor called it which he could not call work—differs from work in some points where it has an advantage. For instance, John took the whole party to Weirs, on Lake Winnipiscogee, for a change. He sent down six new Champollion typewriters the day before; and after lunch they all took the afternoon train to Weirs. It is, you know, a lovely ride.

You can write in a good car on a good railway, not as handsomely, but nearly as legibly, as you can at home. So John did his afternoon stents with Miss Ysabel and Miss Hattie as they rode, and they had the scenery ready to his eye and to everybody's pencils. So he wrote that day the blood-curdling story of Mrs. Dustin and the Pennacook Indians, that you read in *Frank Leslie*. Mrs. Penn, who holds a light pencil, did the illustrations for it evenings. Readers from a distance should understand that as they travelled they were on the route of Mrs. Dustin's captivity, and that they saw the bronze statue of the heroine planted in the place where she killed the Indian.

You get up to Weirs about five o'clock. Their rooms had been ordered, and Mr. Atwood gave them a good supper. In the ride they had picked up any amount of " Personal" from the friends who had come in to interrupt them. And in the evening, while John dictated the " Personal" and the " Calendar," the girls

were out on the lake in canoes or boats.   There proved
to be a good many young men whom they knew who
had come down on the morning train.   Will Watrous
was there, and young Viking, and his classmate Olaf,
and three or four more.   So that evening, and indeed
all the evenings of the week, went very pleasantly.

When the *Globe* announced in its "Personals" of
Thursday that Mr. John Rich was at the hotel at
Weirs, Mr. Poor passed the paper across to his wife,
with a wicked thumb-nail mark against that paragraph.

" That's the way he wastes his time," he said, vicious-
ly—" a man who really has some eye for business."

All the same, when Miss Clara got back to the ledger
Saturday night, she entered on the credit side 242,700
words for the week.   At three cents a word, this made
$7281.   For that week they beat Mr. Gansevoort.   Mr.
Gansevoort's income was only $6730.73 in a week.
And he had all the risk of that President who was so
fond of making wars.

"People will keep on reading short stories and newspapers," said John Rich, "though there should be
eleven rumors of twelve wars."

All this would stop once a week, on Saturday afternoon.   Thanks to the beneficent institution of Sunday,
as John Rich would say, there was one day when a
man did not have to think of leaders, or serials, or memoirs, or reminiscences, or novels.   He said that "Personals" and "Calendars" never required any thought,
any day in the week.

They would all crowd a little on Friday—even on

Thursday afternoons—so that Saturday evening there
was nothing to do.   And then it was that John Rich,
instead of arranging "Personals" and other tric-trac,
took the electric for the Tenterden Junction and walked across to Waban to spend Saturday night and Sunday at his aunt Priscilla's.   She lived, you know, next
door to the Poors.   Mr. Leonidas Poor might be as
grumpy as he pleased.   He could not keep John from
coming in to tea, or from walking up and down the
River Road with Lucy, or from spending the evening
in the sitting-room while she played to him, or while
they sang together, or while Olive read the last Stevenson aloud to them ; or if there was a symphony concert
at Stoughton, from driving over there together.   In
that household Mrs. Poor did much as she chose, and
had things much as she chose.   And as she liked John
Rich very much, Mr. Poor's grumpiness was practically
nothing to anybody but himself.

     And the Saturday evenings were only too short.
And Sunday morning, if Aunt Priscilla asked Lucy to
breakfast, Lucy was not so stuck up but she would come;
and on the alternate Sundays John would go over to
the Poors' to breakfast.   And while Lucy got up her
lesson for her Sunday-school class, John was generally
able to help her.   And it always happened that there
was not room in the carry-all for her, so they generally
started together to walk to church, she and John.   Why,
you know it is only two miles if you go through the
school-house lane.   Then John waited through the
Sunday-school—in fact, before long he had a class there,
the boys were so fond of him!   His subject was the
athletic games introduced at Jerusalem and Cæsarea,

by Herod the Great. He would carry Josephus's *Antiquities* from the library. But practically the instruction was largely in object-lessons. They had that little room to themselves where the sexton stands when he rings the bell.

As for the rest of Sunday, I do not know so much. They were a little apt to disappear. John was apt to have a horse and buggy in which he could go to drive, and it was understood that Lucy had some protégées at South Natick, whom she used to visit. John was himself an officer in the Home for Sick Dogs, and they sometimes went over there to see how Bruno and Bismarck were getting on. Always, however, they arrived at Aunt Priscilla's in time for a late tea, and either at Aunt Priscilla's or at the Candlers', or the Pettingills' or the Poors', they had sacred music if they were not walking together in the shrubbery. There was never a word said about articles of any sort. Nobody asked anybody about the denouement of a story. Nobody talked of Mr. Davis or Miss Wilkins or Miss Jewett, or even of Mr. Howells. If there were any conversation on literary subjects, it was of far-away times.

When August came the staff and John Rich went to Niagara together. As has been said, on a good railway, like the New York Central, one writes very decently, and you can work the typewriter — if it be work to run the typewriter; the Leonidas Poors of this world think it is not. Dr. Holmes once said to me that he thought he wrote better in a moving car than he did anywhere else. He asked if there were not some slight impulse of blood to the head which

quickened the work of the brain. I thought it was
only the impulse of the devil proposing that you should
write when you had no proper implements and what
you wrote was illegible. But Wagner and Pullman
and Mr. Depew have changed all that.

They took ten days at Cape Breton, and looked up
Louisburg. And on this trip Mrs. Poor and Lucy went
with them. They had some grand friends whom they
wanted to visit there. Generally Madame Gutenschrift
and Mrs. Penn matronized the parties; they took their
six little girls with them, who made nice companions
for the working party—if, as has been said, this be work.

They roughed through the winter as well as they
could. You can stand a good deal in our polar latitude through December, and even January. You forget
how bad it was last year, and you say, "the days begin
to lengthen." You buy new arctics, and you get a
good deal of fun out of Thanksgiving and Christmas.
It is not till the liar February appears that hope begins
to leave you. And so, early in February, John Rich
bade Miss Clara write to the Pennsylvania Railroad
for his two palace-cars and the dining-room again,
and went off to Manatee and Punto Gordo and Punta
Rassa and the Fountain of Life, oranges, and orange
blossoms. They came back—keeping pretty near the
fresh strawberry line—by New Orleans and a Mississippi steamer, and Glenwood Springs and Banff, and
so by Point Keweenaw and Mackinaw, in time for the
young people to be at class-day on the 20th of June at
Harvard. Will Viking had the poem that year, and
they were all engaged eleven spreads deep at Cambridge.

"The only way to do it," said John Rich, "is to keep steadily to your hours. Jump out of bed at twenty-three minutes before seven, if that is your time. If your time is twenty-seven minutes after six, get up then. If you have promised Mr. McClure eleven hundred words, send him eleven hundred. If you only promised him nine hundred, do not bother him with more." And to the young authors who came to him with their manuscripts at the stations, or asked him at Niagara to look over them while the others were in the *Belle of the Foam* or under the cataract, John would give like advice.

"Do not try to tell a story till there is a story to tell.

"Then tell it as well as you can, in as few words as will do.

"First, second, and last, forget yourself while you are doing it, and never bother about style."

From which year's career—for this was, in a way, an exceptional year—one triumph came to John Rich. It was after class-day. Miss Clara's monthly return had been larger than ever. The dilatory people were paying up, and there was a new President, who did not make wars. So John Rich bought more sugar, and took more money on collateral than ever.

As he read his *To-day* one morning before he went to after-breakfast work, a note came in the mail marked "Personal and particular." Miss Clara did not open it.

"This is a victory," said John Rich, grimly, as he read. The note was this:

"DEAR MR. RICH,—A mortgage has fallen in, by the death of old Gradgrind. It amounts to three thousand four hundred dollars, and makes all my wife's independent property. Might I have a minute with you before Saturday, to consult you about reinvesting it ?   Always yours,

                              "LEONIDAS POOR."

To which John Rich dictated this reply:

"DEAR MR. POOR,—You know I would do anything to serve you. But really, in a case like this, you ought to consult some man of business."

Then he made lamplighters of Mr. Poor's note.

That exceptional year came to an end on the 7th of July. Exceptional it was, John Rich said, because at the end of it nobody made any objection to his marrying the dearest girl in the world. She had agreed on the place where they would build their little cottage, and then Dr. Primrose married them, and they went on their wedding journey.

As they read their Howells together, just as you pass the oldest rocks in the world, between Schenectady and Syracuse, John shook hands with a sad-looking man who came into the Wagner palace from the smoking car and took his seat. His seat was on the sunny side, three chairs in front of Lucy's. Lucy asked her husband who this downcast-looking man was.

"Oh, you do not know him? He was the year before me in college. That is Gansevoort." And then, after a thoughtful pause, "Lucy, his income is only three hundred and fifty thousand dollars a year. Ours, even outside the investments, the work of our hands,

20

has panned out twelve hundred and thirty-four dollars more than his. There is Clara's figure."

And he showed her Miss Clara's memorandum on the back of a card—

$351,234.

"You see how sad he looks. Don't you think I ought to share our surplus with him?"

"Poor man, I am afraid the girl he wanted to marry would not look at him!"

The only grief about their wedding journey was that they could not stay to Clara's wedding. She married Will Watrous the next day, and she had ten brides-maids—Annie and Louise and Ysabel and Lizzie and Minnie and Hattie and Lilian and Mabel, and the others of their nice travelling-parties.

The next day there were four weddings, and the next four more. And now those young people are Mrs. Viking and Mrs. Olaf and Mrs. Brown and Mrs. Green and Mrs. White and Mrs. Black and Mrs. Gray and Mrs. Bistre.

FROM GENERATION TO GENERATION

A STORY OF CHRISTMAS CHRISTIANITY

I

"COME and see the new moon, grandam! Come, come, thee must come and see the new moon! And put money in thy pocket, grandam, and put thy right foot on the ladder, and face this way and look over that shoulder, and then thee will have money for a month."

"And little good will the money do me," said the poor woman, not moving a finger. "Be there another moon? Then it's fifty-nine days since we started on this weary, weary sea. And in my heart I know we shall never see land."

"Thee knows no such thing, grandam," cried one of the children and another; "and thee must come and see the moon."

"For before she is full thee will be seeing sugar and spice and everything nice, and medlars and pears and plums, and thee will be hungry for all of them, and thee will need all thy money to buy them for Abner and for Willie."

This was the speech of that pretty Anne Fortune, who could make the poor sea-sick woman do what she chose. And she succeeded this time, as she had done so often, and dragged her up the narrow ladder to the deck in triumph.   And so Goody Wakelin saw the third moon of their voyage.

They were all on the *Mayflower*.   Yes, the famous *Mayflower*.   But this was not the famous voyage. This was one of the later voyages of the brave old ship, before she disappeared and was broken up and changed into old junk in some dockyard on the river.   It was to America she was coming; and Goody Wakelin was in theory taking charge of the children.   And really Abner and Anne had charge of her.   For they had the omnipotence of youth, and she, sick and careworn, looked back far more than was well for her, and had to be cajoled or scolded into looking forward.   Her complaining began again as she turned from the new moon.

"But where is my dear Lord?   Why does He not say to the sea, 'Be still'?   Why does He not come to me and lead me by still waters?"

The poor children did not know, and did not tell her.   They could only beg her again to stay and see the people on deck, and so far they succeeded.   They found for their poor captive a lee under the shelter of a big cask, which was a part of the deck freight; and in spite of herself she watched the reflection of the afterglow on the clouds behind.   Just then a group of seamen around the foremast began singing Simeon's hymn :

> "Lord, because my heart's desire
> Hath wishèd long to see
> My only Lord and Saviour,
> Thy Son, before I die."

Some of the women and children gathered round them, and joined in the familiar words. And it was with jubilant joy that they sang the last verse:

> " The Gentiles to illuminate
> And Satan over-quell,
> And eke to be the glory of
> Thy people Israel."

The whole deck cheered, one may say, as the sacred song was ended. For the "Amen, amen, amen!" which rose from so many lips was indeed the cheer of conquerors. And the ship's boatswain, a modest-looking young fellow, with a friendly face and a blazing eye, stepped forward and said, "Let us pray." He spoke perhaps fifty words in the strain of triumph, and again came the glad "Amen, amen!" And then the young fellow said, what lingered in the hearts of those children till they died:

"You see, mates, it is not the hair of His head ye are to look for, nay, nor the grip of His fingers and His thumb. It is as 'twere midnight, black and dark, here, and ye heard the cheer of His voice out of the fo'castle as He called ye from the poop yonder. It is not His face that ye want; it is Him. It is Him I long to see,

> " 'The only Lord and Saviour,
> Thy Son, before I die.' "

"Amen, amen, amen!" rang from the crowd. And as the children lifted their grandmother down the companion-way, the dear old soul said, "Amen, my darling. How wicked I was when I came up-stairs! I see it now, and I will not whine any more."

II

Sixty-five years make more or less, as you take them. The three children—Abner, William, and Anne—were sixty-five years older in the year 1690 than they were in the spring of 1625. But they did not take life any less joyously — perhaps they took it more joyously. Anne Fortune was no longer Anne Fortune. She had been Abner's wife — well, if they had known about golden weddings, theirs would have passed already. Her children's children were tumbling round, some in the great lean-to, sailing boats in the water-tank, some in the cherry-trees, picking cherries and eating them. Will Wakelin had just come across from Plymouth, and had brought some ribbons for Comfort and Ruth, some pepper and ginger for the kitchen, and the new dasher for the churn which he had bidden Silas Meek finish for him at the mill. And he and his wife— Aunt Hitty, as the children called her— had walked across from their house. They all sat together under the great elm as the sun went down. On the common—the green between two roads—the bigger boys were playing the ball-game which we now call lacrosse. There were three or four Sogkonate boys among them, quite enough to give a savage flavor, not to say color, to the game.

"I was telling your wife, Will," says the Anne Fortune of the *Mayflower*, "that the little brats here have been making me tell them old-time stories of the sea and of the old country. And I told them o' that night when we coaxed thy grandmother up

on deck, and showed her the new moon over her
shoulder."

"And, indeed, there is the same moon now," cried
Aunt Hitty—"as new as ever!"

And, sure enough, the faint white sickle, only two
days old, appeared above the apple-orchard. And the
children twisted their necks into absurd contortions,
that they might see it over their left shoulders.

"And did you tell them," said Will, a little seriously,
"how we sang, and she sang, and how they all sang?
Little did I know about the Gentiles then. And thy
mother, Hitty, told me stories that same night about
the old times which I shall never forget."

"And Arnold, the boatswain, spoke to us that night,
and—yes, here is the Elder, Arnold's son, has come just
in time for supper. Hold up, Elder, hold up! We
were talking of your father. Now, Elder, you have
not far to go—John, take the Elder's horse—and,
Elder, there will be a plate and a spoon for you.
Elder, we were talking of the times before you were
born."

And so the boys were called from the ball-field, and
their brothers and sisters from the orchard, and young
Abner and Silas from the barn, as little Hitty and
Salome came out beaming from the great kitchen and
announced that supper was on the table.

The older people sat mostly at one end of the long
table, "Little Hitty," who was five feet seven if she
were an inch in height, presided at the other end, and
the children drew up stools or short settles in the space
between. The party was not large for this hospitable
house. There were but twenty-seven in all. The Elder

asked God's blessing, the mugs were filled, now with cider, now with milk, the meats, cold and warm, were served, and with good appetite they all fell to, with viands such as

> "Kings and prophets waited for,
> And sought, but never found."

"Oh, Anne, do you remember the night when the pea-soup was sour on the ship, and old Watrous threw his plate into the sea?"

"And, Will, I can see thee standing by the kettle, and how thee let David Antrim carry off the long cut because thee knew what was under it"—and so on, and so on.

And after the supper the children gathered in groups on the grass before the lean-to, and the old people brought their chairs under the great elm, and Abner gave to the Elder the Bible, and asked him to read the song of Simeon. And he did. And then all at once children, fathers and mothers, and grandfathers and grandmothers stood in a circle, and the Elder offered prayer. And then, with Abner's lead, they sang as they had sung on the deck of the ship:

> "The Gentiles to illuminate
> And Satan over-quell,
> And eke to be the glory of
> Thy people Israel."

"'Thy kingdom come,' indeed," said the Elder. "The good Lord heard and answered."

"'Thy will be done on earth as it is in heaven.' I think of that every night when the children come and kiss me."

"Indeed," said the Elder, "there is no such heaven as a happy home."

"And do you think, Elder, that the Lord Christ will long delay His coming? Are there not signs in the sky and trembling of men's hearts?"

"Dear friend," said the Elder, "when I see those redskins eating their bread and milk with our children, when I go from door to door and every one praises the Lord because He is good, I see that it is as the good Lord says. He cometh not with observation. He has already come."

III

A perfect September day. A spacious and elegant house on a quiet street in Boston. The large hall divides three generous parlors on the right from three as generous on the left. In the most westerly of the last three is a large company of ladies and gentlemen around an admirably furnished dinner-table. The time is one o'clock in the afternoon, the dinner-hour in Boston in 1740.

At the right hand of Mrs. Arnold, the hostess, sits the Reverend George Whitefield, who is the guest of honor of the occasion. Rightly or not, every one in the company addresses him as "Dr. Whitefield." Mrs. Arnold, dignified, gracious, and self-possessed, is, none the less, more or less dashed in the presence of a guest so distinguished and, for good reason, so much honored. At the other end of the table, at the right of Morton Arnold, her husband, sat Parson Webb of the New North Church, Morton Arnold's minister. Thus Morton

Arnold would have called that gentleman, not meaning
that he owned him in any sense, but rather that when
John Webb preached in the New North Church he
listened.

We are not strangers to these people. Morton
Arnold is the oldest son of that Elder Arnold in the
last chapter, who asked the blessing at Marshfield
fifty years before. Mrs. Arnold is the younger of the
two girls who served the supper to the others, of which
by accident Elder Arnold partook. Morton was one
of the boys who played lacrosse on the green. That
portrait by Smibert, at which Whitefield is looking as
he speaks with Madam Morton, is a picture of Elder
Arnold. The world's gear has prospered in Morton
Arnold's hands; his dunfish are in favor among the
monks at Vallombrosa—see what a noble fish that is
from which Madam Arnold helps Whitefield! And as
the repast closes, these figs and oranges and raisins
have all been selected by his own agents in Alicante
and Barcelona.

Just before they left the table Morton Arnold was
trying to catch his wife's eye, so that she might ask
Dr. Whitefield to return thanks. But she had brought
round the conversation with her distinguished guest so
far as to venture to ask him his opinion on Dr. Bengel's
theory of the Apocalypse, which theory was a fashion-
able one at that moment with regard to the second
coming of Christ. Did Dr. Whitefield think that the
Treaty of Utrecht was the closing of the fifth seal?—
or whatever was the particular question of the hour.
Whitefield felt, perhaps, that this was not a very good
moment for exegetical discussion; he simply said, and

she never forgot it, " My dear madam, if you and I can welcome the dear Lord in our hearts, we need not be troubled if we do not see Him in the sky." And at this moment she caught her husband's eye, she saw his purpose, and she said :

" Thank you, Dr. Whitefield, thank you indeed ! I will try to remember what you say. Now we must not keep all the people waiting. Will you return thanks ?"

And the company all stood with bowed heads while Whitefield thanked the good God for the feast which they had enjoyed, and, in words which faltered, asked for his strength for the duty which was before him.

No one sat down. All repaired to the great hall ; mantles or other outer gear were thrown over the ladies' shoulders, the men took their canes and hats, and in a stately procession they moved towards the New North Church. The whole town and the whole neighborhood knew that Whitefield was to preach there, and as they approached Hanover Street, which had taken its new name from the dynasty hardly a generation old, their way was already blocked by the throngs of people who were passing around the meeting - house. The meeting - house itself had been filled long before.

Morton Arnold was not surprised. He turned back and spoke to Whitefield, who was following him close, with Madam Arnold on his arm, and said :

" It is as I told you, Dr. Whitefield. There will be no room in the church. I shall send forward Michael and Samuel, and the town-crier is in waiting, who will give notice that the meeting will be held and you will preach under the Quaker Tree on the Common."

Little did Whitefield know why he used the word Quaker in connection with the tree. Mrs. Arnold knew that it was because Mary Dyer had been hanged there nearly a hundred years before. All the party turned back to Arnold's house.

He had foreseen all this, and his own chariot and horses were in readiness to take Dr. Whitefield and Mrs. Arnold and two other guests to the Common. They arrived at the tree, near the marsh or pond in the more distant part of the Common, before the great mass of the people. Still, there were hundreds there, who had had the foresight to guess that the New North Meeting-house would not be large enough for the assembly. At Mrs. Arnold's direction the horses were removed from the carriage and led away somewhere, so that Whitefield might stand in the carriage himself as the throng of people drew near. And then there flowed up, in a living stream, the crowd of men and women — yes, of children as well, led by their mothers—each eager to get a front place in the throng, and filling in, thousand upon thousand, thousand upon thousand, around the speaker.

Whitefield was pale—he did not seem excited; he sometimes said a word to the three ladies with whom he had come. And they, with reverent understanding that they were not to sit in this accidental pulpit, stepped down from the chariot, and grouped themselves with those who were in the front. A little circle of grass, not ten feet across, separated him from his hearers. The gathering of the crowd was rapid, it was silent as the gathering of the same people in their churches might have been, and there was but little

delay, therefore, before, in a voice which broke sometimes with emotion, Whitefield led the prayers of this
assembly in a fervent appeal to the present God.

The service went forward much as it might have
done in the new brick meeting-house. An occasional
cry of "Amen!" or "Praise the Lord!" breaking in on
the preacher's voice, made indeed the only exception
from the ordinary decorous conduct of Sunday service.
The sermon was an eager, passionate description of the
Saviour's personal presence and movement in Nazareth,
at the well of Samaria, in Edom, by the seaside at Tyre,
and at last at Jerusalem. Whitefield made the Divine
Man live, even for the dullest negro who listened to
him with open mouth and unwinking eyes. It was as
if He spoke to them; it was as if He took them by the
hand. And then, not in many words, but with intense
feeling, he showed them that the love with which Jesus
spoke was God's love, the power with which He acted
was God's power, the eternal wisdom of His instruction
was God's wisdom. "This is incarnation," he cried.
"You see the living God lives and moves and has His
being by the side of the brook of Sharon, on the hill-
side in Nazareth, and in the streets of Jerusalem!" So
passionate and eager was this statement that a chorus of "Amen! amen! amen!" fairly interrupted the
speaker. He almost trembled as he stood silent, but
he waved his hand as if to quell the half-applause
which thus expressed itself, and, pointing with that
thin, bony finger quite into the middle of the crowd,
then almost frowning, as if he could hardly find words
for his message, he cried, "You say 'Amen!'—and
what is the use of my showing you how God can be

present in the form of man as He walked in Nazareth
and Jerusalem unless you are willing that God shall
be incarnate in your own lives, as you go and come
under these trees or in those streets of Boston? Is it
any use for you that God should have been incarnate
then, if you mean to resist the Holy Spirit and will not
let Him be incarnate now? Now is the time accepted,
and this is the day of salvation, and you will know
what it is to be saved if, as your Saviour did, you will
speak God's word, you will do God's deed, and will go
about your Father's business. O God, my God, that
Thou wilt incarnate Thyself in the hearts of Thy servants here to-day!"

And so that address was ended. A moment more,
and in eager words of prayer, words which poured over
each other as if he could not hold them back in his
passion of love and reverence, he continued the same
appeal. The men around him knew that he saw God
and heard Him and was alive with the infinite life.

That evening as Madam Arnold's grandchildren gathered around her, as she kissed them before they went
to bed, her husband read to them the passage which
came in order in the Bible, and the children felt that
his prayer had in it an eager reality to which they
had not been accustomed in the evening service of the
household. And their grandmother kept them for a
moment, as she did not always keep them, and said to
them:

"Do not forget this day—do not forget this day. He
said to me that we are not to look in the clouds for our
Saviour. And I am sure, John, you will remember
what you heard on the Common. You know that you

are one of the children of God; and when you choose,
God lives and moves and has His being in you."

Our business with this story is that John Arnold
never forgot those words. And in a thousand straits
of his after-life—boy, youngster, adventurer, emigrant,
and leader of men; in sorrow or in joy, in weakness
and in strength—John Arnold knew how to find the
infinite companionship, and to go about his business as
those do who are almighty.

IV

Fifty-two years more. John Arnold, this very boy
who saw and heard Whitefield, is standing, a little
nervous, at the door of a great " frame house," not far
from a hospitable log-cabin. From the great chimney
of the cabin pour torrents of blue smoke, which indi-
cate an important function within. John Arnold is a
tall, handsome man, whose hair is hardly grizzled; he
looks ready, is ready, to tramp his five-and-twenty
miles through the woods any day. Yet John Arnold
has been left at home this time while the boys went
to the campaign.

He is dressed in a well-preserved blue uniform coat,
rather old-fashioned, but of French cut and Revolu-
tionary times, and in clean and new buckskin breeches.
He looks uneasily at the sky, to see how far down the
sun has gone, and once or twice walks to the corner of
the barn, listening.

And at last he is rewarded. "Tap, tap, tap," the
sound of a drum is heard; and then four great lumber

wagons rattle across the corduroy road, each flying an
American flag, and well filled with jovial young men,
cheering and waving their hats. This is the party which
John Arnold has been waiting for.

They are the contingent from all this neighborhood
to Mad Anthony's army. And Mad Anthony—General Wayne—has crushed the Shawnee forces in de-
cisive fights. One might almost say the Shawnee
army, so well trained and so elated by their victories
over Harmon and St. Clair were the enemy, and so
well supplied by their English allies. But now they
are utterly beaten and utterly broken. Now there is
some peace for the settlers, so far as Indians go, for
a hundred thousand years.

And Colonel Arnold—"old Colonel John Arnold,"
as the boys call him—has declared that his new house
shall never offer food or drink to man or beast till the
boys come home.

Now, on this bright September day, the boys have
come. And the tin-kitchens in the log-cabin have been
roasting meat all day, and the great potash kettle has
been boiling hams, and the very ashes have been baking potatoes, and the new cider is already drawn, and
every woman and girl in the neighborhood is in her
best gown to wait on the table. Well might John
Arnold wish to hurry their coming. And here, at last,
they have come.

No! One does want to describe the color of every turkey poult, the brown crust and the black clove of every
ham, the flood of red gravy which followed every knife
as every haunch of venison was cut. One wants to tell
how every Phœbe blushed, or every Hitty, when her

own John or Silas or Cephas found her and hugged her and kissed her. One would be glad to repeat the words with which Parson Meigs, who had come all the way up from Marietta, thanked God and asked His blessing. But we must not make the story too long. Enough that the boys and the girls and the boys' fathers and mothers sat at a more than royal feast. For indeed few kings can give such feasts. They are reserved for States like Ohio, one of whose proud mottoes is, "In Ohio no man was ever hungry."

It is after the feast that we have to do with a few of the party. Colonel John is still within, trying to persuade some little boys that they can eat some more doughnuts, and cutting for them some more squash pies. But here, on the western side of the old log-house, a little secluded from the rest, is a group of a dozen, half of them soldiers and the other half "sweethearts and wives." The men are smoking their cob pipes. The women, neither appalled by the smoke nor ashamed to be where they are, are pretending to open the knapsacks, pulling out what they find there, and commenting on the campaign.

But the talk grew more serious. Captain Nat, as the boys called Arnold's son, had told of Wayne's speech when he dismissed them. Then with a good deal of feeling he said, choking a little as he began:

"I was glad when the old man said he had no more use for us, and that there'd be no more use for us in a million years. I tell you, Sally, it's these old graybeards, who've smelt powder all their lives—it's they that pray for peace. 'Now, boys,' says he, 'your homes are your own, and you've nobody to fear. Make 'em

21

homes as is homes,' says he.   And that's what you and
I are for."

"'Bring in the kingdom,'" said James Southworth.
And his wife, Alice, pressed his weather-beaten hand,
from which the forefinger had been shot away, a little
more closely.

"Yes, bring in the kingdom.   That's as good a word
as any.   No more drums, no more wars and fightings.
'Thy will be done on earth as it is in heaven.'"   And
he looked up into the western sky, and pointed to the
white sickle of the moon two days old.   "They do
things without trumpets or drums up there."

"Why, there's the new moon," said Alice Southworth.
"Constant, your grandsire used to tell a story about the
new moon on the *Mayflower*."   And then she looked
round, and with great satisfaction said, "Why, we were
all there!   Constant, you were there, and you, William
Holmes, and you, James, and you, Captain Nat; Cephas
Collier, you were there, and your wife—of course the
Brewsters were there."   She pointed, as she spoke, to
the Hitty Meek of this generation, as if all men and
women knew that she was a Brewster.

"Do you remember, Cicely, how your grandmother
used to sing:

> "'My only Lord and Saviour,
> Thy Son, before I die'?

"I thought I saw him, Thursday night, though it
was pitch-dark, when Hiram knocked, knocked, knocked
so loud at the door, and I started out of bed all frightened.   'Victory,' said he, 'victory!   The war's done,
and the boys are coming home!'   Dark it was as mid-

night; but when I waked up my baby to tell him his
father was coming home"—here the young mother's
voice broke—"I thought I saw my Saviour's face, and
I thought I heard the angels singing, 'Peace on earth
and good will among men.'" And all excited, and
with tears and sobs, she flung herself on her husband's
knees and threw her arms around his neck.

Every one was hushed for a moment, and then in
his clear tenor Cephas sang:

"Israel's strength and consolation,
  Hope of all the earth thou art;
Long desired of every nation,
  Joy of every waiting heart"—

and all the rest, men and women, joined in.

"And now," said James, "we are not the men and
you are not the women to go round singing them
hymns without doing something about it. And we've
talked it all over, we boys have, and you girls will
all come in. We know that without asking. You
see, we've seen the place. Why, we camped there
Wednesday night, and we talked it all over round
the fire. We'll go and take out our claims there next
week, and we'll have the cabins built by Thanksgiving.
Cicely, there's just what you want; the south wind
blows over a bend of the river, which cools it. Hitty,
there's just what you want, for there's a little swell
of the land and great thick woods of black-walnut that
keeps off the northwest wind. Why, it's the kingdom of heaven now, if you can only keep sin and the
devil out of it. I says to Cephas, says I, as the sun
went down that night, says I, 'Cephas, there's nothing

in the Book of Revelations that beats that! I don't
know nothing about chrysoprase or chalcedony, but
there's nothing finer than them maples and chestnuts
and oaks and hickories—and that's where we're going
to make our town.'"

> "The Gentiles to illuminate
> And Satan over-quell,
> And thou to be the glory of
> Thy people Israel."

Cicely interrupted him as she half sang and half said
these words.

"And, first of all," said her husband, "nobody is to
be hungry there. Nobody is to ask God's blessing on
his breakfast any day if he thinks there's one cabin in
the township where there's not enough to eat."

"And, in the second place," said Hiram Meek, "there's
to be no fools there. There's to be a nice, pretty school-
house; and, Cicely, your sister is to come from Ipswich
and teach in it."

"And, in the third place," said William Holmes,
"there's to be no drunkards there. "There's to be no
'eleven o'clocks' nor 'eye-openers,' nor no other devil's
drinks."

"In short," said his wife, "all this means that everybody is to love his brother as himself."

"And his sister," said that demure little Hitty, who
always had the last word, and was, without knowing
it, stroking the back of a great sunburnt hand.

"And that means," said Captain Nat Arnold, who
from a sort of childlike integrity and purity had become regarded as a father of these boys—"that means
that the whole town shall love God and love man.

Boys and girls and their fathers and their mothers will grow up to love God because they love man, and to love man because they love God. And this will be at the ferry and the blacksmith's shop, and when they are hoeing corn, and when the girls are husking it, just as much as in the meeting-house or at the Friday meeting."

" And where is the place, and when shall we go there, and what is its name?" said Mary Chilton, the youngest and the prettiest of the girls, with a far-away look, as if she were trying to make real the figure in a dream.

" We might call it Bethlehem," said her older sister.

"Or we might call it Nazareth," said Alice.

" Let's call it Mayflower," said Hitty.

" No matter, no matter," said Nat—" Old Nat," the boys called him, because he was almost twenty-seven— "no matter what we call it, so it is only Kingdom Come."

"Amen," said Cicely; and she sang, and they joined her in singing, the old verse which her grandmother's great-grandfather had sung on the *Mayflower:*

> "Lord, because my heart's desire
> Hath wishèd long to see
> My only Lord and Saviour,
> Thy Son, before I die."

And as September and October and November went by, the young men went out with their axes. They took with them their brothers and their cousins, and they had built ten new cabins before Thanksgiving-day. It is one hundred and two years since Wayne's

victory. Yet no word that was spoken on that afternoon has been lost, nor any song that was sung. And
the cheer and thanksgiving of that evening have repeated themselves a thousand thousand times in the
pretty village which gave thanks that day.

No canal ever passed through their meadows. No
railroad ever sought a track through the valley. I
do not know on what page of the post-office register
you will find it, and we cannot turn it up in the right
county in the census. But on Thanksgiving-day, in
John Arnold's barn, they held an old-fashioned Thanksgiving. The mothers carried their babies to the meeting, and the babies did not cry. And Morton Arnold,
the great-great-grandson of the other Elder Arnold—
he preached to them that day. "On these two com-
mandments hang all the law and the prophets." I do
not know what the old Elder would have said. But
when Morton Arnold had finished his sermon he said:

"Dear brethren, if the time allowed, I would go
back to the deck of the *Mayflower*, and tell you what
my grandsire has told me of the coming over. And I
would tell you a story of the Old Colony—how my
grandsire's father played ball with the redskins. Or
I would tell you what my father has told me, of the
day when the great George Whitefield preached on
Boston Common, and the captain heard him. But
now there is no time," he said. "But the elders will
not be hurt if we take another day for that, and hold
a special meeting. And on this day six weeks hence
we will call in all the neighbors, and I will tell those
old stories. Every one of them will show us how the
Lord has visited and redeemed His people. Every one

of them will show how He has truly come to every heart that was open to His coming. If they sought their God, they found Him. And in every age the dear Lord Christ has set up His altar and has been present with His own. And now," said he, "we will not sing from the new hymn-book. We will sing one verse of Simeon's hymn, as the elders sang it on the *May-flower*." And he deaconed out the words they sang:

> "The Gentiles to illuminate
> And Satan over-quell,
> And thou to be the glory of
> Thy people Israel."

And it was as the Elder proposed. When Christmas-day came round, the girls hung the barn with red and yellow ears of corn, and outside the men built a great bonfire. And the people came in from the Crossing, and from Hound's Ferry, and some from the village at the Mill. I believe it was the first Christmas celebrated in Ohio. And it was that festival which gave, in all that region, to that sort of religion the name of "Christmas Christianity."

THERE were six caps to be trimmed, and, by some accident, Lucinda had bought ribbon enough for only four.

Mrs. De Laix was not so very sorry. She would not for the world tell Lucinda that she did not fancy that shade. Rather than have Lucinda suspect it, she would wear all the caps in turn, till she could craftily be rid of the ribbon and get more. As this was to be so, she determined to go down-town herself for the ribbon for the other two. And, lest she should wound Lucinda, she took Clara with her.

She determined to try Stearns's shop, which is at the corner of Temple Place.

So she waved her hand and stopped the electric car. The street was horribly crowded. But the car stopped at just the right spot, and Mrs. De Laix and Clara worked their way through the crowd of passengers to the door. But when they came there, Mrs. De Laix said :

"Clara, dear, I think I will go on to Whitney's. I believe Lucinda bought her ribbon here. I should like to see that nice woman at Whitney's to thank her for the crochet needles." And then, to the car-conductor, "I am very much obliged to you. But I believe we will go on to Winter Street."

Alas! it was not so easy. The South Boston cars which had been waiting for their turn at the curve were now running in. Mrs. De Laix's car had lost its right of way. It was fully two minutes before the South Boston cars ran through. And then only could Mrs. De Laix's car and Clara's start again. When they started—well, it is not two hundred yards to Whitney's —they were there in a minute. Half the car had to leave at that corner. Mrs. De Laix and Clara left. They were not more than an hour in buying satisfactory ribbon—"fair and square." And it will not be till the last chapters of this little tale that we shall meet them again.

Readers in that small section of the world which understands the transit arrangements of Boston will know that the stoppage of that particular car at the corner of Temple Place delayed not only the passengers in it, but the passengers in twenty or more cars behind it, which had to stand in what we call a "block" in Boston —a quarter mile of cars waiting—until that South Boston procession could hurry by. In these cars there were some six hundred persons, each of whom lost from his day's work one, two, or three minutes, as it might happen. It is with the fortunes of two of these persons, and with other fortunes connected with theirs, that this story has now to deal.

When the late Mr. De Laix died, he left his property —half a million dollars, more or less—to a trustee, to pay to Mrs. De Laix the income in monthly payments. It was admirably invested, so that, one year with an-

other, even in these days so wretched for capitalists,
Mrs. De Laix received two or three thousand dollars on
the first of every month from her faithful friend, Mr.
Mahsteff. His father had been a clerk with Mr. De
Laix in St. Petersburg.

But such high interest means constant watchfulness.
On the other hand, constant watchfulness was the delight of Mr. Mahsteff; and on this very afternoon, two
cars behind Clara and Mrs. De Laix, he was in his car,
on his way down-town, to a meeting of the committee
of the bond-holders of the first mortgage on the K. and
L. L. Railroad. His friend's investment in these bonds
was so large that his presence, of necessity, would control the action of this meeting. Indeed, at all the pre-
vious meetings of this little syndicate he had been, of
course, chairman, and had, in fact, directed the whole
procedure. At his motion, in truth, it had been determined that the bond-holders should act together, and
that all their bonds should be sold or held, when the
moment came, by one order.

When, at last, Mr. Mahsteff's car arrived at Scollay
Square, he looked at his watch, to find that it was already four o'clock, the moment for which the bond-
holders had been summoned on his own motion. He
leaped from the car to call a cab. Alas, no cab! He
lost a minute by running back to the museum. Alas,
no cab there! He must go on foot—he who had not
run since he strained his sartorial muscle. Perhaps he
should meet a cab—or overtake one! No, poor Mahsteff—no such luck! It is fully six minutes past four
when he arrives at the double elevator in the lofty Exchange Building.

Can that be Mr. Snapp who leaves the descending elevator just as Mr. Mahsteff ascends? Impossible—they cannot have adjourned!

But, alas! they have adjourned. From a dull office-boy, who pretends to know nothing, and perhaps does know nothing, Mr. Mahsteff learns that at four precisely Mr. Snapp had called the four gentlemen present to order. In a moment he showed that he represented a quorum of stock. In two minutes more he had voted—the others doubtful and yet non-resistant—that a telegram should be sent to Denver, before the close of business there, to accept the terms of the D. P. and I. road for the purchase of this block of bonds. Then he had said he would carry the telegram himself, that it was but two o'clock at Denver, and there would yet be time.

Clear enough it was that faithful Mr. Mahsteff had been sold, as well as his bonds and Mrs. De Laix's. He thought of this, he thought of that, of an injunction here, of a "combine" there. But his adversary had not been thinking, he had been acting, and Mr. Mahsteff and his friends had been given over, by Mrs. De Laix's unfortunate indecision, to the tender mercies of the great railway market of the Rocky Mountains.

In the electric car next but one behind Mr. Mahsteff had been sitting and dreaming Alfred Skimpole. Alfred was a tall, pale boy—growing six inches a year—whom his father was trying to make practical, by intrusting him with the humblest detail of the business of his office. He was an affectionate boy, and he want-

ed to do right.   But to-day, as he came in from Brook-
line, he had seen, for the first time since October, a red-
crested nut-hatcher, and he had not refrained, perhaps
need not have refrained, from the pleasure of crossing
Muddy Brook in pursuit, to see where she was building.   All papa had bidden Alfred do was to take the
parcel to the Boston office before four, and give it personally to Mr. Reddiman.   Alfred knew his watch was
a little fast, and he would have "plenty of time," as
dreamers always expect to have, and as they never
have.

As the electrics went and stopped, as one woman
and another conversed with the conductor before she
came on board, even Alfred's dreams began to take a
somewhat dismal color.   He looked at his watch more
and more often.   He persuaded himself that it was six
minutes fast, not four.   At last he was so nervous that,
when they arrived in time at Winter Street, he left
the shebang altogether, and, with speed for which nothing but the six inches' growth of last year prepared,
ran down the middle of the street, cursed by teamsters
and cabmen.   He arrived breathless in High Street, a
minute and a half after Mr. Reddiman had gone.

"Said he would be back at five.   Said he dussn't
wait no longer.   Said perhaps ye father 'ad sent um
heself.   Said perhaps et was no matter.   Said he would
be back at five."   Such were the oracles of the porter
who was left in charge of the office.

Alfred Skimpole's father was the celebrated head
of the engineering firm of Skimpole, Adgers & Hornblende, to which had been intrusted by the city of Bos-

ton its case to be brought before Mr. Cleveland's commission on harbor improvement. The commission had the last of its many meetings that day, and took the pleasant boat for New York and Washington that night. On the boat, between Fall River and Boston, the three members — one of whom was from Texas, one from Washington Territory, and one from Philadelphia — drew up their report on such documents as they had. They were rather annoyed that the city of Boston had given them so few reliable statistics.

The statistics were in the parcel which Alfred did not give to Mr. Reddiman.

They arrived in Washington late at night on the next day, after the report of the commission had been presented.

Mr. Reddiman and Mr. Hornblende and Mr. Adgers and Mr. Skimpole made twenty visits to Washington as the summer passed, hoping to get a supplementary report presented, explaining that the claims of the city of Boston had not been properly attended to. Such a supplementary report was at last got in, as the reader may remember, as the last year of Mr. Cleveland's second administration passed. But, alas! the River and Harbor Bill was then well forward, and although at two o'clock in the morning a desperate effort was made to bring in an amendment, the Senate threw it out on a conference, and the appropriation was never made.

It is to the lack of this appropriation, joined with the unfortunate sinking of two coal barges in the most critical points of the harbor, that the steady decline in the foreign and coastwise commerce of Boston, for the end of the nineteenth century and the beginning of the twentieth, was due.

If the Recording Angel would give us an opportunity to look in at his day-books and ledgers, so that we could show the reader what happened to five hundred and ninety-eight other people in the twenty cars which were held back on that eventful day, the stories would be interesting, as are all stories of human life. But the space given to us is limited, so that these two specimens must be taken as an illustration of what happened to all.

There was John Sidney, on his way, with a lovely bouquet of flowers, to see Alice Vernon before she took the carriage for the train to Mount Desert. John Sidney missed her, and in fact never saw her again. Before the summer was over, she had given her hand, and let us hope her heart, to Wallace Carruthers. There was Dr. Morton, whose cab had broken down, who was on his way to meet Dr. Fothergill in consultation at East Boston. Morton is a courageous person, and always presses forward; but he missed the proper ferry-boat, the driver, waiting for him at the dock supposed that he would not come, Morton was too late in consultation, Fothergill missed the proper artery, and the patient died. There was poor old Johanna Stevenson, with her basket of clean clothes, on her way to the Benedict Club. Poor soul, she came in late, and the porter was cross to her. He said Mr. Whymper had waited till the last minute, and then had gone without one of the shirts which she had promised. Poor Whymper, I am sorry to say, thought he was the worst-dressed man at the Round Robin Club when it met;

his spirits were depressed through the whole evening; he made an unfavorable impression upon Mr. Threadneedle, who was watching him all the time, and Mr. Threadneedle engaged for his confidential book-keeper that other man who had come from a Western college, and who cheated him and his of all that belonged to them before five years were over. All such incidents are at the service of the writers for the *Spider's Web*, *Two Tales*, and of other persons who are on the look-out for plots for their stories. There are plots enough for stories, if only we would keep our eyes open, and would only ask ourselves what follows, or what might follow, on the different contingencies of human life which we are pleased to call commonplace.

As for Mrs. De Laix, with whom we began, she and Clara went happily home from Mr. Whitney's. She had seen the nice girl at the counter, and had had a pleasant conference with her. It was true that Mr. Whitney had not established the shop intending that half an hour should be given to friendly talk across the counter between nice and rich old ladies and hard-working women clerks. But such things happened; and in this case it happened. Mrs. De Laix was never very prompt or quick in such conversation.

She and Clara went home, and for a few days succeeded in concealing the new ribbons from Lucinda. When the caps finally appeared, Lucinda expressed the proper surprise at the shade of ribbon which she had not seen before, and Mrs. De Laix, on the whole, enjoyed her triumph.

But, alas! she enjoyed this triumph as the lady at

the head of a Southern plantation might enjoy her success in baking a batch of cream cakes, when her husband announced that the cotton-worm had got into the
fields, and that there would not be a boll of cotton in
the autumn.   Mr. Mahsteff had kept secret for a week
or two the fatal sale of the bonds to the Denver wreck-
master.   Then he had been obliged to confess to Mrs.
De Laix that on the 1st of June he should not be able
to send her any dividend.   He said, however, cheerfully,
that she must recollect that, however these Western se-
curities came out, more than half her fortune was in
real estate in Boston, and that it was in those parts of
Boston about which there could be no contingency in
the future.   He told her that if she wanted money for
her summer expenses, he could readily advance it to
her on a mortgage of some of her landed property.
But Mrs. De Laix, of course, had money enough in the
bank to carry her down to Boar's Head, and to carry
Clara and Lucinda, and all the others who were in the
habit of making their summer holiday with her.   It
was not in that summer, and it was not in the next
summer, that Mrs. De Laix saw fully what happened
when half her property was swamped by the Denver
speculators; nor was it for two years that she knew
what was going to happen when the coal barges sank
in the harbor of Boston, and the coasting trade of that
city was transferred to the harbors of Salem and Port-
land.

But as year passed after year — particularly after
poor Mr. Mahsteff went home one night perplexed and
troubled, and was found dead in his bed the next
morning because a clot of blood had stuck in the

wrong place in the back of his neck—Mrs. De Laix's outlook on the world appeared, even to herself, optimist as she was, darker and darker with each new day. She did not sell her elegant house on Commonwealth Avenue, although it was taxed awfully and she had nothing with which to pay the taxes. She did not sell it, because there was nobody in the world who would buy such a castle. Half the houses on Commonwealth Avenue had signs upon them indicating that they were for sale. But even these signs were becoming illegible with the stress of weather since the time when they had been placed there. And as you passed in the evening you saw that there was no longer electricity or gas in the parlors or chambers; there was only a snuffy light in some basement, which was inhabited by the keeper of the house, who was waiting in the hope, not very sanguine, that a purchaser might appear. Eventually, however, any question of sale was settled, when the authorities of the town, doubtful how they should meet the annual necessities of their city debt, seized the house, and pretended to sell it at a sheriff's sale. Mrs. De Laix could not remain in it while an auction was going on; and after conference with such of her friends as had not emigrated to Europe, or gone to Denver or to other places to escape the destruction which was settling down over the city of their birth, she determined that she and Clara and Lucinda must leave the house which, as she said, had always been fatal to her. There were a good many homes open to her. There was her sister in Canada, there was her brother in the Fiji Islands. She had a cordial letter from her uncle in Valparaiso, and a proposal was made to her that

22

she should make a long winter visit in Paris with a
lady who was acquainted with the second Madam
Mackay. But all these invitations involved ready
money. Ready money was the first thing which had
disappeared in Mrs. De Laix's calculations. The very
little that she had was needed for postage-stamps, to
pay for such distant correspondence, and Lucinda and
Clara had always been dependent upon her for their
pocket-money and for the modest milliners' bills which
they contracted from year to year.

Mrs. De Laix, Clara, and Lucinda, the minister of
their church, and the president of the sewing society
connected with that church, had one final conference
on the day before the sheriff's sale was to take place
in her mansion. It appeared that, in the old prosperous times, Mrs. De Laix had made herself a life member of the "Society for the Protection and Care of Old
Ladies who had Known Better Days. It proved that
from this life membership it resulted that she had a
right to name an inmate once in four years. It proved
that in the last twelve years Mrs. De Laix had never
named her inmate. The society maintained an agreeable home on the heights of Dorchester, and yet there
were not a great many people living in this home.
For some reason or other, the persons who had lived
there had gone to other places; they had found spending-money, and they had accepted the invitations of
their Valparaiso relatives. Mrs. De Laix would gladly
do the same, but she had no spending-money. It was
therefore determined, quite readily on the part of all
persons, that she should name herself and Clara and
Lucinda as the three inmates for the home. And that

afternoon, with the scanty remnants of their clothing, and a few photographs which reminded them of the past, they established themselves in the pleasant parlors of the institution.

The next morning they occupied themselves in putting their rooms to rights, and in laying the articles of their clothing in the drawers of the neat bureaus and wardrobes. As Mrs. De Laix took out the six caps, which still remained, with the history of which this little story began, her attention was called to the difference between the gray ribbons of one and the lavender of another. She called Clara to her.

"Clara, my dear," said she, "do you remember the day when we bought these ribbons?"

And Clara said she did.

"Clara," said Mrs. De Laix, "do you know, I sometimes wish that, instead of going on to Whitney's that day, we had bought the ribbons at Stearns's."

KING CHARLES'S SHILLING

I

I HAD come up the Congo to a point, well, say sixty miles below Housa, when something happened to the connecting-rod of the steamer, and she was laid up for repairs for twenty-four hours. I was glad of the chance to stretch my legs and to try for game, and started off, as soon as the engineer made this report, with my two boys, as they were called, Philip and Mendi John. Philip was of no great use but as an interpreter with the other, who has a great deal of good woodcraft in him and other working capacity. We had great luck. as how could a man fail to, going through meadows and woods which never saw an entomologist before? I had bagged and chloroformed and stuck, well, twenty-five fine butterflies, and had left a dozen traps for moths, to be examined when we came back the next day. We had lunched under a grove of pepper-trees, when I saw — what I afterwards knew better, but what then I had never seen—a magnificent specimen of Vanessa, larger than Erckhard's, and, as I supposed, rightly, wholly new. I simply called to the boys that they were not to leave the place, and started after him.

A blessed tramp, he led me up hill and down dale.

Hot—oh, how hot it was! Bamboos here, pepper-trees there, plantains, bananas, palm-trees—now in the shade, now in the sun, and this lovely, flattering flutterer ahead of me with the wiles and wit of a siren and an oread combined. But I was too much for him. After an hour I had the splendid creature — there he is now, framed and under glass, hanging on the wall, opposite where I write. I slung my box on my back after I had chloroformed him and fixed him, and then started back to my men.

If I had found them, there would have been no story. The truth was that my handsome wood-nymph there, the Vanessa, had bewitched the brooks and the paths so that everything ran the wrong way. Even the sun in the heavens, when he shone at all, shone in the wrong quarter. Most of the time the sky was overcast, so that the poor sun himself could not shine at all. And who was I, to know my road there, in the kingdom of Mandara, upper or lower, if the sun in the sky did not know his? I tramped and I tramped. I had lost my own tracks long before. At last I came to a path tolerably well beaten, and it brought me out—on the river in sight of the smoke-stacks of the *Princess Beatrice?* Not a bit of it. It brought me out on the slope of a hill, in a large banana patch, with a village of sixty or seventy huts just below me.

I will not say I was frightened, for there is no good in telling tales out of school. But I will not say I was not, for there is no good in lying. The sun, wherever he was, was well near setting. For it was six by my watch. I could not keep it up much longer. So I boldly went down into the village.

Half a dozen little curs snapped at me, just as if I had been in a village of the Yanktons or in the Sahara. I made nothing of them, but pressed on; and then, meeting a pleasant fellow as black as the knave of clubs, with a handsome, good - natured face, clad in a long, blue nightgown, made in a Manchester print-shop for a bed-curtain, I made a salaam to him in the best fashion of Bel-el-djerce. And he, restraining his laughter, made one in quite another fashion to me. Then he advanced and boldly offered me his hand as an Englishman might have done, much to my surprise. He said something, also, but I knew not what, and I took precious good care not to lisp a word of Arabic.

What I did was to lay my head on one side, as if I were desirous of sleeping, and to put my finger in my mouth, as if I wanted to eat. I had learned the first signal from the ballet and the second from Mother Nature and the Navajo Indians. He laughed good-naturedly and pointed to the village. A group of boys and girls, with a few uncles and aunts, fathers and mothers, were assembled already to see the wonder. For myself, I was asking myself whether they would sing, as they did to Mungo Park:

> "Let us pity the white man;
> No mother has he to bring him milk,
> No wife to grind his corn."

But I am not writing for Mr. Fewkes or the Ethnological Society. So I will only say that my guide was evidently a top-sawyer in the crowd, and that he made them march right and left as he would. Before ten minutes had passed I was lying on two or three nice,

sweet mats of an indescribable perfume, and a gentle
black woman, dressed also in a high-colored Manchester
chintz, had brought me a cup of coffee. After this
there was enough to eat, and of the best, too. And, to
make the story as short as I can, in this house I spent
the night, on these same mats, indeed. Conversation is
very hard when it has to be confined to pantomime.
I described the river as well as I could, and the play of
the walking-beam of the engine of the *Princess Beatrice.* Of one thing I may say I am certain—that my
friend had seen her or had not. But whether he had
seen her or not I do not know. At one time I thought
he had, and went on with inquiries as to the distance
that might part me from her at that moment. But
afterwards I had reason to think that he supposed I
described the jumping up and down of some monkeys
who had been playing upon the tree. Such are the
dangers of sign-language.

After a little conversation of this sort I intimated
that I would like to go to sleep. He intimated that
there was no better time or place. With a consideration I had not expected, he stretched a mat, or sort of
curtain, across the room, or house—for there was but
one room under the roof—and I found myself in my
bedroom. I cannot say that I went to bed. I was already in my bed, a rapidity of comfort which I have
not found in more elaborate forms of civilization.

It was the next morning that the revelation came
which I am trying to write out in this story. I was
wakened early from a sound sleep by the singing of
the birds, I believe it is called by the poets. It was,
in fact, the rasping and exasperating screaming of

cocks, guinea-hens, geese, and ducks, for these African villages are nothing without their poultry. It is easy to dress when you have not undressed, and it was scarcely six o'clock when I found myself, not at table, for we were all on the ground, but at breakfast, with a larger company than the night before. The fare was much what it was then. There were plenty of bananas, much finer than the newsboy ever sold me on a train. The resistance piece was a platter of rice, with boiled chicken and butter, all together. The chicken was jointed, so that one could take hold of any piece he wished. For we ate as Adam and Eve did, if indeed they had come as far as kabobs of chicken.

As I bent forward to take a side-bone which looked attractive, a fine old fellow in a white nightgown happened to see, hanging from my watch-chain, an old, very old, silver shilling. It was a shilling of Charles I., in perfect condition, which I had dug up years before in our orchard when I was setting out some quince-trees. When the old man saw this he bent over eagerly and begged me to show it to him, that he might examine it. His manner was perfectly courteous, but I confess I thought I looked my last on my shilling. All these tokens of Manchester were enough to show that they had learned the value of money. This was the first time they had seen that I had any, and I was graceless enough to think that it would be long before I handled my luck-penny again.

But in this I thought as a Philistine thinks, as you shall see.

I gracefully unhitched it from the chain and gave it to him with my best manner. What says Jacob Ab-

bott: " When you grant, grant cheerfully." Old Nightgown showed it eagerly to Blue Nightgown and to
Red Nightgown, on the other side. Their faces beamed
with astonishment and delight. Then they pointed
out to each other the stamp on the obverse with evident joy. Then, with great ceremony, they handed
back the piece to me. If it had been sacred it could
not have been more reverently handled. Then Blue
and Red Nightgowns scrambled up from their haunch-
es, more rapidly than gracefully, and hurried from the
house. What all this meant I could not guess.

And I was more mystified when they returned, this
time again with a certain ceremony, for what I might
call an escort, rather than a body-guard, came with
them. Through the great open doorway I could see
the procession come, of ten or twelve men. I could see
it open to the right and left to make a passage for Red
and Blue and stand fixed as they two came in. Instantly the mats were cleared from all platters as if
the meal were done. Then they put down a great
covered basket, tightly tied.

With endless manipulations and ceremonies it was
opened. The covers and cloths, napkins and mats
taken out from it were numberless. But at last we
came to a handsome necklace, made of three gold coins,
and, say, thirty silver coins. This really elegant thing
they handed fearlessly to me. You know I am a bit
of an expert in coins. The three gold pieces, which
were made, so to speak, the centre of the necklace,
were perfect Portuguese joes, as perfect as if they had
been struck yesterday. The silver coins, also fresh
from the mint, were English shillings, exactly like

mine, but that they were not in the least worn, of the coinage of Charles I. As everybody knows, these are, if in good condition, among the very rarest coins in the world, poor Charles having, for reasons well known to history, very little silver to coin. If my hosts had shown amazement, certainly I showed much more. The joes, as I said, were fresh from the mint of King Joannes of Portugal, the fourth of that name.

In another wrapper, where I found a husk or two of Indian corn, was a very handsome wampum necklace, of Narragansett manufacture. It has been my business to study wampum, not to say to make it, to buy it, and to sell it. I have never seen more perfect beads than these, white and black both, and all in the best forms. I have no doubt that the string was in the same condition as when it was traded away by Canonicus or some of his men.

This revelation was more extraordinary than the other. Silver and gold, almost of their nature, go all over the world, but wampum does not. How did this necklace—it was not a belt—come here?

I expressed by every sign — by raising of the eyebrows, holding up of my open palms and radiant smiles — my interest, curiosity, and surprise, I might say puzzled amazement. Then I handed back the two necklaces, respectfully, to Red-Gown. Then the ceremony continued. More mats were withdrawn from the basket. Another parcel was reached, larger than the first. This was carefully opened, with sundry prostrations, and a knock or two of the forehead upon it. When all was opened it proved to be a bound book, which was handed to me reverently. I opened at the title-page, to find a perfect English Bible. For an instant I thought it was a waif from Mungo Park's equipment. No, it was of a date much earlier than he. "Cum Privilegio. London, 1642. Published by the King's Printer."

How, when, or why—by what agency of church, state, or trade—had these things found their way here?

II

I did not choose to abate the reverence with which I saw this book was regarded. I am as little given to bibliolatry as any man. But in this case I made no scruple. I bowed as low as Red-Gown had bowed, and touched my forehead to the volume. Then I commanded silence. I opened at the Sermon on the Mount. I read the first three beatitudes and the Lord's Prayer aloud, as solemnly and with such dignity as I could express. By a signal I made them all bow their heads. And, with all my heart, I am sure, on my knees I said: "Father in Heaven, tell me what to do, what to say, and how to lead these people." I am sure they understood that I offered prayer.

I gave back the book to the curious and dignified old chief, who was, I think, a priest of some kind. I carefully watched the folding of it in its mats and the business of laying it away with the necklace. Then I began a series of signs, and such interrogatories as can be expressed by them, wishing all the time that I had the skill of Harlequin or of Columbine or of Mr. Bell in translating into "visible speech" the language of the ear.

They led me out into the open air; they showed me
the sun, which was by this time half an hour high; I
was made to understand that he rose at one spot in
one part of the year and at another at another season.
Then I felt that we were advancing. I had, the night
before, been made to understand that two doubled
fists made ten. Now, by repeated pilings together of
the fists of one and another chief and priest I was
taught that it was twenty - four tens of years since
these things came into their possession. The son
of Red-Gown was brought forward, a vigorous man
of fifty, and his son, a small lad of fifteen. I was
made to understand that Red-Gown's father's father's
father, seven generations back, brought these sacred
things from a country beyond the sunset. He had
preserved them, and, as I found afterwards, by oaths
the most sacred, in formulas more binding than anything which is known to book - ruled lands, he had
bound his children, and his children's children's children, to preserve them.

I say, " I was made to understand this." How much
I really gained from that long and trying conversation
in pantomime I do not now precisely know. But
when my interpreters appeared, my guesses were con-
firmed or corrected, so that I find it now hard to say
at what moment I gained the correct ideas.

By this time they had missed me from the ship.
My black fellows had gone home at ten o'clock at
night, and reported that I was lost. At sunrise they
sent these two out again and some volunteer skirmishers. By nine o'clock some of Blue-Gown's people met
some of these scouts, and by ten I had Phil and John

to talk for me. Red-Gown produced a man who had taken a Mendi wife, and so, with four languages and interpreters, we understood each other in a way.

The first time I was at home in Connecticut, some five years after this happened, I made a run down to Boston, and there, in their archives, I got their part of the story. Strange enough it is, and you shall hear it now.

It was in the year of grace 1645 that, in this same village of Lower Mandara, looking much then as it looks now, there was to be a first-class wedding. This young fellow, as he was then, who is the hero of this story henceforth — his name was Telega — was to be married. And he was to be married to his sweetheart, as it happened. I am afraid it did not always happen so. But all the accounts agree that it was a match of his making. Nay, I believe they think, as I do, that this is the reason why we ever hear of him again.

Well, the forms of marriage were not ours. But in all countries lingers the tradition that the bridegroom seizes the bride as, with her maidens, she goes unescorted by him. So Pluto seized Proserpine in Enna. And so to this day in a high wedding at church the bride and her maidens walk up the aisle with the flowers they have gathered in their walk, and the bridegroom, rightly dressed, with his men, perhaps, steps out and takes her for his own. So the bride walked with her maidens that day; so at an ambush, prepared and known of all, Telega and his men seized her, and then the procession passed on, he leading her to the great central house of the village, where the rite would come to an end.

Well, just as the tomtoms and banjoes were doing their best that day, and the dancing-girls dancing their best, down came a dozen Portuguese slave-drivers, with quilted cotton jackets on, such as turned arrows, and with guns loaded and matches burning. The dancing-girls shrieked and ran. The tomtom men and boys ran. And Telega and his father and his friends fought like wild-cats. But what had they to fight with? They were not even armed. It ended in the Portuguese rascals clapping handcuffs on seventeen of them and marching them off to a dhow which was waiting for them on the river. It was, as the traditions agreed, at the very bluff where the *Princess Beatrice* was mending her connecting-rod the day I wandered so far. Tradition is far more accurate, before books, paper, and ink come in.

What happened then I do not know. But it is clear enough that Telega and his neighbors were not used to being slaves, and that they led the Portuguese a wretched life. They knocked them down, they jumped overboard, they set the barracoons on fire, and at the last the Portuguese captain was glad enough to trade Telega off to a man whose language he could not understand, who had been blown south from Sallee, a Moorish port where he had been trading. This man of the unknown language was no other than Nathan Gibbons, a master who had sailed out of Boston in a ship rigged as a brigantine, whose name I do not know. He looked around him in the Bight of Benin, he picked up some cotton and some palm-oil and a little gold-dust. He watered his vessel and went back to Lisbon with her. What happened then I do not know. I do

know that four or five months after the wedding was
broken up Master Telega, the bridegroom, was landed
at Gibbons's wharf, in Boston. I know that Gibbons's
uncle was selling off the cargo, and that Telega was
advertised by poster and by town-crier to be sold as a
hearty, strong negro boy, just arrived from Africa.

III

Thus it is that I am able to fix the date much better
than if I had to rely on that business of the double
fists and the rising and setting of the sun.

There were no newspapers in Boston, but there was
a great deal of conversation, and whatever was posted
on the town-pump or at the town-house hard by, or
above the whipping-post or on the front of the meeting-
house, was rapidly repeated from mouth to mouth. So
was it that the week had not ended before all the town
knew perfectly well that a "Ginny black" was offered
for sale. And in one and another conference, in which
Winthrop and Dudley and John Cotton took the lead,
as they came out from the Thursday lecture, the matter was discussed in all its relations. When John Cotton and John Wilson went into the meeting-house
Thursday morning they did not know much about this
matter, and far less did they know what they thought
about it. But after the informal conversation with
the other Elders after the meeting was over and before
they left the house, both of them knew very well.
Winthrop knew what they thought and Dudley knew,
for in a fashion Winthrop and Dudley had had their

share in telling John Cotton what it was as well that
he should think.   And so when people went to meeting
on Sunday there was quite a general impression in
the congregation that before they came out they would
know what was to be done with the black man.

The meeting-house was always as full as it would
hold.   On this occasion Wilson led the congregation
in prayer; then he "deaconed out" one of the Psalms,
as versified for the congregation.   Then Cotton led in
prayer, and after the prayer he announced the text of
his discourse.   It was from Revelation, xviii., 10, 11,
12, and 13: "Alas, alas, that great city Babylon,
that mighty city! for in one hour is thy judgment
come.   And the merchants of the earth shall weep and
mourn over her; for no man buyeth their merchandise
any more: the merchandise of gold, and silver, and
precious stones, and of pearls, and fine linen, and purple, and silk, and scarlet, and all thyine-wood, and all
manner vessels of ivory, and all manner vessels of most
precious wood, and of brass, and iron, and marble, and
cinnamon, and odors, and ointments, and frankincense,
and wine, and oil, and fine flour, and wheat, and beasts,
and sheep, and horses, and chariots, and slaves, and souls
of men."

The first head was a description of Babylon in all its
glory.   The second head showed that, although Boston
was but a small town now, nay, had been called "Lost
Town" in the sneers of the people around her, there
was every reason why, if Boston held firmly in her
loyalty to the living God, King of kings and Lord of
lords, Boston should have more wealth and trade and
rule and dominion than any of the principalities and

powers of the heathen. The third head showed that
all this was impossible for Boston if she did not cleave
to the living God and did not live by His commands.
The fourth head showed, by full reference to the books
of the Old Testament, that God's people made no
slaves excepting in war. The fifth head pointed out
the denunciations of the prophets against the Syrians,
because they bought and sold slaves from the islands
of the West. And the sixth head brought all this to a
close in its denunciation of Babylon because she traded
in souls and slaves.

"I have read to you," he said, "from the Word of
God the names of some of those things which perish
with the using, which this great Babylon bought and
sold. I have read to you also the names of treasures which do not perish in the using, which this
Babylon pretended to sell and to buy. It is all as
Boston can buy corn and fish and fur, as Boston can
buy beaver and otter and skin of mink and skin of
bear, as Boston can send out her sassafras to England
and buy her cotton from the Indies; so could Babylon
buy and sell cinnamon and frankincense." And then
he read the whole verse. "But woe to Babylon, because she bought, or tried to buy, the souls of men!
Babylon the Great is fallen, because she bought those
slaves which her merchants captivated far away. And
woe to this town, which we thought the Lord founded;
woe to His kingdom, which we thought was to come
even in this wilderness, in the day when our shipmen
and our merchants shall carry away from us our furs
and our spices, and shall bring back to us, for a recom-
pense, slaves and the souls of men!" Then, pausing

23

for a moment, he went on to address the King of kings in prayer. The whole congregation, thrilled and excited, rose to their feet and stood as he prayed, pouring out the anger of his eloquence in eager words:

"O Lord God, spare Thy people, and save Thy heritage! Let not the curse and the damnation fall on this place which fell upon those heathen. Let not Thine own people, the sheep of Thine own pasture and the flock of Thine own hand, stray in the waste in which the Gentiles strayed. Let them not taste the fruit that was forbidden; let them not drink of the waters of Marah. Save, O God, save in this Thy time! Blot out from the book of Thy remembrance our follies and sins in the days that are past. Remember Thine own infinite mercy, and hold fast to Thine own purpose in the redemption of this land; and show Thy people, in the light and majesty of Thine own Holy Spirit, how to undo the chains that they have bound; how to turn back from the paths of their weakness and how to proclaim liberty to the captive. Oh, rule in this Thy land, Thou who art King of kings and God of gods, Thou Lord of hosts! Rule for our good, and do not trample us under the feet of Thy vengeance. Save us, save, we beseech Thee, O Lord! Lift up him that is oppressed; break the bonds of him who is enslaved and set the prisoner free. Save us, Lord Jesus, who hast been pleased, in Thine own flesh, to lead captivity captive, and Thine shall be the glory and the honor, the power and the dominion, forever and ever, world without end. Amen."

And then he directed them to sing the Forty-fourth Psalm. Wilson, as before, gave out the lines one by one, and the congregation all joined in a fashion in the singing. Wilson pronounced the benediction, and the assembly was dissolved.

There is no diary nor note-book which gives any account of the conversation in excited circles on that day or the next day. But in the colony records, brief as fate but no less decided, is the memorandum:

"The Court wrote to Mr. Williams, of Pascataq, requesting him to send the negro which he had of Mr. Smyth, that they might send him back to Ginny."

IV

It was this promptness of the General Court which brought about the dramatic close to the story, as it was finally told me by my four interpreters.

At the first, even after the interest I had shown in the necklaces and in the book, they had not understood how intense was my curiosity and how eager I was to gratify it in every detail. As I have intimated already, they had one detail and another of it to give me, such as I should search for vainly, though I should go up and down among the oldest people in Boston and ask them to tell what they remembered of October, 1645. Alas! so soon as we give ourselves over to printing-presses and libraries this matter of tradition from father to son and from mother to daughter dies out. But this tale of the days and weeks and months which Telega, the "Ginny black," spent in Boston, while they were waiting for a mast-schooner to sail from Piscataqua, which might transfer him to a Guinea trader, which should take him to the Congo, this tale had been repeated, without any "Russian scandal" and without any vagueness of detail, for seven generations. Cotton and Wilson and Winthrop and Dudley, with all the pride of paper and ink, have been more reticent. They have not told whether he dined with them or breakfasted with them or took his tea with them. Winthrop has not told by what efforts of interpreters he tried to find out whether this man knew that he was a grandson of Ham or whether he did not know. This is certain, that Telega picked up some words of English, and I found that they still had the name of the shillings in the necklace; they still knew and could speak the word Smyth in a fashion, and more plainly the word Cotton, and they knew as well that the wampum necklace was a treasure of a different sort from the string of silver and gold.

Telega had seen and driven horses and oxen; Telega had been taught to sail in a boat and to fish with English fishing-tackle; Telega had once been trusted with the care of sheep; Telega had been able to tell of the cocks and hens for whom he had scattered corn morning and evening; and, at the last, when Telega had been sent, as I found, to the Piscataqua for his farewell — sent with the blessings of priests and the hearty hand-shaking of many others—he had been told that the money that was given to him was to be used for any purpose of his passage, if he should find himself in a strait. But, as the reader will see, he fell into no misfortune which an intelligent black like himself, with a smattering of two languages now, besides his own, could not fairly meet. He had, carried in a bag at his neck, concealed under his clothing, the three Joes

and the thirty-one shillings which had been given him
by the Treasurer in the town-house in Boston, and he
had brought them out safely when he arrived at his
home. He had also brought with him a copy of the
Scriptures, which he had been made to understand was
more precious by far than the Joes and the shillings.
After he had gained some little knowledge of the English language I suppose that one and another attempt
had been made to rescue his soul from its certain
danger. But it was clear enough that nobody pretended that he had thus gained any understanding of
the vital truths of the religion of John Cotton. There
had been no blasphemous baptizing, and he had been
left, unwillingly, I dare say, to worship such gods as he
found in the streams or the stars. Only John Cotton
had borne his testimony in a fashion by folding up and
giving him, as a precious keepsake, the copy of the
Bible which had with such reverence been shown to me.

As soon as I had been made to understand this I
begged that the book might be brought to me again.
I opened and examined it carefully, hoping to find
John Cotton's name or some notes from his hand. But
there was hardly a written word. Once or twice a
palpable printer's error had been corrected. For the
rest, it was as it had been when sent to Boston from
London. Why, oh, why, did not dear John Cotton, if
it were he, write something on that fly-leaf, which
seemed made for writing? Or, putting it in general,
why did people who wrote so much that is dull and
said so much that there was no need of saying — why
did they hold the pen just when we, their children, are
most eager to read and to hear?

V

This ends the story, so far as the Massachusetts records go. A year after the Bay people had to send back a "Ginny interpreter" and another black, who had slipped into their hands in much the same way. Telega, who had had the name of "Cotton" given him also—in sign, I suppose, of the friendship of that great preacher—went, I think, to Bristol in England. Certainly it was to some English town larger than the American Boston. Clearly he was no fool, and in Bristol he needed no one to take care of him. There were enough of his own race there, though, I suppose, none of his own village. For a special reason he was eager to be at home. He had, however, to take care what vessel he chose. Fortunately for him he did not choose wrong.

Whatever the vessel was, as they passed the latitude of the Strait of Gibraltar they fell in with a pirate rover from Sallee, one of the Moorish ports. Of the fight which followed, all my story-tellers had much more to tell than of anything that happened to him in Piscataqua or in Boston. In that fight poor Telega had a bullet shot through his chest, and of this shot, I was told, he bore the mark when he died, seventy years after.

His real dangers did not begin—and this he knew—until he was in the Bight of Benin. Had not his English captain been true as steel, he would have sold him there to the first Portuguese trader he found. But Telega had not chosen a knave or a pirate among the

Bristol ship-masters. He had chosen a God-fearing man who would have kept his promise though he had "promised to his loss." I was told, in delightful detail, how he was kept below until the ship was fairly at her anchorage off the mouth of the river. Then I was told how on a dark night in July he was called, and how the English captain bade him good-bye. He was put upon a boat, with a good store of hard bread and a bit of dried beef, and, what he prized more, what we might call a carbine, a short fire-arm or long pistol of that time, with a horn of powder, a pouch with match and bullets, and a flint and steel. The captain fell on his knees on the deck and prayed to his God, and bade Telega good-bye. A sea-breeze was blowing, so that the sailors could put sail on the boat, and when morning came she was well up the river. I was told how long they hid themselves from Portuguese marauders, and then, at length, which I could have well spared, I was told where, at last, he was landed on the northern bank—not an hour too early, as it proved.

In what followed, in this long story, the reason appeared for his pressing haste. On the morning of the fourth day after he parted from his Bristol friends, he came out on the hill-side where I first saw the village. It was a year to a day since his wedding procession had been interrupted so wretchedly. He knew that, and he knew what depended on the passage of a year. By all the customs of his tribe his sweetheart, his almost wife, was a widow for that year. But it was for that year only. When the year was ended she might be betrothed again. Telega did not believe that there would be any careful astronomy in this affair.

He knew very well that when twelve moons were over, every man in the village would think he had a right to the prettiest girl, and the most charming in the village. Here was his reason for refusing to wait with the English captain till he should have gone on to Fernando Po, and till he should have come up the river to trade for ivory.

As I have said, he was not an hour too early.

As he approached the village no one met him. " He was afeared, it was so still." This was Philip's phrase to me in interpreting. He hurried all the faster. He passed a close grove of pepper-trees, to see in it the pretended ambush of a bridegroom and his men in full dress, waiting for the bride's procession.

Telega had been stealing along as a cat does, and this merry group did not see him, but he seems to have seen his advantage. He passed them on the instant, he went twenty paces farther, he hid himself under a heavy tuft of banana plants, and he had not to wait long. The bride came, wretched enough, for all her bridal toggery. She had insisted on wearing two or three sea-gull feathers, which were tokens of deepest mourning. She wept as if she were at her husband's funeral. She flung away a bunch of flowers which the new bridegroom's mother gave to her. None the less was this a bridal procession. Banjoes and tomtoms and the whole village behind and before made this certain.

A large stone to-day marks the corner where Telega, gun in hand, sprang out like a tiger, and, in literal fact, seized his bride. Pluto was not less expected in Enna. The girl screamed now to some purpose, and in a minute was sobbing with her head upon his shoulder. The banjoes and the tomtoms were silent, and bridegroom number two, with his handsome cohort of " best men " —hearing nothing after they should have heard music and song—after a mysterious minute or two came out from their lair to learn what had hindered the procession.

At this point the story, which I heard two or three times at least—once as we went up the river, twice as we came down—varied in its forms. Who can wonder, after nearly two hundred and fifty years? But there can be no doubt that when Telega caught his bride with his left arm, and when she sobbed on his shoulder, his right hand held the matchlock, and he blew the match to be sure that it was a live coal. And when that braggart bridegroom number two came up, howling and storming, Telega turned over his bride to one of her women, dropped the gun to a level, and, in the very classic language of Mandara, told bridegroom number two that if he did not keep a civil tongue in his head he would blow his brains out. Nay, more, I am afraid that Elder Cotton's seed had sprouted so ill that Telega would have done what he said had there been occasion.

But there was no occasion. The game was played through. There were elders in the village who had as much to do with its affairs as in that other village of mud-walls and thatched roofs called Boston, where John Cotton and John Wilson and Thomas Dudley and John Winthrop did the thinking for the rest, and told them what was right and what was wrong. Nay, the evident public opinion of the procession was in favor of the handsome young traveller, who had been in Europe, not to say America, and had brought home its latest fashions. There were bride-maidens, as you saw, and they whispered, " 'Twere better by far to have matched our fair cousin to her old sweetheart." And so, after some flourishing of clubs and knives, much scolding, swearing, threatening, and other debating, three or four elders, much like those I have described, I think, stilled all voices and bade the tom-toms and the banjoes begin again.

I doubt if it were the march in *Midsummer-Night's Dream*, but it answered every purpose of that midsummer noonday as well. Bridegroom number two sulked off. But all his men joined in the procession, and afterwards, I fancy, partook of the banquet. And, though his cabin was not occupied for a day or two, a sufficiently good cabin was found for all purposes of Telega and his bride.

This happy conclusion to a story so sad was brought about when the General Court in the Bay voted to send the " Ginny black man" home. But I should never have heard of it but for King Charles's Shilling.

FROM MAKING TO BAKING

I.—MAKING

"What is it, Arundel?" said the president, kindly. "Take a chair, Arundel. I hope you do not want to go as all the rest do."

"I am sure I do not want to go, sir," said Arundel, with a little hesitation; "but I cannot stay. When I saw you in January I thought it was all arranged. Indeed, it was all arranged, as perhaps you remember I told you. But I have had bad news from home. My younger sister has been sick. My mother must take her to New York for an operation in the hospital. And—in short—there is no money. I am afraid this is the same story which all the others tell you."

"Indeed, indeed, Arundel, I am very sorry for you. But you must not be discouraged, my boy. Modern surgery has resources which we knew nothing of five years ago; and because your sister goes to the hospital you must not think she is not to come out again. New York, you say? Does your mother know them all there? Let me give her a letter to my brother there. He is a real top-sawyer, Arundel," said the kind old man, who wanted to make his favorite laugh. In an instant, indeed, he was arranging for the sister, as if she had been his own daughter, and as if this was the affair Arundel had come upon—as it was not.

All this happened in the president's office of Lansing
College, which, as all the world knows — or ought to
know — is one of the best schools of practical agriculture in the world.

When the doctor could not think of more facilities
for John Arundel's sister — or when John Arundel
would not let him—the matter returned, about which
John Arundel had come. He had determined to leave
the college for Dakota for the summer, and to see
something more of the practice of agriculture. So
many of the other fellows had done the same thing,
that he knew very well what he was proposing, and
so did the president. It was no question of "if,"
"whether," or "maybe." It was a plain bit of necessity. And though the president hated to have him go,
as Arundel knew he would, there was nothing for it.
When the interview had ended, which was all kindness
on the part of the older man, as it was all respect on
the part of the other, the young fellow had full leave
of absence for six months, and as many letters of introduction to be used in his own behalf in one pocket as
in another he had for his sister's advantage. A farewell night with the Sigma Phi, and then John Arundel
was at the station in the gray of the morning, waiting
for the night express to take him westward to Chicago
and towards the bonanzas.

His first sight of his new home was not one of glad
omen.

"You will have to wait," said the foreman, to whom
he had been sent from the first office where he applied.
"I am going to a funeral, and so is Mr. Cutter—indeed,
all of us here are; but at one, if you will be here—or

you can wait. There is the *Tribune*. Only, I suppose, you brought this with you."

"Let me go with you," said Arundel, he hardly knew why. But he had been alone for forty-eight hours, and it was the instinct of companionship which spoke. It was then explained to him, as they walked along, that a balky horse had shied or started or backed, nobody knew what, and this Mr. Keating, an Englishman, whom nobody knew much, had been pitched suddenly from a harrow he was driving. He had broken his skull and never spoke again. Such was the welcome which greeted Arundel; and in the offices of sympathy, as the heads of the farms came around the dazed widow and her children, he spent his first hours at his new home.

But life in that region was not largely given to offices of sympathy, or to other ceremony. Before night fell, Arundel was himself handling two half-broken horses as well as he could, wondering whether either of them was the particular brute that had cost Keating his life. From time to time he met another man on duty like his own, as they passed and repassed in the occasions of their long tours of service. At eight in the evening his day's work was over. He took his horses to the stable, and rubbed them down, and waited until he was sure that they were fed. Then, and not until then, he found his own fodder and his own bed.

A neat enough bunk, in a great barrack where twenty or more men slept — this was the bed. He had his choice between an under bunk, where a Swede, snoring loudly, was already asleep above; or an upper bunk, where the man below did not snore at all. Wisely or not, John chose the latter. There was little question of dressing or undressing, and little discussion in the morning as to whose was this cardigan or that shirt. For every man slept in the clothes he worked in. There was no doubt whether one should wake or not, for the hours when different gangs were needed were distinctly proclaimed as approaching fifteen minutes precisely before they came. If a man were as careful as Arundel was about his work, he went himself to the stable, to make sure there was no delay or stupidity about the harnessing of the span he had to begin work with. He was fond of horses, and they soon knew it. There were some sad screws on the place, but the owners' interests were the same as those of the workmen in this matter, and, on the whole, John's four-footed partners in this business were not a bad company. He soon knew them all and they knew him. And he soon knew the stable-hands well enough to do much as he chose in the selection of teams, when any change was made. He did not dislike his work, and knew it must be done. He had no companionship but his horses in their long drives. But generally he knew them and they trusted him; and for his thoughts there were always home and the boundless future.

With thrashing he had nothing to do. He was one of the last gang of reapers, and when he reported his last day's work in that affair he knew that the immense winter crop was in.

"They drove their handsome horses down, they drove them back again,
　While click, click, click, the rattling knives cut off the heavy grain.
　Before it falls the waiting straw with tightest tie is twined,
　And the well-ordered sheaves are left in still array behind."

II.—CARRYING

"Mr. Arundel," said the boss, "I sent for you to ask you if you could go with this wheat to Philadelphia?"

"Certainly, sir," said John, and he started as he said so, for he had been wanting for a week to go to the East, and yet he could hardly account for the wish. He knew it was, to some degree, sentimental. For a week he had been at work with the gang of men who had been loading these very cars of which Mr. Pegram had spoken. He had amused himself in wondering whether one particular wheat grain or another which walked home in his shoes with him was, or was not, his own production. Had he, or had he not, a share in its harvesting? By and large, or speaking in general, he had now done wellnigh everything in this business of giving men their daily bread. Thus he had been on the harrow in those first days, he had driven seeders for other days, he had taken all his turns with corn-planting and cultivating; and, when he was transferred to the wheat-harvesting side, he had not lost a quarter of an hour from his own stents, while more than once he had taken work which belonged to fellow-workmen. So the fancy had taken him, that it was in a way unkind to let these creatures of his hand go off on their long journey without offering them an escort at the start. Indeed, he knew enough to know, not, of course, which cars his own children were in, but that it was certain that these three last trains had, each of them, hundreds of bushels of wheat which would not have existed but for him.

So he answered Mr. Pegram's request with a certain readiness which surprised even that leader of men. But in that office there was little reference to sentiment. If the young man would go, that was enough.

"If I could have my way, Arundel, those four cars you loaded last should not go at all. The stuff does us no good, and I would not like to have any man know who shipped it. Anyway, it must not be mixed with the rest. That is the reason why I want some one to go with it to Philadelphia and be there. Of course, I have written. But I know what letters are. If you are there, you will see that a separate delivery is made and a separate receipt taken for it. Here are the numbers—C, 12,211, 23,419, 21,501, and 11,798."

Arundel understood perfectly. He did not say so, but he knew that no one ought to be surprised if all this wheat sprouted before they came to the Delaware, and appeared as a lovely green meadow might when the cars were opened. Again he said he should be glad to go. And Mr. Pegram gave him a note to the local superintendent to ask that he might have a "drover's pass" to go with this train to the sea.

The local superintendent honored this request, and John found himself for a week or two a resident of the several cabooses which carried the stern lights of the trains that drew the four fatal cars that held the musty grain of which the firm was so thoroughly ashamed.

The company in the cabooses was not large, but was of all sorts and conditions of men whom this moving world brings together. In each caboose were eight or ten bunks for sleep; four seats which commanded the bunk above, so that those who sat there could look forward or aft like pilots in a little pilot-house, and other seats on the ground-floor; a stove where you could warm up your coffee or a plate of hash for which you had foraged at some station, or could even scramble an egg, if you were luxurious; two packs of cards, black beyond belief with the thumb marks of firemen off duty; one or two old newspapers, and a train directory of prehistoric times — these were the essential appurtenances of these moving palaces. Imagine a nine-cornered bit of looking-glass tacked up by the side of a window, a colored lithograph of the battle of Resaca, a pretty cigar girl in flaunting colors of the gaudiest chromo, each nailed up for study and admiration, and a few comic scraps from newspapers pasted on the walls of the car, and you have the non-essentials.

This particular caravan was bound to Philadelphia; for it was foreordained, though John Arundel did not know this, that the wheat of his harvesting should be shipped from that port to Antwerp. Thirteen days were enough for the land journey, and on the fourteenth day John had taken his duplicate receipts for the several cars of the several trains, and he could report with absolute certainty that the idiotic or abnormal wheat had gone to its own place. The truth is that it was not nearly so bad as its reputation, and there was no spring garden of verdure when the cars were opened.

It was John's first visit at the seaboard, if an arrival in landlocked Philadelphia may thus be called. When he left the elevator office, he pushed his inquiries up and down the river, and soon found himself at the pier

24

where the steamship lay. He wondered whether he might go on board, tried the experiment, and found, as in a busy world one is apt to find, that nobody cared if, whether, who, or what he was, and that he might go where he chose. So that he had the amusement of examining, for the first time in his life, the interior of a great ocean steamer. It was then and there that he fixed an idea, which had floated vaguely before him in his long caboose journey. He determined that he would go to Europe in the *Arteveld* if, as it proved, she carried to Antwerp the grain which was the fruit of his three months' industry.

In a couple of days more this was determined. He learned, at a second visit to the elevator office, that the *Arteveld* would take several thousand bushels of wheat. And though, of course, no man knew which particular kernels would go to that contingent, John easily figured out, from what he knew of the elevator compartments, that some of his handiwork, if he might call it so, was to cross the water.

So John put on a cardigan jacket and a tweed cap, and went to the engineer's room on board the *Arteveld* and engaged himself on the outward trip as a stoker. As he reported for duty the day before the ship sailed, carrying his little kit with him to the gangway, a cab-horse at his side fell and some confusion followed. Arundel himself helped the passengers from the cab. It proved that they were coming to see the *Arteveld*, and he showed them the passengers' gangway. The faces of the two women haunted him for half an hour before he could fix them. Then he recollected that they were the widow and daughter of Keating, whom he had seen at the funeral which began his service on the bonanza farm. The dice-box of life had been so shaken that he fell in with them again at the beginning of this second act in his drama.

III.—SHIPPING

Yes, it is a very hard life, this of a stoker on an ocean steamer. John's wardrobe was not large, but it was much larger than he needed. A pair of drawers, a pair of shoes—these are enough. The watches, at that time, were four hours each, of steady wheeling of coal from the bunkers to the furnaces—back and forth, back and forth, with hardly a change. Then, while a man was off duty he slept, or played cards, or read, or loafed alone. No one cared, so only when the watch was called again he was on hand. At that time, on that line, there were but two daily terms of duty, the stokers being divided into three watches. And at this they had all the work which even stout young men like them cared to do.

But nothing lasts forever. The mere dead monotony of this thing helped, in a way, the hours to go by, though it would be hard to say that they ever flew. The men of the watches cared, in general, little for the history of the passage of the ship, and knew less. But Arundel was inquirer enough to put himself now and then into a costume which would be visible on the upper decks, and he found that they were making a passage better than was usual with the *Arteveld*. Indeed, on the thirteenth day from Philadelphia they were at Antwerp. On the next day the ship was deserted by all these butterfly travellers who had supposed that she was rushing through the ocean for their satisfaction, and that more serious business of giving the world its daily bread began. For Arundel, he declined all invitations to return in the ship. He took his well-earned wages and receipted for them, went ashore and dressed himself like an Aryan of the nineteenth century, abandoning the costume of a savage of the Garden of Eden, and went to see the Antwerp Cathedral.

He spent a day in sight-seeing, and then returned in thought to his Dakota kernels. How were those quarts, pecks, and bushels faring which had no friend in Europe excepting him?

Sure enough, at the pier ("on t' wharf" is what Ant-werp means) he found his children. He did not, in the bottom of his heart. much approve of the way in which they were handled. Antwerp had not then the facilities she has now, and things were done in what seemed a primitive-fashion to this young critic who had seen Chicago and Milwaukee. But he knew life and his own limitations too well to offer advice. He went from place to place, following the wheat along as it travelled, till he found a squad of men and of women shovelling the grain into bags, in which it was to be carried inland. The force of workmen was ridiculously small, and John Arundel, determined to see what he could see, went to the foreman, took off his hat as he saw the others do, pointed at himself, at a shovel, and at an empty bag, and looked an inquiry.

The Dutch boss, who might have been called so in

his own language, took in the situation in an instant, laughed good-naturedly, and said, in perfectly good English:

"You want to go to work? Certainly, and bring a dozen others, if you will." Then he took John's name, appointed him a shovel, and in five minutes more he was shovelling corn like the rest. Only, he said to himself, "How in the world did he know I was a Yankee?" As if, from the crown of his head to the sole of his foot, in the twinkle of his eye and his gait as he walked, he was not pronounced to all men around as an American.

Before a week was over he could make himself understood, when he asked for his bread-and-butter at the workmen's lodging-house to which the friendly boss had directed him. Every night at some theatre of the people, Sunday at church, he listened with all his ears to the new dialect; and it did not seem so unfamiliar to him. And when, at the end of ten days, in which his grain and much more grain had been "sacked" at last, by the joint efforts of some dozens of them of both sexes and all nations, John was quite ready for a new adventure.

He was standing in the office, with the afternoon report of the bags which his gang had filled, tied, and delivered, when a well-to-do Flemish miller was talking with the boss. John understood, after a minute, that the miller wanted to hire a hand. Without a second's thought, finding that his employer was looking at him, he said, as the miller stopped speaking, "Ask him if I shall do." The boss laughed, and said he was thinking of proposing it. The miller was easy to please. He expected to pay little, and he knew the world too well

to expect to receive much. American wheat was
wholly new to him. And perhaps an American mill-
hand might give points for the grinding. The bargain
was soon made, and John bade his friendly boss good-
bye forever, to report on Friday morning at the train
for Little Merode.

IV.—GRINDING

American wheat was certainly a novelty in all that
region. Indeed, if Mr. Fraikin had not been a very
new-fangled and impetuous man, it was generally
agreed that there would be no American wheat there
now. But the truth was that the local harvest of all
that region had virtually failed. Of course, a few
bushels of wretched grain would be found here and
there. But unless people meant to live on roots and
acorns and oatmeal, the stuff of which white bread is
made must be brought from somewhere else. And so
Mr. Fraikin had determined that he might as well
grind it, as he had the stones and the mills, as let his
stones be mould-worn for want of use, and his machinery
rust before his eyes. Great were the wonderings, in
more languages than one, as the bags of foreign wheat,
seen here for the first time, were transferred to his
simple granaries.

It was Saturday night when this transfer was com-
pleted, after a day of hard work by the very limited
force of horses and men which had it in charge. Arundel recommended himself at once by his handiness with
the great Flemish horses that took so large a part of

this business. He tried his new accomplishment in speaking Flemish with the other hands, had his neat quarters assigned him, and thanked God that the next day there would be no work to do. At breakfast he appeared in his Sunday suit, a queer enough contrast in appearance to his fellow-workmen in theirs. When the bells rang, a group of them walked to the church together. In the church porch and outside they all lingered. John did not know why; but he did know that "The dumb man's borders still increase," so he asked no questions, waited, and learned. After a minute or more, the family of Mr. Fraikin drove up in two carriages to the little church, and with some ceremony alighted. Then John saw that all the group with him uncovered themselves, for the first time, and, as the family entered, joined themselves to the little procession as if they were of the family also. In the church, a dozen or twenty chairs, together, seemed to have been waiting for them. In these they all sat down, and after hats and parasols and shawls had been arranged, and hymn-books handed from one to another, John saw that the young woman who sat next to him, who was one of those who came in the second carriage, was the daughter of John Keating, the same with whom he had crossed the ocean, and whom he had first seen at her father's funeral.

Grinding by wind-power is a very different business from grinding by steam. And the quaint, queer windmills where John Arundel was now at work always seemed to him as if they had stepped out of one of Rembrandt's pictures. There are days when no whistling will bring a breeze, and after all has been done

that can be done in the way of holy-stoning floors and
other cleaning up, of patching and other repairing, a
good deal of time goes by, with this or that hand lying
on the shady side of the mill, smoking or lounging, or
singing with the others.   On such a day John Arundel lay on the ground reading a copy of the *Journal
des Enfans* which had strayed into the office, when a
party of children from the house came running up in
their play.   John caught a ball which one of them
·threw, and gave him a return ball, to the little fellow's
great glee.   In a moment the boy had run up and was
talking to him, and so in a minute more he found himself on his feet, with his cap in his hand, talking to
Lucy Keating, the children's governess.   To both of
them, of course, it was a pleasure to talk English.

A minute more, and another of the children reported.
This was the oldest of all, Hilda, who had torn the
ribbon from her hat, and brought it up for repairs.
Miss Keating was not unused to such accidents, produced needle and thread, and set things in order, while
John, on his part, stood the cross-questioning of all the
children, who knew the mills well and all their belong-
ings, as to the American wheat and how it came there.
It was quite natural for him to turn to Miss Keating
and say, " I do not know if you know that this famous
wheat came in the *Arteveld*.   I saw you on board of
her."

She started with some surprise, and owned she had
not seen him.   He laughed and said she would not be
likely to see him, and told of his engaging himself as a
stoker.   " No," said the girl, " I certainly saw nothing
of your under-water place of torment," and then she

paused, and said almost unconsciously, "but I was sure I had seen you somewhere, when we met in the church on the first Sunday." Arundel did not say, of course, that it was at her father's funeral that they had met, but something in the sad expression of his face reminded her how she had looked up once as she had stood by an open grave and had seen his expression of sad sympathy. But she only said, "Ah, yes! I remember now," and at once called the children to go farther on their walk.

You see it had happened, as we say for convenience, that on the famous journey to Antwerp, on which Mr. Fraikin had bought the American wheat, his wife had commissioned him to bring her an English governess. And so it happened that he had gone to his cousin, the wife of the Reverend Herr Pastor Somebody, and it had happened again that she had been told the week before of Lucy Keating and her wish to find a place as English teacher, and so it happened that she and Mr. Fraikin and John Arundel had all gone together, in different cars of one train, to Little Merode, and so it happened that they were talking together in English here and now.

V.—MIXING

" You teach so sweetly the English, dear Mees Lucy, and you show so well Karl his algebra, and he so delights the playing with you his duets, that it is indeed wicked that no one has taught you also the Latin." Such was the intelligible statement, meant to be complimentary, which was made to Lucy Keating by Ma-

dame Fraikin, when it was determined that Karl must
go to the Lycée at Bruxelles for his Latin.

He was a quiet boy, but when he heard this he said :
" Why does not Jan teach me my Latin—Jan at the
mill, I mean ? He knows Latin better than the Herr
Pastor does, or any one else. He reads Latin in a little
book he has in his pocket." In fact, Karl had found
Arundel reading from his pocket Horace, in one of
those days of calm.

Lucas, the cross cousin who lived with them, learning
to be a miller, and snubbing the children by way of
relaxation, laughed at this, and said Karl did not know
the difference between Latin and English or French.
His interpellation was fortunate, for it enlisted the
boy's mother on his side. She did not want to send
him away from home, and would not have thought of
it but that his father had made a point of the Latin.

It was known that Mees Lucy had known Arundel
in America, and now she was summoned into council.
By this time she knew that he was a senior from Lansing, and had taken the "academical course" there.
She said that he could not have gone so far without
knowing Latin well. She had heard him say he had
been a teacher, but what he had taught she did not
know. In truth, she had only met him two or three
times, as the younger children had, when she had them
with her out of doors.

But this was quite enough for Madame Fraikin.
And when the new week began, it was quite settled
that John should begin every day at the house, with
two hours' teaching of Karl in his Latin. At the mills,
also, his functions changed, and, as he came to speak

Flemish more and more easily, he found himself assigned to those hundred and one duties of detail or supervision which come of course in an old-time establishment like that, where there is none too much system, but where, somehow, if you are not impatient, everything gets itself done in time.

And when Christmas came, this mad but wise speculation of M. Fraikin in the American wheat had been repeated once and again, with a success which surprised every one who does not know how to combine madness and wisdom. At first he went to Antwerp to buy the wheat himself; afterwards he sent Monsieur Jan, as Arundel was generally called. Then Monsieur Jan told him how he could send his own orders by telegraph to America, and land his own wheat sometimes in Havre. And there was not a baker in Hesdin, or Hasebrouck, or Arras but had come to see the milling, to feel of the flour and taste it, and at last to buy. And when the great French army contractors, Badaud and Vaurien, actually were forced by their principals to buy, because General Boulanger had seen some of the American bread at a dinner given by the mayor of Guise, then the triumph of M. Fraikin and of the wise madness was complete.

As to the prosperities of family life which followed, such as Madeleine's new pony and her mother's dog-cart, the children associated them all with the arrival, side by side, of Monsieur Jan at the mills and Mees Lucy in the school-room; for which theory of theirs, as the reader knows, there was less or more foundation.

What became clear enough to Monsieur Jan and Mees Lucy in long walks together of Saturday afternoons, in reading Shelley and Tennyson together, in puzzling over Egmont and Wallenstein together, by way of helping Madeleine in her German, was that they did things together a thousand times better than they could do them alone. He found out that he could not live without her, and it seemed as if she could not live without him. He told her so one day, and she blushed and smiled, and tried to speak, and at last did speak, and told him that he made her very happy.

But when he came to speak to M. Fraikin about this, and to say that he wanted to return to America to provide a home for her, that mad-wise man would not hear of it. Home in America, indeed! Belgium was emptying herself that people might make homes in America. There were more empty houses in Belgium than in the United States. Why, here was the old cottage—that they say Louis XIV. slept in—with a little new shed for the cow, and a piazza in front, and a bow-window at the side, it would be a charming place for a young couple. Monsieur Jan should stay on a salary, and introduce those steel buhrs he was always talking about; and they should be married at Easter.

VI.—BAKING

Married at Easter they were. Mrs. Keating came over from Bromwich for the wedding. When it came to the making of the cake there was a great ceremony, half Belgian, half English, and half American. All

the ladies proceeded in state to the kitchen to assist
and superintend.   Behind them, M. Fraikin and Karl
and Monsieur Jan lugged a sack of wheat flour.   Then
it was formally opened, and Lucy herself thrust in a
tin scoop once and again and lifted the good flour herself, and poured it into the pans.   And then, by arts
known to them, she and Madame Fraikin and Mrs.
Keating mixed the cake and baked it.

And Karl concocted a jingling poem, which may be
translated thus:

> " This is the cake mamma made ;
>   It was made from the meal papa made.
>   It was ground in the mill you all of you know,
>   Which grandmamma's grandpapa built long ago ;
>   And the good God sent all the winds to blow,
>   And make the wheels fly round, that so
>   We should have the meal papa made.

> " The corn, it came in Miss Lucy's ship
>   In which she crossed the terrible deep.
>   They sailed by night and they sailed by day,
>   Till they all had sailed the whole of the way ;
>   And the corn has never stopped nor stayed
>   Till now in the cake mamma has made.

> " The corn was made by Monsieur Jan—
>   A very wonderful corn-making man.
>   He took a spade and dug in the ground,
>   And planted some grains of corn he found ;
>   And the good God sent the winds to blow
>   And the sun to shine that the corn might grow,
>   And He told Monsieur Jan the wheat to take
>   And give Miss Lucy a wedding cake,
>   And here is the corn that Jan made."

And at the wedding supper Master Karl was made

to read his ode, with great applause, before Lucy cut
the cake.

And when, the next morning, she and Jan had their
first breakfast in the King Louis cottage, she would
not let him touch a mouthful of anything else till he
and she had broken a biscuit which she had made from
the *Arteveld* flour. This was their wedding sacrament.

THE girl sang cheerily, as she took her place in the canoe:

> "The squirrel said 'chee' to the wood-thrush,
> The wood-thrush said 'whee' to the squirrel,
>   And the sun rose.
> The squirrel hid in the bark,
> And the wood-thrush flew to the south,
>   But the sun rose."

And sure enough, as she sang, the first bright line of the sun's disk could be seen above the horizon's edge.

She pointed to it gayly.

The boy was evidently more fond of his sister than we are taught to believe is the habit of these people. And it was clear that she knew how to make him fond of her. She sat in the bow of her canoe, now humming the refrain of her song, if it may be called so, and, once and again, when he asked her, singing such words as she fancied at the moment. All the time, with split porcupine quills, she was embroidering for him an ornament for the handle of a canoe-paddle. The quills of different colors lay in the lap of her deerskin coat, and the quaint, simple pattern came out, to his delight, more and more plainly, as she sang and as he paddled the boat along.

The canoe had been lying in a little ditch, cut for the purpose in the black mud of the bank of what we should now call a bayou. They pushed out under the heavy shade of the canebrake, upon the waters of the motionless lake, which had, in fact, been left by the river, in an old change of levels, but was still three or four feet deep. The surface was covered in some places by large, round, green shields, the leaves of lotuses, and both boy and girl looked curiously for the great seed-vessels. Now and then, as they shot by, he cut off a ripe head with the copper knife which hung at his belt. He would toss the very ripest to her, and she would open the great cup and shake out the seeds, to crack and nibble as they sailed. On the velvety surface of the great, green leaves of the plants were round diamond drops, beautiful as if they had indeed come from Golconda. Close before them, on the dull surface of the lake, were thousands upon thousands of water birds, quite indifferent to the neighborhood of the voyagers until the boat was close upon them. Then one and another, perhaps a hundred at a time, would rise, always facing the wind. It seemed for a moment as if they ran across the surface of the water till there was momentum enough, if joined with the movement of the wind in the opposite direction, to lift the bird into the air. It was precisely as a boy runs with his kite, to give it, by his earthly running, a chance to fly. The air once caught, the bird stopped the motion of its web-feet, and the wings lifted it on its way, long streams of white foam following after the fugitives, the babble of which was like the babble of a mountain stream. The boy pushed his canoe along through

lilies, lily - pads, lotus leaves, and the bubbles left by
the escape of birds, and two or three minutes of such
rapid paddling as his brought them both into the very
heart of the great plantation (shall one call it?) of wild-
rice, to which he had promised to bring her.

The exquisite plants rose above the girl's head, even
when she stood in the canoe, four, even five times as
high as she was. The wild-rice can hardly be described
to one who has not seen it, so delicate and fine are the
highest stems, each bearing a beautiful chandelier of
the blossoms and of the ripened fruit. A leaf of delicate green hangs right and left from a round stem as
green, and on the very top stem of all are clustered the
long spikes of rice, daintiest of food for ducks and teal,
and not to be despised by men.

The girl clapped her hands as she saw how plenteous
was the harvest, and, in joyful smiles, she expressed
her pleasure to her brother. Into the mouth of the
smallest and narrowest creek which can be conceived
he drove the boat. She helped him, by pulling hard
at the stems of rice on the right hand and the left,
until they were completely embosomed in it, he at his
end and she at hers. Then he took the paddle which
he had been using, and, as she bent down the tall stems
in a line over the boat, he beat them thoroughly. Or
she herself used the paddle of which she had worked
the handle, while he bent down stems for her to work
upon. Then they pushed the boat farther and farther
in. The ripe grains piled up upon the bottom and
around their feet. It was rough harvesting, but was
ample. When the boat would go no farther up that
particular creek, he backed out into the lake again and

25

found another. It was not half an hour before the canoe had all the cargo she could float, and boy and girl both sat gingerly as he turned her head homeward to her little dock, and again drove the congress of web-footed senators away. As they came into the trench which had been cut in the hard mud, the graceful girl sprang lightly ashore, but turned again, with what in opera we should call a gesture of good-bye. He knew he need only wait for her a moment. Sure enough, she was back again as soon as she had time to run to the tepees and to return. And this time she was heavily laden with a great string of baskets, which she had fastened together and carried on a long hickory stick above her head. The load was indeed too heavy for her, and her brother ran up the path to help her.

"Now you see why I have been so busy all the summer, and all through the time of harvest, while the other girls have been singing and dancing and fooling away their time."

"I see that the baskets are for the rice, and I see that they will empty the canoe, but I do not see why you and I should gather rice for the others. And I do not know why we should go before the others are ready."

"The others? The others?" said she—this with a merry laugh, but with a gesture of scorn. "As if I meant to work for them! For them, indeed! Let them work for me!

"No, White-wings," and now she spoke more seriously, "none of our rice will go into their storehouse. I will do my share when the time comes, but this is not for them.

"White-wings, keep my secret. Help me build my
grain-house and cover it. Go with me two more mornings, that we may have three canoe-loads in all. Help
me pack it in the baskets—I have baskets enough—
and be ready to move it when the time comes.

"White-wings, do this for me, and you shall have
the white totem. You shall have the white pine-tree."
And the girl put her hand under her leather jacket,
and drew out, hanging to a cord of deer's sinew, a
round bit of silver, on one side of which was a rude
image of a pine-tree.

The boy knew that it was the most precious thing
she had. He had coveted it as the rarest of treasures,
and now she offered it to him for his own.

"White-wings," she said, "before I made the first
basket I had a dream. I dreamed that six black
swans — oh, so large!—would come down the lake
shore. And in the dream they stopped and bent their
long necks, all of them, where I stood. And I knew
they wanted rice, and I gave them rice, and the tallest
swan of all gave to me a kernel of yellow corn.

"I waked from my dream, and that morning I began
to make my baskets, that I might have the grain ready
for the swans when they should come.

"And I dreamed another dream. This time there
came six blue herons, and they bent their long necks
as they stood on their long legs. And I gave each of
them a fish, and they flew away. Then I worked all
the harder, that I might be ready for the herons when
they came.

"And three nights ago I dreamed again. And this
time six red deer came running from the east. And

they were not afraid of me. They came and nibbled grains of ripe rice from my hand. And I woke up when I felt their cold noses on my fingers.

"That time I came to you, and my good brother has helped me to fill the baskets."

As she talked they filled the baskets with the ripe grain, and carried them where they could cover them with corn-leaves, under an old willow. In hard work for the rest of that day they palisaded them stoutly, and made their enclosure so secure that it was safe from rabbits. Of deer, so near the tepees, there was no danger.

Carefully did the Indian girl watch the sun, morning, noon, and night, as the days grew shorter. She had driven a long peg into a cottonwood-tree, as high as she could, and, day by day, on the ground, she made her mark at noon, when the shadow was the shortest. At last she summoned her brother. "See, White-wings, see! The mark was here three days ago, and, see, now the shadow is here—so much shorter. They will come soon."

Every morning at sunrise, while the village was still at its laziest, the girl had, for a week before this, climbed to her eyry in her own selected bare cotton-wood-tree, to be sure that no one escaped her eye upon the larger lake. It was near a mile's walk for her every day through the prairie, but she never hesitated. Snow, rain, ice, or sunshine, it was all one for her.

And the very next day after she showed to White-wings the telltale shadow which proved that the days were growing longer, she was rewarded in her outlook.

Far to the north, on the quiet lake, which was still not frozen, were one, two, three — more specks than she could surely count. She hardly waited to count them, indeed, so eager was she to find her brother, and to bring him to the shore.

It was not an hour before they were both there. They built a fire, of which the smoke curled above them. They stood out on the bank, hardly high enough to be called a bluff, and, with tall canes, the tallest they could cut, waved signals of welcome; signals which were readily discerned in that white, flat wilderness.

Within an hour or two more the strange canoes drew near, in two lines. The strangers also waved signals of recognition, and the leading boat ran fearlessly up to the shore. Robert Cavalier de La Salle landed, and freely took the offered hand of White-wings, the boy, who knew already that such was the white man's signal of welcome.

For Waketa, she had been recognized, on the moment, by a tall, well-built, handsome Indian of the leading crew. He was one of the eighteen Massachusetts Indians whom La Salle took, with their squaws and pappooses, because they had been to the Mississippi before.

The girl looked gladly up in the face of the tall stranger, welcomed his expression of eager joy, looked up again and smiled, as any man might be glad to have such a woman smile on him.

"Yes, I knew you would come. And I knew you would come to-day.

"My dream said that when the sun was four days towards the south the six black swans would come, the

six white herons would come, the six deer would come.
And to-day is the fourth day, and you are here."

"And where is the token?" asked her admirer, proud
of the eager eyes and curious gaze of those who looked
on.

The girl looked down a minute, and hesitated.
"Which was best, Waban? Which was best?

"He has the token. It is safe; no one else has it.
I am sure," she said, proudly, "you do not fear me.

"Waban, I knew that you were coming. I knew
you would not come alone. I knew six canoes would
come with you, for I saw six swans, six herons, and six
deer in my dream.

"Waban, we are ready for you. Tell the black chief
that we are ready." And she pointed to Cavalier de
La Salle.

Then White-wings and Waban, in a mixture of the
Winnebago language and French and English, explained to the great leader that the village was but a
mile back behind the canebrake. He readily accepted
the invitation to a feast which, in his father's name,
White-wings gave him. Taking two of the whites
of his party, Waban, and the three babies and their
mothers, La Salle followed his guides to the encamp-
ment, and, with his own civility, received the hurried
welcome which was offered. Stores of berries and rice
and corn were brought out, fifty fish were placed upon
the coals, and a sudden feast of welcome was impro-
vised.

And Waketa took her lover, and led him to her
palisade, and showed him the hard-packed baskets of
rice which she and her brother had made ready.

Waban, delighted with her foresight, ran back and called the great chief.

It was hard to explain to La Salle that this welcome store of provision was thus all ready for his winter passage across to the Mississippi.

When, in three languages, the story of her dreams was told to him, he held his hand over her, and blessed her and hers.

"*Dominus tibi benedicet, filia mea.*" It was a Christmas blessing.

And from his pouch he took a Portuguese joe of gold, ten pine-tree shillings, and placed them in the hand of the girl, compelling her to take them, though she would gladly have shrunk away.

For this little story there is, alas! no written authority. But if it can ever be authenticated, here is the record of the oldest harvest, and that of the first sale on the Corn Exchange of Chicago.

And thus was consecrated that Christmas Day.

"Land at last! Look round, Patience; look round, Jack, and see how you like your new home."

The young man spoke to a boy ten years old and a girl of twelve, as they cautiously climbed a rickety ladder from a flat-boat which rose and fell on the waves. The two children stepped on a rude wooden wharf, which ran out over the rocks. It was their older brother who addressed them. He then left them to their fate, while, with a sailor in the boat, he lifted to the wharf two or three bags of grain, on which Patience and Jack had been sitting.

As soon as the first of these was on the wharf, Patience took her place on it, while Jack rendered such help as he could in landing the others. All went well enough until, by a slip, the last bag fell heavily on the boards. The leather cord, which was tied around its mouth, gave way, and as much as half a peck of grain rolled out upon the wharf.

"This will never do—this will never do. We must not waste good English wheat in this fashion." This was the warning giving by a sunburned man in his shirt-sleeves, who had just come down to the landing, and who revealed himself for the first time.

"We will waste nothing," said Martin Coram, the oldest of the three. "But a land of plenty, like yours,

will not grudge a few handfuls of grain to the sparrows
—eh, neighbor?"

And he lifted the heavy bag upon its end, opened
the mouth, and with his hands began scraping up the
wheat which had escaped. Patience and Jack helped.
He took a bit of stout whip-cord from his pocket, and
began with his knife to make holes, through which he
could lace it into the buckram. By the time these
were made and the cord inserted, the children had
gathered almost all which fell, and he drew up his cord
and made all safe.

The landsmen answered him, with a certain surliness
of manner: "The sparrows have enough, but we do
not mean to teach sparrows or hawks the taste of
English grain." And he turned away. As he did so,
the girl, Patience, rose, with her hands full of wheat,
which she had been gathering from a corner between
two bags. But she was too late for her brother. She
would have thrown it back for the birds but for the
surly words of the stranger. As it was, she put it
carefully in the great pocket which was fastened at her
waist. And on the future of those two handfuls of
wheat is built our little story.

I

The family of Corams, to which the two children
and their brother Martin belonged, were of the English emigration, of near a thousand men, women, and
children, who arrived in Massachusetts Bay in June of
1630. After a fortnight of varied experience, sleeping

in a barn to-night and under canvas to-morrow night, riding on a pillion behind one brother, or steering a boat for another, Patience found herself, with her father and mother, her brothers and sisters, and especially with the precious baby of the party, under the shelter of a tent on the shore of Charles River, where, two hundred and fifty years after, stood the house of one of her descendants, on the land which her father staked out on the morning of that day. The older brothers and sisters were at work here and there, as the regimen of a well-disciplined English yeoman's family directed. And to Patience was left the oversight of the three children younger than herself. It was not hard to set Robert and Jotham to digging holes in the sand beside the river, with the big shells they had found there. The baby was too small to dig, too big to go to sleep, and too resolute to be left alone. Patience had built houses of pebbles on the chest on which she sat, she had extemporized jackstraws from the big pine-needles; but one sport failed after another, and, at last, with unwearying good temper, such as befitted her name, she said, "Well, Tommy, let us see what we have in our pocket." And from the great pocket which hung from her belt appeared a spool of thread, the comb which the other children knew only too well, three or four nails which she had picked up in one cruise or another, two or three little kerchiefs which were tied round their necks in one and another crisis, and at last a good handful of the wheat which Patience had placed there on the day of the landing. This served her purpose best of all. The wheat was ranged in armies, it was pushed to and fro, it was dropped through holes, to be recovered by the baby's fingers, till, happily and suddenly, the child developed drowsiness, gave way to one skilful, slow rendering of the ballad of *Robin Hood*, and, in a minute more, was sleeping under a veil, on the rough bed which he shared with his mother. Patience was left to her own devices. She hastily pocketed again the various treasures which had been the baby's playthings, till she came to the armies of wheat-grains. "I mean to plant these," she said. "I mean to have some bread of my own. Thee knows, Martin," she said, gravely, to her brother, "the Bible says, 'some an hundredfold.'" And she rapidly counted her grains. "Here are forty-three grains. A hundredfold will be a great many."

Martin laughed good-naturedly at her confidence, and said, "Thee must be careful, Pashe, or the sun will burn them or the weeds choke them. The sun seems to me hotter than it was yon, and thee sees how the weeds grow. And who knows, dear little Pashe, where next spring will find us? 'Up and away,' may be the order."

"I do not know," said the girl, good-naturedly. "But where we go, I will take my farm. See here, Martin, I have this big basket, which the Indian woman gave me for a little bit of ribbon. Thee will show me the good ground, I will fill the basket with good ground, and I will plant my seed there. Then, if we go to another plantation, we will carry the basket. See how strong it is."

Martin was fond of the child, as well he might be, and always humored her. They filled the basket together, and then he bade her pick out the very largest and plumpest of her grains. "Thee does not want a mean harvest, Pashe," he said; "good grain or none, and good seed, if we are to have a hundredfold." So the basket was filled two-thirds full from the rich soil left in some overflow of Charles River. Thirty plump grains, such as would have delighted the vizier Joseph, were planted in it, the basket was set away under the slope of the tent, and, to tell the truth, it was forgotten by everybody.

A cabin was built, after a fashion, partly of logs and partly of planks, which had been diligently sawed out by Jotham and Martin and Stedfast and their father. Poor Mrs. Coram began to feel the joys of a stable home, after seven months of ships and boats and tents and bivouacs, and to say, between tears and prayers, that it was a comfort there was wood enough to burn. But alack and alas! as March came in, as the ice in the river melted, as the children brought up from the river-bank prince's-pine and bits of green moss which seemed as if summer might come, the goodman came in, one night, quite excited, with one more proposal for removal.

One of the magistrates, and two other men of sub-stance, had come on from the South River, as they called it, to ask him if he would not come and direct the setting up of their mill there, as he had so well directed this at Watertown. There was a modest pride in Coram's face as he told this to the family, while he knew that the proposal would not be popular. But the end of all was that it was agreed that he ought to go. He would take Martin with him till the house could be ready for the little ones, for house there was this time, or the beginning of one. And then, "by the time you want to make your garden, mother," Martin should come back with their own horse and with another horse which could be borrowed, for mother to ride upon and the little ones. The establishment at Watertown was turned over to Stedfast, and Stedfast should marry Hope Garfield a little earlier than had been expected. By such bribery was Stedfast's vote secured for the scheme. And, of course, Goodwife Coram consented, as she had consented to so many schemes before.

"And thee will have a good patch of wheat here," said the father to his son, as he left in the gray of the morning, and looked around, with a certain regret, on the improvements of the hard work of last October and November.

Patience heard the words. Childlike, she said nothing. But, so soon as her brother and father left, she ran back into the old tent, which had stood all winter long as a storehouse, rummaged under the ropes, and dragged out the Indian woman's forgotten basket. She set it in a sheltered place, fenced it carefully from chickens, and, with a gourd of her own, watered it every day when she did not forget it. When, upon May-day itself, she lifted her little sister on the pillion behind Martin, for the emigration to the South River, she gave to her care the heavy basket. "If thee will take it, Polly, all the way, I will walk all the way. Thee need not give me thy place at all." And Polly gladly fulfilled her share of the contract.

II

And it proved, as it will prove in the world, that the party who went on foot had quite as easy a journey as those who went on horses. First of all, they had some miles in a great birch canoe, which a friendly Indian squaw on the river had lent Goodwife Coram. When it came to the carries, the children did their part with the best. There were two more than when they landed at Salem. For the gentle Madam Skeats had died before Christmas, and that quiet gentleman, her husband, had coughed his life away before two months more. Here were the two orphans, Lawrence and Mildred, whom Goodwife Coram had taken into her shelter and into her heart, of course. With her eight children, these two made the journey to Dedham.

The new home was further advanced in the beginning than the old one had been when they left it. The men of mark who wanted Coram's help had known enough to know that he would be likely to stay if they made things attractive to his family. Two or three acres of meadow had been ploughed, a log-cabin built, and thatched with marsh hay and reeds, and, as the day of arrival chose to be one of the days in a New England May when the wind blows from the southwest, where the Indian's heaven lies, everything seemed cheerful and hopeful.

Coram's two horses were by far the most valuable part of his wealth. At once he made for himself a rough harrow, and, under the moonlight, with the

boys' help, broke up the newly ploughed land. He
would try oats, he would try barley, he would try
wheat. As for the new corn, which the Indian boys
showed him, he was incredulous. They might plant
that; good old English wheat was good enough for
him. Patience said nothing while these larger labors
went on. But the next day she chose her own garden-
spot behind the house. She found a pick and a spade—
both far too heavy for her, but a fortunate rush of
water in the spring had broken up the surface so that
it was not sodded beyond her strength. In one interval and another, between baby-tending and plate-
washing, and other cares invented or suggested by her
mother, she made herself a bed big enough for all the
seeds she had and more. She planted apple-seeds which
her grandmother had given her in Kent. She planted
scarlet-beans which she had saved a year ago in the
old cottage in England. And, with most care of all,
she broke into a dozen bits the hard block of soil which
had caked together in the Indian basket, and set them
in her new garden, as she might have done as many
precious tulips, had she ever heard of such wonders.

Fortune favors the brave. And is there not indeed
a divinity among the powers set to rule this world who
has a special love for children and their enterprises?
Who shall say? But it seemed so. Before June was
over Goodman Coram had reason to wish that he had
listened more carefully to the Indian boys. They had
warned him that the meadow where he planted, which
seemed wholly out of reach of the stream, was, in exceptional years, flooded when a freshet came. They
even showed him logs which had been floated there;

but they had to confess that these had been there ever
since they remembered. Coram had said, in his easy
way, that if the freshets had held off for ten years,
they would hold off a year longer. Anyway, he must
build the town mill and tend it; he could not be felling timber for his fields and crops, as the others were.

And so poor Coram had the dismay, when he woke
one morning in the middle of June, of seeing that the
rain of the last week had started up in the hills sources
and streams such as he had never dreamed of in England. At night he had simply taken comfort that the
roof was so well thatched and the house so dry. But
in the morning here was the stream within a foot of
his little field, so carefully planted not four weeks
since. He looked wistfully on the field, sorrowfully
on the river. "No good crying for spilled milk," he
said, as he led Patience and her mother back to breakfast. "Lucky that I am a better millwright than I
am farmer." Lucky, indeed, for before an hour had
gone by some new rush of water came down, as some
beaver-dam gave way above, and all the little field was
under a torrent which even floated the logs which had
lodged in it in the freshet of old days.

And so it happened that, in Patience's little patch
behind the house, there ripened all the wheat which
the Coram family made in their second summer in the
bay. The seed, because it had been chosen of the best,
and because it was diligently watered with the slops
which Patience carried from her mother's kitchen,
throve marvellously. Goodman Coram and Martin
would praise Patience's farming almost every day.
"Thee will not have thy hundredfold, Pashe," Martin

would say, good-naturedly; "I do not know what the
man sowed who got that, but not such wheat as we
sow. But thee will have a good twentyfold, and,
maybe, thirtyfold. And that is enough for a beginning in farming."

"The good Lord did not say that all bore a hundredfold, even then and there," said the girl's mother, laughing. "Some had a hundred and some thirty. And I
believe he loved one as much as the other."

When Martin told her the time had come, Patience
cut her tall wheat with her own scissors. Her mother
kept the thirty tall stalks of straw, and laid them by
under the eaves for the time when Patience should
learn to braid them. And Patience with her own fingers, in the autumn twilight, picked all the big grains
from the husks. Martin himself marvelled that they
were so large, and his good-natured father praised Patience that she picked her seed so well. So, as she
picked, the girl made two piles, one for "the best, the
very, very best," and another for what her father told
her to mark as second grade. She counted the full
grains which she called the "Pharaoh wheat," and she
had five hundred and seventy kernels. She made for
herself a little bag from a dish-clout, and sewed the
ends together, and hid it away with her treasures.

III

So, when October came, and the mill was running
briskly, if only there had been grain enough for it to
grind, Patience called Martin one afternoon and asked
26

him how she was to plant "Pharaoh." "'Lean kine'
I will not plant at all," she said, laughing. "It shall
not be said of me that I started poor crops in this
brave, new world, which hath such wonders in it."
The scrap of Shakespeare had stolen to her ears from
a sailor on the ship. Neither she nor her brother
guessed where the sailor heard it, and still less that she
had misquoted it. Martin always petted her, and
would have done much more for her than make a
garden-bed. He went out at once, surveyed her present
possessions, and saw at a glance how they could be
enlarged. "I must bring thee some of the posies from
the woods," he said, "if there is ever a time when the
sun will not burn them before we can move them.
Thy beans do thee credit, like thy wheat, my darling,
and thee is the best farmer of us all." So he brought
his spade and his pick, he drove in pickets strong
enough to keep off any wandering pig, he warned her
that her worst enemies were the fowls she loved so
well, and then made her a bed big enough for her
heart's most earnest desire. He dammed off the strag-
gling water which came down from the wood above.
There was space for the posies which were to come
from the swamp, there was a large corner where she
was to plant in the spring the Indian-corn which the
old squaw had given her, there were a dozen poles for
her beans, which were to be glorious in another summer, there were long beds for her peas, and, in the
midst of all, well away from the rush of water from
the thatched roof, was a space especially raked and
sifted, where Pharaoh was to have his five hundred
and seventy-two full stalks of grain. "Thee shall have

a stalk for each day of the year, little one, and two hundred and seven stalks more. With such good luck as thee has had, we will have thirtyfold this time." And with her own hand Patience planted Pharaoh as he bade her. She had a bit of worn-out net which one of the fishermen gave her, and she pinned this carefully over Pharaoh's bed and the parts around it. She drove off cocks and hens with unflinching perseverance, and even taught the little spaniel who had followed all their wanderings, that he must not leap inside that enclosure. Little had the girl to call her away from home, and her watchfulness, therefore, was easy, until the snow fell and protected all. If she had known it, it enriched all; "snow is the poor man's manure."

With that fall's success in the mill, and with work which knew no such petty limits as twelve hours, or even thirteen, Coram and Martin cleared a farm where no freshets would sweep away their planting. Between the stumps they compelled the horses to drag their light plough. And, in a fashion, they got in their oats and their barley, and their wheat. By this time, also, Coram was willing to plant as much of the Indian's corn as he planted of all the rest. "But this we will make ready for in winter," he said. "We will keep ourselves warm by felling the great pines yon, and by burning them when they are felled."

And all was as he said.

His wheat harvest made but a poor show compared with what he would have seen in Kent. His barley was poorer yet. But the oats were full and strong. "But nobody has such wheat in this land," said he, after their little Harvest Home, "as the lasses do.

How big is thy farm, Patience, and are there three yards of it, or six? I only know that I must buy all thy crop for planting another year, even if thee weighs it against sixpences. 'Brave new land,' is that what thee calls it? It is a land where the lasses have better farms than their own daddies have."

And little Patience, who was not so little now, blushed crimson, and flung her arms around him without saying a word, and kissed him.

IV

Perhaps the origin of the "Pharaoh grains" has been told in too much detail. But it seemed worth while for younger readers, at least, who eat their daily bread as if it came to them of course, without anybody's special effort or care, to be carried back to some of the chances and difficulties of a beginning. The story need not be told with the same nicety for a year or two more. For enough has been told to show why and how it happened that the little girl's handful came to be planted separately, and why, from year to year, the product was kept separately. It was no trifling task, after her third harvest, to lay out in succession, on the large kitchen table, one and another measure of the great yellow grains, and to put upon the floor, in the old Indian basket, those which were a little shrivelled, or for any reason not so full as the others. A dozen, perhaps, had been pierced by a miserable little worm, hardly bigger round than a large pin, who had worked his way out of them. Patience buried these behind the coals in the smouldering ashes of the fireplace. Her beloved grains were far beyond her counting now. And while she kept her first bag, with a certain superstitious love or respect, she had to make a much larger bag to hold the increase of her harvest. Thirty times fifty is fifteen hundred, and in another year thirty times fifteen hundred made forty-five thousand grains. Patience, who is no longer little Patience, but tall Patience, and, be it added in a whisper, pretty Patience, did not even make this calculation. But she did weigh her bags, and laid them in the corner of the great meal-chest, of which she was now the mistress. And thus she knew that Pharaoh had kept up to his old standard. Not a grain of all that was thus chosen was ever made into meal. No, it was saved for autumn sowing. And all Patience's original garden, and more, well manured by Martin's loving care, was needed for Pharaoh's tyrannical requisitions.

But two years was a long time for Goodman Coram to remain in one home. He was one of those who "hunger for the horizon." And so soon as men began to suspect that the sandy gravel of the bay shores was not even equal to old Kent for farming land, so soon also there began to be great rumors of "The Great River of the West," as watering meadows to which the little freshet-washed fields of the Neponset were as a handkerchief pinned on the mainsail of a man-of-war. This was not the great river of which we know the name as Meschachipi, or Mississippi. It was a river which the Minneapolis and St. Paul people would think a very little river, but which was big to an Indian of the bay, and which from its meadows fed young New

England as the Mississippi valley feeds the New England of to-day. Coram had not been at the Dedham home for two years before he was sent for to New Plymouth for some advice as to their mill-gear. There he met some of the traders to the "great river" and came home full of enthusiasm with what they told him. There was to be the place for a miller; there was to be the region from which the country was to be fed.

Here it proved he was right, and, accordingly, he led his vagrant family there when they had lived little more than three years in their home on the Neponset river. But this was a long time for an adventurer like Goodman Coram.

And, once more, the family was divided. This time Patience and Lawrence and Mildred and Martin were of the party which went across the land, while the little children, with the mill-gear, and their mother and the various stores, went in a trading vessel, out through the bay, around by the perilous passage of Cape Cod and Nantucket, anchored once and again in the Vineyard Sound and in Long Island Sound, and then, by favorable winds, pushed forward for a fortnight to the great river. This time the marching party came in ahead of the sailing party, and this time Martin and the boys, who could swing an axe with the best of the men now, had made a good beginning for their father and mother, in cutting the logs ready for lifting, so that the cabin was soon built and there was but little tent-life for the women before they were fairly established. That valley was as beautiful as it is now, and Goodwife Coram hoped that this time they had come to the home where they were to remain. Surely her goodman would hear of nothing that was better than this. Here was to be the home which she had prom-ised herself so long.

Of all such emigration, the temptation is to the new settler to come somewhere where he may plough at once, without that irksome or tiresome business of cut-ting down the timber, burning it, and so creating a farm. On the other side, as poor Coram found to his cost, in the little Mattapan valley a meadow was a place not to be trusted too fully, even if one go up on the second terrace. Here, in their new Eden, they had the ex-ample of the squaws, who were the Indian farmers, and were able to profit by some of their rough hydraulic enginery. That is to say, their custom was to take a good bit of land on an upper terrace, and to fortify themselves by a low log rampart, which would not, in-deed, bear the pressure of a heavy freshet, but which would be able to keep an accidental flood from the highest water levels from ravaging the field. Even before the cabin was well covered in, Coram and his boys, who were as good to him as men, felled one and another tree, so that it should answer such a purpose of protection for a few acres, resolved not to be caught again as they had been caught before. Nor were they. The cabin itself stood on ground somewhat higher than this terrace. For it is one of the peculiarities of that beautiful river, pointing back, I suppose, to bits of its geological history, that, as one lake after another gave way in the formation of New England, different ter-races rose from the river, and you may take your choice at what height you will live above the stream. This time the father sowed his wheat in his field, and

Lawrence and Martin sowed " Pharaoh" in what they knew as "the upper garden." Pharaoh had become an important element in the family life, and it was understood that Patience would not like to have her crop mixed in with the more vulgar crop of the larger field. It was no longer a crop to be watered with the suds of the wash-tubs. It had to take the chances, with the most democratic wheat, of the rain and the dew. But when spring came, Patience was delighted to see how firmly the stalks came up and how bravely they grew under those hot suns and under those healthy spring showers. Her father was as proud of her harvest as he was of his own, and was willing to confess once and again that she had the best show of them all. It was really quite a large patch which grew from the careful sowing of Lawrence and Martin, and when a hot July crowned the work of the showers of May and June, Goodman Coram himself confessed that never in his best English experience had he seen better grain.

V

It was half-past three of a July morning. The eastern sky was all a sea of pale pearly light; in the lower edge of it just the first suspicion of yellow. From his tent, half hidden under some low patch pines, came Lawrence Skeats. now a tall, handsome young fellow, more than six feet high, with a paddle on his left shoulder and an axe in his right hand. He was browned with the sun, but the English glow still shone in his cheeks, and such a mass of curly auburn hair blazed round his head as never glorified Apollo. He sat on the rail-fence, with his axe and with his paddle at his side, watching the door of the log-cabin, over which climbed scarlet-beans and ground-nut and Virginia-creeper. The young fellow's thoughts were carried back to his father's cottage at Hampshire, in the old home. He sat whistling at first, and then humming the song which he had heard his father sing in those days:

> " Hark ! hark ! the lark at heaven's gate sings,
>   And Phœbus 'gins arise,
> His steeds to water at those springs
>   On chaliced flowers that lies ;
> And winking Mary-buds begin
>   To ope their golden eyes,
> With everything that pretty bin ;—
>   My lady sweet, arise !"

He looked round at the last words, but on the high ridge there was no Phœbus yet, only the long golden streak which made it sure that Phœbus was coming.

Patience had promised her lover that she would be up before sunrise, and go with him to the little bayou, almost a pond, from which he had brought her her pond-lilies, so that she might see the pretty daily mira-cle of their opening. She was, let us hope, not quite so impatient as he was for the appointment—at least, it would not have been like her to say so. But, on the other hand, she was not too late, and, by the time the boy sang of the "winking Mary-buds," the girl pushed open the door and came smiling towards him, offering him her hand, and then insisting on carrying the pad-dle. A little walk—not half a mile—in which they brushed the dew from the grass in the narrow path,

and then the birch-canoe which Lawrence himself and
some friendly squaws had built the autumn before,
clean within as Patience's kneading-table, with a prettily dressed tasselled deer-skin for her to sit on, and a
bunch of wild roses on one side, and of white azalea
on the other.

"How sweet they are, Lawrence, and how nice in
thee to have them ready!"

The proud lad only blushed, intimated that they
were not half sweet enough for her, stepped into the
boat and pushed off, and in a minute they were in the
middle of the little lake.

What loving things he said to her, or what kind
answers she made to him, who shall tell after two
hundred and fifty years? Guess if you can, Maud and
Maurice, but they are not here written down. The
balance of the boat does not permit him to put his arm
around her, even if she would have permitted, and he
cannot press his lips upon her cheek, as sometimes he
had done. But there were only five or six jealous cubits between them, and he could see the play of the
blood as it went and came in her cheeks, and hear what
she said, though it were only in a whisper. And he
could sit and wonder how the good God himself could
make anything so beautiful as she. And the girl, hardly conscious of the intensity of his admiration, was
happy because he was happy, was happy because the
lake and the trees were so beautiful, and the reflection
of the trees in the still water. Was the morning dawn
always as exquisite as this? If it were, why, it was
wicked in them that they did not come out to see it
every day! Something like this they said. But neither

of them said much. Both of them were the good
God's children, and had been so trained that they were
not afraid of Him. Each of them would have liked
to say just the words which John Milton — perhaps
that very morning—was thinking of putting into the
mouth of Eve:

"These are thy glorious works, Parent of Good."

But, of a sudden, the miracle was perfected for which
they had come. It was the girl who saw it first.
" There is one!" she cried, as a great white lily opened
itself to the sun. " Surely, it was not there before !"

No, pretty Patience, or it was only a bud before.
And lily buds open to the sun as quickly as girls change
into women.

Lawrence looked over his shoulder to see the " chal-
iced flower" floating on the lake, and skilfully drew
the boat to it, so that Patience might take it for her
prize. In the minute in which she did so, half a dozen
more had opened, and, as she looked up she saw them.
" There—oh ! and there ! There Lawrence, look there !
Oh, they are everywhere ?"

Yes, that is the beauty of morning on such a lake,
where there are so many of these maiden-queens waiting to meet the sun - god. And Lawrence, delighted
that she so enjoyed the new pleasure which he had
prepared for her, skilfully pushed the boat from one to
another as she pointed. At last, indeed, there needed
no pointing or exclamation. The surface, just now
brown, or blue, or green, as it reflected shadow, or sky,
or tree, was everywhere flecked with the pure white of

the lilies, as they waited, hoping that the girl would need them.

The space between them in the canoe was filled with the mass of them which she had collected, when Lawrence for the first time looked northward in the sky. In an instant his face changed.

"Patience, stand up — look yon! What is that — smoke?"

"Smoke indeed," cried she, in dismay, like his own. "Not near the house, thank God!"

And already he was driving the boat to the landing. Three minutes and they are there; two more, with no thought of their cargo now, nor of axe or paddle, they are running up the sloping bank. The smoke, and even tongues of fire, were only too visible, just beyond the northeast point, where the mountain had turned the course of the river.

"I will run to the house and warn them," cried he. "Do thou go right to the tent and wake Martin," and, as he spoke, he threw back to her his whittle. "Cut all the cords, bid Martin roll up the canvas, and we will come for it." The girl caught the knife, and ran, like Diana herself, to call her sleeping brother.

Yes, and neither of them had a minute too much for what they had to do. Lawrence thundered at the cabin door. His cry waked all who were there, and some sort of clothing was wrapped round the little ones. Goodman Coram himself was away, caring for the Windsor Mills. But the two boys who slept there were made to put on shoes and breeches. Mrs. Coram, with the girls, carried to the safe covert of the trees such things of worth as women could handle. The new baby, most precious of all, and the other little ones were left there, under the care of the wondering Robert. And in a few minutes more—in time, thank God!—Martin and Lawrence and the rest appeared, stumbling through the thicket, with the great roll of the tent-cover. Two of the young fellows climbed upon the roof of the cabin. There was time still to do their work well, though they could see that the fire had turned the point, and could plainly hear its roar as it rushed through the tall grasses of the meadow, on which no rain had fallen for a fortnight. Before a single burning leaf or straw fell upon it, the dangerous thatch was covered with the canvas, and Martin at his post, Lawrence at his, on the leeward side of the roof, were throwing water over the sheet, as the hard-working women supplied it in buckets from below. The air grew hotter and hotter, but the women and the men were wet from top to toe, and hardly felt or knew whether they were hot or cold. Within thirty yards of them there was nothing to feed the fire. A little line of maples, which had been spared in chopping, from some Indian's talk of their sugar, parted the homestead lot from the broken field. And, after a terrible hour, they knew that the fire storm had passed them and was speeding its way down the valley. Men and women, boys and girls, their faces were black with smoke and with the crock of cinders.

The house was saved! But the harvest on the meadows was gone!

Jotham and Robert were sent down in Lawrence's canoe to call back poor Coram to the scene of desolation, and on the night of the third day after the fire he was with his wife and children. Such men—hopeful and eager to make a change when none is necessary —are always the more depressed when misfortune falls upon them which they have not expected. And now it was Goodwife Coram who was encouraging her husband, and Patience who was trying to make him understand that things were really not as bad as they were on the night when they gathered so hopefully at Watertown, glad that the voyage was well over.

"For now, dear father," said the girl, "we have a house over our heads, we have enough to eat and to drink, we have a field all broken up and ready to plant again, and we have neighbors and friends within five miles, to whom we can go to borrow salt or sugar."

"And what are we to do," said poor Coram, gloomily, "between this time and next summer, when the crops will be ripe, Patience, if so be another fire does not sweep down the valley and finish them again?"

But here the good wife put in a word. She reminded him that there would be as many shad and salmon in the river as there had been in the spring, that there would be as many pigeons and turkeys in the sky as there had been for a thousand years, that they had in the out-house, which had been preserved so skilfully by the boys, the tubs of salt fish which they had all worked together to lay down in April. "Thou shalt not say that we are going to starve in a land flowing with milk and honey. What was it, Nathan, that thee told me of this Tartar wheat which people plant in July and harvest in the early autumn? We will send the boys to the fort with these skins and they shall bring up enough to us for all that we can eat, and all that we can sell to the redskins here."

They were all sitting where they looked upon the black ground, which was not even stubble, where the fire had burned so savagely all Nathan Coram's standing corn. Not a straw was left of the yellow acres which had been so promising to his eye only eight days before. This was the field which, in his wife's simple husbandry, was to be covered with buckwheat before the summer was over. "And then, father," said Patience, "it will be time to put in our winter wheat." And the sad man answered his daughter without any smile this time. "Neither love nor money will buy wheat for the planting at any of the forts. None of them had our luck; there was a blast here and a blight there, and if our new mill cannot grind oats, and these hard Indian-corns, I might as well have built them a pigeon-coop as a windmill."

"But, father dear," pleaded Patience, "thee does not remember anything. Thee thinks that all is gone when all is not gone. Come up with me and see how thy little apple-trees have been growing, and see what is growing all around them and almost hiding them." So she led the way to the upper garden, and there, sure enough, screened from the cinders by a stretch of the maple forest, was the gorgeous yellow of "Pharaoh's" harvest, just ready for the reaping. "If thou art as wise, dear father, as I think, we will not cry over spilled milk any longer, but we will all take our sickles and attack Pharaoh on four sides. And this year he shall be threshed and winnowed as men thresh wheat, and not as women do in their farming. See if there

is not seed-corn for another summer, and tell me if, at
the mill, anybody brings in better wheat than the miller's daughter?"

And her father took her in his arms and kissed her.
And, after the harvest of the next summer, when there
had been no freshet and no fire, and no mildew and no
weevil, when Nathan Coram's crops of oats and barley
were such as he had never dreamed of in Kent, when
his great bins of Indian-corn were so big that he did
not know how it was to be husked or to be shelled,
first of all he and Lawrence and Martin threshed out
the English wheat, which had grown as never English
wheat did before. And they tied it in great bags and
stacked it, and Nathan Coram said to Lawrence: "We
will not eat a kernel of it, Lawrence. But when the
new house is finished and the wedding-day comes, the
boys shall carry it over there and Patience's wheat
shall be Patience's dowry."

And it was all so. And if any one, stumbling over
the old accounts of Governor Haynes or of Mr. Pyn-
chon, finds the credit or the debit for so many pecks or
so many bushels of "Pharaoh," it is because these old
settlers, for their planting, bought Lawrence Skeat's
best winter wheat, the best which was ever yet seen
on the river.

THE END

www.ingramcontent.com/pod-product-compliance
Lightning Source LLC
Chambersburg PA
CBHW030953110726
47900CB00004B/1256